after
THE END

Good
but very
repetitive
7/08

BOOKS BY NATASHA PRESTON

SILENCE SERIES

Silence
Broken Silence
Players, Bumps and Cocktail Sausages

CHANCE SERIES

Second Chance
Our Chance

STAND-ALONES

Save Me
With the Band
Reliving Fate
Lie to Me
After the End

YOUNG ADULT THRILLERS

The Cellar
Awake
The Cabin
You Will Be Mine

THE END

NATASHA PRESTON

This one is for my husband.
Actually, this is the second book dedicated to him because of the
offended look he gets every time he's not mentioned.
There, Joe. Now, stop pestering!

1

Tilly

I have been stuck inside two alternating nightmares for the last four years. Today, one of them is going to come true. Today, Lincoln Reid is moving home.

Four years after Lincoln; his brother, Stanley; and my brother, Robbie, were in a car accident that resulted in Robbie's death, he's moving back.

Even the thought of seeing Lincoln or Stanley again makes me break out into a cold sweat.

Does Lincoln think that all is forgiven? That the town has forgotten what his brother did? What he and his parents did?

When Robbie died, life as I had known it ended.

You can't come back from something like that.

My family used to be happy. We would go on holidays, go camping, or spend nights watching movies or playing board games. Robbie was the one I went to with boy troubles because, although he was protective, he was also supportive, open-minded, and nonjudgmental. My friendship group was tight, close, and untouchable. Lincoln was part of that, flitting between hanging out with my circle and my brother's.

But, now, my family is empty and lifeless. My parents don't want to do anything we used to do with Robbie anymore. I can't blame them. I don't really fancy sitting around, playing Monopoly either. And my friendship group now starts and ends with Hanna and Mel.

Logically, I know it's not his fault that Robbie is dead, no more than it's Robbie's fault anyway. Neither of them was behind the wheel, but Lincoln is alive, and my brother isn't.

"Has he arrived yet?" Mum asks, tugging on her sleeve. She's sitting on the sofa, her knee bouncing up and down.

Dad is at the window with framed pictures of Robbie on either side of him. "Not yet," Dad replies gruffly.

Mum's back is to him, so she can't see the way his hands are curled around the windowsill.

Robbie's death has gutted them—and me. He was my big brother by two years, and although we argued sometimes, we got along really well. He was my friend as much as he was family, and now, he's gone. Mum is openly heartbroken, breaking down in tears often and refusing to move on. Dad hurts every second of every day, too, but he works so hard to show the world that he's strong.

This last week, since Martha Reid called to let us know that Lincoln was coming back, Mum has been on edge. She's barely eaten, her nails have been bitten to the quick, and I've heard her crying herself to sleep more than once. Mum didn't ask if Stanley was coming, too, but Martha definitely only mentioned Lincoln.

I hope Stanley doesn't come back. If he does, I'm going, and I don't care where to. I can't face my brother's killer.

Dad's breath catches. I know what that means, and I can see anyway because, although I'm deeper in the room with Mum, I'm facing the window. The way I have been for the last thirty minutes. Waiting.

My lungs deflate.

"I can't go out there," Mum says.

Dad turns around. "You don't have to."

She doesn't want to leave her home.

Fire burns in my veins, so hot that I want to rip at my skin to relieve the pressure. We can't lock ourselves away until he's gone. We're not prisoners here, and I won't hide.

I'll go out there.

I don't really know what I'm doing or why I'm doing it, but my legs are moving, and I'm ignoring my parents calling my name. Something has taken me over. *Am I possessed?* I'm sure I'm running purely on adrenaline.

I storm out of the house as Lincoln tugs on the hand brake like it's wronged him.

He cuts the engine and shoves the door open.

The sight of him, inky-black hair tousled and messy in a short style and full lips turned down, stops me dead. He really came back. After everything that happened, he drives home like his drunk brother didn't ruin my life.

Lincoln looks over the roof of his car. His eyes meet mine, and every muscle in my body locks in place.

Shit.

Seeing his deep, dark blue eyes is like being punched in the gut. We were friends. He was the boy version of me. We both loved all things old horror and old rock. Lincoln used to joke that we were born in the wrong decade.

He rounds the car. I'm catapulted back four years, and all I can see is him walking toward me at the hospital. Back then, he had blood on his face, cuts and bruises were everywhere, and his eyes were haunted and red.

This time, he's pale, and he looks like he's walking into the lion's den.

His super-dark hair is actually a little longer than he used to wear it, but it's still styled well, leaning more toward surfer than hipster. He must have spent most of the four years working out because his body has changed *a lot*.

"Tilly," he whispers, his chest expanding in a deep breath.

I swallow the football-sized lump in my throat. "What are you doing here, Linc?"

Wait, don't use his nickname!

"I'm here for the house, I swear. Someone had to come back and sort it out. Figured it would be better, being me."

Over Stanley? For sure.

"What are you doing to the house? Are you moving home permanently?"

He raises his eyes to the sky. "That's what my mum wants." With a sigh, he looks back at me. "But no. I'm renovating it, so my parents can sell."

"Why do you have to do it?"

They could have hired someone.

"Finance," he replies. "How are you?"

I dig my nails into my palms. "Fine," I lie.

Even though it's been four years since Robbie died, I'm not over his death the way some people think I should be. My friends, Hanna and Mel, think that, at twenty-one, I should move out and move on. But I can't do that yet. My parents are still *so* broken. How can I leave the house and leave them with nothing but silence?

Unhealthy to live my life purely to make theirs easier, yes.

"I've missed ..." He presses his lips together, and his shoulders sag with the weight of the world.

He's missed me? Is that what he was about to say?

I used to miss him. Well, his company. When he was with my friends and me, we got on so well. We liked the same movies and music, walking along the beach, and getting lost in the forest. Okay, not *lost*, lost, but walking around aimlessly for hours.

Those times were special to me, but the night he got into a car with his drunk brother and my drunk brother marked the end of our friendship.

I've stopped missing him because he reminds me of what I've lost.

Three of them got into that car, and not one of them thought it was a bad idea for Stanley to drive when he was over the limit.

"Look, I'll stay out of your way as much as I can, if that's what you want?"

"That's what I want," I confirm. "It's what my parents want, too."

That much is one hundred percent true. My parents would rather never see Lincoln, Stanley, or any other member of the Reid family ever again.

"Of course," he breathes. "I didn't come back here to intentionally hurt *anyone*, Tilly."

"Then, what did you think coming back here would do? Stanley is the reason Robbie is dead."

We both fall silent, and Lincoln squeezes his eyelids shut.

What did he expect?

Sighing, I run my hands over my face. "Look, I didn't come out here to argue."

"Why did you come out?"

Dropping my arms, I reply, "It doesn't matter."

I came because I was angry that my mum wanted to hide from him, but I don't have a goal here. Lincoln has never been a malicious person, so I know he will keep his distance. I invited this little meeting.

Can I blame the adrenaline?

"I know you can't forgive me for what happened, but believe me, I can't forgive myself either. There are so many things I wish I'd done differently that night—"

"Don't." I hold my hand up, and he clenches his jaw. Maybe I'm just not ready to talk to him, but I so don't want to have this conversation. I don't want his excuses or apologies. "There's nothing you can say, so save it."

Raising his palms, he backs up a step. "Okay. I get it, Tilly. I'll keep away."

He turns away and walks to his house with his shoulders hunched and head low.

The house has been vacant for four years. They moved away shortly after Robbie's funeral. I don't like mob mentality, but most of our tight-knit town turned on them. Martha and

Cliff fought hard and spent a lot of money on a lawyer who could keep Stanley out of prison.

That didn't sit right with anyone. Stanley had chosen to drink and drive, and as a result, someone had died.

My someone had died.

They weren't exactly run out of town with pitchforks, but there weren't many places they were welcome anymore. So, they chose to leave.

I think we could have gotten past things a whole lot easier if Stanley had been forced to take responsibility. He blamed everyone but himself. Lincoln and Robbie certainly weren't innocent, but Robbie is dead, and Lincoln held his hands up to his part in it.

I'm planted to the floor, my feet unmoving, watching him as he walks into the house with two shopping bags and slams the door shut.

Breathing heavily, I double over at the stinging in my stomach.

Jesus.

"Tilly!"

Shit.

I turn.

Greg, an old friend, is jogging toward me, his car parked on the road outside my house. "Are you okay? Lincoln is back already?"

Standing straight, I nod. "I'm fine, Greg. He just got back now."

Out of the corner of my eye, I can see my parents standing at the front door, huddled together like they're waiting for a child to come home from war.

"What did he say?" Greg asks, firing bullets from his eyes into Lincoln's house.

Greg has kind of taken it upon himself to be my knight in shining armour. Unfortunately for him, I'm not a damsel in distress.

"Nothing much," I reply, standing tall despite feeling like I want to curl up and hide.

"Let me take you inside, and we can talk about it." He glances at my parents. "They want you inside, too, by the looks of it."

What I want is to run away, but Mum and Dad need me.

"Okay," I reply and let Greg lead me into my house. It's not like I have a lot of choices anyway because Greg is not going to go away yet, so why waste energy in fighting it?

I step over the threshold and clench my trembling hands. Greg closes the door behind us, my parents backing up but still cautiously watching me.

Turning from the three of them, I head to the kitchen, passing pictures of Robbie staring at me.

What would my brother think of Lincoln being back? Would he be as angry as I feel?

Who am I kidding? Robbie would have forgiven him. He would have; I have no doubt about that.

My brother forgave. He never held grudges and always saw the best in people, even when they didn't show their best.

I don't know how he did. Lord knows, I've tried, but I can't seem to follow through with the logic I tell myself. I can say that I've forgiven Lincoln for his part in my brother's death, but deep down, I know I haven't.

"Are you okay?" Mum asks, pulling me into a hug.

Resting my chin on her tense shoulder, I reply, "I'm fine. He said he would keep out of our way."

"Good," she replies. I pull back, and she looks at me through tears. "I don't want anyone from that family near you."

I gulp at the perfect mixture of despair and fury in her voice.

"Don't worry, Emma; I won't let him near her," Greg says, smiling and standing slightly taller, like he's my protector.

I don't need protecting. I'm not scared of Lincoln. I'm sad because I miss my brother, but that doesn't mean I'm some broken woman, unable to take care of myself. The sooner Greg realises that, the better.

I look at him smiling like he's won some prize.

Trying to keep my irritation out of my voice, I reply, "If I see Linc again, I'll deal with it."

Greg's jaw clenches at the mention of Lincoln's nickname, which, apparently, I'm using again. Greg has only just stopped using Linc's full name when talking about him.

"I'll put the kettle on," Dad says, sensing the tension. He squeezes my shoulder on the way past me.

I follow him into the kitchen, stealing one last look at Lincoln's house, my heart twisting in a tight knot.

Linc

I don't know exactly when I fell in love with Tilly Drake, but I didn't even realise it until it was too late. I'd already moved away with my family, and she hated me.

Every couple I know can tell me exactly when they fell for each other. I can only remember the moment that I realised I loved her. We had been in the new house, a hundred miles away, for four days, and I couldn't shake the gripping ache in my chest. I knew I missed her, but when I realised *why* I missed her so much, I could barely breathe.

I stand in the study after bringing in some food I picked up on the way here, watching Tilly from the window. I've been here for the last thirty minutes while Greg has been in her house. She asked me to stay away, and I will, but I can't help staring at her right now. For four years, all I've had is the memory of her and a few photos saved on my phone.

Facebook stalking is one level I won't sink to, and she deleted me soon after Robbie died.

Greg is outside with her as she stuffs crap from her car into a plastic bag. Before I left, she'd recently passed her driving test, and I remember her using her car as a second bedroom. I don't know why she's cleaning out her car thirty minutes after going inside, but I think it's because I'm back, and she wants to keep busy.

I spend a long time cleaning and rearranging.

Tilly's long white-blonde hair is tied in a messy bun on the top of her head. A few wavy tendrils hang down either side of her neck. She was beautiful before, but now, she is something else. I have never seen anything so perfect.

She stands up and straightens out her back. Slamming her door, she turns to the dickhead who's staring more at her chest than her eyes. Greg is her age and has always had a thing for her. I see nothing has changed there. I have no idea if she didn't realise or just didn't care, but she never seemed to be into him.

I don't know if they're a thing now, but I'm certain I don't want to keep looking in case I find out they are.

So, why can't I stop watching?

Because it's been too long since I've been this close.

My feet are glued to the floorboards, eyes pinned on Tilly's face. I find it hard to look away from her, especially after only seeing her in photos these last four years, but if I see her with him, it's going to hurt like fuck.

One moment is all it took to make her hate me, to ruin any chance I ever had of asking her out. We'd always gotten along. Every time we had been together, it had been fun and easy. I think that maybe she could have felt something for me, too. I think, before Robbie died, I could have had a shot with her.

Timing is a bitch.

Greg says something, and she laughs. I want to crack the window to hear them, but that would probably draw attention to myself. I lay my palms against the wall and hold my breath as he gets a little too close.

Don't touch her.

Tilly stops short and says something.

They haven't embraced. They would have if they were together.

My lungs fill with air. She's not going to be single forever, and she doesn't owe me anything, but, Jesus, I hope she stays single until I'm gone. I don't know how I would cope with seeing her with someone and wishing it were me.

I would give anything to change that night—and not just for me and Tilly.

Greg now laughs at something Tilly said.

Every muscle in my body screams to go out there and intervene. But it's not my place. It's never been my place. Besides, she told me to stay away from her.

I don't really know how I'm supposed to do that, as we live next door to each other, but if that's what she wants, then I will do everything I can to make it happen. I would rather be in agony from being so close yet so far than have her feeling one ounce of pain from seeing me.

Four years I have spent of loving someone I never really had.

I've not told anyone either. I've kept it inside because it's pathetic. Stanley and I don't talk about Tilly. To be fair, we don't talk much at all. We've never verbally agreed on anything, but we both know she's off-limits. I think he suspects that I like her, so he won't bring her into a conversation. He knows that night—the night he chose to drive over the limit, and Robbie and I let him—that any chance I had of starting something with Tilly died.

Greg raises his hand and gets in his car. Tilly starts to back away, and that's when I see the tendons in my wrists poking out of where I'm gripping the edge of the wall by the window so hard.

I step back and drop my arms. She disappears from my view, and my gut twists. I've missed her so much. Looking at the pictures she uploads on Instagram, the one place she hasn't banned me from, has in no way prepared me for seeing her in the flesh or diminished how much it makes me crave her.

I turn around, ready to get back to work, when someone hammers on my door. It's Jack's knock; he always was impatient.

Jack is in a relationship with Tilly's friend, Hanna. I've wanted to ask him about Tilly so many times over the years, but I've forced myself to hang back. She probably wouldn't want anyone telling me about her life, and I don't want to put Jack in that position.

I head out to open the front door. Sure enough, it's Jack.

"Nice of you to tell me you're back, fucker," he says, scowling and running his hand through his light hair as he pushes past me. "You should have let me take care of the house; it's dusty as fuck."

"Good to see you, too, mate."

The house is covered in four years' worth of dust. We had a pipe burst a year ago, which was repaired by a friend of the family, but the flooring in the kitchen and living room needs replacing, the cabinets are broken, and there's mould on the walls that needs to be treated before I can redecorate.

"Why didn't you tell me, man? I had to find out through Hanna that you're back now."

I shrug. "I don't know. I was kind of hoping to get in, sort this house out, and leave."

"You didn't think we'd run into each other?"

"I would have told you eventually."

"Just because Hanna is friends with Tilly doesn't mean you have to keep your distance from me."

"You've visited me."

"Yeah, where you live now, but we've not hung out here. What are you doing tonight?"

I raise both hands up, gesturing around the room. I'm going to be working pretty much flat-out to get the house done.

He sighs. "You're allowed to leave the house, Linc."

"I know, and I will."

"How are your parents and Stanley?"

"They're fine," I reply.

I'm surprised he mentioned Stanley. We don't often talk about him. I don't know if he hates Stanley, but his usual silence speaks volumes.

"You're going to need help with this place. Why didn't your parents hire anyone?"

"For four years, they've been paying the mortgage on this place as well as rent on the place they have now. They can't afford to hire anyone."

"Why didn't they sell years ago?" he asks.

"I told them to, but they wanted to wait and see if they could come back. But they don't feel Stanley will ever be welcome back in this town, so they decided a few weeks ago to sell."

He clears his throat. "It's not up to anyone else where Stanley lives, and it sure as hell isn't your parents' fault that he made a shitty decision."

"It wasn't just him though, was it? Robbie and I should have known he'd had more than a couple of beers and stopped him. We could have called a taxi. Hell, we could have called my parents or Robbie's parents. But we didn't. We all got in that car. *Fuck*, Robbie lost his life, and we put everyone else on the road that night in danger. We did that. How could we move back here?"

My heart plummets to my feet every time I think about how fucking stupid we were that night. I should have done more.

We'd been in a pub garden for most of the evening. Robbie and I were drinking beer. Stanley had a few before switching to Coke. We ate after, hours after. He should have been fine. Only I didn't find out until after the accident that, every time he'd gone for a round, he would add rum to his Coke.

Robbie and I didn't know the extent of his drinking, but that doesn't excuse our part. We shouldn't have let him drive, knowing he'd had any alcohol at all.

He blows out a breath. "I get it, mate, but it's not quite the same."

13

"That doesn't make it okay."

Nothing will ever make that night okay. There is no do-over. Robbie is gone, and I just have to live with the crippling guilt.

"You want to meet up tonight?" he asks, changing the subject.

I shake my head. "I need to make a dent in this."

"Fine, have it your way. We'll order in and … work."

"Jack, you don't need to help."

He holds his hand up. "I'm helping. Have you seen Tilly yet?"

The sound of her name being spoken aloud is sweet torture.

"Yeah."

"She cool?"

I watch him, trying to gauge how much he knows about Tilly's feelings toward me being back here.

"She doesn't want to see me," I reply, forcing out the words as they slice along my vocal cords.

"I'm sure it's just the shock of you being back, you know?"

No, I think it's because I had a hand in the death of her brother.

"Whatever," I say. "I'll do what she wants and leave as soon as I can. I don't want to make anything more difficult for her or her parents."

"Tilly is one of the most forgiving people I know, Linc. Don't write her off yet."

I walk into the kitchen, and he follows.

"Do you want a drink?" I ask.

"Coffee, please. Do you want me to talk to Hanna?"

I look over my shoulder. "No. I want you to leave it. Tilly and I haven't talked properly in four years."

"But you want to though, right?" He frowns. "You guys were close."

"Not that close."

He watches me for a second longer than is comfortable, his dark brown eyes searching for the truth.

Shortly after he got together with Hanna, Jack asked me once if I liked Tilly as more than a friend, and I told him no. At the time, I wasn't sure. When he asked, we hadn't been hanging around each other for too long. I found Tilly attractive—I'd always thought she was pretty—but I didn't have feelings for her back then. Or so I thought.

"All right. I miss our group, you know?"

Oh, I know.

I dip my eyes. "Yeah, I do, too."

Filling up the kettle, I flick it on and get two mugs from the cupboard. Most of our things are still here—we bought a lot new when we moved—but I obviously had to pick up food on the way here.

Out of everyone I hung around with, I always enjoyed being with Tilly, Jack, Hanna, Ian, and Mel the most.

"How are things with Hanna?" I ask, turning around and leaning back against the counter.

He smiles. "Good. You'll have to come see our place while you're in town."

"That'd be great."

Jack and Hanna bought a place together last year, and he has been inviting me over since they moved in. I didn't want to come back here, but now, I have no choice but to visit. It would be good to see his house.

"Where are you living now? Last time we spoke, you were back with your parents."

"Jesus, that's an experience not to be repeated. Never move back home after you've left, even for a short period. The second I leave, I'm finding a flat. I can't be there much longer."

He nods. "I wouldn't mind moving back home. Hanna refuses to do my washing."

Chuckling, I start making the coffee as the kettle clicks off.

I look up out of the kitchen window, and Tilly is outside again. Her stunning amber eyes lock with mine for a second, punching me in the gut, before she spins around and gets into her car.

I suck in a breath.
She's going to kill me.

3

Tilly

Lincoln has stayed true to his word, and for the past three days, I haven't run into him at all. Nothing. Not even outside his house. I don't know if he leaves it, but if he does, it must be in the dead of night.

The fact that I've not physically seen him doesn't stop me from seeing him everywhere though. Figuratively. There are so many memories of him all around. As kids, we all played outside in the street. He's all over town—in the café where groups of our friends would get milkshakes and the park where we'd hang out in the summer. The forest that I can just about see in the distance from my house is where we walked dozens of times.

When there was no threat of running into him, it was easy to ignore where he'd been. Now, the ghosts of him around town could turn to flesh.

I work at the local restaurant where we hung out just four years ago. I made it through my A Levels, finishing just six months after Robbie's death, but I didn't go on to university. Now, I have to figure out my next move.

Do I apply to uni like I've always wanted and study Criminal Law?

That would mean leaving my parents.

I tie my black apron around my waist and head out into the restaurant. My best friend, Hanna, also works here. She's on a gap year from uni after finding the second year really tough. She's going back next September to continue the nursing course.

"Quick, which one?" Hanna says, nodding to a table of three guys by the window.

Since the restaurant's makeover, making it more modern with avocado almost in every dish and a cocktail list that took months to memorise, it attracts a slightly older clientele than teens. We would have hated the change four years ago. But it's still called The Café, paying homage to its roots.

It's misleading, but it's kind of iconic to the town, and since we don't get many people passing through, the owners decided it wouldn't hurt business. It didn't. With the added bonus of serving alcohol, business has been better than ever.

I lean on the small bar and take a look. "Er, none of them."

"You're no fun this morning."

Tilting my head, I glare. "Well, Linc came home, and then Greg turned up at my house, playing the white knight."

She turns up her nose. "Tell me you're not starting to fall for Greg."

"No, but lay off him, okay? He's been a good friend."

"He's a good friend because he wants to be a good *boy*friend. You need to cut him loose."

Must we have this conversation every single month?

"Hanna, I've been very clear on where we stand."

"Clear with me or clear with him?"

Slapping her arm, I shake my head and walk past her to my section where someone has just sat down.

"Tilly, wait!" Hanna grabs my wrist. "I'll take that table."

"What? Why do you …"

He turns, and that's when I see why she wants to take it.

Lincoln Reid.

"It's cool, babe. I've got this," she says, pulling me back a step.

"No," I say, tugging my wrist from her grip. "That's my section."

"You don't have to."

Frowning, I disagree, "Actually, I do."

She takes a step back and grabs a cloth to wipe the bar down. "Go get 'im."

I've got this.

Rounding the bar, I walk confidently to Linc's table and hold up my notepad. He looks up and stills.

"What can I get you?" I ask, giving him the brightest smile that I can muster while my heart flips over.

"I-I didn't know you worked here," he stammers.

I close my eyes for a second. *Can we please just get through this?*

"That's okay. Do you want a drink while you decide on what to order?"

"This place has changed."

Lowering my notepad, I meet his gaze. "Do you miss the old chipped tables and aqua-coloured seats?"

The corner of his mouth kicks in a smirk. "A little actually. It does look better now."

It does. Now, it's super modern with clean lines and a black-and-orange theme, and the old counter is now a shiny black bar.

I bite my lip.

"Do you want me to leave?" he asks.

Yes.

"No, it's fine."

"I said I would keep my distance."

"You didn't know I worked here."

"I thought you would be in a big city, living in a penthouse and working some high-flying career in law."

His words feed the failure inside me.

"Nope, not yet," I snip.

"Sorry." As he takes a breath, his eyes close, like he's in pain. "I'll have a coffee for now, thank you."

"You don't want a beer, Linc?"

His eyes, blue and dancing, snap to mine. The use of his nickname yet again. It's not a fluke. I'd stopped using it after the accident. He would wince every time I called him Lincoln.

Apparently, that's over.

He frowns. "Tilly, it's ten in the morning. Do you serve alcohol this early?"

"Yes, but not often. I'll go and grab your coffee."

He opens his mouth, but I spin and run before he can say anything else. I already need some space from him. Maybe I should have let Hanna take the table.

"How did that go?" she asks, placing two mugs under the coffee machine.

I grab an oversize mug. "It was fine. Weird, I guess."

She takes a quick glance over her shoulder. "He's looking at you."

My face heats, but I don't raise my eyes. I already know that; I can feel it. I'm not sure where his head is, but I can't see us being able to go back to the casual friendship we had before.

We were never mega close, so I don't know why I feel like I've lost something there. I guess because the accident marked the end of our extended group. Things haven't been the same. Jack and Ian are still in contact with Linc, and they're friends, but Hanna and Mel never mention anything. They both respect the fact that their boyfriends are still friends with him, but they no longer are.

Not that I ever asked them to stop talking to him, but sisterhood solidarity and all that.

I finish making the coffee and go back for round two.

"Thank you," he says as I place his drink on the table.

"Are you ready to order?"

"Tilly," he breathes.

I don't want to look directly at him.

"Please."

Against my better judgment, I do look up. His eyes are pained, like it physically hurts to look at me, and my stomach twists.

"What do you want, Linc?"

"To reverse time. To do something to stop you from looking so sad now."

The ache in my stomach grows.

"What do you want to *eat?*"

Sighing, he hands me the menu. "All-day breakfast, please."

I take the menu and nod. "Okay."

Hanna watches me as I walk past her and into the back to give the chef Linc's order rather than passing it through the hatch. I do just that. Then, rather than going back into the restaurant, I go to the staff room.

Pressing my palms against the wall, I close my eyes and try to breathe through the tightening in my chest.

Breathe slow.

I stay like that for a minute until Hanna comes in.

"Oh God," she says softly. "What did he say?"

Shaking my head, I stand up straight. "That he would change things if he could. I knew that already. It's just that I haven't heard him say it in so long."

She wraps her arms around me and squeezes a bit too hard.

"Thanks, Han. I'm okay now, I promise," I lie.

Pulling back, she raises her black eyebrows. "You sure?"

"Yeah. We'd better get back out there."

"Are you really sure? I can cover for a while. It's pretty slow this morning."

"No, it's fine. I'm not hiding from Linc." I swallow.

"Do you think that maybe you should have a conversation with him? Like a proper one about everything, if he's sticking around?"

Shrugging, I reach for the door handle "Maybe, but I don't even know where to begin with that." *Or what my parents would think.*

"In your own time, Tills." Hanna follows me back into the restaurant.

There are never very many customers in on Wednesday morning, so it's always a pretty easy shift. Clearly, the universe has other ideas for me on this particular Wednesday though because Linc is silently watching me.

His gaze burns into my skin, sending my pulse into a frenzy.

Maybe I remind him of that day, too. I would never diminish the horror that he went through just because he's partly to blame for the whole thing. He watched his friend die.

I have dreams of what it was like in that car after it crashed; Linc has memories.

Pushing the thought away since I need to get through the day, I grab a cloth and wipe down a few tables. They're clean already, but right this second, there's nothing to do, and with him in the same room as me, I need to keep busy.

The chef seems to work at lightning speed because I swear, he has never made a breakfast faster than he's made Linc's. I need more time before I face him again. I'm holding on by a thread here. I pick it up from the hatch and hold my head high as I walk over. He lowers his phone and puts it down on the table.

"Do you need anything? Sauce?" I ask, handing him the plate.

"Thanks, Tilly. This is good how it is."

I linger for a minute, my mind going blank, feet refusing to move. He watches me like he's not sure if he should start defending himself in case I attack. I breathe heavier.

Not really sure what I'm doing myself and not wanting to look like a creep, I take a step back. My eyes never leave his, like he's magnetic or something. Him being here stirs up so many feelings and brings everything back to the surface that I've fought to suppress.

I've dealt with Robbie's death in *a lot* of grief therapy sessions. My therapist, Jennifer, took me through each feeling I had over Robbie's death, including how I felt about Linc and Stanley. Though I've accepted that I can't forgive them, I thought those feelings were done.

"Are you okay?" he asks, his intense gaze burning through me.

With a soft shake of my head, my heart drops. I murmur, "No," and walk away.

Those feelings aren't done.

Tilly

After I picked at an old wound by admitting to Linc that I wasn't okay, Hanna took over the table, and this time, I let her.

That didn't stop him from looking over at me when Hanna took his plate away. He knew why she was there; he knew that I'd swapped because I couldn't go back, but he thankfully didn't try to talk to me. He simply watched me with an unreadable expression.

Very Linc—Lincoln. Very Lincoln.

As if he were controlling time, when he left, the rest of my shift seemed to fly by.

Time is in slow motion whenever he is around, prolonging the pain of my having to see him, as I have to relive the worst moments of my life.

Hanna is meeting Jack after work for drinks in a bar near the restaurant. And she's somehow managed to convince me to go along, too. Don't get me wrong; I love going for a drink, but going for a drink with a couple sucks.

"I'm going to be a third wheel," I grumble even though I can really do with a drink.

She links my arm. "Shut up. I think Mel and Ian are going, too."

"So, I'll be a fifth wheel," I mutter.

Mel and Ian are the other members of our crossover group. Mel is my age, and Ian is two years older, same as Linc. He and Jack are the reason Linc started to hang out with me and my friends more.

I stop outside the bar and grab her wrist. "Wait. Linc isn't going, is he?"

"Jack hasn't mentioned it. I don't think he would invite Linc without asking if I was cool with it."

"You don't have to hate him, Hanna."

She gives me a sad smile. "Neither do you."

So, why do I feel like I do?

I avert my eyes, but she tugs my hand and forces me to look at her.

"I get it, Tilly, but don't let Robbie's death take over every aspect of your life."

"I haven't," I reply, frowning as my back stiffens.

"You're living at home with your parents and putting uni on hold."

"It's just not the right time yet, Han."

She tilts her head. "You don't have to rush anything, but you have to do things for the right reasons. Your parents will be fine if you move out, they'll be fine if uni takes you a little further out, and they'll be fine if you don't hate Linc."

I'm not sure my conscience will be fine if I don't hate Linc.

"I really, *really* need a drink," I say, wanting this conversation over with.

"Okay." She sighs. "Neither of us has to be at work early, so let's get drunk."

"Best idea ever." I push the door open and immediately spot Jack, Mel, and Ian at a table in the corner of the room.

It's still relatively early in the evening, so it's not too busy, but there is a small crowd at the bar, and the whole place smells like beer.

Jack stands up and greets Hanna with a kiss while I hug Mel.

"I'm so glad you've come, too," she says. "How are you doing?"

She knows that Linc is back, but we haven't had a chance to meet up and talk about it yet.

"I'm fine."

"She needs a drink, so I'll go to the bar," Hanna says.

Jack gently pushes Hanna onto a chair. "No, babe, sit down. I'll get this round."

I take a seat, too, after thanking Jack.

"How's it going?" Ian asks, shifting on his seat. He scratches his chin like he's guilty of something.

Instantly, I know he's seen Linc. There's no need for him to feel bad about that though. I understand Linc still has friends. I never wanted the hostility he received from the town. I just wanted them all to go.

"I'm okay," I reply, preferring a lie to spilling everything that's on my mind right now. No one wants me to bring the evening crashing down. "You?"

"I've seen him," he blurts.

Laughing, I nod. "I figured. He is your friend. You don't owe me an explanation, Ian. You don't even have to tell me."

"Right." He winces. "It's just that I told him we'd be here tonight—"

"What?" Mel snaps.

He looks at her. "You said you were okay with him."

Her eyes flick to me like I'm not supposed to know that. "I said I wasn't going to make your friendship with him difficult, so I'd be civil, Ian."

"I'm sorry. He just seems so …" Ian trails off, snapping his mouth shut.

"Please don't argue over this. It's fine if he comes." The words flow from my mouth like I mean them.

His eyebrows rise. "Yeah?"

"Are you sure?" Hanna asks. "We can have a girls' night somewhere else and leave the men here, if you want?"

"Totally," Mel adds.

"I love you both for that, but I'm fine. I mean, I'm going to see him around, and we do share some of the same friends."

I will have to see him, no matter if I'd rather not. Besides, once his house is sold, he'll be gone again.

Maybe, with the sale of their house and them being gone permanently, my parents will breathe a little easier. Things might start to resemble some version of normal.

"He might not even come," Ian says.

Yeah, right.

"Who might not come?" Jack asks as he puts a tray of drinks on the table.

"I ran into Linc and mentioned we'd be here tonight."

Jack's eyes slide to me.

"It's fine, honestly," I say. "Thanks for the drink."

Taking my wine glass, I swig a really big mouthful. It's definitely a wine night; it gets me drunk a lot faster than beer does.

Would Robbie care at all that I'm possibly about to spend an evening with Linc?

"You really are on it tonight," Mel says, watching me chug.

"Certainly am." Even more so now. It's not even a definite that he will come, but let's face it; I'm having a shit day, so he's going to.

Hanna starts a conversation about the festivals we need to attend this year, and I could kiss her. She's taking the limelight off me because we both know Mel was going to say more things. I love the girl, but she does tend to want to talk everything through then and there, which isn't always convenient.

I sip my drink, injecting myself into the conversation when necessary, but mostly, I just listen.

I'm too distracted to keep up because I feel nauseous, and no matter how many times I sip my drink, my throat is still bone-dry. I wish he would hurry up, so I could get this over with.

My stomach clenches with another sip of my drink.

Ian's eyes flick behind me.

"He's here," I say, watching Ian's reaction.

Slowly, he nods. "But he's not moving." Ian stands up and walks around the table.

"What's going on?" I mutter.

"He's watching you again," Hanna replies. She puts her hand on my arm, squeezing for comfort.

I want to curl up in a ball. Robbie would tell me to snap out of it, that I was friends with Linc before all this, and I shouldn't let his death affect everything. How could it not though? He was my big brother.

"What are they doing?" I whisper, staring ahead like there's a Picasso hanging on the wall rather than a stock image of a random boat.

"Ian is talking to him. Linc looks like he's going to leave."

Sighing, I put my drink down. My legs, seemingly forming a life of their own, get up and turn around.

One of those adrenaline things again? What are you doing?

"Tilly," Hanna calls after me as I take uncertain steps toward Linc.

He looks up like he senses me approaching.

Ian follows his gaze and stands straighter, ready to defuse an argument. But I'm not here to argue. I'm tired of being angry, so for tonight, I just want to ignore the past and have a drink with friends. It's been so long since I've done that.

Besides, I can ignore him.

"Tilly," Linc breathes, deep blue eyes seeking something in mine I can't quite grasp.

"You good?" Ian asks me.

"I'm fine. Can you give us a minute?" I reply.

He hesitates for a split second but then retreats to our table like he's being chased.

Linc grips the back of his neck. "I didn't know you'd be here."

"Seems to be a theme with that, huh?"

Wincing, he takes a step back. "Are you okay with me staying?"

"I am." At least, for tonight, I'm working on it. "Can we just have a drink with our friends and ignore everything else?"

"Ignore it?"

"Yes," I reply sharply, my heart aching at the thought of him trying to talk about Robbie to me. I can't discuss my brother's death with one of the people responsible for it.

Linc takes the hint, his shoulders hunching a fraction, as he understands my need to hide from it right now. "All right." He clears his throat. "Do you want a drink?"

"I have one, thanks, and look, Ian is at the bar, so I assume you're going to have one in a second, too." I twist my body but keep my eyes on him. "Our table is this way."

I avert my eyes, and that's when I feel the burning of my lungs. Letting out a breath, I walk back to the table, a little light-headed. Being around Linc still hurts so much, but I intend to be drunk tonight, so it won't matter.

Hanna looks like she has a lot to say when I sit down, and Linc takes a seat next to Jack. At least he's not next to me.

Giving my not-so-subtle friend the side-eye, I pick my drink up again. Hanna's lips are pursed, holding in everything she wants to say. Tonight, I do not want to hear it. Besides, I'm sure she would prefer us to all be able to be in the same place again. It does make things easier for her and Jack.

To Hanna, Jack, Mel, and Ian, my friendship with Linc is probably a bit like parents separating. I couldn't be in the same room as Linc after the accident, and up until this morning at the restaurant, I haven't been.

Jack and Linc are talking about football. Neither one of them is massively into football—unless that's changed for Linc—so it's painfully obvious the subject is for my benefit.

What would they be talking about if I wasn't here?

Frowning, I grip my drink in my hand.

Does Linc talk about Robbie?

He does I bet.

I lick my dry lips, as the room seems to shrink to half the size.

Mel leans in and whispers, "You okay?"

"Fine."

My eyes rise, and against my better judgment, they seek Linc. He's not looking at me anymore, but he looks about as relaxed as I am. This evening is going to be no fun for anyone if we're both on edge, tension seeping from our every pore. The air is so thick; I could choke on it.

Tell him to stay, Tilly; great idea.

I don't know how he feels about me—whether he still wishes we were friends or if he hates me, too—but he must want to be anywhere else.

This is my fault really. I was the one to learn he would be here first, so I should have left.

"Here's your Coke, mate," Ian says to Linc, placing a tray with five shots on the table.

Can I take them all?

"Who's driving?" Hanna asks, pointing to the shots and noticing we're one down. She then notices Linc's Coke. "Ah, you are."

He dips his head a fraction. "I don't drink."

My breath catches in my throat. *He doesn't drink alcohol anymore?*

"Since Robbie?" I ask. The words slip from my mouth before I can engage my brain.

We've been sitting down for about three minutes, and I've already broken my rule.

Linc's eye twitches at the mention of my brother's name. "Yeah, since then," he confirms.

I put my drink down because the glass was wobbling in my trembling hand as Linc's eyes cloud. Silence cloaks our table.

Tilly

Clearly, I've lost my voice, and it seems everyone else around the table is suffering from the same fate. This has never happened before. We can always count on Hanna to say something but not now. No one speaks.

How long has it been now? Ten seconds? Thirty?

Linc hasn't had a drink since the accident.

I wonder if Stanley has given up drinking, too.

I still drink. Alcohol isn't the problem. It's getting behind the wheel after that's the issue.

"You don't have to—" I clamp my mouth together.

Sure, he doesn't have to give up alcohol forever, but it's not my decision. What he does with his life is none of my business.

Linc shakes his head. "Actually, I do have to. I can't …" Frowning, he picks up his Coke and looks away from me.

He has to stay away from alcohol? There's something or someone making him? A medical reason? Is he sick? What illness would make him have to give it up?

Air leaves my lungs like they've been squeezed in a vise.

No. He can't be sick. I don't want anything to happen to him. That wouldn't accomplish anything. Nothing will ever bring Robbie back. Linc can't be ill.

"Will you be here for the cabin, mate?" Ian asks Linc, breaking the silence.

Every year, since they were seventeen, my brother, Stanley, Linc, Ian, Jack, and a couple of other guys I didn't know that well would go to a cabin on a cliff. Jack's family is pretty wealthy, and they've owned the acres of land for generations. They built a cabin there about ten years ago.

I've never been since it's a boys' weekend. All I know is that they play a lot of poker and drink beer. Though I'm sure they go out and find a bar to entertain women they find there.

"Maybe," he replies. "I don't know how long the house will take, but I'll meet you guys there wherever I am."

His eyes flit to mine for a second, unsure if I'm okay with him being around for months, let alone weeks. Their trip to the cabin is always in June, which is six weeks away.

Can I be around him for that long? More importantly, can my parents?

His house is right next door, so there is no way they can go that long without ever seeing him. At one point, he will walk out of his door at the same time as them. I think Dad would be able to handle it a hell of a lot better than Mum.

How would either of them handle knowing that I'm sitting around the same table as him now? Let's not think over that betrayal, shall we?

"I think, this year, you should make an exception, and we should come, too," Hanna says, raising her eyebrow at Jack.

He coughs. "Do you?"

There is room for us since Robbie and Stanley won't be there.

Unless Stanley will.

The thought makes me almost lose my dinner.

I don't know if Jack and Ian are still in contact with him. They were always more Linc's friends since they were in the same year at school.

Mel gasps. "Yes! Come on. It's time ladies are included in this weekend. You're all older now."

"What does our age have to do with a lads' weekend?" Ian asks, playfully nudging his girlfriend.

I don't think it's going to take much for him to cave.

"What do you say, Tilly? Are you up for it, too?" Hanna asks like it's already a done deal.

There's nothing I want less than to spend a weekend stuck in a small space with Lincoln Reid.

"Okay, you're inviting people to a weekend that you're not even invited to," Jack says. "No offence, Tilly."

I hold my hand up, not at all offended. I don't want to go anyway.

"Baby, us girls are coming, and you know it. You can still do everything you used to do with us there ..." She frowns. "Not the things you did before we got together though."

He rolls his eyes and looks to Ian for help, but all he gets in return is a defeated shrug.

"Perfect!" Hanna claps her hands together. "You definitely need this weekend, too, Tilly, so don't even try to get out of it."

Does she somehow assume that, because I waited on Linc this morning and I'm tolerating him now, I want to spend real time with him? Nothing is forgiven or forgotten. I'm *not* spending time with him. Right now doesn't count since I didn't know he would be here.

I give her a weak smile. "Whatever you say."

I'll tell her later that it's not happening, but I can't be bothered to argue it here. There is no point, and the night has already taken the most awkward turn, so there's no need to add to it.

"I might take off soon. I'm pretty tired," I lie.

Tired is the last thing I feel. I'm so very awake, my thudding pulse nowhere near calm enough to allow sleep. But the air is getting even thicker, and I need to leave.

I've done, what, ten minutes in Linc's company. That's plenty.

"What? You've not even finished one drink yet!" Mel replies.

Shut up.

I give her a pointed look. If she takes three seconds to think, she'll understand why I need to get out of here. I can't sit around a table and make plans with one of the men responsible for my brother's death.

Jabbing my fist into my stomach, I try to take away the pressure that's coiling inside.

"I'm going after this one anyway, Tilly," Linc says, tilting his almost-empty Coke in my direction.

"That's not …" I clamp my lips together. He won't believe me if I try telling him that he's not the reason I want to go. "I just want to go home."

My parents won't like me being here. They're more important.

I thought I could handle it. I thought I could push it aside, but I can't. Robbie's death isn't something that can be ignored. I feel it in every breath I take. Being around Linc only makes it that much harder to breathe.

"I'll come with you," Hanna says, always having my back.

"No, you stay here and have fun." I drain the last of my drink and stand up. "Night, guys."

I don't wait around long enough for any of them to respond. I hightail it to the door, gripping my handbag tight. Why I thought that would be a good idea, I'll never know. Maybe I'm going crazy.

The cool late-April air hits me as I reach the outside of the bar. Closing my eyes, I focus for a minute on the light wind moving my hair, the smell of Italian food leaking from the restaurant next door.

Grounding, my therapist, Jennifer, called it.

I open my eyes and look up at the sky. It's a clear night, the dark sky dotted with thousands of stars.

Ground, ground, ground.

I'm okay.

"Tilly." Linc's voice sends ice creeping down my spine.

I turn.

He steps closer, his eyes burning a hole in mine. "If anyone leaves, it's me. I can't ..." Sighing, he pinches the bridge of his nose. "Just ... I'm the one to leave."

Right now, *I* want to be the one to leave.

"I don't ..." *Jesus.* I take a breath. "Linc, I want to be okay with being around you."

"But you're not," he finishes. "I get that, Tilly, and I am *so* sorry."

"I know you are," I whisper.

"Tell me what you want me to do. I can get contractors in to renovate the house, if it's too much, me being here."

My parents would jump at that, I'm sure.

I shake my head. "No, I don't want this situation," I say, clutching my heart, "to have that kind of control over me."

Besides, he said they couldn't afford to get contractors in.

"Should I do better at staying away from you, or do you want to have it all out? Shout and scream at me, if that will help." He steps closer, and my heart plummets to the floor. "Hell, go full-on and hit me. Do whatever you need to do."

From here, I can smell the woodsy scent of his aftershave.

I clear my throat. "If you're still needing to ease the guilt, I recommend therapy. I'm not going to be the one to do that for you."

His eyes flicker with pain and then determination. "I don't want you to shout at me for my benefit. I understand my part in Robbie's death, and while I will *never* forgive myself, I have accepted it. There is nothing I can do to lessen the guilt; I have accepted that, too."

"Robbie wouldn't want you to spend your life feeling guilty." I'm not really sure why I said that. But I know that it's true, and I know that my brother would have wanted me to tell Linc that.

A ghost of a smile touches his lips. "He wouldn't, but it's not something I can control. Robbie wouldn't want you to spend your life in pain."

I dip my eyes, my heart almost ripping out of my chest. "Yeah, well, that's not something I can control either."

"Why don't you go back inside with your friends and enjoy being out? I'll go."

"Did you drive here?" I ask.

He frowns. "I walked."

We're only twenty minutes out from the town, but I wouldn't walk it alone at night. I always get a taxi.

"Can I walk with you?" I ask.

He watches me for a second. "Sure."

It's like I've left my body, and I'm staring down at this scene below me, screaming. *Why do I want to walk with him?* I just spent ten minutes in a bar, wishing I were anywhere else.

Linc starts walking first, and I keep with his pace.

We walk in the direction of home in complete silence.

Linc steals a look at me about every seven steps. He's probably as confused as I am. If I hadn't blurted out the words, I could have been in a taxi right now, away from him.

But here we are.

I should really call Jennifer ASAP because something is up with me.

"Are you okay, Tilly?" He sounds like he's asking a bit more than about my immediate health. Like he thinks there's something mentally wrong with me.

"I think so."

"One minute, you're practically sprinting out of a pub to get away from me, and the next, you want to walk together."

"I remember what happened back there."

"All right. Care to share *why* it happened?"

"I don't know how I really feel about you," I say, the words falling out of my mouth before my brain has time to engage.

Linc stops. His hand reaches out to stop me, too, but he hesitates and drops it back by his side. I plant my feet anyway and turn to him. We're alone now, on the edge of town before the long, stretching path to our little village ahead.

"You can't forgive me, but you also can't forget that we were friends. You're angry because I was so stupid that night and didn't stop Stanley from driving, but you also know that blaming me isn't helping anything. You want to hate me, but our past stops you.

"We were friends, Tilly. We got along so well. When our group was together, it was always you and me messing around or talking until someone made us stop and join in with everyone else. We spent hours watching old horror, listening to old rock, or walking around aimlessly. I miss that. I miss the ease of our friendship and how, no matter what kind of shitty day I had, you would always be the one to snap me out of a bad mood."

His words might as well be razor blades firing at my body. Everything he just said is true. I miss our friendship; I didn't really know how much until I saw him again. Missing someone who was part of something so awful shouldn't be possible.

Why isn't there something wired into me, something that stops me from wanting to be his friend again? I love my brother, so why can't I fully hate Lincoln Reid?

"You're right," I say. My shoulders sag. "I'm angry with you, and I miss you. I don't know how those two things fit in the same space. They shouldn't, but they do."

His eyes flicker with different emotions—disappointment, guilt, sadness, and maybe hope. "What do you want to do about this, Tilly? I'll follow your lead."

I shrug, the impossible situation weighing me down like lead. "I don't know what can happen."

I'm not sure how to get past the anger. It's so much stronger than everything else. Robbie's death was preventable, and that's not something I can get past. All Linc had to do was tell Stanley he shouldn't drive.

How hard is it to not get into a car?

"Things will never be the way they used to be," I say to myself as much as him.

He wets his dry lips and swallows hard. "I'm so sorry, Tilly."

"I know you are," I reply and turn in the direction of home again.

6

Tilly

Linc and I walk the rest of the way in a tense silence that makes me want to run in the opposite direction and never look back. This is all my own stupid fault.

Why did I think this was a good idea?

Walking home together was an old Tilly and Linc thing—back when we'd hang out in a small pub in town with loose morals and an entire lack of respect for underage drinking laws, and then we'd walk home tipsy, grinning from ear to ear. The new us doesn't do that. We're strangers now. We knew each other as teens, but I'm twenty-one, and he's twenty-three; we're adults.

At this point in our lives, I should be finishing up uni, and Linc … well, he never spoke about what he wanted to do. It was part of the mysterious thing he had going on, but I doubt this was part of his plan.

He keeps a healthy distance between us, walking almost on the kerb. One wrong step, and he would topple over, but that seems to be preferential than getting too close to me. I don't really know how to take that, so I try not to obsess.

Up ahead, our houses come into view. His looks like it's been vacant for years. Linc's neighbour on the other side mows the front lawn when he mows his own, but that hasn't been in a while, so even the front garden doesn't look too good anymore. At least it fits with the dirty windows and dead flower beds.

"How are you getting on in the house?" I ask.

It's nice to have a safe topic. Maybe, if we can stick to surface-level conversations when I run into him—or walk home with him—I can get through the few months he's going to be here.

Or I could do what I'm supposed to and ignore him completely.

He steals a look at me, arching his eyebrow. He's on to me, but I know he will play along. So much about Linc has changed, and so much is the same. He's quieter and withdrawn, and he looks like he's constantly in pain. When we used to hang out together, he would always joke with me and wear a smile. And, now, he doesn't drink. But not because he's ill.

Please.

"Progress is slow. But Jack and Ian are helping next week, so hopefully, we'll be able to get the kitchen floor ripped out and made good."

I want to know what it looks like inside. Linc's parents were house-proud; nothing was ever out of place. It's been left for years, so it must be so different now, especially with four years' worth of dust. It definitely will look different after the floor is replaced.

But I can't go in there.

"You couldn't just clean, refloor, and paint?"

He shakes his head. "Some of the kitchen cabinets were … damaged." His voice deepens toward the end of the sentence, hinting at something more.

How were they damaged?

"Sounds like there's a story there?" I ask.

I watch him to try to see if I can detect a lie. Most of the time, Linc is a closed book, and I don't have a clue what he's thinking, but very occasionally, like an eclipse, I can tell.

There are things I preferred to tell Linc instead of Hanna and Mel. Not now, of course. I can't talk to him about anything deep and real anymore.

So, why do I still feel like I can trust him with my secrets?

Because you can.

Linc is loyal.

"Do you want to hear it?" he asks on a sigh.

"Do you want to tell me?"

A hint of the old him shines through as he smirks, making his eyes lighten. "We don't bullshit, Tilly."

"We don't bullshit."

Those words have been spoken between us many times before. We always demanded the truth from each other, probably because we both equally hate when people don't say what they mean and waste time in being hurt and angry over it.

I suppose our friendship was an odd one. We didn't spend nearly enough time together to be as open and close as we were. But it was easy, and us hanging out together, those are some of the best memories I have.

"No. No bullshit," I say, stopping because we're getting dangerously close to my house.

My parents can't see this. They're not ready to be around him … if they ever will be.

He stops and digs his hands in his pockets. "*I* happened."

"We said, no bullshit. What does '*I* happened' even mean?" *Oh.* "Wait, *you* damaged the kitchen?"

"It was a *really* bad day."

"Which one?" I whisper.

He averts his eyes, suddenly finding something across the street incredibly interesting. So, we never bullshit, but we can and have chosen not to talk if we're not ready.

Whichever day it was—and I have a pretty good guess— he isn't ready to talk about it. I have a hunch it was Robbie's funeral. That was the worst day of my life. There was no more pretending that he could wake up. When a body is buried in the ground, that kind of kills any chance of hope even if that hope was an impossibility. It was also the first time I spoke to Linc since the accident. I told him to go to hell. Three days later, the Reid family left.

"What happens now, Tilly?"

I instantly know what he means as he looks over his shoulder at my house. We're three doors down.

"My parents wouldn't …"

"Yeah," he rasps as his eyes finally meet mine again, but I have to look away because the agony behind the dark blue is too much to bear.

My breath catches as I *feel* the pain he's in.

"You go first, so I know you're in safely."

I still don't look at him as I walk past. "Thank you," I whisper, darting along the path while jabbing the heel of my palm into the searing pain in my chest.

Linc

I watch Tilly enter her house and wait another five minutes before I start walking again. Partly because I want to make us walking home in the same direction as inconspicuous as possible and partly because I can't move.

She's still not okay with me, and I don't know if she ever will be.

This afternoon, at the restaurant, she admitted that she wasn't okay, but then she didn't want me to leave the pub, and she let me walk her home.

What do I do with that?

There's no clear path with her. I don't know if she really wants me to stay away or not.

I don't know what any of that means, but I feel a spark of hope ignite in my gut.

I've known for years now that nothing will happen with Tilly. There's too much bad history, but that doesn't stop me from wanting everything.

Where she is concerned, I'll always want more.

I trudge the final steps home, my boots thudding against the path.

Her house is on my left, but I don't dare turn my head in case I see her parents. They shouldn't have to make eye contact with me. I owe it to them to make my presence as pain-free as I can.

My phone pings with a text message as I let myself into the house. It's strange, being back here. I never thought I would come home. My parents wanted to, but Emma and Dan lost a child, and that's not something you get over. We could never move back next door to them.

That is another reason Tilly and I could never be together. Her family wouldn't want to be in the same room as mine.

I slam the door with a little more force than needed and tug my phone from my pocket.

Ian: You cool?

Linc: Yeah, man. See you later.

Chucking my phone and keys on the side table, I head into the kitchen to make a coffee. Since Robbie died, I've not wanted a drink, and I've not touched a drop, but seeing Tilly and knowing I'm hurting her make me want to get off-my-face drunk.

I won't. I would never do that to Robbie's memory. My friend is dead because of alcohol, so what does that say about me if I take up drinking again? Even the smell of alcohol takes me back to that day.

I boil the kettle and look out the window. I can't see her house from this room, only her front garden, and that's probably a good thing.

Shit, I need to get this house finished as soon as possible.

Seeing her again has made me as obsessed as I felt when I first realised I loved her. It was fucking awful back then. I can still feel the gripping pain of not only the realisation that I'd lost someone I loved, but also that I'd never see her again.

Now, she's here, in the flesh, and it's taking every ounce of control I have not to beg her to forgive me.

I want a chance.

I want it fucking all.

The odds of her giving me a chance for what I want are nonexistent. I'm not stupid enough to think that, even if she were open to more with me, it would work. Families get involved when you're more. If she and her parents managed to forgive me, they probably wouldn't forgive Stanley. And what about my parents? Emma was devastated when my mum and dad managed to get a top lawyer to stop Stanley from doing any prison time.

He's my brother, and I never wanted to see him behind bars, but I understood why he needed to be there. You should never be able to kill someone and walk away. But Stanley walked away with community service, a fine, and a driving ban.

Six short months of picking up rubbish for Robbie's life. Even I can see the injustice in that.

My hands are itching to reach for my phone and send her a text, so I busy myself with making my coffee. We managed to have a conversation, but that doesn't mean she wants me to contact her. Besides, I don't know if she still has the same number.

If she does, I know it by heart.

I'm not as sad as that sounds. I have a near-identic memory and can probably recall every phone number I've ever had.

I take the coffee into the living room and sit down. It's been a while since I've sat in here. I've actively refrained from coming here. There are a lot of memories in this room. My parents always worked long hours, so on the occasions when Tilly hung out at mine, our group would be in here, watching old horror movies.

Her ghost is stronger in this room than anywhere else.

I stretch my legs out and sip my boiling hot coffee.

This room needs a lot of work, so I'm going to have to get used to being in here. Tilly is just next door, so I shouldn't feel so shitty, being here with her memory.

Fuck this. I put the coffee down and head upstairs.

Sleep—that's what I need. In the morning, things will be better. Maybe Tilly will be open to talking again. Maybe I'll get a grip.

God, I need to shake that girl off. I've tried to over the years. I might love her and miss her like crazy, but I've hardly been a saint in her absence. Every woman I've been with since I moved has been a blonde, and every time I wake up, I drown in misplaced guilt.

Tilly isn't good for me—not because she's a shitty person, but because of what she does to me. I won't get what I want with her, and it's about time I work on getting over her.

Bad timing though, considering I'm going to have to see her for the next few months. But I tried forgetting about her while I was away, and that got me nowhere.

How can I make a decision about moving on from her and then change it the next second?

You don't want to let her go.

I use the bathroom and get into bed with my phone.

Mum texts as I'm about to lock the phone in a drawer to stop myself from reaching out to Tilly.

Mum: How are things?

Things. I get the distinct impression that *things* refers to Tilly and not the house renovation. If she were asking about the house, she would have said.

Lincoln: Things are fine. How are you and Dad?

Mum: Good. We miss you though. Have you seen Tilly?

48

Ah, I didn't take the bait the first time, so she went straight in for the kill on the second round.

Lincoln: Tilly is speaking to me.

Kind of speaking to me anyway.

Mum and Tilly were close when she was a kid. As Mum only has boys, she loved spending time with her. In fact, my mum was better than anyone else at braiding hair and that shit, so Tilly would often pop over in the morning if she wanted something more than a ponytail.

Mum: That's great. I miss her.

Lincoln: I know you do.

Mum chose Stanley. He's her son, so of course, she did, but that meant that she had to completely let go of her friendship with Emma and Dan and, in turn, Tilly, too. I don't know how Tilly feels about my mum now, but she's only just talking to me, so I'm not going to push anything.

Not that I expected a reply, but Mum doesn't text back, and I'm glad because I'm trying to forget about the blonde for a while here. At least, long enough to sleep.

Tilly

I wake up before my alarm for the first time in years. Miracle. Tilting my phone toward me, I see that it's five in the morning. *What the hell is that about?*

Groaning, I drop the phone back on my bed and run my hands over my face. I'm never up *this* early unless it's because I need to leave for a morning flight. When was the last time that happened? We've not had a holiday anywhere since Robbie died.

God, we've not done *anything* since Robbie died.

Of course, I'll not be able to go back to sleep now.

Kicking my covers off, I get out of bed and walk to my window. I open the blinds and glance outside. The sun is rising, casting an orange glow over the clouds.

Movement from the ground captures my attention. My heart slams to a halt.

Linc.

He's outside, getting some materials from his car.

What's he doing up so early?

Until yesterday, I'd not seen him leave his house. Is this why? Has he been going out early in the mornings to avoid running into me and my parents? He's not doing a great job of avoiding me; we're constantly running into each other, it feels.

I don't want him to have to get up before dawn because he's worried about upsetting us. At least, I don't think I do. Sure, it would be easier to not see him around, but working early mornings and late nights doesn't seem all that healthy.

People do like being up at the crack of dawn though. Not any people I can relate to, but it happens. Maybe this new version of Linc enjoys it. I don't know everything about him now. I didn't even know everything about him then. I never would have thought he would get into a car with a drunk driver. My brother either.

I shake my head, clearing haunting thoughts. I still care about Linc. I don't want him running himself into the ground, getting up too early and working too late just to get out of here sooner.

Gripping the windowsill, I close my eyes as the ache in my chest intensifies to the point where it might swallow me whole. All Robbie had to do was call someone else to pick them up. Now, I'm stuck with missing him so much that I can't see a way of returning to any semblance of normal. I walk around every day with this feeling of being so completely lost, and Linc being here is making it worse, much worse.

Why am I worrying about his sleep patterns and when he works? He's an adult.

I leave the window and throw on some clothes. I usually shower first thing in the morning, but it's too early, and I don't want to risk waking my parents.

Grabbing my phone, I freeze. On my bedside table is a picture of me and Robbie. It was taken about six months before he died. We're pulling funny faces, and he looks so content. Closing my eyes, I wait for the wave of fresh grief to pass.

What would he be doing now?

He was super smart, so I have no doubt that he would have been starting some high-flying career. He never really got the chance to do anything.

Clenching my fist, I take off out of my room and down the stairs.

I have to talk to my brother. My skin buzzes with the need to visit him. To let him know that I care and that I'm here. I hate that he's alone there. I've always taken comfort in talking to Robbie by his grave. He was such a good listener. He was the person I turned to when I had a problem because he could find solutions instantly. It takes me a lot longer, which is why I've struggled over the years to sort my own shit out. Give me someone else's problem, and I'll Dr. Drew that shit in three seconds flat.

I grab my keys from the side table by the front door and head outside.

Out of the corner of my eye, I see Linc watching me. He stills and straightens his back. I don't look over there because I can't have him try to talk to me right now.

Don't look at him.

Pressing my lips together, I focus on the job in hand. *Get into car. Drive car. Forget Linc.*

I just need to go and visit my brother.

With tears burning my eyes, I unlock my car and get inside. My hand shakes as I shove the key in the ignition like I'm running from a killer in a movie.

Just go.

Linc walks around his car and watches me head-on as I peel out of the driveway.

I got away.

I press my foot on the accelerator pedal, and Linc slowly gets smaller in my mirror. Then, he disappears completely, and my lungs empty.

Robbie wouldn't have cared that Linc was home. Actually, he would have. He'd have loved that he was back, and he would have wanted him to slot right back into our friendship group, but that's much harder to do in reality.

How I would love to have my old friend back in any other situation.

It only takes five minutes to get to the car park opposite the cemetery. The walk to Robbie's grave is long. He is buried right near the back, morbidly on our family's plot, near greenery. A light splattering of trees backs onto the end of the cemetery. It's super peaceful.

I get out of my car, lock it, and then make the walk along the gravel path to the very end.

His headstone has been maintained; we make sure it's always clean and looking tidy. For a teenage boy, Robbie was a neat freak.

With a heavy heart, I sink to my knees.

"Hey, bro," I say, placing my palm over his name.

Robert Drake.

No one ever called him Robert though, just like no one calls me Matilda.

"Sorry I didn't make it earlier in the week. I'm sure you know why."

Linc's arrival threw me completely.

"I know what you'd say to me, but honestly, Robbie, it's *so* hard to see him. I thought that I would be able to handle it. Sometimes, I can pretend a little better than others. Over the years, I even considered contacting him, but I'd stop before I pressed Send or Call every single time."

Robbie would have wanted me to reach out and tell him he wasn't to blame.

"I was on his Facebook page a few days before we knew he was coming home, Robbie, ready to send him a message, but I couldn't do it. My finger hovered over that damn button for five minutes before I deleted it. I can't pretend like I don't hold him accountable, too."

It's been a long time since I've felt like I *need* to hear Robbie's response. Right now is one of those times. There's nothing in this world I wouldn't do for one last conversation with my big brother.

"I have a problem here, and you know how much I suck at sorting those out, right?"

I don't think chucking Ben & Jerry's ice cream at this whole Lincoln thing is going to work.

"If the situation were reversed and it were me who died, would you forgive Linc?"

Maybe the question should be, *Would I want Robbie to forgive him?*

I'd like to think I would, but I don't really know how to answer that honestly yet.

"Doesn't matter, I guess. I can't force myself to want to be around him. Everything has changed. He'll be gone soon. He's working on the house full-time, so I don't think it'll take him long at all. The house will sell, and that will be the last I see of Lincoln Reid."

I curl my toes in my shoes. *I'll never see Lincoln Reid again. That's what I want. Right?*

I should never want to see him. But a part of me can't let go of the people we once were. I miss who he was to me. I don't miss what he turned out to be.

On a sigh, I kick my legs out and lean back against his headstone. I rest my head where his name is forever carved into stone. "I wish you were here, Robbie. Everything is falling apart. Mum and Dad still barely smile. They're scared of me going out in case anything happens to me, too, and I'm pretty sure I'll not be able to go to uni now. It's been three years since I was supposed to go. I don't know *how* to leave."

I'm stuck.

The day Robbie died, time stopped. My parents treat me like I'm seventeen still, and I let them because I'm too scared that they aren't coping. I don't want to make things even worse. If they knew how I felt, if they knew they were the reason I'd not yet done anything with my life, they would be gutted. But I don't plan on telling them, so I pretend like all is well, and I'm just not ready to go out into the big, wide world.

I've been ready for at least two years now.

I wish I'd taken the leap and gone to uni the following year I was supposed to. One year late would have been no big deal. People take a year off all the time. People don't often take more than three.

Fuck's sake, get ahold of yourself, you twat.

Gritting my teeth, I bang the back of my head against Robbie's headstone in replacement of him gently whacking the back of my head when I needed to pull myself together. He would never let me wallow.

"Okay, Robbie." See, this was exactly what I needed. A conversation with my big brother always gives me a bit of clarity when I feel like I'm walking around, blind. "That's enough, huh? Time to stop moaning and make changes."

I don't really like change anymore. It's kind of petrifying. But scary doesn't always have to be bad. I have to figure out what I'm doing and where I'm going because I can't stay working in a restaurant for the rest of my life. There is so much more that I want to do.

I want to help people. Law still interests me, but my experience with bereavement has made me want to counsel people going through the same.

To do that, you have to be qualified.

Now isn't the right time to leave my parents, not until Linc has gone.

Way to talk yourself out of it again.

"I should go, Robbie. If Mum and Dad get up and notice I'm gone without letting them know, they'll freak out." Standing up, I brush my fingers over the top of his headstone. "Love you. I'll be back soon."

I turn to walk away, and my heart takes a dive, slamming into the dirt below me.

Standing at the far end of the path is Linc. He's watching me but nowhere near close enough to hear what I was talking to Robbie about.

Thank God.

Why is he here?

This isn't somewhere he should be.

Shut up. Robbie would have wanted him to visit.

I ball my trembling hands and take small steps toward him. Seeing Linc near Robbie's grave has my stomach twisting in knots so tight that I want to hurl.

Linc doesn't approach. He keeps still, watching me with haunted eyes.

"What are you doing here?" I ask when I'm close enough for him to hear.

"I'm sorry. I didn't want to disturb you."

"Why are you here, Lincoln?"

His eye twitches at my use of his full name. "You looked upset this morning."

"So, you followed me?"

"No, not at first." He rubs the back of his neck, his dark blue eyes burning into mine. "I was coming here anyway when I noticed your car parked over the road. I was going to leave and come back later, but I was … worried about you."

"You don't need to be worried about me. I'm fine," I reply, my voice ice-cold as I stare back at him. I don't like him being here.

Though he has a right to visit his friend.

"Have you been here before?"

He drops his arm from his neck, eyebrows slightly pulled together, almost like he's in pain. "Yes. I come early."

"When there's less chance of running into me or my parents?"

He nods his confirmation. "I've come almost every morning I've been back, and I'd like to continue doing that."

He's asking for permission now. That's not really up to me. I don't get to decide who Robbie would have wanted here. My forgiving brother would have probably allowed Stanley to be here, too; he was his best friend. But Stanley, to my knowledge, has never been.

"Okay," I say slowly.

Linc breathes, "Thank you, Tilly."

"It's not up to me. Robbie would have wanted you here."

His lips kick at the corner, almost smiling. "I often talk to him. If anyone heard me, they would think I'm crazy because I talk to myself."

"I talk to him, too," I admit. "Though I do it here and not randomly at home or in the street."

He laughs, and the sound punches a hole in my heart. It's not a sound anyone gets to hear much, even before Robbie died when everything was perfect. Lincoln has always been a closed book, preferring to be on the sideline and observe. He's hard to read. Getting a laugh out of him is rare for everyone else. It used to be a little easier for me, and on the rare occasions when we were alone, his laughter seemed never-ending.

"I don't exactly do it in the street, Tilly."

"What do you talk to him about?" I realise that I've asked an incredibly personal question, and I don't have a right to know just because he's talking to my brother's ghost, but I'm curious.

"Anything and everything really. I need him to know how sorry I am and that he'll never be forgotten. Sometimes, I do things that I think he would have liked purely because I think he would have liked it, so I tell him about it."

I swallow back the tears prickling my eyes.

What does it say about me for never thinking of that?

Robbie's life stopped at nineteen. He can't do anything anymore, and I've not done anything he would have wanted to do.

"You do that?"

He nods, his expression sombre.

"I think he would have liked that. I … don't do things he'd like." *Why don't I do that? I'm his sister!*

As he takes a step toward me, his eyes soften. "There are no rules here, Tilly. You honour your brother in whatever way you feel."

"I don't really know if I'm honouring him at all." I'm not doing anything.

"You're here, talking to him. That's enough."

Is it?

"Well, I should go and leave you to visit Robbie."

Linc dips his head, his body tensing as I walk past. I don't look back.

9

Linc

Tilly walks away from me, and it takes every ounce of control I possess to keep my eyes forward.

I hate that she doesn't feel like she's doing enough for Robbie.

What was I thinking, telling her what I do for him?

I shouldn't have said anything, but I wanted to keep the conversation alive. I crave interaction with her, and I'll take whatever I can.

Even if I end up feeling like shit after.

Robbie's headstone looks brand-new, even four years on. Tilly and her parents have really taken care of it, like I suspected. I've been here every day since I got home, but before that, I hadn't visited him in months.

It was always a risk, coming back here to visit him. I only ever did it in the early hours of the morning, but I did worry that Tilly or her parents could be with him.

Every time I was here, I'd avoid my house. I'd go out of my way, so I didn't have to pass it.

I walk to my friend and sit down on the grass. "Hey, man. Sorry I didn't come yesterday. Things have been crazy, getting ready to renovate the house."

Shaking my head, I continue, "As you know, my parents decided to sell. I knew they would, and I don't blame them. As much as it pains me, this isn't home anymore. I wish it were."

Laughing, I nudge the stone above him. "Hey, at least Tilly's talking to me, right?"

Robbie asked me if I had feelings for Tilly about three months before he died. I denied it at the time because, although I liked her, I didn't realise I *liked* her. He must understand now how I feel. I've talked to him about her almost every time I've visited.

"I don't really know what to do with her, bro. One minute, she's cold as ice, and the next, she's looking at me the way she used to, like she still sees her friend."

Chuckling, I shake my head. "It'll always be weird, talking about your sister with you."

I'm sure he knows everything that is happening now. I'm not a great believer in the afterlife, but I can't believe that nothing happens when we die. I wouldn't talk to Robbie if I didn't think he was somewhere, watching and listening.

"Last night, when I arrived at the pub, she barely said two words to me, and then she left. I followed her to tell her to go back in with her friends and that I'd go. She pulled a one-eighty and asked me to walk her home. It seems she has more mood swings now, hey?"

Tilly has always been cool. While other girls we hung around with were more worried about breaking nails, Tilly would get stuck in whatever we were doing. She would be the one drinking cheap beer rather than cheap wine.

"I think that maybe she'll let me in again. In the few times we've spoken since I've been back, she gets to a point where she forgets herself, and things are normal for a moment."

I tap the stone below his name with my knuckles. "It's a start, right? And I can't deny that it's fun to watch her remember that she's supposed to be mad at me."

Frowning, I kick one leg over the other. "I mean, it's fun until she gets really irritated with me. I wish she didn't carry around so much sadness. I can see it in her eyes. It used to drive your mum crazy, how laid-back she was. She was always so carefree."

Why has everyone around her let her stop?

She's morphed into this angry version of the seventeen-year-old her. Now, she's twenty-one, and her life has been passing her by for the last four years.

How can her parents not see it?

"Do you worry about her, too? I knew she wouldn't be the exact same girl as before. None of us—me, my parents, or Stanley—came out of that the same, but we've all moved somewhat forward."

I can almost feel Robbie's judgment because I haven't moved that far. I've spent four years beating myself up over that night and missing Tilly until I think I am going to go crazy.

But I still have a job in the field I want to work, and I have my own place—or I will have one again when I move back near my parents. Tilly has none of that.

"I don't know what to do. I don't know what is reasonable for me to do. Telling her to get on with what she planned seems like a bit of a slap in the face, coming from me. But you're not here to do it."

Robbie could be quite tough on Tilly because their parents never were. They were happy as long as Robbie and Tilly were happy, which is kind of what you shoot for when you're a parent, but it didn't push them to be the best versions of themselves. So, Robbie did it for them. Emma and Dan are clearly still taking the same stance because Tilly isn't in her final year at uni, which is where she should be.

"So, if you could send me some direction, that'd be great. Or invade one of her dreams and tell her to sort her shit. Can you do that?"

Robbie would be laughing if he could hear me and probably telling me that I was a dick.

"I can't move on, Robbie," I admit with a sigh. "Not from her, not from what happened, not from wishing I could go back in time and stop Stanley from driving. We were *so* stupid. Silly decisions aren't supposed to end in death. Why did you have to die, and we didn't?"

That's never made sense to me. I was on the same side of the car as him, sitting in the back, but I walked out of there with minor cuts, some bruising, and a slight concussion.

How is that fair?

"I wake up every morning and tell myself that today is the day I move on. I can't change anything, so it's pointless, beating myself up, right?" I laugh bitterly. "If only it were that simple. Mate, I am so sorry."

When I think back to how idiotic and reckless we were that night, it makes me feel sick. We were in our late teens and thought we were indestructible.

"A few beers seemed like nothing. Stanley had no trouble with walking in a straight line, did he? He wasn't slurring his words; he didn't seem anything other than his usual, larger-than-life self. How were we to know?" Closing my eyes, I lean back. "Of course, we should have known he'd had more. His blood alcohol level was through the roof."

I tap my knuckle on the headstone. "There are no excuses, are there, man? We were all dumb that night, and you're the one who paid the ultimate price. At first, I thought I could help you. You weren't breathing, but I really thought I could change that. I thought I could get you breathing again, and I'm so sorry that I couldn't."

The events of that night flood back, darkening my mind and stealing my breath. I can still see Robbie clear as day, lying on the grass while I tried to awake him up. His eyes, so similar to Tilly's, were hollow. He was so pale, like the life had already left him.

Shaking my head, I attempt to cast away the images, but they're burned into my mind. Not even intensive therapy sessions can make these memories fade. They're here to stay, and I've accepted that I'll watch Robbie die every night before I fall asleep, every morning when I wake, and randomly throughout the day. It's always there, and it's my penance.

I've offered wondered if Stanley sees it as well. He came around and got out of the car while I was with Robbie. He watched him die, too. Unlike me, he never talks about it. My brother refuses therapy; he refuses to talk at all.

I don't know how he feels about that night. I'd like to think it's guilt, but I honestly don't know. Stanley has never taken responsibility for anything, so in his mind, he could have made up a scenario where it wasn't his fault. Like Robbie and I could have refused to get in the car with him, or someone could have stopped him from driving. He's never to blame though.

"I should go now. I have a lot to do, but I'll come back tomorrow morning, earlier. And I'll try to sort something out with your sister. I'll try to help get her back, I promise you."

Planting my palms on the grass, I push myself to standing.

"See you later, mate," I say, tapping the top of his headstone.

10

Tilly

Mum and Dad left for work after trying to get me to talk about why I was so "quiet" this morning. They had still been asleep when I got home, so I didn't have to have that awkward conversation, but they could sense something wasn't quite right.

The house is silent. Leaving Linc at Robbie's grave felt … weird, like I should have stayed, but I don't know why I would have needed to stay.

I walk from the kitchen to the living room and back.

Usually, my days off are spent properly, doing whatever I want—shopping, having my nails done, or binge-watching shows on Netflix—but today, there's nothing.

I stop at the fridge.

Food. I should eat.

Ugh, I don't want to bloody eat.

Turning around, I head to the front door. I can't stay in here. I can't wander around this house all day with only my thoughts and lack of appetite.

Slipping on my shoes, I grab my keys from the hook and head outside. Linc still isn't home, and it's now been three hours since I saw him.

Is he still there? What is he talking to Robbie about?

I would love to know.

Does he talk about that night? Does he tell him he's sorry? Does he avoid the subject altogether and focus on lighter things?

Robbie never dwelled on the bad. He wouldn't have wanted Linc to feel guilty forever. He would have wanted to hear about what he was doing now and dumb shit that he'd done. Robbie would have wanted funny stories.

I can't see that Linc has had many of them in the last four years. We were always having a laugh when we were younger, especially when we walked in the forest. I haven't been in there since he left.

Linc has never been super carefree or the life of the party, but compared to the brooding loner he is now, old him was larger than life.

Town is about a twenty-minute walk, and while I usually drive, today, I need the distraction. I hold my breath as I walk past Linc's house. A part of me still wants to go inside. He's only just started renovations. I wonder if it still looks exactly like it used to.

There was a flood, but I don't know how bad the damage is.

Yeah, I can't go in there. It'd be another reminder of what I lost. I think I can count on both hands the amount of times I've been in Linc's room, but the pull I feel to sit on his bed and listen to old bands or watch old movies makes me grit my teeth.

Most of those times we were alone were when I was having a shit day. When I'd had an argument with my parents or Robbie, when I was stressed over exams at school, and one time when I had been dumped by an old boyfriend.

Mel and Hanna always want to hang out as our trio and have a girls' day when they're feeling down, but back then, I wanted to go to Linc and listen to music. I suppose I was doing it all wrong, going to the moody one to make myself feel better when Hanna and Mel would have been a whole lot cheerier, but I would have felt pressure to feel better. I wouldn't have wanted to rain on their *fix Tilly* parade by wallowing in whatever issue was going on, but Linc would let me. Then, by doing nothing at all really, he would make things better. With each song that played, I would smile a little, and then he would make me laugh.

By the time we got through an album, I would have forgotten what was wrong. Then, we would put on something scary.

That was the power he had. I didn't appreciate it at the time. I didn't really think too much about what he did for me and how much I needed him. If Robbie had died under different circumstances, Linc would have been the first person I went to.

Songs wouldn't have been able to fix Robbie's death though, and they can't fix the vastness between us now.

I'm power-walking, almost breaking into a jog, trying to outrun memories. My feet hit the concrete hard, and I know, if I go any faster, I'll end up with shin splints tomorrow. Maybe I should. The physical pain would be a welcome distraction.

I used to run, but I've not been in a few weeks. I know I'll definitely be paying for it tomorrow.

Before I know it, I've arrived at Greg's workplace.

Why am I here?

He's working, damn it. He can't leave to talk me down from the ledge again. I've relied on Greg too much. If he knows I'm struggling, he will leave work. He's done it before, so I won't ever let him know what's going on during his work hours. It's not fair.

Besides, I know that I could listen to a million albums with Greg, and I wouldn't feel half as healed as I did with one song in Linc's room.

Shit, what am I doing? Am I going mad? Is this what it's like to lose it?

Here I was, thinking I was doing okay. Linc comes home, and all of a sudden, I realise how okay I'm not. Like, really bloody not.

I turn away from the big glass door, but before I can move, Greg calls my name.

Grimacing, I spin back. He's half-outside, holding the door open in one hand. He must have been walking past just as I was there.

"Hey, Greg," I greet with my most cheerful voice. I sound a little too much like Hanna as I channel her unicorn personality.

"Are you okay?"

"Yeah, I was just walking."

Letting go of the door, he takes a step, and he's outside. "Walking where?"

Good question.

"Lunch."

"Tilly, it's not even ten in the morning."

"Right. Obviously, it's morning. Brunch. I mean, I'm going for brunch. It's my day off, so I thought I'd go out. It's a nice day after all. Don't want to waste it."

Shut up, you lunatic!

He tilts his head to the side, keeping his eyes on mine, like he's trying to read my mind and find the truth. "You're going alone?"

"Yes. People do that."

"They do. You don't."

I stretch my arms behind my back. "It's good to try new things. Get out of that comfort zone and all."

"Are you sure you're all right?"

"Absolutely. I should let you go; you're working."

"Okay. Let's get together sometime soon."

Is that a request or a demand? Who knows?

But I nod along anyway. "Sounds good. See you later."

"Bye, Tilly."

He retreats back into the building, and I hightail it the hell out of there.

Why was that weird?

I felt like I'd been caught out. Okay, I kind of was, but I overreacted, and he now probably thinks I'm on drugs.

I should not be allowed to talk to people when I'm all worked up.

I take off again, jog around the corner of Greg's building, and slam square into a chest. Squealing like a chipmunk being tortured, I fly back. I'm inches from the hard floor, about to break my arse, when two hands grab mine and end my fall.

Gasping, I look up.

Linc pulls my arms, and I stand. *What is he doing here?*

He would usually smirk or come out with some witty one-liner, but after this morning, he's looking very sombre.

He lets go of me the second I have my footing again, like I've burned him.

Can I not catch a break today?

I stand straight. "Sorry. I wasn't looking."

"Why would you need to look when you run?" he mutters.

So ... sarcasm, or is he being a dick? It's hard to tell with Mr. Poker Face.

"About this morning, I know I was a bit weird, but I am okay with you visiting Robbie's grave."

You didn't tell him you weren't sure about it, genius!

His lips purse as he undoubtedly reaches the same conclusion. I'm replying to something I thought in my head.

"You weren't okay with it?"

"I ..." Frowning, I try to dig down to the bottom of my backward little mind and find the answer. Sodding blank.

"Tilly?" he prompts, his lips thinning with impatience.

"It's complicated, Linc."

He scratches the back of his neck and takes a deep breath. "It's not actually. You're either okay with it or you're not."

"Well, I think you'll find, I know my own mind better than you." *Debatable.* "So, when I tell you I'm unsure, I'm unsure."

Shaking his head, he looks up to the sky for help. I would do it, too, if it worked.

"I'm sorry," I say, my shoulders slumping at the weight of my words. "I don't want to feel like this."

His eyes meet mine again, and he looks sad, like he's just realised we haven't come as far as he thought.

One step forward, three steps back. That pretty much sums up my whole life right now.

I'm wading through mud, and I know I'll come out on the other side, but I don't know how or when.

11

Tilly

Hanna and I are sitting in a quiet café after a busy morning shift in the restaurant. The new breakfast menu is going down really well, but my feet are screaming from the rush, so I was glad when Hanna suggested we grab something to eat.

It was a solid idea, and I'm usually always down for food. Except now when I still don't feel like eating anything. So, I'm hungry, but I can't eat, *and* I'll be tired all day.

It doesn't help that I slept like a newborn last night, waking every couple of hours. My traitorous mind kept reverting back to my meeting with Linc at Robbie's grave yesterday.

Did he go back there this morning?

I wouldn't know, as I stayed well away, lying awake in my bed, wondering if he was sitting by my brother's headstone.

"I hate that it's too early to drink," she says, stretching her back.

Me, too. I could do with a Coors Light about now. Or three of them.

It's a little after midday, and we've ordered coffee and the all-day breakfast here, but I'm dreading it coming because my stomach is churning, and if I don't eat, Hanna will have questions.

"Technically, it's afternoon, so that's not too early," I offer.

"Yeah, but I have to go to Jack's parents' for dinner tonight, and I cannot turn up drunk. His mum will say things. She already thinks I'm not good enough for her *precious son*."

"She's crazy."

Hanna nods. "I know. So, have you spoken to Linc any more?"

"Yesterday. He was ..." Sighing, I loosen my shoulders. "He was at Robbie's grave super early in the morning. Then, I ran into him in town."

Her eyebrows shoot up. "Oh. Wait, what were you doing there super early in the morning?"

"I couldn't sleep, so I got up. He was outside, getting some stuff in from his car. I felt like the walls were closing in, so I took off and ended up with Robbie. Linc turned up shortly after. He admitted that he goes there either really early or really late, so we don't run into him."

"Does it bother you that he goes there?"

"Um ... sort of, yeah. I know they were friends, and I won't stop him because Robbie would have wanted him there. But ... ugh, I bloody don't know, Hanna. Everything surrounding Linc is so foggy. I miss my friend, but I can't see past what happened. How dumb is that?"

"It's not dumb. Do you blame Linc for Robbie's death? He didn't know that Stanley had kept drinking."

"I understand that, but he knew that he'd had a couple. Stanley was *three* times over the limit, and no one knew. Even if he hadn't seen Stanley order the alcohol in his Coke, you can tell when someone has had too much."

"Can you? I mean, I could tell if you have, but Jack can really put it away. He could be over the limit after one, but he needs at least seven or eight before it shows. Besides, Stanley always seemed drunk."

Hanna's defence of Linc leaves an unsettling weight in my stomach.

"Am I being unfair to him?"

She pauses and then shakes her head. "No, I don't think you are. You told him to stay in the restaurant and the pub rather than making him leave. I get it, Tilly, and no one can blame you for not jumping straight back into the way things were. You can't help how you feel about him, so don't beat yourself up over that."

I would love to jump back into the way things were. Back then, I didn't appreciate it enough, but life was pretty close to perfect. My whole future was stretched out before me.

"I don't want to feel like this, Hanna."

I'm sad all the time. I honestly don't think I know how to be happy anymore. Every day, I walk around with a big grey cloud over my head, waiting for it to rain heavier. There is no break, no sunlight shining through.

Right now, I'd even take feeling nothing.

"Okay." Her voice turns serious, eyebrows knitting together. "How are you feeling exactly?" She leans forward, ready to dissect everything I'm about to say.

I lick my dry lips. *Keep this about Linc, or she'll stress.* "Sometimes, I want to talk to him, and other times, I want to run in the opposite direction when I see him. I want to go back to being friends and having a laugh, but I know I shouldn't."

"Why shouldn't you? Linc didn't kill Robbie."

"He didn't," I confirm.

I get that, I really do, but he was part of it. He could have prevented it from happening.

"But?" she prompts.

"But he was there, and I'm so angry because the whole thing could have been avoided if they'd just called someone to pick them up. All Linc had to do is say no to Stanley driving. How is that difficult?"

Hanna reaches over the table and pushes my coffee mug toward me. Rolling my eyes, I pick it up and take a sip.

"Anger like that is going to eat you up. I'm not saying they weren't stupid that night, but they never intended for anyone to get hurt. Robbie and Linc believed that Stanley was okay to drive, or they wouldn't have gotten in that car. They trusted him, and let's face it; they'd probably done the same thing before without incident. They were young and stupid and thought they were indestructible. It was a horrible accident, babe. Most are preventable—that's why they're called accidents—but you can't predict them. I'm not saying you have to go back to being BFFs with him, but at least don't keep making yourself hate him even if it's just for your own sake."

"We were never BFFs, Han."

"Damn straight! That's my job. But you know what I'm saying."

"Yes. I just need to figure out a way to stop wanting to slap him and hug him at the same time."

"He is pretty hot."

I deadpan, "Not what I meant."

Linc is more than hot. I've always thought he was gorgeous with his black hair, dark blue eyes, muscular physique, and full lips. God, those lips are sinful. He's tall, dark, and brooding, which is sexy as hell. But he is part of something that shattered my heart even if he hadn't meant to be. That's really hard to get past.

I'm trying though because Hanna is right, and I don't want to walk around with anger weighing me down. It's exhausting, and it kind of gives me a permanent headache right behind my eyes.

"Whatever. The dude is smokin', and if I wasn't with Jack, I would take every opportunity to press my body up against his rock-hard chest."

"Okay! I get it. He's a fucking Adonis, and I should get over myself, so I can feel his six-pack." I'm joking, of course.

I love Hanna, and she's my person, but she doesn't get it.

Grinning, she shrugs. "I think it would help. On a serious note, I do think forgiving him and letting go of the blame you place on him will help you. Robbie would have wanted you to be happy, and he would have wanted you to have your friend back. Linc was always good at bringing you out of yourself."

"I'm not *in* myself." Smirking, I add, "There's a really bad masturbation joke in there somewhere."

"You loosen up when he's around. It's not a bad thing, Tilly. You feel comfortable with him."

"*Felt* comfortable," I correct.

"Nah, you still feel it. That's why you're so stressed. You think you should give him a wide berth, right? But you clearly don't want to. I vote you stop listening to your head and give him a chance."

"Maybe," I reply to appease her.

Hanna means well, so I'm not going to argue with her.

"All I ask is that you try. Why don't we all do something? Cinema? No, bowling! We used to bowl all the time."

"Um ..."

"Stop overthinking, Tilly!"

"Fine. All right, count me in."

"Good girl. Shall I get Jack to invite Linc, or do you want to?"

"Jack," I say. I'm not quite at the point where I'll ask Linc to go somewhere again. It's not something that's ever bothered me before, and I don't wait to be asked because I'm female, but things with Linc are still strained.

"Okay."

Our food is brought out, and that thankfully takes Hanna's mind off me for a while. Nothing she said is wrong, but the truth isn't always well received. When it comes to Linc, I don't have a very level head.

"Have you seen much of Greg lately?"

"No, not properly, but I'm going for a drink with him tonight. He texted me after we briefly ran into each other ... right before I ran into Linc."

"Oh." She bites the inside of her cheek while hacking apart a sausage.

"You mad at that?" I ask, dropping my eyes to the shredded sausage.

She looks down. "Oops."

"What's going on? Why did you say, 'Oh,' like you wanted to say a whole lot more?"

"What are you and Greg?"

"Friends," I reply. "I've always been very clear about that."

"Yes, I know you've told him you guys are only friends, but does he believe that? He's been hanging around for years."

I roll my eyes. "Han, we're friends. He's not hanging around."

"Would you be bothered if he was one of the friends from high school that you didn't see anymore?"

"I'm starting to wish you were," I mutter, narrowing my eyes.

She laughs. "I'm sorry. I'll ease up on you. I knew I should have brought up only one man today."

"Okay, we should eat in silence now—unless you want to discuss something about *you*."

"No fun." She pouts. "But there's nothing new with me. Jack is driving me crazy with this whole engagement thing."

"What?" My eyes bulge. "You're engaged? What the hell, Hanna?"

Holding her hands up, she shakes her head. "No, we're not. I would have told you. He wants us to be."

"He proposed?"

"No."

"Okay, I'm confused."

"He's been talking about the future a lot, and apparently, engagement is the next step."

Huh?

"You guys live together, so yeah, I'm with Jack on this one."

"Logically, it is. But isn't that boring?"

"What would you want to do next then? Kids?"

"Fuck off, Tilly. I'm twenty-two."

"You're giving me a headache." I put my knife and fork down and frown. I've barely eaten half. That's not happened before. I always finish an all-day fried breakfast here.

Hanna notices, too. "You're done?"

"Yeah, I can't eat anything else." I push the plate away and sip my coffee. My appetite has been nonexistent recently, and it's annoying because I totally planned to grab a Krispy Kreme before going home.

Hanna and I part ways after we've eaten—her going home to Jack and me going back to my parents'.

I spend the rest of the day in my room, researching what I need to do to attend university as a mature student. I'm in my early twenties but considered old for uni. I'm so going to be the sad, single woman crying into her large glass of wine and constantly swiping right on Tinder.

Greg asked if I wanted him to pick me up, but I told him I'd meet him at the bar, so that's where I'm going now.

I take a taxi because I don't know where tonight will lead. I don't have to be at work early, and I could really use a few beers.

Greg's already sitting at a table with two beers. Greg isn't bad-looking. He's tall with blond hair, blue eyes, and a strong jaw. Women fawn over him. He's had a few girlfriends over the years—none of them have liked me because he and I are friends—but he's never gotten serious with a girl.

Hanna's words haunt me as I head over to the table.

She thinks Greg likes me.

He does.

I shove the thought out of my mind, not having the capacity to overthink that, too.

"Hey, Greg."

Jumping to his feet, he gives me a hug—*nope, not overthinking that*—and we sit down.

"How's your day been?" he asks.

"Long. Yours?"

"Good. I got a promotion. You're now looking at the office manager," he says proudly.

"Greg, that's awesome! Congratulations. Why didn't you tell me earlier? Then, I could have picked you up, so you could celebrate."

"I don't need alcohol to celebrate with you, Tilly."

What does that mean?

Oh God, don't start!

"How's everything at home? It's been a while since we've met up."

"Yeah, things are ... weird."

"Is Lincoln keeping away?"

I shrug, grimacing at the awkwardness of covering this topic with Greg. "Well, he's trying to, but it's difficult since he lives next door."

Greg frowns. "How much longer is he going to be here?"

"A couple of months perhaps. Hopefully, shorter."

"Maybe I should offer to help him, so it's done faster, and he can get out of your life once and for all."

There was a point where I would have jumped at that. But, selfishly, I can't say it's been awful for me, having him back. Mum and Dad would hate me if they knew how I felt about hanging out with Linc ... or sometimes feel anyway.

I sip the beer. "Thanks for this, by the way. I appreciate the thought, but it's okay. Having him back isn't the worst thing in the world. Besides, I can't make everything I'm not happy with disappear."

Laughing, Greg leans over the table. "No, but I can."

"You have Mafia connections you've never mentioned?"

"Good one, Tilly. I mean, I will sort it if you want me to."

Sort it? Like he would make Linc leave? I'd like to see him try.

What would he even do? I can't see Linc rolling over and letting Greg intimidate him. Or anyone for that matter.

Linc doesn't really have many close friends, not too many people he would fight for, but I have no doubt that he would go to the very end for the ones he does.

Greg is mistaking quiet for weak.

"I'm fine," I reply, cringing at his attempt to be macho.

Greg could definitely take care of himself, but my money will be on the brooding guy who's always thinking.

Greg nods. "Let's forget him tonight."

"Sounds good to me. How are your parents?"

"My mum misses you. She's desperate to pass on her recipes to someone."

"You've not told her I can't cook yet? I get that from my mum."

"She would only see that as a challenge and …"

I stop listening—not because I'm not interested, but because I suddenly spot a pair of dark blue eyes burning into mine.

Although I'm not looking at Greg, I do register him following what I'm staring at.

He growls. "Seriously, he comes here?"

His hostility snaps me out of my trance.

"He didn't know we would be here."

This town is small, and now that Linc is back, it seems so much smaller.

"Whatever. The prick needs to leave."

"Don't! You came here to have a drink with me, so let's focus on catching up."

Greg turns back to me, and I smile.

My mind is now anywhere but on catching up with him.

Linc

This is exactly what I didn't ever want to see.

Ian walks past me to the bar.

I swallow hard through the painful tightening of my throat as I try to ignore Tilly and Greg.

Are they here on a date?

"Dude?" Ian slaps my upper arm. He came back to see what's kept me planted in the same spot. "What're you drinking?" He turns his head, looking for the cause of my distraction. "Ah."

I take a few steps to the bar, breaking eye contact with Tilly. "I want a beer and a whiskey, but I'll have a Coke."

Ian rests his elbows on the wooden bar and leans closer. "Do you want to leave?"

Yes.

"No. Why?"

He tilts his head like he thinks I'm a dickhead. "They're just friends."

"She can do what she wants." The words burn.

She can, of course, but I don't have to like it.

"I think you should tell her how you feel."

"I think you should shut up."

Laughing, he places our order and looks for a table. "There's one near them ... or we're standing."

The table he's talking about isn't right next to them—there's another couple between the tables—but it's still a little close for comfort.

"We're standing," I reply.

"Fuck that, mate. I've been on my feet all day."

Ian orders and pays for our drinks, and I reluctantly follow him toward the free table right in the centre of my own personal hell.

Tilly's eyes meet mine, and she looks at me with so much hate, I barely recognise her. Greg's jaw looks about ready to snap as he grits his teeth. So, there's someone who hates me more than she does in this room. I'll take that.

I nod. "Tilly. Greg."

Ian stops and raises his eyebrow, clearly not thinking we'd stop for small talk.

Greg only glares, but Tilly takes a breath and says, "Hello, Linc."

Linc.

So, she's not as mad at me as she wants to be right now. That's a good start.

"How's it going, Tills?" Ian asks.

I envy that he can be so casual when he's talking to Tilly. That used to be my relationship with her.

She nods, her eyes losing the tension when she looks at Ian. "Good, thanks. What are you guys up to?"

That can be translated to, *Why the hell is Linc here?*

"We need a drink."

Tilly's amber eyes immediately seek out the drink I'm holding. Her shoulders relax when she sees the Coke. I'm not ever going back on my decision to quit drinking. My friend is dead as a direct result of alcohol, so it's not happening. Not ever.

I clear my throat. This is awkward as fuck, but I don't really want to leave them alone. In fact, I want to pull a chair over and sit between them.

"I think your table is being taken," Greg says, straightening his back. He sounds desperate to get us away, his voice hitching a couple of octaves toward the end.

Ian and I turn, and sure enough, someone is sitting on the table we were going for.

"Damn," Ian mutters. "Do you guys mind if we join you?"

I would object, but I was about to say the same. Sure, she might be pissed off with me, but at least they won't be alone. I sit down before either of them can reply.

Ian takes the seat between me and Greg and says, "Thanks."

Tilly glances at me out of the corner of her eye, and the tightness is a kick to the gut. She's still mad. Whatever. She's often mad.

"How are you?" I ask her, wanting to add, *after the other day*, but refraining.

"Fine. You?" She's being polite, but the clipped tone to her voice and death stare tell me she's anything but.

What the fuck is she doing with Greg?

They've been friends ever since I can remember, but, like me, he wants more. He's always wanted more though, and she's never been interested. I don't even think she knows how he feels; that's how off her radar he is.

"No Hanna or Mel tonight?"

"No," she replies, sipping her beer.

"Tonight, Tilly is having a drink with me," Greg says, interrupting our conversation.

His words sound an awful lot like a big, *Fuck off*, to me and Ian. But we're not going anywhere. The thought of her leaving with him makes me want to punch something and then chuck up.

She's mine. I don't care about the circumstances. I don't care about the past or what the future might be. Tilly is mine. She's mine until she sends me away with no hope of anything ever happening.

Even then, I'm not sure I'll fully let her go.

"Nice," Ian says, settling back in his chair.

I grin behind my glass of Coke.

Ian strikes up a conversation with Greg about cars. Greg has always been super into cars, thinking he was going to be the next Ayrton Senna, so he can't resist being sucked in.

"Have you been back?" Tilly asks me.

She doesn't need to expand because I know she means to Robbie's grave.

"This morning," I reply. *Every morning.*

Nodding, she takes a long swig of her drink and closes her eyes.

"Are you really okay with it?"

"I think I am." She gives me a smile. "I'm working on it."

"Thank you."

"So, Lincoln," Greg says.

Obviously, Ian's conversation has run its course, or he's just remembered that Tilly is here, too. I wonder why she's not into him …

"Yes, Greg?" I say and grit my teeth.

His mouth lifts in a smirk that is begging to be punched. "You didn't think it would be better to hire someone to work on your house? I mean, you must have better things to do than renovations on an old house."

"Nope, I'm good here."

"Really. There no job back home?"

"I recently left it."

He smirks again. "So, you're between jobs."

"Yep."

"Sounds expensive to take a few months off."

I shake my head. "I have plenty of money to keep me going, but thank you for that heartfelt concern."

Ian looks between me and Greg with amusement in his eyes. He lifts his eyebrow to show whose team he's on, and I laugh.

Tilly doesn't miss the look, but I don't think she gets what it means. Ian knows how I feel about her; she doesn't.

She puts her drink down and folds her arms. "I thought you were super busy with the house." Translation: why are you here?

"All work and no play makes Linc a dull boy," Ian says, slapping my arm with the back of his hand.

Greg snorts, but I ignore it.

"Will you need a lift home?" I ask her. It's been five minutes, but I'm ready to go.

"I have my car. She's with me!" Greg spits.

"And you have a beer," I grit.

Tilly's eyes snap to Greg. "You're planning on driving?"

"We'll get a taxi home. I can come back for my car tomorrow."

Whose home is he planning on going to?

"I have my car, and I'm not drinking," I tell her.

"I've got this," Greg snaps.

Sighing sharply, Tilly says, "Stop. Greg, Linc lives next to me. It makes sense that he drives me."

"You can't get in a car with him."

I ball my hands into fists, heat flushing through my body. "Why the fuck not?"

"Don't, both of you." She stands up. "I'm ready to leave now, Linc."

"What the hell, Tilly? You came here to have a drink with me, and you're leaving with *him*? Let's tell them to fuck off and get on with our evening."

"No, thanks. Neither of you is playing nice, and I don't much feel like being social anymore. Linc, please take me home."

I'm on my feet before she finishes the sentence.

"Later, guys," Ian says, holding his beer up.

He came with me, but he'll find another way home, so I can take her back on my own.

I give him a nod and make a mental note that I owe him one.

Greg tries to move toward Tilly, but she holds her hand up.

"I'm over the pissing contest already. I'll talk to you later, Greg."

I follow Tilly out of the pub. I know I shouldn't get cocky because she's probably going to be angry and yell when we get into the car, but fuck, I feel cocky. She wants me to take her home. Who cares if it makes logistical sense?

He's her friend, but she's still leaving with me.

Tilly gets in my car the second I unlock it and slams the door so hard, the car moves.

Here we go.

I get in, too, and press the ignition button. She buckles the seat belt and takes a deep breath.

"Tilly—" I start, but she cuts me off pretty quickly.

"What the fuck was that?"

"That was a drink in the pub with—"

"Don't be cute, Linc; it doesn't suit you."

"Ouch."

She growls, and I clench my stomach muscles and my jaw, so I don't laugh.

"You were a dick back there!"

"I think I was perfectly pleasant actually. It was Greg who started with the hostility."

"Because you crashed our …" She frowns.

"Your what, Tilly? Date?" The word tastes foul on my tongue.

"No, not a date." Closing her eyes, she exhales and slumps back against the seat. "He's a friend."

He'd better be. The thought of them together makes me feel violent.

"Does he know that?"

"Don't start, Linc. It's none of your business, what's going on between me and Greg."

"So, there is something going on between you two?"

"That's not what I'm saying! The point is, if there were, it wouldn't have anything to do with you."

"Why are you still mad at me?"

She folds her arms and looks out the side window, her head facing as far away from me as she can get it. If she's not careful, she's going to end up pulling some *The Exorcist* shit.

"Tilly," I say on a sigh. My God, she is more up and down than a prostitute. "Tilly, talk to me."

"Just stop talking because it's making me more irritated."

I take off out of the pub car park. Greg runs out the door, but we're already gone. Tilly's phone rings the next second.

"That Greg?" I ask, already knowing the answer.

Tilly doesn't reply, but that's hardly a surprise. She does hang up the phone, ignoring his call. It seems we're both getting the silent treatment.

I pull down our road five minutes later and stop three houses from hers. "Tilly," I try again.

"Linc, please, I really need you to give me some space for a while."

I hold my hands up. "All right."

"Thank you for the lift," she whispers and gets out of my car.

I watch her walk away and disappear into her house.

13

Tilly

If Linc's car didn't give him away, I would think he had left town already. He's gotten really good at hiding over the last week. I've not seen him at Robbie's grave either, but I've purposefully not gone early in the morning again. I did ask him to give me some space.

Even Greg has been giving me space. He texted me a couple of times, which I replied to, but I haven't met up with him since the pub. There was no need for all the hostility from either of them. They don't like each other, and I get that. I've hardly helped by complaining about Linc to Greg, but that doesn't excuse his hostile behaviour.

I'm going to have to speak to them both soon. Linc is still here and will be for the foreseeable future. Personally, I would prefer he didn't leave town. I think. It seems wrong … or maybe it's right. All I know is, Robbie would have been happy with Linc visiting his grave. Mum and Dad don't know, obviously, and there's no reason to upset them. They were so heartbroken when Linc's parents asked if they could visit Robbie shortly after he was buried, but I don't know how much has changed for them.

Some days, it seems like nothing is different, and Robbie's death is still as raw as the day we got the news.

Mum is in the kitchen, cooking bacon sandwiches—same as she's done every Saturday for years. It was Robbie's favourite part of the week and the only time he ate breakfast with us.

I watch her from behind my mug of coffee. She's a beautiful woman with shiny blonde hair that sits on her shoulders, big blue eyes, and a killer figure. But she's sad *all the time*. Her shoulders hold tension, changing her posture completely. She used to be taller. I can't imagine what it's like to lose a child, but I do know my mum battles to get out of bed every day. I suspect she only does it for me.

"Won't be long, Tilly," she says, turning the bacon on the pan. Her voice is low and raw, like she spent a lot of time crying last night.

Bacon is the least of my concerns right now.

"Are you okay, Mum?"

She looks over her shoulder and smiles. Although she never looks happy with any smile now, her ones for me are genuine. "Of course, darling."

"Have you seen him?" I ask.

Not once has she mentioned Linc since the day he arrived back. My parents talk about Robbie all the time but rarely mention Lincoln, Stanley, or their parents. Hell, my parents used to be friendly with Cliff and Martha. They've not spoken since Stanley got off with a fine, community service, and three-year driving ban.

Stanley has been allowed behind the wheel of a car for a year now.

Cliff and Martha were elated that he wouldn't be serving years behind bars. Mum and Dad were devastated.

Until his recent return, that was the last time I spoke to Linc, too, and I told him to go to hell.

"No, he's stayed true to his word and kept his distance, just like he told you." She turns on her heel, holding the tongs in her hand that she's using to turn the bacon. "Has he approached you?"

"No, he hasn't."

"Why doesn't that sound like the end of the story?"

I put my mug down on the table. "He came into the restaurant, not knowing I worked there."

"When was this? Are you okay?"

She doesn't need to know that it was last week or that he walked and drove me home. I've kept it all from her.

"Not long ago," I reply. "I'm fine. He was apologetic and offered to leave, but I can't force him out every time we accidentally run into each other. I can't walk around town, constantly looking over my shoulder."

Mum gives me another smile. "You're a good girl, Tilly, and so strong."

"Thanks, Mum," I say, not really sure if I should accept the compliment or not.

I suppose it depends on how you look at it. I'm strong for my family, making sure they're okay, but I'm not strong for myself, or I would be in my final year of uni right now, preparing to graduate and start a career.

I think, actually, I'm a bit lost and unable to find a way to get what I want. That was something I used to rock at. I knew what I was doing, where I wanted to go, and what steps I needed to take to get there.

Now, my life is like a game of Snakes and Ladders. Each time I step up, there's a really big slope, ready to slide my butt straight back down again.

Mum plates up bacon sandwiches.

"Thanks," I say as my stomach rolls in rejection of the food. I don't much feel like eating.

I'm constantly on edge, nervous energy taking up residence in my gut and claiming squatter's rights. Until Linc is gone, until there is no chance of my parents running into him, I don't think I'll be able to relax.

"Is there something wrong with the food?" Mum asks when I don't immediately dive in.

I smile up at her and wince as the heartache she carries around blinds me. I miss Robbie all the time, but I can't imagine what it's like for her. She feels it in every cell of her body, every second of the day. Although she would never class herself as a strong person, she is, just by getting out of bed in the morning.

"It's great as usual, Mum, but I don't have much of an appetite right now."

With a deep frown on her forehead, she places her palms on the table beside me. "Are you sure everything is okay, Tilly?"

"I'm fine."

Linc is eventually going to go home, and then things will get back to normal. Soon, our town won't be buzzing with gossip of the youngest Reid's return. I wish I had an end date, so I could cross off the days. Not knowing when I'll be able to breathe properly again makes me apprehensive, my stomach constantly churning.

"You know you can talk to me about anything, don't you?"

Nope. I used to be able to. Mum and I would have long late-night talks about anything and everything. We had such an open relationship, but the second Robbie died, that died, too. She's too afraid of something being wrong in my life, and I'm too scared to pile more worry onto her shoulders.

"Of course. All is great, Mum. Things are just a bit weird right now, but it'll settle down."

"Ah," she says, lifting her head to the ceiling. When she looks down, her face hardens, lips pursing, and she sits down. "This is about Lincoln."

"He just brings back a whole heap of memories that I wasn't prepared for."

"I understand," she whispers, her voice weak and clogged with emotion, her eyes glistening with the shine of withheld tears.

This is why I don't speak to her about things.

"Don't worry about it, Mum. I'm working through it." I've said too much already. "It's all good."

"We can talk about it, if you'd like."

No, Mum, we can't.

"That's okay." I pick up the sandwich.

"Tilly, are you struggling with Lincoln's return?"

I stare at the bacon in front of my face. *Why couldn't I just eat you when she first put the plate down?*

"Not him exactly. We were friends, and it's strange, not being friends now."

"You don't feel like you could be?"

I shake my head. "There's too much."

When I see him, I see my brother. *How do I get past that?*

"Yes. That's how your father and I feel, too. Lincoln wasn't driving the car, but he was there. He walked away, and Robbie is buried in the ground." She sucks in a breath that sounds like she's being strangled through. "My son is ..."

"Mum, it's okay," I say with my heart in my stomach. "Linc will be gone soon."

We need to stop talking about this!

Sniffing, she blots under her eyes. "He will. Then, things will be better."

That has been her mantra for the last four years. We just have to get through one thing and then the next, and things will be better. Nothing has gotten better. I don't really know if my mother has mixed up the definition of *better* with *absolute shit*, but she's lying to herself.

Mum and Dad pushed therapy on me. They even went with me for a short time, but then they soon stopped. Apparently, they felt like they didn't need it anymore. They need it now more than ever.

I think, if Robbie had been an only child, they would have gone with him. I'm the only thing keeping them on earth, but that doesn't stop them from half being with Robbie, too.

Then, I suppose none of us are walking around with our hearts in this life. I've experienced some of the worst that life has to offer, and my parents lost a child. Why would we be excited for what the future held when I can't see a good future right now?

"Yeah, things will be better when he's gone," I repeat, spinning her the same bullshit she spun me.

Mum stands up and goes back to the pan on the hob, ready to dish up Dad's food. I lower my sandwich and sigh.

We're all lying to ourselves here.

Linc

Tilly hasn't spoken to me in almost a week and a half.

I've seen her outside, but I've not gone out. Not once in the last ten days has she looked over at my house when I've seen her, but before that, we had a few conversations. She's so back and forth, clearly struggling with me being home and unsure of what she wants.

I get it. If she could forget, we could so easily go back to the way things were—to the teasing and the movie marathons and the freedom to be ourselves. A part of me wants to go to the restaurant, so she'll have to face me, but I can't bring myself to do anything that could cause her pain.

I love her, and I want to protect her even if that means taking myself out of the equation—for now.

Ian and Jack are over, helping me lay new floorboards downstairs, as the old ones were wrecked by the flood. They might know how Tilly is doing since Hanna and Mel talk to them, but if she hates me, I don't want to hear it.

Jack taps me on the back. "We going for a beer after this? You owe us for free labour, Linc."

"Yeah, sure. Whatever."

I'm going to have to get some beer for Jack and Ian.

They're here every spare minute they have, helping me out and asking for nothing in return. Nothing but alcohol, of course.

"Want to see if the girls will meet us?"

The girls as in Hanna and Mel, or does that include Tilly, too?

"Sure, if you want, man."

Jack and Ian look at each other, exchanging an inside glance.

I straighten my back, pressing my hand into the aching muscle. Working on my knees is killer. "What?"

"If Hanna and Mel come, they'll probably invite Tilly," Jack tells me.

"I figured as much," I reply. I'm hoping as much.

We've got to get past this nonverbal, *avoiding each other* thing. Neither of us can do that indefinitely.

Ian clears his throat. "You're okay with seeing her again? I couldn't help but notice things have been frosty recently."

Frosty? She's gone full-on Ice Age.

I shake my head. "She can't decide if she's okay with me or if she hates me. I think she flits between them. After the pub with Greg, she's pissed at me, so right now, I'm not coming off so well."

"You thought about talking to her?" Ian asks.

"I think the fact that she's ignoring me makes it pretty clear that she doesn't want to talk at the minute, and I don't want to push." *Not yet anyway.*

Jack throws the hammer he was working with down. "Sometimes, you need to jump though, mate. Go and make her talk to you. Clear the air. I think you'll both feel better for it."

God, if we could do that, it would mean everything. If I could just wake up in the morning and know that she didn't hate me …

But I didn't bump her car or anything trivial like that. I was involved in an accident that killed her brother. What kind of conversation can you have that would clear the air of that? I'd do it. I'd do anything to make this even a fraction better for her, but I'm clueless.

Through my life, I've prided myself on not getting involved in anything messy. I stay out of people's business and stay away from people who crave drama. I've never had to deal with situations that get out of hand or are complex, not like some friends who have dated several people at once or dabbled in things not so legal, so I'll freely admit that I'm walking blind.

"That won't work," I tell them. "I'm just going to give her the space she wants for now and figure the rest out later. I won't be here for much longer."

"That doesn't sound like a good plan, mate. Our trio has been reunited," Jack says, whacking my chest with the back of his hand.

"Yeah, well, you guys will just have to come and visit me more."

Ian folds his arms, ready to challenge. "Visit you where? You don't have a place to live yet."

"You make it sound like I'll be on the street. There are plenty of rentals where I was; it won't take me long to find something."

"You're standing in a house your family owns," Jack points out.

"I've pretty much been a hermit for the last four years, but I've not saved enough to buy this house."

"That's why they have mortgages, dumbarse," Jack quips.

"I'm not buying my parents' house." I can't do that to Tilly and her family. "The best thing to do is for my parents to sell up and for me to leave. I miss hanging out with you guys, too, but that was another life."

"Well, who says your next life needs to be somewhere else? You could find a place here. Things will settle down," Ian pushes.

"Let's not go there, Ian."

I have done that a thousand times over in my head. I've thought of scenarios where I get to stay and call this town my home again, but they're just dreams.

Ian sighs. "Have it your way."

"Come on, fuckers. Let's go and eat," Jack says, slapping my back.

I chuck down my tool because I'm starving, and they're not going to do any more work before I buy them lunch.

As the only one of us who doesn't drink alcohol, I'm also always the driver.

"Is Tilly working today?" I ask as I pull into the car park at the restaurant.

Her car isn't here, but I know the staff can park around the back if there is space.

Jack shrugs. "Hanna didn't mention it, and she usually mentions everything."

"Well, that's unhelpful," I mutter, getting out of the car.

"Mate, just chill out with this whole Tilly thing. You're making it harder than it needs to be," Ian says.

He's a twat, but he also has no idea, not really, so I don't want to be too hard on him. Instead, I bite out a smile and follow them into the building.

We sit down at a table in the corner that Jack picks because it's in Hanna's section, and I lean back against the chair, my back protesting the new position. Working solidly on the house the way I have been is taking its toll on my body. I want it done and over, but I'm damn near suffering for it.

Hanna storms to the table. Jack almost stands up but notices her fierce expression and decides it's safer to stay put.

"What's up, babe?" he asks as she stomps her foot as she stops by the table.

"What are you three doing here?"

"We've come for lunch. What's wrong?"

I spot the problem before Hanna has a chance to explain.

"Tilly is here," I mutter, my eyes glued to the beautiful blonde I would die for.

"Yeah, Sasha called in sick, so she's covering," Hanna says.

"Does she want us to go?" I ask, tearing my eyes away and looking at Hanna.

She shakes her head. "No, but I'll be serving you today. What drinks are you having?"

"Isn't this your area?" Jack asks.

"I swapped because Tilly's aunt and uncle were in an hour ago." Her eyes pin me to my seat like I'm a naughty schoolboy. "Now, we're swapping back."

Hanna takes our order and walks off before Jack can talk to her.

"Fuck's sake," I groan. "I knew it would be hard, coming back, but I didn't know I'd be constantly hurting her."

Jack and Ian look at each other again, deciding who's going to tackle this one.

Ian wins.

Jack says, "You're not. A lot of feelings are returning to the surface, but that's not necessarily a bad thing, Linc. If you and Tilly have a shot at being friends again, you need to go through this shitty part."

"She doesn't want anything from me, except maybe for me to leave town."

Ian shakes his head, leaning over the table. "You're wrong."

"You know that how?"

Biting his lip, he looks away.

"Ian?" I slap my hand on the table. "Talk."

"I overheard her talking to Mel. She doesn't hate you; she just wants to. There is a big fucking difference, man. Don't screw this up by letting her push you away. If anything good can come out of this, it'll be you and Tilly being friends again."

We all miss those times. The six of us would hang out a couple of times a month, and I always enjoyed it more than being with any of my other friends. Tilly was so easy to talk to, and her smart mouth and love for life were infectious. She could be impulsive and sometimes reckless, but I loved every second with her.

I would sell my soul to have just one night like the old times.

"Let's all plan something. A trip somewhere," Jack says, sitting taller.

"Where?" I ask, not at all convinced that this is a good idea.

"Legoland," Hanna says, throwing three menus down in the middle of the table.

We all look up at the same time.

"What, baby?" Jack asks.

"You guys aren't quiet. I could hear your conversation from the table I was waiting on. You want to reconnect with Tilly, Linc, and we *all* want our group back together even if it's just for a while. The trip Tilly still talks about when she's drunk is Legoland."

We went there when we were teens—Tilly and Mel sixteen, Hanna seventeen, and Jack, Ian, and I eighteen. We had so much fun.

Jack lifts his eyebrow. "Doesn't it seem a bit weird for six adults to go to Legoland?"

Hanna shrugs. "When have any of us ever cared about how something looks?"

"Fair point," I say. "Do you think Tilly will want to go?"

Hanna smiles. "Leave it with me. And hurry up and order. I'll go grab your drinks."

I pick up the menu, but I can't focus on anything. Tilly is behind the bar, making drinks and chatting with some guy. She laughs, and I instantly hate him.

I fucking miss that laugh. I could have her in stitches within minutes. Now, she looks at me like I've robbed her of so much. If I could swap places with Robbie, I would. He should be here now. He was a damn good guy, and Tilly loved him.

Tilly walks over with a tray and puts it on the table.

I feel my heart thudding harder as she reaches across me to hand Jack his beer.

Why is she waiting on us now?

She takes a breath. "How are you guys?"

"Good. How are you doing?" Jack asks.

She gives him a small smile but doesn't answer. "Are you ready to order? Ian, I assume you're having the double cheeseburger?"

"You know it," he replies.

What is going on? Hanna was serving us. Why is no one else mentioning this?

She looks at Jack, and he orders.

Then, her eyes flit to me, and she swallows. "Lincoln?"

Okay, I'm Lincoln again today.

"Same as Ian, please."

"You want normal fries or sweet potato?"

I turn my nose up. "Definitely not that orange mush."

Tilly's lip lifts in amusement so slightly at the side. "I don't blame you; they're disgusting. I'll place your order. Shout if you need anything else." She collects the menus and walks away.

Am I Linc now that the frost has melted a little?

"I think that went quite well," Ian says.

I deadpan, "In what universe did that go well?"

"She didn't throw your Coke at you, *and* she spoke to you *nicely* at the end."

"She called me Lincoln."

"That's your name, dickhead," Jack jokes.

I reach to my side and thump him on the arm. "You're an idiot. She uses my full name when I'm in the shit."

"You know there is a very fine line between love and hate," Ian says. "Maybe she's secretly, madly in love with you."

Fuck off. Don't even joke.

I shake my head, my stomach knotting tight, wishing his words were true but knowing it could never be.

15

Tilly

"Want to tell me what that was about?" Hanna asks, leaning her hip against the wall in the kitchen.

She's referring to me picking up the drinks and taking them to the guys' table. I had to. Hanna had offered to swap sections again, and I'd let her right up until I realised that I didn't want to avoid him when we were in the same room.

Seeing his face, wide eyes and fraught with worry, put things into perspective. There are a lot of people who would run Linc out of town if they had the balls, and I won't add to that. I won't make things even more uncomfortable for him.

"I'm not going to do anything to actively hide from him anymore. It's crazy, right? Switching sections and avoiding Robbie's grave at certain times?"

Hanna nods. "A little *but* understandable."

"Well, not again. Maybe, if I don't avoid him, other people will be more accepting," I say, sneaking a look through the hatch at a table near the guys.

Two men are talking in hushed tones, their heads bent together over the table, taking occasional glances at Linc and scowling.

No one should have to deal with that when they come out to eat.

My pulse quickens. How dare they be so openly rude. They don't have to like Linc, they don't even have to think that he deserves a second chance, but they shouldn't be dicks about it. I want to rush over there and tell them to get out, but I need my job.

Instead, I march over, my pulse hammering even faster, the closer I get, and I stop dead at their table. "Is everything okay for you?" I ask.

One of them, the one who was doing most of the talking and head-shaking, looks up. "The food is great," he says like there's a hidden meaning. Like the food is good, but the atmosphere is shit because the guy involved in the accident had the audacity to show his face.

"Let me know if I can get you anything." I walk away because I'm about to snap my teeth from clenching my jaw so hard.

Linc is watching me like he knows what's going on. His mouth is parted, hands balled together. When Jack and Ian follow Linc's gaze, I busy myself, clearing plates from a table nearby.

Thirty minutes later, I watch Linc, Jack, and Ian leave the restaurant. My muscles slowly begin to uncoil, shoulders sagging with relief from the freedom his departure brings. I might not want to chase him away, but that doesn't mean it doesn't hurt.

He's gone. You can breathe.

Hanna bursts into the kitchen behind me as I stack the plates on the side. She's beside me in a flash, her hand on my back. "Are you okay?"

"I'm fine."

I should just tattoo that to my forehead and be done with it.

"Hmm, I don't think I believe you." She moves to my side, leans her back against the wall, and folds her arms.

I turn my head. "Hanna, leave it, okay?"

"I thought you were all right with him being here?"

"I am. It depends on the day," I admit. "I don't like people being harsh to him, but doesn't that make me a hypocrite? I can't forget, Han. When I see Linc, my mind goes straight to the last time I saw Robbie, telling him he looked like he was joining a boy band in his white trousers and pale blue shirt. Then, I see my mum falling to the floor because a cop just told her that her son was involved in a serious accident."

She sighs, biting on her lip. "Babe, it wasn't Linc's fault."

"And I'm not going to throw anything in his face, but that doesn't mean I can forgive and forget. I don't want to spend time with him because it hurts too much." I stand up straight. "I just need to get through these next few months without running into him every damn day."

"Of course. Look, do you want to leave early? It's pretty quiet out there, and you only have an hour left."

"Actually, that sounds good. I could really use a scalding bath and a beer."

"Go, hon, and call me later."

I grab my things from the staff room opposite the kitchen and head out the back. As I walk along the alley toward the car park, I notice Linc and Jack standing by Linc's car. They're talking, not moving, not leaving.

Gripping the handle of my handbag sitting over my shoulder, I press my back against the wall.

For fuck's sake. How long are they going to be talking? Couldn't they go somewhere else to chat?

I just want to go home and soak in the bath.

What could they still have to talk about? They just spent almost an hour in the restaurant, talking.

Come on.

My car is parked in the corner, pretty far from where they are, but it's unlikely I'll get to the other end without one of them seeing me. Linc would let me pass without a word; he would silently watch me with his dark blue eyes. Jack would call me over.

He's the perfect fit for Hanna; they both don't care much for boundaries.

I bite my lip and tap my fingers on my chin, waiting for them to finish.

Jack laughs at something Linc said, but all the moody one does is give his signature half-smile.

How is this my life? Hiding out in an alleyway to avoid Lincoln Reid.

If my mum or dad came past right now, they would book me an emergency appointment with Jennifer. Mum would freak out about how I wasn't really dealing with Linc's return and how I needed to talk it all through in therapy even though they hadn't been dealing with it at all.

Right now, I'm totally okay with ignoring my issues. I'd rather get through the storm before I started rebuilding.

My eyes roam in an effort to pass the time. I float up to the clouds and watch as they change shape in the light wind. They slowly turn from white to grey. If it were to rain right now, that would be fitting. Though, at least, it might make the gossiping tossers move it the hell on.

I move back to the boys, and they've stepped away from each other, closer to their respective cars. Progress, I suppose.

The first raindrop lands on the end of my nose. I swipe it away with my finger and huff.

Come. On.

Finally, they nod to each other and turn away.

I wait until they're in their cars. Jack drives away first, being closest to the exit. Linc follows a few seconds later. When his car disappears, I step into the street and cross the car park. The rain falls harder the second I do, of course, and I dash toward my car, lowering my head to shelter myself from the water.

I press the unlock button on the key fob and leap into my car as the rain hammers down. God, this bath cannot come soon enough. I shove the key into the ignition and turn.

Nothing.

Really?

My car is reliable; it hasn't broken down ever, but today is clearly the obvious choice for it to refuse to start.

Stupid piece of shit.

Today can go to hell.

I take a deep breath through the stinging in my eyes and the heat pumping through my veins.

Why now? Why?

"God!" I shout, thumping both hands down on the top of my steering wheel. "Stupid fucking everything!"

You're losing it. Calm down.

With the air kicked from my lungs, I collapse back in my seat, and my arms fall onto my lap.

I'm about to get my phone and call my dad, but someone raps on my window.

Lincoln. He's back.

I open the door because the damn windows don't work unless the engine is on, and since that's not happening ...

"What do you want?" I ask.

"What's wrong with your car?"

"How do you know there is something wrong?"

He ducks down, practically getting in since it's raining and he's getting wet. "I saw you hitting your steering wheel on the way past, so I circled back." Water runs down his hair, dripping onto the floor.

"Get in, Linc."

He flashes that half-smile and runs around the back of my car to the passenger side. I slam my door and turn to him.

"It's not starting at all?"

"Nope," I mutter. "Nothing."

"You're mad."

"You're sharp."

Linc lowers his head, and I wince at the venom in my words. He came back to help, and I'm being a bitch to him.

"I'm sorry; that was uncalled for. It's just been a bad day, but I appreciate you coming back."

"Let me take a look at your car and see if I can fix it."

"Did you take a course in mechanics while you were away?"

Smirking, he shakes his head. "No, but I've had many shit cars I needed to fix."

"Well, my car isn't shit, so what makes you think you can fix it?"

"Your car won't start, and you're claiming it's not shit?" he quips.

"You're insulting my car, but it's keeping you dry right now."

"It makes a good umbrella; I'll give you that."

How quickly we can go from frosty to flirty.

I fold my arms, biting back a smile. "Do you need me to help check out my car, or can you handle that alone?"

He dips his head in a little bow and grabs the door handle. "Pop the bonnet."

I watch him dash to the front of my car and pull the lever near the steering wheel. He lifts the bonnet and blocks himself from sight. He's out there, getting wet, trying to fix my car, and I'm in the dry, waiting.

Damn it.

I open the door and step outside. "Linc," I say, hunching over as the rain pelts my body.

He looks up from my engine. "Tilly, get back in the car."

"You're soaked. Get back inside until it's eased up."

The heavy rain forms a sheet of water, which makes it almost impossible to see, like looking through frosted glass.

"Linc," I say, reaching out and grabbing his arm. "Come on, get back inside."

He drops the bonnet. "Get your stuff. I'll drive you home. The car can wait."

I'd argue with that, but he's right. There is no point in getting soaked out here. My dad will come back with me later to sort the car.

Linc waits out in the rain while I grab my handbag and lock my car. Then, we jog to his truck, two down from mine. I didn't see him come back, but then I wasn't looking.

"Oh my God, I'm soaked through," I say when we get into his car. "Your seat is going to get wet."

He shrugs and runs his hand over his head, and water drops down his back. His black T-shirt clings to every inch of his body, perfectly accentuating his abs.

Eyes. Up.

He turns his key in the ignition, and his car starts immediately. Though there is no snarky comment, the corner of his mouth does lift.

"You know Karma is a bitch, right?"

"I didn't say anything, Tilly." He reverses out of the parking space.

"You didn't have to. This is one of the rare times when I can read your expression."

"One of the rare times?" he asks, pulling out of the car park.

"You can't be surprised by that. You're hardly an open book."

Silence falls over the car as Linc thinks about my words. He accelerates down the road. "Do you want to know more?"

Yes.

I push my damp hair behind my ears. "Know more what? About you?"

"Well, yeah. If you want to know what I'm thinking, you could try asking."

An invitation to get inside Lincoln Reid's head. So many people would snap that up, but getting deeper involved with him isn't a good idea. He makes my head pound.

"Why did you come back for me today?"

Frowning, he looks at me for a fraction of a second. "You were obviously having car trouble."

"I told you to stay away."

"You did. I didn't."

His blatant honesty stifles a laugh out of me. "No, you didn't. Not that I'm not grateful you came back because I am."

"Is that all you want to know?"

"For now," I reply, laying my head against the headrest and sighing.

16

Linc

Tilly turns up the heat in the car, having no issues with messing with my stuff.

She glances at me out of the corner of her eye. "Do you want to ask me anything? Seems only fair."

"Nah, you're not a closed book."

"Oh, you think you know what I'm thinking?"

"Most of the time, I have a good guess. I'm good at reading people, remember? Maybe you don't know what you're doing or what you want, but that doesn't mean no one else knows you."

Just because I don't know what mood she's going to be in from one second to the next doesn't mean I don't know what mood she's in when she's there.

"I don't think anyone else knows me."

"Not everyone, Tilly. *Me*. Your parents see what they want to see. Hanna and Mel see, but they don't speak."

She presses her lips together and stares forward, like the windscreen is the most interesting thing she's ever seen. Her mind is working overtime to absorb the truth in my words. She knows what's going on and what she's putting off—of course she does—but she doesn't admit it to herself. Hanna and Mel are good friends to her, but they're not honest about the situation with her family because they're scared of hurting her.

Tilly needs hard truths. She needs someone to tell her to wake up and start living rather than enabling her to crawl through life, pleasing her mum and dad. Robbie can't do it anymore, and I promised him I would try.

"You're going to need to leave your engine on for a while to dry the car out," she says after a minute of silence.

"Will do," I reply, my shoulders sagging.

What did I think? That she was going to start opening up to me because I called it as it was?

If she's going to talk to anyone, it's not going to be me.

"Do you need me to help you with your car later?" I ask.

"Thanks, but I'll get my dad to sort it. We have breakdown cover if he can't."

"All right. How are the hands?"

"Huh?"

"You were beating your steering wheel as if it were … well, me."

She rolls her pretty eyes at me. "Dramatic much? Besides, I would kick you, not hit you. I've taken up running, and my legs are much stronger."

"You've taken up running?"

"Yes."

"What do you take to stop yourself from breaking out in hives?"

"Oh, ha-ha, Linc."

I laugh with the playfulness of her voice as well as the words. "Sorry. You were always so anti-workout, so knowing you run now is …"

"Yeah, I get it. But there is something so freeing about running. When I'm out there, I feel like I can outrun my thoughts, and most of the time, I can."

"What about the times you can't?"

"Beer."

"Solid call, Tilly. Run or drink it away."

"Hey, I've done years of therapy. This does the same, and it's cheaper."

"Do you want to go running together?" I ask before my brain can engage. It was me who was involved in the accident. I'm partly responsible for Robbie's death, the very thing she is trying to outrun, and I just asked if she wanted to do it with me.

She tilts her head toward me. "Want to run now?"

"I'm kind of driving right now, Tilly."

"Have you taken something? All this joking around is very unlike you."

"Sorry. I'll go back to my usual *moody* self soon," I say sarcastically.

"No, don't. I've always liked it when you're this way. It doesn't happen nearly enough."

And it's no coincidence that I only ever really feel like this when I'm alone with her. Sure, I can piss around with Jack and Ian and have a laugh, but it's nothing like this. No one else can make me feel this good.

"About this run," she presses.

"In the rain?" I ask.

She nods. Okay, I don't want to get wet, but I'm not going to turn down an opportunity to spend time with her. I don't care what we do.

"I'm in." I pull into my driveway. It's still raining but nowhere near as hard.

"Cool. I'll meet you out here in five?"

"I'll be here."

With a fleeting smile, Tilly gets out of the car and runs inside.

I go into the house and get changed into joggers and a T-shirt. Placing my palms on either side of the window frame, I peer outside. We're going running.

She's tipped back onto the pro-Linc side, and she wants us to run. I don't know how long it's going to last, as she could hate me again when I get back outside, but I'll take it.

I walk through the empty house, looking at everything that's changed so dramatically that it might as well be a different place. Gone are our photos or the crap my mum used to buy and hang from walls or sit on the mantel.

The house feels cold all the time.

I have to get out of here as soon as possible.

Grabbing my keys and phone, I head out just as Tilly is coming out of her house. She's dressed in leggings and a longline vest. Her wet hair is tied up, and she's wearing a smile.

My body stiffens.

Jesus, her legs.

"Ready?" she asks.

How did we get here?

I clear my throat. "I'm ready. Where do you usually run?"

"I don't plan it. I just run."

"Ah, nice and safe then."

"What's going to happen to me in our little town, Linc?"

I'd argue with her, but what's the point? Besides, I don't want to piss her off. I'm not going to give her a reason to turn cold on me. She'll do that all by herself soon enough, I'm sure.

She turns around and starts jogging. I follow.

We pass streets lined with houses with perfectly manicured lawns. Her feet hit the floor, face frowning so slightly, like she's running from her mind right now. I'm right here, so that's not going to be possible.

"All good?" I ask.

"Yeah," she huffs. "Let's go right at the end of the road."

Toward Robbie's grave?

That's the only thing that's right. Beyond the cemetery is another town.

"You want to visit him?" I ask.

"No. I like to run past."

She either likes to torture herself or she finds being near him comforting. I honestly don't think she knows which one.

"You're cool with me running past?"

"You visit Robbie, Linc."

"I do. Alone."

"It's okay. I'm fine with that," she says breathlessly as we push harder.

I run faster to keep up with her. "Thank you."

"He was your friend, Linc. Just because you were there doesn't mean you aren't entitled to visit or to be sad."

"I used to do this, you know. When we first moved, I would run and run at all hours of the night, trying to forget. For those few hours, I would be free of it. I wouldn't see the accident over and over on a loop in my head."

She stops dead near the entrance to the cemetery, her chest rising and falling rapidly. "Do you still see it?"

"Almost every time I close my eyes."

"I'm glad it's not every time."

"Yeah, me, too."

What I don't tell her is that, when I'm not seeing Robbie die, I'm seeing her after his funeral, telling me to go to hell. It's no less painful.

17

Tilly

I can't stop letting Linc in. He's like a big, muscular, gorgeous magnet that I can't keep away from for longer than five minutes. Being around him is as comforting as it is painful. All I've felt over the last four years is pain, so it's addictive, feeling something else.

Linc is back at his house after our run, and I'm in mine. Things got a bit awkward when we ran by Robbie's grave; neither of us quite knows the right way to deal with the brother issue—either of our brothers, to be fair.

I step out of the shower and wrap a towel around my body.

We picked up the pace as we were walking home, so my muscles are going to be aching tomorrow. I've missed the burn of exertion.

Towelling off my hair, I change into shorts and a T-shirt and head downstairs.

Dad is the only one home after sorting my car. Mum is in late meetings all week with her team. Something to do with a new product launch at the local department store or whatever.

"Hey, Dad. How's it going?" I ask as I bounce into the kitchen.

He looks up at me over his newspaper and smiles. "You're chipper, love."

I shrug. "I guess."

"It's good to see. I'm about to sort dinner. What do you want?"

"Are you cooking, or are we getting takeaway?"

"Takeaway. Chinese or Indian?"

Well, I guess I did just run five miles. "Chinese sounds good."

"All right. Before I order, I want to talk to you since your mum is working late."

Okay. Why can't he talk to me while she's here?

"Sounds ominous." I sit down and place my palms on the worktop.

"Nothing to worry about. I just want to check in since you're out more often than you're home. If I say anything in front of your mum, she'll only fret."

I raise my eyebrows. "There's no reason for either of you to be concerned, Dad. I'm okay. You know, you often encourage me to go out more with my friends."

"I do. Is it coincidental that you're getting out more now that Lincoln is home?"

My heart stalls at the break in Dad's voice when he says Linc's name. He's still hurting. I want to be honest. I want to tell Dad that I'm on friendly terms with him, most of the time anyway, but he's not ready to accept Linc.

I'm not pushing.

"Yes, it's coincidental. Jack and Ian are spending more time with Linc, so Hanna and Mel are at a loose end." The lie comes easily. I surprise myself. I'm used to telling them I'm fine, and I want to be at home still, but this seems worse.

Dad nods, my lie accepted at face value. "As long as everything is cool."

"You know what's not cool? You using the word *cool*."

Laughing, he puts the newspaper down. "I'm not that old just yet, Tilly. Have you seen much of him? I know he's next door, so it's hard not to, but he seems to keep to himself."

No, he doesn't. I see him all the bloody time.

"He's around, and I see him, but it's okay. I ... I don't blame Linc the way I used to anymore, Dad."

He clears his throat. "All right. Look, I understand what happened that night. I don't place any more blame on Lincoln than I do on Robbie, so if you don't want to spend more energy on hating Lincoln, that is okay."

"Thank you, Dad. Do you think that Mum will have the same opinion? I mean, I'm not looking to be Linc's best friend. I'm just so tired of always feeling like I'm being weighed down. I want to let go of everything negative that I cope with."

"I'm really glad to hear you say that, love. I wish I could do the same."

"You can. It's not easy, but you can. Trust me, it feels pretty good."

Please forgive Linc.

"I'll tell you what. If you spend a couple of extra nights at home with me and your mum, I'll do my best to follow suit. Maybe I'll say hello over the fence when Lincoln is outside."

I laugh. "I can just see that now, you both pausing from cutting the grass to say good morning."

"Does Lincoln cut grass now that he's back? It doesn't look like anyone is doing it since he arrived," he jokes. The fact that he can talk about him this easily, even if he is still using his full name, is a start.

"When I see him, I'll have to mention that you don't want to look out of your window and see a jungle next door."

He grins. "Do you speak with him?"

"We talk when I run into him, yes. Briefly."

His jaw tightens, but his eyes are free of tension. "You were friends before."

"We were. Well, he was Robbie's friend, but we have more in common."

"Ah, the creepy movie stuff. I never got that."

"No, you're a die-hard action fan. Linc and I used to go to Ted's cinema on the edge of town. Every few months, they would have a horror week and play scary movies all day, every day, in one of the two screens."

Smiling, he says, "I think I recall you mentioning that years ago."

"Yep. Linc came by to pick me up, and you gave us the third degree."

Dad assumed we were going on a date, but that was so far from the truth.

"Yes, well, a nineteen-year-old man comes by to pick up your seventeen-year-old daughter, and you have questions."

"Okay, you make it sound gross. We were horror fans, and none of our friends were; that's it."

He lifts his hands. "I know; I know. Now, pick what you want, and I'll order food."

Dad ends the Linc subject, and I don't feel like I can say anything else, or he might get suspicious. I want my parents to be okay with Linc. I want to be able to hang out with him and my friends at the same time without worrying that it's going to get back to Mum and Dad. I would prefer if they just knew, if they were okay with us being friends again.

I reel off a list of Chinese food that is far too long, and Dad places the order. While we wait for our food, we chat about work, mine and his, keeping things on a safe, surface level that we've become accustomed to.

When the doorbell rings, I go to answer, and Dad gets plates and cutlery ready.

I open the door and frown. "Greg. Hey."

"Hey, is this a bad time?"

"Er, no. I just thought you were the Chinese delivery guy."

Chuckling, he shrugs. "Sorry to disappoint. I just wanted to apologise for that night at the pub again—in person this time."

"Yeah, look, I'm sorry that I haven't called—"

"It was my fault, Tilly. That man just gets under my skin."

From behind me, Dad calls, "Greg, are you joining us?"

My parents love Greg. They have always liked him, but ever since Robbie died, they love him. I can see the look Mum gives me when he comes by, all doe-eyed and ready to buy a hat. But there is nothing but friendship there.

Greg is good-looking, sweet, and funny, but I don't feel an attraction to him. Not even the tiniest spark.

Blue eyes settle on me, asking if *I* am okay with him staying. I step to the side, giving him my answer, and just as I do, Linc walks out of his front door. His posture visibly stiffens from across the lawn, face paling.

I lick my lips as I raise my hand in greeting. He dips his head and then steps back, shutting his door with just a little bit too much vigour.

Well, that's great.

On a sigh, I close the door, as Greg moved past me the second I stepped aside to let him through. I turn and smile.

"What have you been up to over the last week?" I ask him.

"Come through, son," Dad calls.

Greg waits for me to go into the kitchen and follows. "I've been working a lot." He lifts his chin to my dad. "Hey, Dan."

"Did you walk or drive?"

"Drive. So, I'll grab a Coke, if that's okay?" Greg replies.

"You know to help yourself by now," Dad says at the same time the doorbell goes again. "I'll get it. Tilly, take an extra plate over for Greg, will you?"

I busy myself with the plate as my stomach flutters with nervous energy, the call of next door buzzing through my skin.

"Are you okay?" Greg asks, sensing my discomfort.

"Yeah. Hungry."

I want to go and see if Linc is okay. But that's stupid. Greg and I are friends. I don't owe Linc anything, and whatever issue they have with each other is none of my business. I can speak to each of them without picking sides. I refuse to be in the middle of bad blood.

"Well, sit down, and let's eat," he replies as my dad comes into the kitchen with two full bags of Chinese food, holding them up like they're some grand prize.

We dig in, dishing spoonfuls of different food onto our plates. I push some noodles around with my fork before trying a mouthful of egg fried rice. My throat closes as I swallow, making me gag.

I press my hand to my chest as my body tries to reject the food.

This is just bloody great!

Neither Dad nor Greg sees me though, so I'm thankful for that. They're too busy talking sports—MotoGP, to be exact. Both of them love to watch motorbikes whizzing around, but neither of them rides.

I like Formula 1. More accurately, Lewis Hamilton.

What is Linc doing now?

Okay, that really isn't any of my business.

He looked pissed when Greg came over.

Maybe I should text him?

Oh, for goodness' sake! I need to eat and chill and forget Lincoln Reid for one night.

"Tilly?" Dad says, his voice louder than usual, signifying that he's probably called me a couple of times already.

"Huh?"

"What's going on? You've not eaten much," he repeats.

Greg watches on with wide eyes, full to the brim with concern. He seems to think that all my problems are down to Linc's return.

They're not *all* because of him. I have all the same problems; Linc has just accentuated them. And maybe added one or two more. But they are my problems, and I'll deal with it all in due time.

Meaning, I will avoid and down Coors Light at every opportunity.

It's not a great plan, but then I've never claimed it would be good.

"Yeah, not feeling it as much as I thought." I scoop a pile of rice and shove it in my mouth to appease them both.

They turn back to each other, picking up their conversation where they left off. Appeasement successful. Now, all I have to do is make my plate look like someone has at least tried.

What is wrong with me?

Dinner stretches on over an hour because they don't stop talking, but that turns out to be a good thing because it gives me the opportunity to slowly force some food in, enough to make it look like I've had a decent meal.

Mum arrives home and tucks in, too, so that takes some of the heat off me.

While I watch my mum chatting happily with Greg, my mind wanders.

Will she ever be accepting of Linc again? Could she sit around a table with him like this?

That used to be such a natural thing for us to do. My family and his, friends and neighbours coming together to eat on a regular basis. She is used to seeing Linc at this table— well, not this one. The old one had to be changed after Robbie died because Mum couldn't eat at it. She also couldn't get rid of it, so it's dismantled and being stored in the loft. But my point is, Linc being here isn't such a crazy idea. I've seen it plenty of times before. Though, right now, it feels like there is more chance of the Queen coming for dinner than Linc.

Not that I care though, right?

Don't. Care.

Linc

For one hour and fifty-three minutes, Greg has been in Tilly's house.

What could he possibly be doing?

You don't want to know.

No, Tilly would have said if they were together. It would be obvious if they were. He's a friend. A friend who is invited in to eat with them. While I'm here, in my bedroom, with the lights off, watching out the window.

This is how low I have sunk. How desperate she makes me feel.

If he touches her, I'm out of here. I can't stay and watch that. I'll get two jobs to fund someone else taking over the renovations here.

It's now nine p.m. They can't have much left to talk about, surely. He didn't have a bag or anything else with him, so he can't stay the night.

My chest is tight, limbs heavy, as I watch on, waiting for some confirmation that they're friends. I don't know if she sees it, but Greg wants her. Maybe I can because there's some weird solidarity thing passing between us. We both want to hold her, to make her smile, and to take away her pain.

Only he has a much better chance because he hasn't put any pain there.

Fuck it.

I hold my breath as my body weakens, energy draining from every pore. I'm not going to get the girl. She might have moments where she stares at my chest or forgets herself and flirts, but she's not going to let me closer than that. Greg is perfect for her—nice, a people person, still gets along with her parents, wasn't involved in an accident that killed her brother. I can't compete with that.

Hell, I can't even get her to forgive me. Not that she should.

Her front door opens, and my lungs collapse.

Greg walks out, and Tilly is laughing.

Jesus.

I want to look away, but my body won't let me. My tight muscles are locked into place, forcing me to watch the girl I love with another guy.

Don't kiss. Don't kiss.

Fuck's sake, they're friends!

He turns back, so he's facing her, and they seem to engage in another conversation.

Just get in your car and fuck off, prick.

Why am I so insanely jealous of her having a friend over?

Right, because he's a friend who wants to get in her pants, too.

I suck in a ragged breath, my eyes stinging with the sudden burst of oxygen.

Stop watching.

He moves closer, too close. If he bent his head, he would be kissing her, and my palm slams on the wall beside the window.

Don't, Tilly. Please.

My chest rises and falls quickly with short, sharp breaths, and I want to leave. I want to get in my car and drive a thousand miles away. That would end up being in the sea, but right now, that sounds just fine.

"Tilly," I whisper, my heart dying.

She laughs and playfully slaps his arm.

I. Can't. Stop. Watching.

Somewhere in my mind, I've already packed up my things. I should go right now. They're close. I didn't see it before, as they weren't alone like this, but I see it now, and it's fucking agony.

I watch Tilly. The beautiful smile on her face, her relaxed posture, the way her mouth moves with each word she speaks to him. And her eyes, those honey-coloured eyes haunt me every night, are smiling.

Not to be dramatic, but if she kisses him right now, this will be the last time I see her. I commit every inch of her to my memory, not ever wanting to forget a single thing about her.

Whatever happens in life, with me or with her, I will love her forever.

She takes a step back and holds the edge of the door, ready to close it. Greg turns and heads for his car.

My shoulders drop, and I exhale. I close my eyes as the relief of him leaving washes through my whole body, giving me air.

I back away from the window as her door closes, my stomach rolling from the whole thing.

This can't carry on. I can't spy on her, afraid that I'll see something I don't want to. If I don't at least tell her how I feel, how can I expect her to stay away from anyone else? Surely, I have to try.

Now, there's a terrifying thought. At least when I've not mentioned how I feel about her, there is no definite end. I can still pretend that there's a chance, but once she rejects me, that'll be it. No more hope.

To be honest, neither option sounds good right now. Tell her and risk having my heart ripped from my chest. Or don't tell her and risk her finding someone else and, in turn, having my heart ripped from my chest.

A third option would be welcome.

I go downstairs and grab the sander. The living room walls need sanding from all the filler I've used, and right now seems like the perfect time for that job. I need to keep busy.

I stick the plug into the socket, and my phone beeps with a text.

I straighten and unlock my phone when I see Tilly's name.

Tilly: My legs hurt already.

The text is short and sweet, but it still makes me smile. She didn't really have anything to say to me, but she chose to anyway.

Linc: I thought you were a runner?

Tilly: I haven't run for weeks. Now, I know why I should never miss one.

Linc: Same tomorrow?

I hit Send on the message and instantly second-guess it. *Was that too forward?* It's nothing I wouldn't have asked four years ago.

Tilly: Day after, you masochist!

A laugh rumbles from my chest. Maybe I was a little too eager there, but I'm used to working out at least once a day. Or working off a certain blonde once a day.

Linc: Sounds good.

Tilly: What are you doing now?

*Linc: About to sand the living room walls.
You?*

Tilly: Same.

I roll my eyes. Her next message comes quickly.

Tilly: Why are you working so late?

Because I couldn't relax even if I wanted to after the whole Greg thing. I have some pent-up aggression to let out, and I don't want time to think.

Linc: It needs to be done.

Tilly: Do you need help?

What? She wants to help? She wants to come over here after having takeaway with her parents and Greg to help me sand walls? We all know I'm not going to say no to spending time with her, knocking that big wall down one brick at a time.

Linc: Come over. Wear old clothes.

I throw my phone down on the sofa and go in the kitchen to put the kettle on to make coffee. She's going to want caffeine, if she's still crashing around ten p.m. Tilly used to need some coffee if we were ever out late, and she wasn't drinking. On beer, she can go all night, like the damn Energiser Bunny.

Five minutes later, when I've finished our coffee and grabbed what chocolate I have from the cupboard, there's a light knock on the door.

Dashing to the front door, I wipe my palms on my jeans and tug it open.

"Hey," she says, ducking under my arm and stepping into the house like she's escaping wildfire. I know it's so her parents don't see her coming here.

"Where do they think you are?" I ask.

Turning to me, she winces. "I'm sorry. I told them I was going for a quick drink with Hanna."

"At nine at night?"

"Totally believable. When Hanna is having a *crisis*, I could be called at any hour. Once, it was midnight."

"Right. Coffee in the kitchen."

"Thanks, Linc."

Greg gets welcomed with open arms, and I get Tilly running into my house, so the lamb isn't seen with the lion.

She pulls a mug to her chest—we take our coffee the same—and hands me the other. "Tell me you're hurting."

I think she's talking physically here.

"Sorry, I'm all good." Again, physically.

"Damn it."

"Never miss a workout, Tilly."

"Yeah, apparently, that isn't just bullshit." She sips her coffee, her eyes staying on mine. "Are we really going to sand your walls tonight?"

"That was the plan. Unless you have something else in mind?"

There are many, many things I can think of that I'd rather do right now.

"No, it's just … isn't that going to be loud and dusty?"

"There's an attachment on the Hoover that will take most of the dust. I've been using tools like this through the night since I got here, and no one has complained yet."

"Hmm, I've never heard you."

"There's your answer." I frown at my snippy tone, my stomach coiling at the residual resentment of her flirting with Greg. Or what I perceived to be flirting.

She purses her lips, her mind working to put together pieces of something she's searching for.

Is she trying to figure out if I'm angry? How she really feels about me? Does being here make her realise that Greg isn't for her?

I don't think she's ever been interested in him, but me coming home might push her to do something she wouldn't usually. We're getting closer—that much is obvious—and I watch her fight that daily.

What if she snaps and gives Greg a chance just so she can stay away from me?

I need something stronger than coffee.

"You okay?" She takes a few steps closer, almost as close as she was to Greg. "You look tired."

"Thanks," I mutter.

"I don't mean that badly. You're pale," she replies softly. Her eyes warm with the concern behind her words. "Maybe you should just sleep and do the sanding tomorrow?"

"I don't feel tired, and this has to be done."

"It doesn't need to be done tonight, Linc. I know you and your parents want the house sold, but you matter, too."

"Tilly, I promise you, I'm fine. I'll finish this coffee and be good to go."

She puts the coffee down and folds her arms. "Make some popcorn."

"I'm sorry?"

"Popcorn. We're watching a movie, and you're relaxing. Besides, my legs hurt, and I want to sit."

"Why did you offer to come and help if you're in pain?"

Her teeth bite down on her bottom lip. "Hmm. Popcorn, Linc."

Deflecting much?

"Fine, you win. Do you want a beer?"

"You have beer?"

"I have Jack and Ian's beer. They can't come over and do anything without having one."

"In that case, I'll definitely drink their beer. Does your TV have Netflix?"

"Yeah. Remote is on the coffee table," I call as we separate into different rooms.

I grab her a beer and three share bags of different flavoured crisps since I don't have popcorn. "You'll have to make do with these," I say, chucking them down on the coffee table and passing her the bottle.

"Thanks." She lies back against the sofa cushions, pointing the remote at the TV. "So, we have a whole heap of new shit, not much of the good stuff. *The Shining* though?"

Dropping beside her, I kick my feet up. "Sounds good."

We settle in as the movie starts to play. This is something we've done plenty of times before, usually with other friends there, telling us that old movies are crap and CGI is the way forward. They have no soul for preferring the new shit.

"You still root for the killer?" I ask, smirking over at her as her eyes absorb everything on the screen, flitting from one side to the other, depending on where the characters are.

"Yep. But only if the victim is dumb. You fall over or split up from your friends, and you deserve it."

I laugh at her logic, though she's not wrong.

Right when Jack is about to get in the bath with a mouldy old lady, Tilly turns to me. "I've missed this."

Staring back at her, I whisper, "I've missed this, too."

19

Tilly

The movie ends with poor, crazy Jack frozen in the snow.

"One of the best," I say, sitting up and stretching out my spine.

I look to my side when Linc doesn't fill the silence ... and he's asleep. His head is tilted to the side, facing me, eyes free of stress and lips pressed together.

He's beautiful. From the silky darkness of his black hair to the strong lines of his jaw and the fullness of his lips. He looks like he should be a model for top brands, his face and body too perfect to be kept hidden away. But he would hate being in the public eye.

I could just picture him now at some swanky red-carpet event, scowling in the corner and avoiding eye contact with everyone else.

It doesn't seem right to wake him, not with him working all hours and not getting enough sleep. He must be desperate to get out of here if he's renovating into the early hours.

My hand itches to reach out and thread my fingers through his soft hair. It's just long enough to be able to get a fistful. My mouth parts as my mind takes a dive into the gutter.

Nope. Stop. Now!

I force my eyes away and swallow the lust burning in my groin.

Time to leave.

I gather up the half-eaten bags of crisps, my empty bottle of Corona, and Linc's glass and carry it all into the kitchen. I throw away the bottle and wash his glass, but I leave the crisps on the worktop since I didn't see where he'd gotten them from. I don't really want to go rooting through his kitchen, though I have a pretty good idea where they would go. I still remember.

On a calming breath because I'm not totally comfortable with being here yet, I walk back into the living room to get my phone and keys.

There isn't a blanket, so I don't know what to cover him with, but it's warm in here, so I don't think he would want one anyway.

Taking my things off the coffee table, I put my phone in my pocket and grab a Post-it note. They're curled at the edges like they've been here for years; they probably have. I write him a note.

You're lucky I didn't draw a moustache and cock on your face.
See you tomorrow.
Tilly.

My eyes flit between Linc and the coffee table where I stick the note. I kind of want to wake him up and say good-bye properly, but I also want him to find the note in the morning. It's something I would have done before … only I probably would have drawn the moustache and cock.

Okay, time to stop staring at his pretty face and leave!

I have an acute awareness of how hard and fast my heart is beating, drumming to its own frantic song. Linc's chest expands in a deep breath, but he doesn't even twitch, too deep in sleep to wake now.

Drawing my lip in between my teeth, I thread my fingers together behind my back.

Go. Get out.

Gasping at the sudden realisation of what the hell I'm doing, I turn and dash to the front door. My shoes are slip-ons, but I still manage to stumble as I shove my feet into them and yank Linc's front door open.

I make it across the grass and to my house in three seconds flat. Mum is in the living room when I get in. It's eleven o'clock, and she's reading a book.

As she hears me approach, she lowers the paperback and looks up. "Hi, darling. How is Hanna?"

"She's okay now. What are you doing up still? You're strictly a *ten thirty to bed* kind of girl." I slump down beside her.

"I was waiting for you."

"Mum, you don't need to do that. I'm twenty-one, remember?"

"Yes, and you're still my baby."

I roll my eyes. "Right. Well, I'm home now, so you can go to bed."

"So, did Greg stop by of his own accord, or did you ask him over?"

"He just came over. Why?"

"Oh, he's always welcome; you know that."

"Then, why do you ask?"

Smiling like she's the only one privy to an inside joke, she puts the book down beside her and shifts to face me completely.

Uh-oh, she's assumed the girl-talk position.

"Over the last six months, he's been coming more and more. Then, over the past few weeks, it's been less. It's nice to see things returning to normal."

"You've been keeping count of the times he comes over?"

"I don't have a tally, but I notice things."

"You are so off the mark here, if you're going where I think you're going."

"He's a decent man."

"He is. But he's not *my* decent man."

"I think he could be if you wanted."

"I don't. Greg is a friend, like Jack and Ian, and that's all I ever want him to be. Okay?"

She holds up her hands. "Okay. I understand. And is Lincoln a friend?"

I swallow. Then, I swallow again.

What exactly is she insinuating here? Is she asking because I didn't include him in the friend zone with Jack, Ian, and Greg, or is she just asking because she knows I've had some contact with him? Or is it obvious where I was tonight?

"Linc is complicated, but we were friends."

"You were. He was the only friend of Robbie's I didn't mind being here anytime." She laughs. "Some of the people Robbie hung around with …"

Would he be welcome now?

"Yeah, stereotypical teenage lads. Different girl most nights."

"I hope Robbie wasn't like that."

I smile at her because she doesn't want the truth. While Robbie wasn't as bad as some of them, he was hardly an advocate for meaningful, monogamous relationships.

"I did hope he would eventually get with Jessica. She was sweet and always had eyes for him."

Jessica was someone who hung around with Robbie and Stanley's crew. She was their age and besotted with my brother.

"They never got together because he was an idiot and couldn't see what was right in front of him," I tell Mum.

"True. Don't you do that, Tilly. Life is too short."

Is that something she would stick to if she knew the guy I was just imagining on top of me was Linc?

I have a feeling she would be giving a very different speech about how we couldn't work because Robbie's death would always be there, eating away at the relationship like a disease.

"I won't, Mum. No Prince Charming yet though."

Her smile spreads wide, the way it did before Robbie died. "You are still young. I didn't meet your dad until I was twenty-four."

"Hmm, so I have three more years of playing the field."

Mum smirks, and I haven't seen the playful glint in her eye in a very long time. I bite my lip as my eyes sting with the best kind of tears.

"Playing the field? Honey, are you even anywhere near the field?"

"Okay. Ouch."

"When was the last time you went on a date?" she questions, lifting her eyebrow.

"Well ... yeah, okay, it's been a while." *Seriously, when was it? Years. It's definitely been years. How sad is that?* "Maybe I should get out more ..."

"To the field, love. At least, meet new people. Somewhere out there is the man of your dreams."

Somewhere out there or asleep next door?

Oh God, don't go there.

"I'll get right on that, Mum. Night," I say, getting up and heading to my room.

She wants me to go out and meet new people, so nowhere in her mind is she thinking that Linc is a possibility.

And he's not. Right? He's not.

"Good night, love," Mum says, sighing like she's sighing out the last four years of anguish.

I don't look back as I go upstairs because I'm confused enough about Linc, and I don't want this moment with her to end. For now, I want things to be okay. Mum was more normal than she had been in a long time, Linc and I were getting on, and I don't feel like I'm struggling to breathe.

If it doesn't last, that's fine. It's likely. But I'll always have tonight.

Linc

I stare at Tilly's note, reading it for the fifth time. Or sixth. Or tenth. I've lost count.

I can't believe I fell asleep last night! What an idiot!

She signed the note with, *See you tomorrow*, like it's a given. We don't have plans, but her note suggests otherwise. It's such an old Tilly thing to say. On a text, she would sign off with, *See you tomorrow*, and we always would.

It's *tomorrow* now. I've not seen her yet, but then it is only nine in the morning. She's probably asleep since she didn't crash before the movie ended. I don't usually sleep well; a good night for me is four hours. But, with Tilly beside me, I was so relaxed, so at home, that my body gave up the fight.

Today, I feel like a new person.

It's a damn good feeling and one I hope will spur me on as I try to see if Tilly wants something to happen between us. I've got to make the jump eventually, so I'm going to. Slowly because this new version of her scares easily.

I stick the Post-it note to my index finger and walk into the kitchen to make a coffee. She tidied up in here; her empty bottle is nowhere to be seen, and my glass is sitting upside down beside the sink, clean.

I put the note on the worktop and read it again as I fill the kettle.

My phone, still in my pocket, starts to ring. I put the kettle down if it's already hot and answer the call. It's not her.

"Hey, Jack. What's up?"

"Legoland tomorrow."

"What?"

"Hanna has been looking online, and there are a few rooms left. The park tickets are free. You in?"

Okay, I knew there was talk of this but didn't know it was anything more than that. "Has Hanna asked Tilly? Can you all get off work at short notice?"

"Hanna said that she and Tilly are working today and then have a couple of days off. Mel doesn't start her new job until next week, and Ian is going to call in sick."

"And you?"

"My boss owes me a favour, so he's giving me late-notice holiday."

He's not answered my question about Tilly yet.

"I'm in," I reply.

"Cool. Hanna is on the phone with Tilly. I'll let Han book, and we can sort it out later, yeah?"

I frown. *Tilly hasn't agreed to this yet then?*

"Sounds good."

My God, does it sound good.

"You need any help in the house today? Han is going out shopping with Mel, so I'm free, if you need a hand."

"I need a hand," I say. There's much more work than I anticipated, and it's slow-going on my own. "Come over whenever you're free."

"All right. Now ... what did you and Tilly get up to last night?"

I freeze, my finger pressed on the button of the kettle. "What do you mean?"

"I heard Hanna quizzing her. She stayed over?"

"Not like that. She came over, and we watched a film. I fell asleep."

"You fell asleep? Dude, what is the matter with you? As if you fell asleep when she was with you!"

I don't know what is the matter with me. "Chill out, Jack. It's not like we would have gone at it for hours if I hadn't."

"You'll never know," he points out.

"Oh, I know."

Though, if she wants to, I'm in.

"See you soon, dickhead," he says and hangs up the phone.

I busy myself, making a drink and toast.

Jack turns up about ten minutes after I finish breakfast. The house is still a mess—tools everywhere and a half-finished kitchen since I ripped the wall tiles off and removed the cupboard doors to paint.

The house is chaotic, but it's what I need to keep myself busy. If I didn't have a distraction, I think the close proximity of Tilly would slowly drive me insane.

I let Jack in and make us each a drink.

"So, you really fell asleep?" he asks, shaking his head with a smirk.

I never claimed to be smart.

"Are you going to let that go anytime soon?"

"Hell no. I can't believe you had her here, in your house, on your sofa, and you fell asleep."

"Nothing was going to happen, Jack."

He frowns. "You believe that? When you're near each other, you can cut the sexual tension with a knife. Tilly might be trying to keep you at arm's length, but in her mind, you've both had sex."

"It's amazing what goes on in *your* mind."

"Whatever, man. You know I'm right. Though the more you both wait, the better it will be when you do get naked."

143

It's been four years. I'll probably come like a rocket in five seconds and then cry.

"I'm not holding my breath." I can't deny that she feels something, but I don't know that it's strong enough to outweigh what I did.

"Have you thought about what you'll do if you don't man up and make something happen?"

He leans back against the worktop. A worktop that, as of yesterday, isn't properly secured to the wall anymore. I'm not telling him.

All the time. It's one of my biggest fears, knowing Tilly is living her life without me in it. But I just want her to be happy, and if she can't let herself be happy with me, then I have to walk away. She deserves the world.

"I'll deal with it," I reply.

He nods, lips pursed, not believing me at all.

"Your poker face is shit," I tell him.

"This isn't my poker face; this is my look of disapproval. You and Tilly have both spent four years doing absolutely fuck all. *Four years*, Linc. You will never get that back, so I guess I'm just surprised that you're willing to waste more of your life."

I wince at the weight of his words.

Everything he said is true. I can't deny that, although I've worked jobs I enjoyed and lived on my own, I've done nothing with my life. I've been on hold, waiting in limbo to see if I would get the chance to see Tilly again.

"That hit home?" he asks, lifting his eyebrow. There is no humour in his expression. There is nothing funny about this.

I clear my throat. "I understand what you're saying ..." *Where am I going with this? What is there to say?* Realising you've lost four years is kind of a kick in the balls, to be honest.

There is so much more I could have been doing. I've spent the whole time working, doing different roles within the advertising industry to prepare myself for starting a business with my dad. I've had aspirations of growing the business, buying a big house, and living a comfortable life, but what's the point in having nice things if you don't have anyone to share them with? Tilly should have been the priority.

I've done this all wrong, thinking the only way to make it up to Robbie is to do something with my life professionally. He wouldn't have cared where I lived or what job I was doing. He would have cared if I was happy. And he would have cared more if Tilly was.

I should have come back for her long ago.

"Look, I'm not trying to make you feel like shit."

"No, you're right. I have nothing real to show for that four years."

My apartment was rented and is now being sold, so I have no place to live. I left my job because it was only a temporary position, and the other guy was returning.

I might have done more than Tilly, but neither of us has done anything that truly matters. Neither of us is happy.

"So, make up for it now. I know Hanna is about as subtle as a tornado, but she only wants to make you guys happy. She spends most nights thinking of ways to get you two back to how you were—and then more." He smirks. "She has quite a few ideas actually."

I bet.

"So, Legoland," I say, my voice low and drained from having my life dissected and finding it to be hollow.

He nods. "Legoland."

21

Tilly

I'm bored. We're only twenty minutes into a two-hour drive to bloody Legoland, and no one will play any road trip games with me. Linc is driving, Jack is in the passenger seat, and Hanna is in the back beside me.

Ian and Mel are leaving later after Ian works until midday because the big boss is in until eleven thirty, and then he's going to fake illness.

I'm still unsure about this whole thing. I mean, we're not teenagers anymore, and I don't think trying to re-create something we once had is the answer to our problems. We're not the same people, we're not carefree, and there is a massive elephant in the room in the form of my dead brother.

And, yesterday, you had some very naughty thoughts about Linc.

Apparently, we're forgetting about the not-so-pleasant past for now and pretending like the last four years didn't happen. And I'm not mad about it.

I love Robbie, but I desperately want this for me.

What kind of shit person does that make me?

He lost his life, and here I am, wanting a normal weekend where there's no pain, no void, and no missing a friend I didn't realise had meant so much until he was gone.

I'll have this time with my friends and deal with the guilt later. It's not easy to be selfish—I haven't done that in a very long time—but I think I've earned this a little bit. I think I can possibly get through this weekend with minimal damage to myself.

When I look up, my heart stills. Linc is glancing at me in the mirror. His eyes are back on the road the next second.

Why does he always seem to know when I'm overthinking?

I'm sharing a room with him too. It's expensive and the rooms are laid out in a way that we'll both have some privacy. At first, I wanted to tell Hanna to book another room, but it doesn't make sense, and I want to do this. I'm trying to be his friend again, and, four years ago, I wouldn't have batted an eyelid at sharing a room with him.

Hanna flicks my leg, keeping her arm down low on the seat so that the boys can't see what she's doing.

But what is she doing?

Frowning in question, I wait for an explanation.

She rolls her eyes, clearly unable to tell me because, whatever it is, Jack and Linc can't hear. Pulling her phone out of her bag, she taps away, writing me a message—because that's not going to be obvious.

She puts the phone on the seat between us and stares at me while jabbing her index finger into the screen and sliding the phone toward me.

Has she been drinking?

I pick it up and read her message.

Hanna: He keeps looking at you.

I tap back, replying to her message.

Tilly: We're not talking about this.

I swing my arm out, handing the phone back. She snatches it and slams it down on the seat. Giving me wide eyes, the look of disapproval, she points to the boys. Linc is looking. He saw me hand her phone back, but he can't read the words.

"Han, go to sleep or something," I say.

"What's going on with you two?" Jack asks, twisting his body so that he can look into the back.

"Nothing!" Hanna snaps. She gives Jack a big, toothy smile, which is going to do nothing to dispel his suspicions.

I roll my eyes. "Hanna is being boring and won't play any games."

Jack laughs. "You really don't do long drives well, do you?"

No, I don't, and this isn't really a long drive. I'd rather be up and doing something than sitting around, which I know seems weird since I'm not really doing much with my life at the moment. Or maybe that's why. If I'm too still physically, I'll think about what a mess my life is.

So, let's not think about that …

"Linc, the girls are up to something, and they won't tell us," Jack says, playfully narrowing his eyes at Hanna.

"You do not need to know everything that goes on in my life, Jack," she replies.

He turns back, laughing and shaking his head. He knows better than to bite back. And he also knows that Hanna has a particularly big mouth and won't be able to hide anything from him anyway.

I raise my eyes and steal another look at Linc. This time, he's focused on the road—like, crazy focused, as if he's scared something is going to jump out in front of us.

What is he thinking?

I would give anything to get inside his head. I think Jack and Ian would sometimes, too. They're pretty transparent, and their facial expressions usually give them away. Not Linc. He has one of the best poker faces I've ever seen.

I find it incredible when Hanna and Mel say the same things about me. I'm able to hide a lot, especially from my parents, but I feel like my thoughts are written on my forehead, only my parents can't read.

The rest of the car journey passes much the same. Hanna and Jack flirt. Linc and I pretend like we don't keep looking at each other in the mirror.

When we arrive at Legoland and park the car, I get out and almost kiss the floor. Almost.

Linc stretches his back, and his six-pack pokes through the thin cotton of his T-shirt.

Okay, I'm going to need him to stop doing that ... and to never stop doing that.

"Shall we get checked in? I really need a shower," Hanna says, pressing her boobs into Jack's chest.

He wastes no time in grabbing their bags and running— yes, running—for reception.

"I hope our room is nowhere near theirs," I say, taking my small suitcase from Linc.

He grabs his holdall and slams the boot shut. "Yeah, me, too. We can request to change because of noisy sex next door, right?"

"Or you could outdo them." I snap my mouth shut so hard that my teeth audibly slam together.

Linc raises his dark eyebrows. "Not going to say no to that, Tilly."

"You know exactly what I meant here, mister," I reply, pointing my finger at him. But I can't quite make a stern expression stick because I'm grinning too much.

He laughs.

This feels good.

Looks like Legoland is working already.

Linc and I walk along the path to the hotel together, him now sporting a smirk rather than a moody half-scowl.

Inside the hotel lobby is a soft play style ring filled with Legos, which a few children are playing in while their parents check in. I know Lego is predominantly aimed at children and all that, but I wish they had adult-only breaks here. I wouldn't mind a day on the rides and then an evening of getting drunk.

"Are you checking in?" a tall, skinny man behind the front desk asks. Behind him is a wall of Lego figures.

Linc lifts his eyebrows, and I get a small glimpse inside his head. He thinks it's obvious that we're checking in. And it is.

"Please," I say before Linc. "We have a room under the name Reid."

Because being on top of him would be awful!

He smiles and taps away on his computer.

"Our friends just checked in a minute ago, under the name Jack Peters. Any chance we can *not* be near them?" Linc asks.

I nudge his side. So, I don't want to be near Hanna and Jack if they're going to have loud sex, but you're not actually supposed to ask that of the staff.

The man eyes Linc like he doesn't understand the question.

"Never mind," I say.

He looks back down and taps again. "Okay, you are in pirate room three-oh-four."

I smile and take the key cards. "Thanks."

Linc and I take our bags to the lift. He smirks at me as he presses the call button.

"What is so amusing here?" he asks as we wait.

"You do know the rooms here are all one king bed and a bunk bed? Shotgun on the king!"

He deadpans. "You think I would make you sleep in a single bunk bed while I'm starfishing in a king?"

"Hmm … no, I don't actually. But I should take the bunks. You're a lot taller than me."

Linc is a foot taller to be exact, far too long for a kid's bed.

"I'm fine, Tilly." He slings his bag over his shoulder as the lift doors slide open, and he waits for me to step inside.

I follow him in, wheeling my bag in with a little more force than necessary and almost whacking it against the wall. He laughs, shaking his head.

"What?" I ask.

"We're sharing a room."

"Why is that funny?" I question.

"Not funny, just … you're okay with it?"

I fold my arms. "I am. Are you? I mean, it's expensive here, and the beds are at opposite sides of the room. The bunk bed is in kind of a nook, so I really don't see how—"

"Breathe, Tilly. I'm joking. But you're not convincing anyone. You know that, right?"

What?

My heart skips a beat.

"I'm going to need you to elaborate," I tell him.

"The room. You do want us to challenge Hanna and Jack."

I breathe a sigh of relief. He doesn't know what I'm really thinking. Or perhaps he's more accurate than even he knows.

"Oh, that's definitely it. I just can't—"

"Ah, we're here," he says, cutting me off as the lift stops.

He walks past me, shuffling to the side to get by. I wait a second because he smells good—like him, like the past, like a million times I've laughed and felt free and safe.

Snap out of it, Tilly!

Gripping the handle of my case, I dash out of the lift and follow after Linc. I hand him the key card, and he uses it to unlock the door, holding it open for me.

"Thanks," I whisper, sliding past him.

The room is smaller than I remembered. Linc somehow seems to take up a lot of space. He's everywhere in here already.

"I need a shower before we all go out," I say, tugging my case into the bathroom.

What I really need is a few minutes away from him to catch my breath and clear my mind. Linc has this foggy effect on me.

I close the door and firmly twist the lock. Turning my body, I lay my back against the door and breathe.

Linc

Jack texted to tell us to meet him and Hanna at the bar in ten. I showered before we left, so I'm just waiting for Tilly to get out.

My head is all over the place. She's naked and only meters away from me. The sound of water spraying from the shower is torture, knowing it's hitting her body and gliding off. There is a very flimsy door between us. How quickly that could be broken.

She's wet and naked!

I want to see. I want to pretend like I heard a scream to use as an excuse for bashing down the door, but I haven't lost full control of my faculties just yet.

She would kill me.

The walkway from the nook where my damn bunk bed is to her king-size bed is short, and I pace it in seconds. I've already tucked away the key in my wallet since I tend to lose those fucking things, put my phone and wallet in my pocket, sorted out my hair a thousand times, and straightened up the room. *Anything* to keep me occupied.

Of course, I pass the bathroom in the middle each way, which doesn't help.

I turn, ready to do another lap, my pulse buzzing from the knowledge of her bare skin on the other side of the door when said door flies open.

When did the water shut off?

Tilly walks out, wearing a pair of wonderfully short denim shorts and a white top. "You okay?" she asks, pulling her case along with her.

Shit, those shorts barely cover her arse.

I've never been more grateful to a clothes designer before.

What a legend.

"Uh-huh," I mutter like an idiot. "Jack wants us to meet them in the bar."

Tilly's grin widens. "Good. I'm ready for a drink."

So am I.

We have park tickets for tomorrow, so today is all about eating and drinking apparently. At least I can do one of those things. I don't drink, so this could be a long night for me. Not that I don't enjoy watching drunk people and then being incredibly loud the next day.

Plus, I love Tilly drunk.

"I'm ready," I reply, gesturing toward the door. "Let's get you to the bar."

She lets go of the handle of the case and raises her arms. "To the bar!"

"You've not even started yet, and you're being obnoxious."

Grinning, she replies, "It's a talent."

Did she pop or snort something in the bathroom there?

She is so different when there's a few hundred miles from home and her parents. This Tilly is the one I know and love.

"How sick are you going to be tomorrow?"

She shrugs. "I'm not going to get too drunk tonight. Probably."

"Great. I'm carrying you back to your bed."

"It's only a few meters past your bed. I think you'll cope."

"What if I can only make it to my bed?"

"You can barely fit on there, let alone both of us."

That would not stop me.

"Oh, I think I could make it work."

She rolls her eyes, and with a wide smile, she practically skips toward the lift. "I'm sure you could."

"All you have to do is say the word," I reply, lifting an eyebrow and leaning against the wall as we wait for the lift.

"I'll bear that in mind when I'm alone and horny," she replies.

Fuck.

I clench my jaw as every ounce of blood in my body heads to my dick. "You tell me the moment you're horny," I rasp without the hint of playfulness.

Rolling her pretty amber eyes yet again, she steps into the lift as the doors part. "Linc, you're more of a horny teenager now than when you were a teenager. What gives?"

I follow her inside and grip the handrail running the length of the wall. Leaning closer, I bend my head and reply, "Beautiful woman sleeping in the same room and talking about lying in her bed, throbbing—" Or that's just what I'm hoping.

Her hand flies up, cutting me off. Her eyebrows snap together in a frown, but her pupils dilate. The temperature in the lift just shot up a few thousand degrees. My mouth parts as I try to get oxygen to other organs.

The lift has suddenly halved in size. My gaze flits to her pink lips.

"When did you get so bold, Linc?"

Laughing, I take a step back and shake the naked thoughts from my mind. "I apologise."

We both know I don't mean that. There is no apology for how I feel about her or what I want. There are a lot of things in my life I'm sorry for, but loving Tilly will never be one of them. I'm not sorry, and she's not really offended over me coming on to her.

But I have to be careful. When she's back to her playful self, it's so easy to get caught up in what I feel, and I need to watch that. She's not ready for anything, and I'm sure as hell not willing to be a regret.

If we get together, she's not going to have second thoughts.

That calls for patience. I've had an abundance of patience when it comes to this girl. She is worth the wait.

Tilly walks out of the lift first, brushing past me while fluttering her eyelashes. Yes, she knows exactly what she's doing.

Hanna and Jack already have a table when we get into the Skyline Bar in the hotel. There's a beer waiting for Tilly and a Coke waiting for me. Hanna looks up and waves her hand even though we've seen them.

Tilly takes off, sits down, and grabs her drink. I could be looking at her four years ago.

Her best friend notices, too, and she watches Tilly with questioning eyes and a smile on her mouth. She sees the difference in her friend, and she likes it as much as I do.

I wonder if Tilly feels it.

"Okay, if any of you gets wasted, I'm not sitting near you on any rides," Tilly says, raising her beer to her mouth.

"But you said you're drinking," I remind her.

She takes a sip, her lips stretching around the rim of the bottle. My dick thickens.

"Yes, but I didn't say I was getting wasted."

"Right. Of course."

"Tills, you're the worst one when you've had too much," Hanna chimes in, nudging Tilly's arm.

I laugh. "I can't wait to talk very loudly tomorrow."

She turns to me, her body twisting to face mine, and we might as well be alone. "Don't you dare!"

"I thought you weren't going to get wasted."

"I didn't think you were middle-aged yet, Granddad."

I lift my eyebrow. "You think middle-aged people are grandparents?"

She purses her lips. "Some are."

"Okay, whatever. Just don't be sick tomorrow."

I'm in love with her, and nothing could ever put me off, but I don't fancy waking up to her being sick in the bathroom. Going from her being wet and naked in the shower to chucking up in the toilet is a bit of a step down.

"I haven't been sick because of alcohol since I was eighteen," she states proudly.

"You should put that on your CV."

Rolling her eyes, she slaps my forearm. "Sad thing is, that would actually be the best thing on my CV."

"You aced your exams. I think an employer would be more impressed with all As than *can get wankered without chucking.*"

She laughs, shaking her head. "Wankered. I haven't heard you say that in a long time."

"I think it was Jack who first called getting drunk that."

"It was, man," Jack says, cutting into our conversation.

Right. We're not actually alone.

Tilly's gaze slides to Jack before returning to me, like she's just realised the others are with us, too.

"Drink up, guys. We've got a long day of acting like children tomorrow," Jack says, sitting down and raising her glass.

Tilly lifts her beer and clinks it to the glass I have against my lips as I go to take a swig. Coke hits my upper lip and seeps down the side of my chin. Lowering the glass, I wipe my face with the back of my hand.

She looks up at me through her lashes as I pat Coke droplets off my jeans with a napkin. "Oops."

I glare. "Tilly …"

"Shut up. You missed me."

You have no idea.

23

Tilly

Stopping drinking after three last night was a stellar idea. My head is clear, and I'm ready to spend the day on rides. At a kids theme park, but who cares? Linc is still asleep in the bunk bed at the other end of the room. He's far too big to be in a kid's bed, but he's a true gentleman.

I grab the kettle because the least I can do for him for letting me take the king-size bed is make him a coffee. While I busy myself with the mugs and sachets of coffee, I allow my mind to wander.

Is Linc naked?

I saw him take his T-shirt off, and when he went into the little nook where his bunk bed is hidden away, I heard other garments hitting the floor.

Last night took me about two hours to fall asleep because I couldn't stop thinking about his nude body.

So, although I don't have a hangover, I am a little tired. And the way my heart is buzzing and with the fire between my legs, I'm pretty sure I'm turned the fuck on.

Oh my God, will you stop?

As much as I'm looking forward to the day, I have a feeling it's going to be a long one.

When was the last time I had sex again?

It must be about ten months.

Right now, it feels like ten years.

I pour milk onto the coffee grains and give it a minute while the kettle whistles louder and louder.

If he's kicked the cover away in the night, you'll be able to see everything.

Okay, that's enough. Time to stop being a massive pervert and focus on making drinks.

Behind me—because that's where he is—Linc takes a deep breath, and I don't know if he's asleep or awake now.

"Linc," I whisper, keeping my eyes glued to the rattling kettle.

When there is no reply, I bite my lip and twist my head to look over my shoulder.

My eyes are greeted with his chest. Lord, that chest. Hard muscles cut perfectly into six slabs on his chest. His lips are parted just enough to make me weak at the knees. The cover is draped over his legs, sitting dangerously low at his hips. I can't see boxer shorts, but they could be lower.

Or he could be naked!

After my coffee, I need to take an ice-cold shower.

I follow his body back up to his face and drink in the lines of his jaw and those dark eyebrows casting a shadow on his cheeks.

He's perfect. Every inch of him.

Linc stretches his back and rubs his hand over his face. I look away before he opens his eyes, my cheeks feeling red hot at the thought of being caught staring.

"Tilly," he says as I pour hot water into our mugs.

His gravelly morning voice sends a shiver of desire down my spine.

I put the kettle down and smile as I turn around. "Morning. Coffee is made."

He sits up, readjusting the cover a little higher, no doubt not wanting to make me uncomfortable. I already am but for an entirely different reason.

"Thanks. How are you feeling today?" His voice is rough from just waking, and it's sexy as hell.

I swallow. "I'm good. You?"

His voice might be pure sex, but my voice, however, is full of helium.

Linc's head tilts to the side as I walk over with his coffee. My legs feel dead, like I've been sitting on them for hours.

Did he have this effect on me before?

I don't think so, but then I didn't used to sleep in the same room as him, and I didn't used to get such an eyeful of that Adonis body.

With unsteady legs—because his lack of a shirt is doing crazy things to my insides—I hand him the drink and mentally high-five myself for not spilling it all over him. My hands, unlike the rest of me, are surprisingly steady.

"Linc, you okay?" I ask, realising that he's not answered my question.

"I'm good, Tilly."

"You slept okay in that child's bed?"

"Children are small."

I blink. "Yes, they are."

His mouth curves at the sides in the cutest and subtlest smile. "I slept fine. Did you enjoy starfishing?"

"How do you know I was starfishing? You can't see my bed from your little corner over here." I cross my arms over my chest and wait for his reply. The thought of him watching me while I slept is, well, creepy, sure, but not entirely unpleasant.

"I spent the night wanking beside your bed," he says, losing it and laughing halfway through.

NATASHA PRESTON

"Oh, you are disgusting!" I throw my hands in the air and turn away.

Linc laughs harder, and I bite my lip to stop myself from joining in.

After caffeinating, we shower—separately, unfortunately—and we head down to meet the others for breakfast in the restaurant.

The Bricks Family Restaurant is a buffet, which is fine because then no one else is in control of your portion size. I hate it when places give you one rasher of bacon. I mean, what's the point?

When we get down, Hanna, Jack, Mel, and Ian already have a table and have grabbed drinks.

"Morning," I say, sliding onto a chair beside Hanna.

Linc takes the other free seat next to me.

She looks at the Greek god beside me first and then settles on me where she lifts her perfect eyebrow. Not one word leaves her mouth, but words aren't needed. I know the contents of the Spanish Inquisition behind her closed lips in its entirety.

"Sleep well, Tills?" she asks.

Thankfully for me, everyone else has struck up a conversation about what rides we're heading to first and which ones to avoid because they'll be riddled with small humans.

"Yes, thank you," I reply politely, pushing my feet into the floor so that I'm not tempted to kick her under the table.

She leans in and whispers, "Well?"

With a quick, sharp shake of my head, her shoulders drop, and she sits back up. Whatever I'm feeling, whatever my hormones are doing—having a rave is my guess—nothing can happen between me and Linc. It's messy, and it can't go anywhere.

"Nothing? Really?"

"Nothing," I confirm.

She purses her lips.

If Hanna had her way, I think Linc and I would be a thing. *Not happening. Nope.*

162

We eat breakfast. I am careful not to overdo it since I don't want to see my food again on a ride. Then, we check out, dump our bags in the cars, and head into the park. School isn't out, so it's not particularly busy. There are quite a few younger children, but they're all too small for the bigger rides, so we shouldn't have long waits. There aren't a massive number of roller coasters here anyway, but there is a lot to see, and there's always the bar.

Ian, Jack, and Linc walk behind Hanna, Mel, and me as we head to a roller coaster.

"There are children everywhere," Jack moans.

"Three children, Jack," Linc replies sarcastically.

He turns his nose up. "Yeah, they'll multiply."

Hanna tuts. "We're at Legoland, babe."

"And whose fault is that?"

Okay, so I'll admit that I feel a little out of place, being in my twenties and here without small people, but Lego boxes go up to age ninety-nine, right?

It was so much fun here the last time. I've missed fun, so I don't really care what we're doing as long as our group is together, and we're laughing.

My eyes catch Linc watching me as we join the short queue for the roller coaster. I bite my lip and look away as the image of his bare chest slams into my mind. I think I'll be able to conjure up that image anytime for the rest of my life.

Though his sculptured chest looked hard, the skin covering it also looked soft and smooth. I want to touch him and see.

"Line's moving, Tills," Hanna says, laughing as she nudges me forward.

Whoops.

"You scared?" Linc teases, nodding his head in the direction of the ride.

I'm petrified ... but not of the roller coaster. Well, not the one I'm about to ride anyway. It's roller coaster Reid I'm scared of.

"I don't know how I'll cope."

163

He laughs at my dead tone and steps beside me. The others are all in front now. The ride seats two next to each other, so I figure it will be Linc and me. After this morning, I'm very okay with that.

"Well, anytime you want to jump on me to protect you ..."

"I'll keep that in mind, thanks."

His smile widens, and it steals my breath.

God, he is beautiful.

He's right beside me, arm occasionally brushing mine as we move along the queue. I can smell the woodsy tone to his aftershave.

He's simultaneously attacking each one of my senses.

We shuffle along again, and we're going on next.

"When was the last time you were at a theme park?" I ask him.

With a smirk, he replies, "The last time we were here."

"Yeah, me, too."

Hanna and I planned a trip to Alton Towers theme park with our friendship group, but Robbie died.

"I'm glad we came here now," I say.

The gate is opened, and we're let in. Linc and I take a seat, fourth from the front, behind Hanna and Jack and Mel and Ian.

I tug on the small rod of metal that seems too thin to adequately save my life, but I'm sure it's fine. The ride doesn't even go upside down.

Linc chuckles as I next push the metal bar down.

"You don't test the ride before it starts?" I ask him.

"No, I'm normal."

"Well, don't come crying to me when you're thrown to a grizzly death."

The roller coaster jolts and then begins to move.

"I'm sure I'll be fine if this ride tips me out."

Okay, so I don't think anything at Legoland can kill you—unless one of those big Lego statues falls on your head—but that's not the point really. Who wants to be thrown from even a gentle ride? You're still going to break something.

The cart zooms forward, and we're thrown from side to side. I'm chucked into Linc, but he manages to stop himself from squishing me. We judder to a halt at the end, and I grin up at him.

Laughing, he pushes the bar off our legs. "Enjoy that, did you?"

I step out of the cart. "It's not the same as a proper roller coaster, but yes, I did."

Being here again has put a smile on my face, and enjoying everything we did last time only adds to that. My heart is light, the way it was back then. Here, there is no pain or guilt. We're young people acting years below our age and having fun.

I needed this.

"Good," he replies as we head out of the gate. "Where to next?"

Hanna bounces. "The fire engines!"

"Oh, we are so kicking your arses this time!" I tell her.

Five years ago, we split into teams, couples and then me and Linc, and we went head-to-head. Jack and Hanna just clinched the win, but I'm physically stronger than I was, and Linc has been working out a lot.

"It's on, bitch," she replies, smirking and grabbing Jack's hand.

Mel scoffs. "Ugh, we have no chance."

"We only have no chance because you refuse to get your hands dirty and help me," Ian replies.

Mel glares at him.

"Come on, let's go!" I grab Linc's upper arm, my fingers stretching over his muscles.

Yummy.

I drop my hand because it would be a bit creepy if I kept holding him as we walked.

Linc keeps up with my pace. "You look different today."

"I feel different today."

"It's nice to see you smile like that again. I've missed it," he admits.

"Thanks. You don't look so moody yourself right now." I bump his arm with my shoulder and arch my eyebrow.

Shaking his head, he laughs. "I'm not that moody."

"Right now, you're not. I've always liked it when *you* smile like that."

We pass various rides and attractions on our way to the fire engines. I want to go on everything.

I'm a child!

"It's good, being here. I'm not looking forward to going home tonight," he says.

My heart sinks at the thought. "No, neither am I."

We can't live at Legoland or any other place where we have fond memories. That isn't real. Eventually, we have to face reality and decide if we can handle our painful, entwined past. In this moment, I feel like we can do anything. I'm attracted to him—duh—and I want to see how our friendship can develop. But the nostalgia of best times is working something fierce here. I can't make any kind of lasting decisions while I'm here.

There isn't a line at the fire engines, as everyone heads to the cars and roller coasters when they get in, so we get straight on a Lego-looking fire engine.

"You're the stronger one, so you pump the lever and make the engine move," I tell Linc.

When we move the engine to the other end of the tracks, we have to get out and spray water from the hose at the fake fires and then go back to the other end and do the same.

Linc stretches his arms. "No pressure then."

"Come on. With that body you've got going on now, you can beat Jack in your sleep."

His dark, stormy blue eyes glisten. "You've noticed my body?"

"Linc, I'm not blind."

His lips curl wider. That's fine. He can be smug or whatever. I'm not ashamed of the fact that I think he looks incredible now or that every part of my being wants to be closer to him. I'm sitting in a fucking red Lego fire engine, wanting to wrap my arms around his waist and be greeted with the comfort I'm sure I'll get.

I press my fingernails into the palms of my hands. I can't go to him like that.

"You're going down!" Jack calls as we begin.

Linc grabs the lever and pumps it up and down so fast; it's almost a blur. The little fire engine moves forward with his efforts, and we shoot off to first place. I stick my tongue out to Hanna, and she gives me the finger.

"Faster, Linc!"

He doesn't stop, but he does raise his eyebrow. Yeah, okay, I'm not exactly helping, but if I did, I would just slow him down.

We hit the end of the track, and I grab the hose. Water sprays out.

"Aim it, Tilly!"

I am bloody aiming it!

He helps, and we knock out the fire in seconds.

"Go!" I shout, my heart pumping double time.

Next to us, Hanna and Jack are bickering. She's bitching at him to hurry up with the hose while hindering him by grabbing it and trying to aim it herself.

We're already on our way back, Linc having the fire engine flying down the tracks.

Mel and Ian are doing well—not as well as us, obviously—but they're giving Jack and Hanna a run for their money. Jack will be livid if they beat them, too. God, I hope they do.

We hit the other end as Jack puts out the last of his fire, and they head back.

This time, Linc takes over, completely absorbed in beating Jack. We look ridiculous, but I don't care because watching him hold a hose and laugh as he squirts water makes me swoon harder than a teenager meeting Justin Bieber.

Our last fire is knocked over, and we've won.

My arms shoot into the air. "Yes! Ha, losers!"

Linc chuckles. "Winning with grace there, Tilly."

"I don't care. And do you think he would have won gracefully if they'd beaten us?"

He frowns and then turns to Jack. "Sucker."

"Fuck off," Jack shouts, thankfully out of earshot of any toddlers.

We jump out of the fire engines, and I basically skip.

"The best team won," I cheer, holding my hand up for Linc.

He gives me a high five and smirks. Although he's trying to look a little discouraged by my behaviour right now, he can't stop smiling either.

Hanna was right; this was a good idea.

"Let's go to Lego Miniland next," I say.

"No, food first," Jack protests.

I tilt my head. "You ate forty-five minutes ago."

"I could eat something," Ian chimes in.

"We cannot spend all day eating."

"Okay, okay," Hanna says. "Me, Jack, Mel, and Ian will go get food and meet you and Linc by the Miniland in, like, ten minutes."

I look at Linc, and he shrugs like he doesn't care what we do.

"Sure, see you there." I walk off with Linc, and the others go in search of food. Jack should be a lot bigger than he is. "I love the miniature world."

Who wouldn't like to walk around tiny buildings from around the world, all made from Legos?

Linc has looked at the map once and seems to know the way, so I follow him.

"Shouldn't these kids be in school?" he grumbles.

I look at their school polo T-shirts. "Linc, they're on a school trip."

He turns up his nose. "Very educational."

"You are such a grump."

He smiles down at me. "Better?"

"Much. I like your smile." *And your chest.*

"There it is," I say, spotting a tiny version of London.

"Have you ever been on the London Eye?" he asks.

"No, have you?"

"Yeah, it was boring."

I roll my eyes. "Of course it was."

He laughs and turns to me, the smile slowly fading as his dark blue eyes delve into mine.

My breath catches, desire blazing through my veins.

I want him. Right. Now.

His mouth parts, tongue darting out and wetting his bottom lip. He's going to kiss me.

Oh God, please just bloody kiss me!

Something passes through Linc's gaze, and he clears his throat.

No.

"The others are coming," he says, straightening his back.

No, I want my damn kiss!

He recovers much quicker than me. My hormones are all over the place. I'm too hot, and all I want to do is drag him to a hotel room.

"Hey," Hanna says, grabbing a crisp from the packet in her hand.

I smile and look away.

Linc and I almost kissed somewhere between London and Paris.

We spend the rest of the day on rides made for children, but we laugh so much that my cheek muscles are aching. After a quick drink in the bar, and Coke for the drivers, we head to the cars to go home.

My heart is heavy as I say good-bye to my friends. Linc is driving me since we live near each other. Ian and Mel are taking Jack and Hanna home because they have to pass their house to get to theirs.

I rub the butterflies in my stomach at the thought of spending a couple of hours confined in a small space with

Linc. I've been desperate for physical contact with him all day—and yesterday, too—so I need space between us, not to be trapped in a vehicle.

Lie. Big, fat lie.

What I need is for him to put his hands all over me. But that can't happen without an abundance of guilt after, so it's best not to bloody think about it.

I wave to the others as I get into the passenger seat of Linc's car and sigh.

Linc gets in, all smiles and relaxed shoulders. "Let's hit the road."

Yeah, I would rather not. But we will always have this. Linc will eventually leave again, and life will return to *normal*, but Hanna's meddling has given me good memories of my friend, post-Robbie's death, and nothing will take that away.

"Yep, let's go."

24

Tilly

My head swims with confusion. The night away has been amazing. I've not laughed and been free like that since I was sixteen.

But we can't stay in a place that was part of my teens. We can't live in the past, and one weekend of getting along with Linc doesn't erase what happened.

I wish it could because having a taste of the past was incredible.

We're now driving home and going back to reality. In about twenty minutes, we'll be outside my house, and the weekend will really be over.

Linc and I are alone in his car. Perhaps it's what we need though because, when we go home, we have to go our separate ways again.

I won't hurt my parents by letting them see me hanging out with him.

"You all right?" he asks.

The last ten minutes have been travelled in strained silence, both of us understanding that this weekend was a one-off and that it's almost over.

"Fine. You?" I reply, fiddling with my fingers.

"Uh-huh," he mutters, though he sounds anything but okay.

"What are you thinking?"

On a sigh, he shakes his head. "You really want to know?"

"Wouldn't have asked if I didn't."

"What happens when we get home? Can I talk to you, or do we go back to the way things have been?"

"You've been talking to me," I say defensively. Honestly, that was a bit of a dick move on my part. I know what he means. But I can't make promises. "Okay, I'm just going to put it out there, Linc. I'd love for things to go back to how they were. We had an amazing friendship group, but I don't know how to be your friend with Robbie's death hanging over us."

The words lift a weight off my shoulders. There's no need to sidestep the subject with him. It's only eating away at me, making me feel worse for wanting a friendship when I feel like I should hate him indefinitely.

Then, the weight is back because this just reinforces the fact that we can't go back.

"Tilly, if I could change what happened, I would do it in a heartbeat," he says. His voice is low and strained, almost like the words knock the air from his lungs. "I am so sorry I didn't do more. It's something I have to live with every day. The guilt never, *ever* lessens."

I close my eyes as my heart rips. "I'm not solely blaming you, and I know that Robbie made his own choices, but it's hard. He's not here."

"I know," he whispers. "I hate that you're hurting. You are the last person in this world I want to hurt. Tell me there is something I can do."

"You can talk me through that night."

His head snaps in my direction. "What?"

"I know the facts. The police told us what happened, but I've never heard it from you."

He looks back at the road. "I ... I'm not sure."

I wring my fingers. "Look, I know it's a lot to ask of you, to relive that day, but—"

"What? No, that's not what I mean. I don't care about me."

Well, I do.

"I need to hear it. Please, Linc? All I have in my head is what I think happened, and it's so painful."

"You want to talk about this now?"

"Not in the car."

"Mine?" he asks.

"Um ..."

Do I want to go in there? What if my parents see? If Linc and I are going to attempt some sort of friendship again, I'm going to have to tell them. *But how do I tell them?*

"I don't know where else," he admits.

"Yours is fine," I find myself saying. "I'll come tonight."

"You're going to sneak out of your house?"

I roll my eyes. "Crazy, right? I'm twenty-one. They need time, Linc. I don't want to push my friendship with you on them, but I *will* eventually tell them."

Time to grow the hell up, I suppose. I don't ever want to hurt my parents, but we have to move past this limbo we're in.

"Nothing about you is crazy. Well, not in a bad way."

"So, is tonight okay?" I ask.

"Yeah, anytime, Tilly."

He pulls up just before my house.

"Anytime? You're going to regret saying that when I'm throwing stones at your window at three in the morning."

He smiles but doesn't reply. After a second, he shakes his head. "I knew that was you."

"You heard me that night? Why didn't you look out your window?"

It was about three weeks before Robbie died. I'd been on a night out with Linc, Jack, and Hanna. When I got home, I realised that I wasn't one bit tired and didn't want the night to end. So, I snuck out and threw stones at Linc's window, but after ten minutes, I figured he was asleep.

"By the time I realised there was something there, you'd gone. What did you want?"

I shrug. "I don't know really. I couldn't sleep."

"Ah, so you thought I shouldn't either."

"Precisely," I reply, laughing at him.

"Well, I'm sorry. I wish I'd gotten up sooner. We could have hit up the old haunted house."

I scrunch my nose. "Absolutely not."

There is a house in town that has been vacant ever since I can remember. It's big and creepy with ivy growing all over it. And it's supposedly haunted. A few people have been in there and come out, telling tales of ice-cold wind blowing where doors and windows are closed, things falling or moving of their own accord, and strange scraping sounds.

I don't know if I believe in ghosts, but I'm perfectly okay with never finding out.

"One day, Tilly."

"Nope."

"I didn't think you were scared of anything ... besides spiders."

"I'm not scared of spiders, just that one spider. It was the size of a cat. You didn't see it."

Chuckling, he tilts his head in my direction. "I might not have seen it, but I sure heard your scream."

I was in my room, looking out the window, waiting for thunder after a strike of lightning, when the massive bastard dropped down from above. And I'm pretty sure it was growling, too.

"Whatever. I'm not scared of spiders, but ghosts freak me out."

"You believe in them?" he asks, his eyes sharpening, ready to dissect my reply in his head.

"You're asking if I think Robbie is a ghost? If I think he's still here?"

Linc doesn't respond, but his silence speaks volumes.

With a sigh that sounds heavier than I feel right now, I reply, "I have to believe he's somewhere. I couldn't stand it if there was nothing for him now."

"I don't think he would go far, Tilly." He playfully narrows his eyes. "He once said, if he was invisible, he'd hang out in the women's shower at the gym."

"Ew. I didn't need to know that."

He had better not.

And why the hell have I never thought about pervert ghosts before? They could watch everything.

So, I'm never having a shower, a bath, or sex again.

I'm already not getting the latter.

"You should get home," he says with a smile. "I'll see you tonight when you break out."

Rolling my eyes, I salute. "See you later, Linc."

I get out of the car and walk into my house, feeling even lighter, like someone has removed a ball and chain that was shackled to my ankles. Even through all of the confusion, I feel good right now.

Linc being home should have been the worst thing to happen. My parents and I always hoped they would sell the house without returning, but having him here, it's ... freeing. Somehow, he's opened the door to healing. He's making me want to sort my life out, and I want to move forward. All the things that stopped being super important to me after Robbie died are slowly reappearing.

I open the front door and immediately know something isn't right. The lights are off, all of them, but I can hear deep breathing in the living room.

"Mum? Dad?"

They're not supposed to be home yet.

My pulse hums as I move deeper into the house, approaching the living room door.

I poke my head around the doorframe and grip the wood with the tips of my fingers. Mum is sitting on the sofa with her head in her hands, sobbing quietly.

The ball and chain is firmly back.

"Mum," I call softly, stepping into the room.

Her spine stiffens, hands frantically wiping her eyes. She faces away from me, but I can see well enough.

"Tilly, darling, how are you?"

When she stands and turns around, she's smiling, but her eyes are red and puffy.

"What happened?" I ask.

"Oh, nothing, just a little cry. I take it Legoland was good? Are you hungry? I'll put the kettle on and then make you something to eat." She whisks past me like she's on a time-sensitive mission.

"Mum, why were you crying?" I ask, following her into the kitchen as she switches lights on.

She's not getting away with crying her heart out in darkness and trying to pass it off as a *little cry*.

Her hand circles the handle on the kettle so hard; her knuckles turn white. "I miss him; that's all."

She cries for Robbie a lot, but what I just witnessed—the all-consuming, crippling grief that threatens to swallow a person whole—hasn't happened in a good year.

"That's not it. You were in the dark. How long have you been in there, crying?"

It's been dark for about two hours now, and she must have gotten in that state a while before that to have not turned any lights on in the house. I'm taking steps forward, and she's taking steps back.

Am I stealing hers? Does something have to give for me to be able to move?

Could Linc be the best thing for me and the worst thing for her?

He will have to go if that's it. I will finish the Reids' house for them if my mother's mental health is at risk.

She has worked so hard to pull herself out of her deep depression and only been off her medication in the last six months. She can't go back there.

"Tilly, he's my son, and sometimes, I miss him so much, I can't breathe, so I let it out."

"I'm worried."

Tilting her head to the side, she smiles. "Don't be."

"You were doing so well."

"I still am. Bad days happen."

Bad days happen, sure, but that was something else entirely. That was raw pain, like it had just happened, not like four solid years and a lot of therapy had taken place between.

This doesn't feel right.

"Is it Linc?" I ask, going in for the kill. Best to get it all out there and be honest.

That's what we were told in our group therapy sessions, that we had to be open with each other. We only ever did that in those sessions, and when that hour was up, we'd go back to pretending we were fine.

She flicks the kettle on and turns around. "What do you mean?"

"Is Linc being home opening old wounds?"

"Those wounds aren't going to go away."

"No, not for me either, but they're healing. You were dealing better than you had been."

When she came off the tablets, there was a period of time when things got worse as her body adjusted to the hormonal change, but she worked harder to wade through those emotions and take them head-on. She's not all right, but she's making progress.

"Sweetheart, I'm okay. I don't feel the way I did before, but there will always be times where it's unbearable. That doesn't mean that, when my tears dry, I won't get up. I made a promise to you that I wouldn't allow myself to go back to a place where I couldn't get out of bed. You're just as important to me as Robbie, and I will be there for you."

"I'm not trying to imply that you aren't there for me again."

"I know." She steps around the worktop and tugs me into her arms. "I'm okay, and it has nothing to do with Lincoln being home."

I hug her back until she lets me go. "All right." Smiling, I realise I believe her. She's not bullshitting, like she got so good at. "Want to make some popcorn and watch a movie?"

"That would be lovely," she replies.

"Cool. I'll go and pick something."

And I also need to message Linc and let him know I won't be sneaking out tonight.

25

Tilly

I haven't seen Linc in two days. Not a peep. He replied to my message, letting me know that he was fine with me cancelling, and we've texted a couple of times since then, but apart from that, nada.

Late last night, Greg called and asked me to meet him for breakfast. He wouldn't give anything away, but I could tell from the sober tone in his voice that it was going to be more than a casual meeting.

Greg is now opposite me in the restaurant and sips his coffee. Since I got here five minutes ago, he's barely said a word. Anything I say, he responds with simple one-syllable words.

I'm not sure what's going on, but it's pretty pointless and kind of rude to invite me somewhere and ignore me.

"So," I prompt, "is everything okay?"

His eyes twitch, and his hand tightens around the mug. "Why wouldn't it be?"

"You seem … distracted."

"How was your weekend away with your friends?"

Ah, is that it? Is he pissed off because he wasn't invited?

He's not really friends with any of my friends, only me. It wouldn't have been a very fun weekend with him, particularly since he hates Linc.

"It was good, thank you. Greg, are you upset because I didn't ask you to come?" I cringe as I ask.

The only real and deep conversations we've had are about Robbie and how I'm dealing with his death. Everything else has been somewhat off-limits. We have just never opened up about our feelings.

His eyebrows almost touch his hairline. "Is that what you think? Tilly, I can't stand Lincoln, Ian, and Jack, and I barely know Hanna and Mel. No, I'm not *upset* that you didn't ask me to come, too." The snarky tone in his voice has my spine stiffening.

"Then, why are you being so hostile? You've asked me here, but you don't seem to want me here. Has something happened? You can talk to me, you know."

"You've forgiven him then?"

"I'm sorry?"

"Lincoln! You went away with him, and you're keeping it from your parents. Have you forgotten what he did?"

My fingertips dig into my mug. *Have I forgotten?*

"I'm choosing not to spend the rest of my life being angry. Linc was stupid that night, but no more so than Robbie and certainly no more than Stanley. I don't want to punish him for the rest of my life. It's exhausting, Greg, and it only makes me feel worse."

"So, that's it? All is forgiven because he moves back and lays on the charm?"

"Lays on the charm? I'm not sleeping with him!"

There isn't much charming going on, but Linc isn't really the kind of guy who needs to charm a woman. There is something about his height, muscular physique, gorgeous blue eyes, and nonchalant attitude that have women falling at his feet.

But I don't need to mention that to Greg now.

"Tilly, he's bad news. He moved away with his family. He chose his murderer of a brother over—"

I slam my free hand on the table, seething. "Don't. Things aren't that black and white, and you know it. Everyone turned on the Reid family, but the person to blame for Robbie's death is Stanley."

"His parents kept him out of prison, Tilly!"

"I remember, Greg. As much as I hate their decision back then, you can't seriously tell me you're surprised. They're his *parents*, and none of that has anything to do with Linc."

He shakes his head, clenching his jaw. "So, everything goes back to the way it was with you and him? He might not have been driving, but he was drinking, too."

"Also a fact I remember." My chest burns. I press my fist against the fire. "I don't know what you're not hearing, but if you want to blame him for someone else's actions forever, then go ahead, but it's not going to get you anywhere. This isn't even your fight, so why are you so angry over this?"

"*I've* been there, Tilly! Over the last four years, I've been there for you when you've fallen apart. That's why I can be fucking pissed off over this."

"And I've always thanked you for being there. You know how grateful I am for that. But Linc isn't Stanley. We've all done things we're not proud of, and every single one of us has made mistakes, but how long are you people going to make Linc suffer for his?"

"Have you had this conversation with your parents?"

"That's none of your business."

He laughs bitterly. "So, no. You don't know what you're doing, Tilly, and that worries me. You want to forgive him, and you want things to go back to how they were before, but that can't ever happen. Deep down, you know it's not that simple. What does being friends with him mean? You'll have to hide from your parents and his parents. You'll have to hide from the whole town because the second someone sees you and him getting pally, it's over."

"You're overreacting."

"Am I?"

No, he's not really. Everything he's saying is true even if he's a bit melodramatic. Being friends with Linc isn't going to be easy, but that doesn't mean it's impossible. We might have to keep things on the down-low for a while, but I'm sure my parents would be okay with it in time. Lots and lots of time.

But that's not really going to be an issue since Linc is leaving once his old house is renovated. He has another life, one I'm not part of, a hundred miles away.

"Everything you're saying, I've said to myself. They are things I battle with on a daily basis, but I'm not going to let fear rule my life. Linc was my friend."

"*Was*, Tilly."

Oh my God, I can't believe I'm having this argument with him like we're in high school. My life is filled with bullshit drama, and I'm tired of it.

"Look, this is how things are now. I'm friends with him, and I'm friends with you. It's fine if you don't like it. I won't hang out with you together anyway. I don't see why this has to be a big deal."

Greg pushes his mug into the centre of the table and stands up. The metal chair scrapes against the stained flooring. "I need to leave then." He throws some cash down to cover the coffees.

"What? Greg?"

Shit, he's actually going. What the hell?

I reluctantly let go of my coffee since I've not had nearly enough caffeine for this shit and jog to the door where Greg has just burst through.

He can't just go all crazy boyfriend on me when he's not even my boyfriend and walk away. Not happening.

"Hey!" I snap, running until I catch up with him outside the entrance to the park. "Greg, what are you doing?"

Spinning around, he throws his hands up. "I'm not doing it, Tilly."

"Doing what?"

"You want him. I get that loud and clear now. You wanted him then, and nothing has changed ... even though *everything* has changed."

"What are you saying? Linc and I are friends."

"Of course you are. I'm not blind. I thought things might change for us, but seeing how quickly you let him back in proves it won't."

I don't like where this is going at all.

Taking a breath, I hold my hands up, and Greg relaxes a little.

"You want things to change for us? Greg, I ..." *I don't feel that way!*

"Oh, I get it, believe me."

"I'm sorry," I whisper. My stomach turns stone-cold. "Can we still be friends? You've been so good to me. I don't want to lose you."

He rolls his eyes. "You can't have us both."

"I don't have either of you. I want to be friends with you and him."

"It doesn't work that way, Tilly. I can't stand by and watch you get closer to him. If there is no chance for us, then I need to walk away for good."

"Tilly?"

Oh, he has the worst timing.

I turn my head toward the sound of my name. Linc is standing still, fists clenched by his sides just enough to show his displeasure at the sight of me and Greg but not too much that he looks threatening.

Greg, however, looks like he wants to rip Linc's head off. His face is red, and his blue eyes look almost black as he glares.

"Hey," I say, squirming at the awkward energy buzzing between us all. "What are you doing here?"

Linc's eyes flick from Greg to me, chest puffing, as he assumes I asked him why he's here because I've been caught out. Even if there was something between me and Greg, it wouldn't be Linc's business. Nothing has happened between us, though it feels like everything has happened between us.

"I'm meeting Ian and Jack."

"Cool." I wince, rubbing my lips with my index finger. *Cool.* That's the only word that came to mind. I am so *un*cool.

Greg scoffs, his nose turned up. "I'm going. You might as well go inside with her and sit down, Reid."

"Greg," I start, but he holds his hand up, asking for me to stop.

There seems to be no point in dragging this out and making anything harder for anyone, but Greg is my friend. He's been there for me so many times. I appreciate that, and I don't want to lose him. Still, I can't force him to want to stay friends, and I can't give him what he wants if my heart isn't into it.

"You win," Greg says as he storms past Linc.

My hand hits my forehead, and I groan. I head back inside because there are people out here, and they're looking.

Linc follows as I shove the door open and head back to my table.

I don't look, but I hear Linc take a seat at the table.

"Hey," he says tenderly. "What just happened?"

I lift my head. "Greg just walked away from our friendship. He's been here through so much. He helped me a lot when Robbie died. Now, he's gone."

Linc's chin dips, but his face is blank.

Is he feeling guilt over Robbie? Because he wasn't there?

Because we all know the reason Greg has cut me off now has everything to do with Linc being back.

"I'm sorry, Tilly."

"You ever feel like your whole life is one big ride, and you're watching parts of the rail fall off, but you can't do anything about it?"

His eyes meet mine, and the rail seems a bit steadier.

Why is he my rail mechanic?

"I feel like that all the time," he admits.

"What about before Robbie?"

"Yeah, I felt like that before Robbie died, too."

"That's why you've always been so brooding?"

"Brooding?" His face brightens a fraction with a ghost of a smile.

"Tell me you know you're moody and brooding."

"Can't say I've thought about it much. I don't like many people, and I'm happy to be alone, but I didn't think I was that moody."

He doesn't think he's that moody. Amazing.

"Well, you are. That was the appeal for all the girls when we were growing up—who would be the one to make you laugh."

"I laugh, Tilly."

"You know what I mean." I roll my eyes. "You never seemed happy, though you never really seemed unhappy."

"Can't say I was either. I was just me."

"I don't think I've felt happy at all in the last four years."

He takes a breath that sounds like he's been inflicted with pain. "Have you been unhappy the *whole* time?"

"Not exactly. At first, I was, of course, but I haven't been constantly unhappy."

"Greg helped with that. Are you going to be okay now?"

I smile at Linc and curl my fingers into my palms to stop myself from reaching for his hands. We're in a very public place. Thankfully, everyone else seems more interested in their drinks and company to notice me and Linc. Yet.

"Greg did a lot. I won't take that away from him, but I'm in a different place now."

"Are you?"

My spine stiffens. "You didn't see me before, Linc. Maybe I'm not totally together like I was, but I'm not the same as a year ago either."

"All right," he says, conceding. "I just worry; that's all."

"Because I'm wasting my life here, doing nothing?"

"Not exactly the words I was going to use. If you want to be here, Tilly, be here. But you want more, don't you?"

185

"I'll have more. My life isn't quite over yet."

He looks away and purses his lips, irritated with my tone. I'm getting defensive when I shouldn't be.

Linc is right to be concerned. For years now, I've buried my own nagging worry about where I'm going. When someone else comes to the same conclusion as me though, I feel like a loser.

"Do you want a drink?" he asks, turning his head back to me.

"A really big one, please."

"You know it's ten o'clock in the morning, yeah?"

"Are you judging my drink choices, too?"

He leans in, getting a bit dangerously close. I can smell his aftershave and his hair.

"I'm not judging your drink choices, Tilly."

Oh, great.

"It's fine. I want a Coke now anyway."

Linc's eyes search mine for agonising seconds before he gets up without a word and heads to the bar in the corner of the restaurant.

Is my life some sort of Truman Show? *Are there people watching this train wreck right now, some shouting at me to follow Greg, some wanting me to get with Linc already, and others turning off because they can't take how stupid I am?*

While Linc has his back to me at the bar, I unlock my phone and tap a quick text to Greg. I should just leave it, as he walked away for a reason, but my stomach is heavy, nerves buzzing with uneasy energy.

I have to at least apologise for how messy things have gotten. We were friends, and I hate that I've hurt him.

Tilly: I'm sorry. I hope you're okay.

The time on my screen ticks by another minute. He lives close by, so he should be home now. I can't expect a reply. He seemed to want nothing to do with me.

Tears burn behind my eyes, but I can't be that tragic, so I take a breath, feeling my chest expand and then deflate. I concentrate on my lungs getting bigger and smaller.

Ground yourself.

I only stop when Linc puts a bottle of Coors Light down in front of me with a little more force than necessary.

"Beer?" I ask. It's far too early for beer, but I don't want to lose face. Besides, I could really do with one after losing a friend.

"You want a drink, Tilly, so drink."

"Why are you mad at me?"

I blink, and the tears for Greg have been replaced with contempt for Linc because he's pissing me off … and I'm not too sure why. It'll be the shortest bout of contempt in history because, no matter what happens, I can't stay angry with him.

He slumps back in his seat. "I'm not mad at you."

"Could've fooled me. But thanks for the drink." I grab the cold beer and take a swig. "I'm also going to need a lift home."

His lips smile around the rim of the glass. "I know."

I wonder if he thinks a little less of me for still drinking. It's my brother who died, but he's the one sitting with a Coke. He said he doesn't drink, and for the most part, Linc doesn't judge anyone, but perhaps that's because he doesn't really pay attention to anyone.

Okay, time to stop overthinking that one.

"You don't like Greg." I don't ask him because I already know the answer, but I want to explore why. I can take a good guess and say it's over me, but back in the day, we were all purely friends.

"I don't like most people."

"Glad I made the cut." I lean over. "Have I still made the cut right now?"

"You're still there, Tilly," he replies like I asked the dumbest question ever.

I straighten up again and smile. "Good. Back to Greg …"

Linc puts the glass down on the table and folds his arms. "You're intelligent, Tilly. Don't ever pretend you're not."

"There has never been anything between me and Greg."

"Not from your point of view," he counters.

"Okay. So, maybe not, but nothing has ever happened between us."

"Yeah, I know that, too."

"Have you spent the last four years stalking me?"

That stifles a low, dark laugh out of him. It's a good sound.

"Nah, you've not made the stalking cut."

"Hmm. Who is on your stalking cut? I have Tom Hardy, Stephen James, Brant Daugherty, any Hemsworth, David Beckham—when he's wearing his Royal Wedding suit—and Kit Harington."

His shoulders are free of the tension Greg put there. "Anyone else?"

"Probably. The list keeps growing."

"Wow, you're a little bit of a stalker slut."

Gasping, I slap his upper arm as he laughs freely. "That's rude."

"I'm only kidding. Stalk however many people you like."

"I plan to. You've still not told me who is on your list."

"I don't have a list of people I want to stalk, and if I did, I would probably be on a list."

"Well, there's a surprise. Hey, aren't you supposed to be meeting Ian and Jack?"

He shakes his head. "Not anymore. I texted them when I went to the bar."

"Aw, you ditched your boys for me. Isn't that, like, some sort of treason? Hanna would have a lot to say if I ditched her."

For about ten seconds, time sits still. I wait for Linc to respond, but he stares at me like he's seeing me for the first time. My smile fades as my heart starts to pound.

"What?" I say, brushing my long hair behind my ears. "Linc?"

"Nothing." He lowers his eyes and grabs his drink.

"No, what was that?"

His scrutiny has made me self-conscious.

"You just sound like you."

Huh?

"Who do I sound like the rest of the time?"

"I wish I knew."

His sharp words seep through my skin, deep into my bones, and leave me cold. Linc isn't the only one unsure of who I am now.

How do you get back to who you once were after losing so much? It's like expecting a human to breathe underwater just because they don't want to die.

I duck my head and grab my beer, my half-drank coffee now completely abandoned.

26

Tilly

It's been a while since I've been to a party on the beach. Mostly due to the fact that I'm not seventeen anymore. But, tonight, I'm going back. A lot of us are actually because it's Mel's birthday, and she wants a night like the old days.

There seems to be a lot of old-day reenactments going on recently. It's like Hanna and Mel have a plan. That plan being to get things back to how they were. To remind me of how good things were. As if I've forgotten. It's something I think about and mourn on a daily basis.

I'd be lying if I said I wasn't looking forward to it. The sun is heating up; the beginning of June is usually kind to us here. So, I'm wearing a knee-length white sundress and flip-flops with a denim jacket in case the temperature drops.

Ian and Mel offered to give me a ride, but since Linc is going and lives next door, it seems silly to make them come out of their way.

So, that's how I find myself walking to the end of the road where Linc is going to meet me. I've not broached the subject of him with my parents yet. I need to, and I know that, but it's always so hard to talk to them about anything Reid-related.

I sigh as Linc pulls up on the road beside me. Taking a breath, I get in.

Sweet mother …

He's wearing a white T-shirt, black jeans, and a black leather jacket. I'm momentarily stunned.

"Hey." His mouth curves as his eyes flit a little bit south.

Definitely the right dress.

"Thanks for picking me up," I say, chucking my bag on the backseat. I'm going to stay with Hanna and Jack tonight, so I've brought my stuff.

He nods and pulls off toward the beach. It's only a fifteen-minute drive to where I spent so long as a kid. Though I used to enjoy walking it.

"Did you get much done in the house today?" I ask, biting on my lip as I watch him grip the steering wheel just a little too tight.

What's up with him?

Sighing, he shakes off whatever was just eating at him. "It's been productive. What have you done?"

"Nothing quite so productive," I admit. But then my days are filled with working a job I don't particularly want to do and tiptoeing around my parents.

"That doesn't sound like you."

"I'm not the same person you knew, Linc."

He glances at me out of the corner of his eye. "I don't know; I'm seeing a little more of her each day."

When did this topic get so heavy?

"Are you staying at Hanna and Jack's, too? A bunch of us are."

"I'm not sure. I won't be drinking, so I don't really need a place to crash."

"You don't have to be drunk to stay there."

"Will you be drunk later?"

I wish I were drunk right now.

"Probably."

Dipping his chin in a curt nod, he accelerates as we join the main road for a short stretch.

"You don't like drinking yourself or you don't like anyone drinking?" I ask.

"Myself. I don't really care what anyone else does."

Okay, ouch.

"You're in a bad mood. Why?"

If I've managed to piss him off in the two minutes we've been in the car, I think it's a record.

"Everything is fine, Tilly. I just need to relax and forget."

"What are you forgetting?"

He cuts me a look, but his eyes are back on the road a nanosecond later. "The house."

"Okay. Well, if it's worth anything, I think the house is looking great."

With a sigh, he nods. "Thanks."

And he doesn't think he's moody.

A very long fifteen minutes later, we pull into the car park at the beach, and there are already a few cars here I recognise.

"Looks like the party started without us," I say as I unbuckle my seat belt.

Linc grumbles something that sounds like, "Good," and gets out.

Great.

He's going to be a bundle of laughs tonight. It's times like this I wish he would drink, so that would lighten him up a little.

Grumpy fucker.

"Are you going to stand around all night with your arms folded, looking like someone just kicked your cat?"

"No," he replies. "I don't have a cat. And I planned on sitting."

Irritation bubbles in my stomach. I turn and walk toward the steps that have been worn into the terrain over time, leading down to the beach. Linc is behind me. I can hear his heavy footsteps.

"You're a regular comedian, Linc," I say as he catches up.

He chuckles, and—*hallelujah*—his face looks a little happier. "You used to tell me that all the time," he says overtaking me and walking backwards so we can talk.

"You have a shit sense of humour," I say.

He stops dead in his tracks, so I have to grip his upper arms or fall forward into him. He fake gasps. "How dare you."

Mayday.

We're close.

We're too sodding close!

He's a step below me, so that puts us more or less at the same height.

"You falling at my feet, Tilly?"

Rolling my eyes at him, I let go now that I have my balance. "You stopping like that nearly made me fall, you psycho."

"You said I have a shit sense of humour. That wasn't very nice." His dark blue eyes glow with the reflection of the setting sun. They're even more devastating in orange light.

My insides flame.

He is so fucking gorgeous. I just want to jump him.

This is a very bad idea. But then I've never been a massive fan of the good ones.

Robbie. Think. Of. Robbie.

My brother popping into my head is like a bucket of cold water being chucked over my body—and not just because he's my brother.

I straighten and avert my eyes because I know, if I keep looking at Linc, I'll end up doing something I'll regret. I'm not ready. I'm working on my feelings for Linc—between being scared, excited, and trying to hide from them. I don't understand why I feel like this or what it means for my loyalty to my brother. If it even means anything at all.

"We should get to the party. I can see the fire from here."

Something passes through Linc's stunning eyes, and he knows the moment, or whatever it was, is now over. He turns and replies, "You think the fire will last longer than thirty minutes?"

I follow him as we continue our decline. "I hope not. We need to relight it at least three times; it's tradition."

"You remember when I offered to light the fire, so it wouldn't keep going out, and you lost your pretty mind."

Inside my head is the word *pretty* in big, flashing letters. But, on the outside, I'm going to be ice cool. The seventeen-year-old me who thought Linc was the hottest thing on the planet is back out to play, it would seem.

"I did not lose my mind." My *pretty* mind. "You were about to ruin two years' worth of tradition, and I couldn't have that."

"It doesn't make sense to keep relighting it."

"Of course it does. We'd get cold if we left it."

His steps falter a little as he looks at me like I've grown another head. "Sure," he replies.

"You never seemed to like the parties on the beach," I say as we head across the sand to the fire in the distance.

At the other end of the beach is another fire surrounded by teens. That used to be us. Now, we're the older ones on the sand.

He shrugs. "I don't dislike it, but some of your friends are annoying as hell."

"Which ones?"

"I like Hanna and Mel."

"Just those two?"

"Yeah. And you."

I roll my eyes. "Duh."

He grins. "Well, you do think a lot of yourself, don't you?"

Not as much as I used to. I've let so much of myself slide. A part of me died with Robbie, and I've let the rest of me remain stagnant. Moving forward is hard; it means letting go.

"Someone has to," I reply sarcastically.

195

"Oh, please, golden girl." He sees that I'm about to protest and gets in there first. "Don't even try to deny it. Everyone loves you, Tilly."

I snort. "You should tell that to Shawna Ferguson and her band of big-boobed clones."

"The girl in your year who thought she was the next Beyoncé?"

"Yeah. She did not like me."

"She tried to get me to go home with her at a beach party once."

"Did you? Because, if you did, I'm going to need you to never touch me again."

Lies. I want his hands all over me, no matter who has been there before.

"Nah. I could tell the kind of person she was. Besides, a try-hard is not attractive."

"Hey, I'm going to use that one when my parents are on at me to do something."

"Do what?"

"We've not had the uni conversation, as that will lead to many more Robbie-related questions since I'm only home still because Robbie is gone, but they constantly ask me what I'm doing, and I know it's more than them wanting to know what I'm doing that day."

Linc stops and folds his arms.

"Ah!" I point at him. "That's the stance! Getting some practice in?"

"Now, who's the comedian?"

I wave my hand toward him. "Go on. You're obviously about to say something, so let it out."

"I'm not afraid to have that conversation with you."

"It won't be a very long conversation. I don't know what I'm doing."

"It's not my place, and I know that, but you need to go to uni like you planned. You have so many more things to do than work in a restaurant, Tilly."

I grind my teeth and pick at the only thing I can. "There's no shame in—"

"I'm not saying you should be ashamed, but you shouldn't stay there when you don't want to. Your parents will be happy for you if you move out for uni."

My parents fall apart when I'm home late.

"Linc," I whisper, "you haven't been here, so you don't know."

"I haven't been here," he says, stepping closer and getting into my personal space again. "But I do know you. You'll stay here despite wanting more than anything to leave because you don't want to hurt them any more than they've been hurt. But, Tilly, that's not on you. It's not your responsibility to protect your parents."

"This isn't getting me into the party mood."

Smirking, he shakes his head. "Rain check?"

"Or we could just forget it?" I suggest hopefully.

Linc is the last person I want this conversation with, but apparently, he's the only one willing to have it with me.

He lifts his dark eyebrow. "Rain check, Tilly."

"Fine. Pass me a beer. I need one already."

Linc tears a hole in the cardboard box on the floor and grabs me one. "You drinking more now that I'm home?"

"What can I say? You drive me to it." I pop the lid and start to walk. "Do you never think about drinking again?"

"I'll consider having a beer after you apply to uni."

"Wow." I take a swig. "You really aren't going to drop this, are you?"

"Not a chance. Before I leave here, you'd better be back on track."

My lungs deflate. The thought of Linc leaving again leaves a nasty taste on my tongue.

I want him to stay.

27

Linc

Water gently rolls onto the sand and slides back out to sea. It's calm tonight. The gentle breeze ensures it doesn't get too warm. The sea is about the only calm thing here. Well, that, and Ian and me. Everyone is drunk, including Tilly. We've been here for one hour, and the girl is hammered. I have gotten to her.

I'm sitting off to the side with Ian. He's not exactly the life of the party either. I just don't like a lot of people, and obnoxious drunks who think they're God's gift or the funniest thing on the planet make me want to shoot myself in the face.

Ian is drinking the same beer as Tilly though not quite as many of them. The more time I spend with her, the more I can see her internal struggle regarding me. She subconsciously reverts back to the way we were—the easy, fun friendship that we could pick up if we'd not been hanging out together for a while. Four years have gone by, but it feels like only minutes when we're together.

"Mel is going to puke tonight," Ian says, turning his nose up in the direction of his girlfriend, who is doing the robot around the fire with an almost-empty bottle of white wine in her hand. It's not her first bottle either.

I nod. "Yeah, I think she might."

"You and Tilly staying at Jack's?"

He said, "You and Tilly," like we're a couple.

I take a breath. "She is."

"You're going home? But post-birthday breakfasts are the best breakfasts."

The morning after is one big grease-fest with mountains of food cooked in a lot of oil. Best hangover cure in the world. But I don't drink anymore, so there's not much point in my clogging up my arteries. Though I will if I go.

"I might stay over. She's pissed at me again."

Or did it start with me being pissed at her? I can't remember now.

"What have you done now?"

Nothing new.

I shrug. "Just being here, I guess."

"I swear, you two just need to get naked."

I wouldn't say no.

"She's too angry with me for that."

He looks at me and raises his eyebrow. "Nah. Where does most of that anger come from?"

"Robbie."

"This has nothing to do with Robbie, Linc, and you know it."

Sighing, I look over at the girl I'm fucking obsessed with. She's dancing with Hanna. I use the term *dance* loosely since they look like they're being electrocuted. There's a big smile on her face, but it doesn't fool me. Tilly's amber eyes always smiled along with her mouth when she was genuinely happy. Right now, she's just having fun, and there is a huge difference.

"I need to talk to her, don't I?"

We've been tiptoeing around each other for the last two months. She's not willing to admit what we truly are, and I'm too pussy to push the matter.

We're so close though. I have *us* by the tips of my fingers. One wrong move though, and she could be out of reach for good. Tilly is my own personal minefield.

"You need to talk to her," he confirms. "Then, you need to fuck her."

I roll my eyes, but that does sound like a plan. I would love to lay her down and run my hands and tongue all over her body and then turn her onto her stomach before entering her from behind.

That's one of my greatest fantasies with Tilly. It gets me off so fucking fast.

Time to stop thinking about that!

"Come on, man. I get hot, just watching all the sexual tension between you guys."

Turning my nose up, I mutter, "Thanks for that. I'm just not after a shag here, Ian."

"Mate, I can practically hear wedding bells every time you look at her."

"Glad it's that obvious."

But it's not to Tilly. She's too preoccupied, trying not to like me and struggling like hell when she lets her guard down.

Ian and I have stayed pretty much in the same place, catching up properly on four years. Although I've been back two months, we've not had many opportunities to talk in depth since we've been busy with working on my parents' house when he's been over.

I've missed him and Jack. Where I live now—or *not* since I don't have a place to live anymore—I've not made any lasting friendships. It doesn't help that I don't go out and get off my face.

Tilly stays away for the most part, only venturing over to pull Mel away from Ian so that they can dance with Hanna and some other girls I've forgotten the names of but never liked anyway.

Maybe she's right, and I am moody.

It's almost one in the morning, and everyone is trickling out. Hanna and Jack left fifteen minutes ago to unlock the house and wait for their many sleepover guests to start arriving. Ian and Mel have just gone, leaving me with Tilly.

A few others are walking away, heading in different directions to either go home or go to Jack's.

Tilly stumbles over after picking up her flip-flops from the sand. She grins as she leans into me. The response to her is fierce. My fingers curl into the small of her back, holding her close.

My head dips, spurred on by the overpowering desire coursing through my veins to kiss her. I lock my muscles in place in a desperate need not to screw this up between us even more.

What if she wants you to kiss her?

Could she?

"Tilly," I groan as she leans flush against my chest.

The alcohol has given her permission to let go of the reservations she has over us being something.

The beach has now cleared completely, everyone has gone, and I'm supposed to take Tilly to Hanna and Jack's, but she's making it very difficult.

I want to take her back to mine.

She looks up at me, and her amber eyes lose focus. "It's you, isn't it?" Her voice is barely a whisper, but I feel the fear in each word.

"What's me, Tilly? You really should have stopped drinking about an hour ago."

"I couldn't stop."

"Drinking? Why not?"

"Because I know this is the only way that I won't feel immediately guilty for being this close to you." Her eyes flit closed. "I want so badly to be this close to you."

My breath catches. I want to pull away because her words are gutting me, but my body needs to be closer to her, too. My fingers dig further into her flesh, holding her closer, tighter, never wanting to let go.

"Tilly, there is no need for you to feel guilty. Robbie would have been okay with this."

"I know. It's not him I'm worried about." She leans forward and lays her head against my chest. "My parents are having a hard time with you being here."

I rest my chin on her head. She's tucked so closely into me. "Have they told you that?"

"They don't need to." Her arms wrap around my back like she's scared I'll walk away after hearing this.

There is nothing she could ever say to scare me off. I love her unconditionally.

"I don't want to hurt them, but I don't want to hurt you either. It's such a mess, Linc. I wish we were just two normal people without a past."

"Everyone has a past."

"Not everyone's past is all mixed together," she replies. Her voice is a little slurred, but our conversation seems to be sobering her quickly. "Ours is messy."

"Yeah, it's messy."

But she is admitting she wants me!

With raw emotion clogging her throat, she breathes, "I don't want our families to fight."

I bend my head and whisper in her ear, "I'm not giving up on us. It's worth the fight, Tilly."

"Then, fight hard, Linc, because I don't know how to stay."

I left it four years when I should have come back sooner. I want her, and she wants me. The rest of it will have to work itself out.

"You're not going anywhere," I reply. "I understand that you need time, and I'll give you as much as you want, but I need you to know that I'm in. Whenever you're ready, just say the word, Tilly, because I'm so in."

She tips her head back. "How can you be so sure that this will end well?"

"Because it already ended, four years ago when I left. Now, we're after the end, Tilly, and that shit is eternal."

Her lips curl into a smile that brightens her troubled eyes. "I think I like it when you talk like that, you know?"

"Do you now?"

"How do we do this?" she asks, biting on a lip that I very much want to be all over.

Shrugging, I lower my head until we're barely an inch apart. "I don't have all the answers. I only know that I want this so bad, and I don't care what anyone says about us."

The change in her is instantaneous. My words are like a bucket of ice being dropped on her head. She steps back like I've burned her and rips out of my arms. I stumble forward a step but correct myself. I'm not going to grab her. Right this second, she needs the space, but that doesn't mean I'm going to let her go that easily.

"You're worried about how your parents will react to us," I guess. "I might not give a shit what anyone thinks, but you do."

Tilly drops her eyes like she's ashamed. "I don't want to lead you on, Linc."

"Are you serious? I just told you I was going to fight, and *you* told me to fight hard. And you think I'm letting your fear change anything? Back off all you like, we both know you're not actually going anywhere."

"I think you should take me to Hanna's now." As she says the words, the sky opens, and rain starts to drop. Tilly looks up and closes her eyes. She's always liked the rain.

"You want to leave or stand here, getting wet?" I ask.

Her eyes open. "I should leave. Seems kind of dangerous, being here at the minute."

"You're scared of me? I know you don't care about a bit of water."

"My head is foggy, and I don't really know what I'm saying. Alcohol, remember?"

Is she fucking joking?

Gritting my teeth, I step closer, watching her like prey. Tilly standing there, trying to convince me and her that what just happened between us was a drunken mistake, makes her my prey.

Screw waiting.

Reaching out, I grab her upper arms and cement my chest to hers. She doesn't get a chance to protest or talk herself out of this. I clamp my mouth down on hers.

I drink her in, the feel of her soft lips wrestling mine for dominance. Tilly isn't one to back down, or she wasn't, so I'm loving the battle again, feeling more parts of the girl I fell in love with still in there.

Tilly wriggles her arms, and I let go to slide my hands around her back.

The way she is kissing me, like she can't get enough, like she's making up for every second we've been away from each other, ignites a fire in my soul. One touch from her soothes every part of me I was afraid would never feel whole again.

I press my lips against her harder, bruising, as the kiss turns wet and molten hot.

Her warm body is plastered to mine in desperate need to be as close as possible. I feel it, too—the almost violent need for me to be inside her, to have no distance between us, to plug a hole we've both had since I left.

Nothing but each other will heal the pain we've been through.

Tilly's lips part, and I slide my tongue in her mouth. I moan in the back of my throat as my dick presses eagerly into her stomach. I arch my hips into her, curling my fingers in her lower back.

My heart is wild, and my dick is begging to sink inside her heat.

"Tilly," I murmur as her tongue massages mine.

Groaning, she drops her head and breaks the kiss.

Looks like her mind has caught up with what's going on.

Please don't regret this.

"You done?" I ask her, smirking.

Her eyes light up, making her look free. "Really, Linc? How can you tease me about this?"

Laughing, I let go of her but hold my hand out. "Because I'm finally okay. Let's get you to Hanna's before we get soaked."

She watches me with a frown, water droplets running down her face and dripping onto the sand. "That's all you have to say? I'm a mess and go back and forth like—"

"Tilly, I'm getting wet. Can we please go back to my car and get you to Hanna's?"

I start to walk, and she turns and follows.

"You're confusing me right now."

Tilting my head, I smirk. "Welcome to my world."

Tilly is constantly battling between wanting me and wanting to protect her parents. It's a mindfuck but one I'm willing to ride out because there's a chance. Now that she's opened up, albeit under the influence, I'm not keeping much distance.

She folds her arms as we walk. "You really feel confused a lot?"

"All the time, Tilly. It's more frustrating now that I know that you actually want this. If *you* weren't sure about us, it would be easier, but you're trying to please everyone else. You're at home for your parents; you're at the restaurant for your parents. What do you actually do for yourself? Do you allow yourself anything you want?"

"I wanted that kiss," she grumbles.

"I could tell, babe."

Narrowing her eyes, she says, "Don't get cocky."

Too late. She wants me.

Tilly

I wake up with my head in a vise. Or that's how it feels anyway. A massive vise that won't stop turning and tightening. Too many beers.

Wait. What the ...

This isn't my room.

Squinting my eyes, I try to focus on my strange surroundings.

Where am I?

Oh, Hanna and Jack's. Their living room sharpens, and I can see everything again. In the kitchen next door, I can hear voices. I should move, go and find Hanna, but I don't want to. I think I'm still a bit tipsy.

I've always been a lightweight, but it seems I'm worse today.

Did I drink more than usual? Probably.

The night is a bit of a blur though.

No. Oh no. I do remember the end.

My face sets on fire, and I'm sure I'm the colour of a tomato. Linc and I kissed. I mean, we *really* kissed.

Is he here still?

All I remember when I got back here is falling asleep on the sofa. He wasn't going to stay. He was going to drive home, but he could have changed his mind.

Maybe he wanted to stay with me?

But, if he did, where is he? Where did he sleep?

I'm on the long sofa. The other one is much too short for him to properly lie down on.

Okay, I can't sit here forever, too scared to go and face him.

And he might not even be here.

I chuck the blanket off and swing my feet down onto the floor. There are a few people in here, crashed on the floor. The voices get louder as I very carefully walk through the living room like there are explosives planted under the carpet.

"Coffee isn't breakfast, Linc," Hanna says. I can hear the shake of her head in her words.

He's here.

I freeze outside the half-closed door and bite my lip. He was all over my lips last night. Closing my eyes, I push the memory away before I combust.

When I push the door open, Linc, Hanna, and Jack all turn their heads.

"Morning, pisshead," Hanna greets. "Coffee and pastries?"

Holding my delicate stomach, I shake my head. "Just the coffee, please."

Hanna raises her eyebrow at Linc because I'm having the same as him, no doubt. It's too early for food. There is still too much alcohol in my system.

"Morning," Linc says, lifting his mug to his mouth.

I want to be lifted to that mouth.

Taking a breath to calm my sizzling hormones and racing heart, I reply, "Morning."

I wait for the weird to kick in, but it doesn't. Linc isn't acting like this is weird, and he stayed the night after planning on going home, so he clearly doesn't want to avoid me this morning.

Hanna hands me a large mug of coffee.

"Oh God, I love you, Han."

"Suffering?" she asks, amusement dripping from her word.

"I'll be fine after this." I turn to Linc as Hanna wraps her arms around Jack. "Where did you sleep last night?"

"On the sofa."

"On my sofa or the little one?"

As he chuckles behind his mug, his eyes pierce into mine. "You were starfishing. Again. I slept sitting up on that stool they call a sofa."

"Oops," I mutter.

This might not feel awkward, but I don't know if we should talk about it. Then again, a lot was said last night, potentially too much. I didn't hold anything back, and that will need to be addressed. I told him I wanted him, so it's unlikely we can move forward without that little fact popping up. Not that I want to pretend like last night didn't happen. I don't think I could even if I did want to.

"And you snore," he adds.

"I do *not* snore!"

He laughs and casually leans back against the counter. "No, you don't snore."

Thank God for that.

I don't actually know since I'm proper sad, and I haven't had a boyfriend in a *very* long time.

"You can't tell me if I do, can you?"

His dark blue eyes look different. He's free, like he's no longer carrying around the weight of the world. There is no pain in his eyes today, and that does crazy good things to my insides.

"No," I admit. I don't even remember falling asleep. "God, my head hurts. I am never drinking again."

Hanna laughs and throws a pack of painkillers at me. I catch them on the rebound as they hit my stomach.

"You say that about every three months, Tilly."

"This time, I mean it. Beer sucks."

"The beer isn't the problem. The shots of Jäger were the problem."

Oh, yeah, there were shots. What was I thinking?

I chuck two painkillers in my mouth and swallow it with a massive swig of coffee. "I need to lie down and sleep until tomorrow."

"No can do. We're going bowling today," Hanna replies with a smile in her voice.

Linc and Jack groan in response.

"Bowling?" I question. Another thing we've not done since before the accident. How quickly we can fall back into our old lives like the carefree teenagers we once were.

"Yeah, we love bowling, Tilly. Remember?" she says pointedly.

Am I missing something?

She's talking like we've had a previous conversation about this, and I should know what she's clearly hinting at. Well, I don't bloody know, and I'm not privy to this inside information. Maybe she dreamed it. Maybe we actually had the conversation, and I really am going insane. Or I was drunk. The latter is the most likely.

"Sure," I reply slowly.

Hanna claps her hands together. "Great! Let's get ready."

"Now? Hanna, my head feels like it's going to implode."

"Well, you should learn to handle your alcohol better, shouldn't you?"

Gently shaking my head, I reply, "You're too happy in the mornings. You should work on that."

She smiles and grabs Jack's hand. "Come on, babe. Let's kick everyone out and go and get dressed."

Her eyebrow arches as she walks past me.

Does she know what happened between Linc and me last night?

I mean, I remember bits, but if Linc told Hanna everything, then I want to quiz her before I look like a drunk idiot in front of him for not remembering.

Okay, so I definitely looked like a drunken idiot since I was the very definition of the phrase.

Jack and Hanna leave the room and take all the oxygen with them. I turn to Linc and bite my lip.

What do we do now?

"So ..." I say. "Last night was interesting."

With a smirk that illuminates his whole face, he puts his coffee down and folds his arms. "It certainly was interesting. Do you want to talk about it, or are we going to pretend like it didn't happen?"

I narrow my eyes. "Guess which one I'm leaning toward right now."

"I think I can guess." He keeps his eyes on me, his tone light and playful, though his words aren't. "But will you talk about it anyway?"

"Yes." I take a sip of coffee, needing the caffeine hit before I open up without the aid of alcohol. Admitting my feelings for Linc is scary. Though, apparently, super easy when I'm under the influence.

"You surprise me, Tilly. I thought it would be harder than that."

I put my coffee down and fold my arms, mirroring his posture. "I can make it harder, if you want."

That cracks a laugh out of him, and in turn, it has me relaxing. We can do this. Slowly because I have to tread carefully until my parents are okay.

"I don't think you can make it harder, Tilly."

"I could walk out that door."

He pushes off the worktop and takes one step closer. "Yeah, but then where would you go? You don't have a car here, and you live about a thirty-minute walk away. I can't see you doing that with a hangover."

"My legs aren't hungover," I reply, narrowing my eyes.

His smile widens. "Tell me you meant everything you said last night."

I place my palm on the counter because the pleading in his voice makes me light-headed. He told me he wanted this, but hearing that, understanding how much he wants me, is something else entirely.

I swallow damn razor blades. "I meant what I said last night."

His chest caves with the release of a long breath. "Good."

"Next question?"

"When are you getting dressed? We have bowling to get to."

My eyebrows knit together, and I stand up straight. "*That's* your question?"

"Yes."

"Okay." *Surely, there are other things he wants to discuss?* "Are you getting dressed? You wore those clothes yesterday."

"I'll go home, shower, and change, and then I'll meet you all there."

"Okay." I turn on my heel and walk out of the kitchen because the way he's looking at me is making my heart pound.

29

Tilly

Hanna, Jack, and I arrive at the bowling alley first, so we set up the game and wait for Linc to join us.

I rub the dull ache behind my forehead and sip a Coke. Something fizzy is supposed to be good for headaches, right? It'd better be because I've tried just about everything else. I drank so much water back at Hanna's before we left that I've been dashing to the toilet every five minutes.

"Maybe he's not coming," Hanna says, tapping the screen, finishing loading our names onto the computer.

I look up at the monitor hanging above us. "Really, Han?"

Instead of inputting our names, she's written *Hot 'n' Broody* for Linc, *Smokin' Abs* for Jack, *Coors Slut* for me, and *Loves Jack's P* for herself.

Unfortunately, I already know how much she loves Jack's penis because it's a topic she enjoys bringing up frequently.

She shrugs. "If *Hot 'n' Broody* even turns up."

He'll be here. He'd better anyway. He's the only reason I'm here in these god-awful clown shoes, ignoring two irritating children telling their parent that they're bored. The dad seems to take the stance that they've paid, so they are staying despite the fact that none of them are having fun, and they all look like they'd rather be anywhere else.

"Linc didn't have a cute dictator forcing him out of the house, babe, so he'll be here in his own time," Jack says, sipping on a beer at eleven in the morning.

I'm still not okay with beer yet. Beer and I are taking a break.

"Well, next time, we'll have to send Tilly back with him to hurry him the hell up."

Going to Linc's house is less daunting than it used to be, but I still don't feel completely comfortable, so I don't know how often I want to be there. Especially since it would be so easy to get caught. All my parents would have to do is look out of their bedroom window or the living room window, and they could see the front of Linc's house.

Then, there would be tears and a whole heap of questions I'm not ready to answer yet. And one particular question I don't think I'll ever be ready for is, *How can you want him when he was involved in your brother's death?*

For real, how?

I don't think I'll ever know the answer to that. All I know is that I don't blame Linc for Robbie's death. I've missed him so much, and I like him more than a friend.

That might make me a shitty sister or the worst person ever, or both, but I can't lie to myself anymore.

I'm facing our alley, so I don't see him, but I feel him approach. His boots thud against the wooden floor. I turn slowly, needing a few seconds before I face him again.

When I look around and our eyes meet, my heart stops. I tap my fingers on the palm of my hand.

God, he's beautiful.

His dark blue eyes follow me like a hawk as I step closer to him, my feet like jelly. He's wearing a black T-shirt and dark denim jeans with black boots. Simple yet so bloody effective that I feel faint.

"Hi," I say, coming to a stop about five feet away from him.

"Hey, Tilly. Nice shoes."

"Don't get cocky. You've got to wear some, too, and no one looks good in those shoes."

He tilts his head to the side, his eyes falling down my bare legs. "I don't know …"

"Hey," I say, playfully swatting his arm. "My face is up here, and now, I know you're just being nice. These shoes make me look like a clown." They're a size too big because my regular size is all in use. I could probably swim like a mermaid in these.

"Oh, I wasn't looking at the shoes, Tilly."

"Okay, let's start!" I turn to Hanna. "Who's up first?"

"Casanova over there," she replies, smirking so much that she's probably going to get muscle strain in her cheek.

I hate her.

"I'll go and get clowned up then," Linc replies and retreats to the desk.

I hope they don't have his size either, so he has to go up one. Not that he'd look bad. It's incredibly hard to look at his feet when there is so much else going on. Like the face, the eyes, the strong arms, the abs, and *that* V I'm desperate to get a proper look at.

Calm down, girl.

"You need to stop," I hiss, tugging Hanna's arm.

"Babe, you can cut the sexual tension with a knife. You want him, and he blatantly wants you. And we need to have a conversation about last night. What happened when we left? You guys were at the beach for ages after. Did you … you know?"

"No, we did not have sex at the beach!"

"You should. But lay a towel down because sand will be everywhere. Literally *everywhere*," she says as if I didn't get what she was hinting at the first time.

"I get it, Han, and I have no desire to shake sand out of my hoohoo."

Throwing her head back, she laughs. "Hoohoo. You can say vagina."

"I can," I confirm. "But it doesn't have the same ring to it."

"Seriously, bed him soon, please!"

Rolling my eyes, I let go of her wrist. "I'll get right on that ... just for you."

"Ha. Just for me, I'm sure." She looks over my shoulder and takes a step back from me.

Linc is coming back, and she doesn't want it to be obvious that we've been talking about him. It's doubtful that her looking at him and then moving away isn't suspicious. She's crap at subtlety.

"Are we doing teams or every man for himself?" Linc asks.

Don't say you want to be on his team, you desperate fool.

"Every man for himself," Hanna replies. "Jack sucks, so I don't want to team with him."

"Right here, babe," he says to her, raising his hands.

"It's not my fault you can't throw a ball straight." She leans into his chest and kisses him.

They're so good together, so in love, and everything is so easy. It isn't, of course. They have their own set of issues and arguments, but the fact that they can be together in public without people talking makes my heart ache a little.

I want that.

People are already looking at me and Linc. There is a middle-aged couple at the end lane, who keeps glancing up. They probably know my parents and are wondering if they should bring it up or mind their own business.

They should totally mind their own business, but when did that ever stop people from gossiping?

Linc ignores Hanna and Jack's flirting and heads to get a ball. I follow him because I actually don't want to watch them being cutesy—and not just because I'm borderline jealous, but because I've never been big on PDAs.

"Make sure you focus on the ball and not my naked body," I tell Linc as he swings his arm back.

He stills like a mid-bowling statue and stares at me. "Is that how this is going to go?"

I nod once. "I'm not above cheating."

"Your competitive side is coming out, I see."

"Usually does eventually."

"I think I'll be fine." He leans a little closer and whispers, "This wouldn't be the first time I've imagined your naked body." Turning back, he rolls the ball down the lane and knocks all but one pin down.

I don't move because my heart is pumping blood around my body so quickly that I feel my head go a little dizzy.

How often does he imagine me naked?

Is it as much as I imagined him naked when we were at Legoland?

Now, I'm thinking about him naked.

"Who's up?" Linc says after he throws his second ball and gets a spare.

I jump at his voice, my heart rate picking up. The image of him naked in the shower with droplets of water running down his six-pack vanishes, and I want to cry.

"Jack is," Hanna replies, nudging Jack's arm.

Linc steps around me, but he doesn't go far. His chest is inches from my back; I can feel his body heat. To stop my brain from short-circuiting, I keep my eyes on Jack as he takes his turn.

"You okay?" Linc asks quietly.

"Uh-huh," I mutter in reply. "Fine."

Not fine! Definitely not fine.

"You're tense." His voice is low, speaking in hushed tones so that no one else can hear us, "What's changed?"

I turn my head to the side because I'm not really sure what he means. I don't feel tense. Besides the whole naked thing. "Nothing. I'm fine. Really."

Linc watches me with purpose. He's trying to work out if I mean what I say or if I'm covering up. Let's not dwell on that because I'm okay at this particular moment in time. I tend to want to take those moments whenever I can. It's not going to be long before my mind has caught up, and I'm freaking out again.

"Okay," he replies. "You're up."

His face is relaxed and emotionless, so it's anyone's guess if he believes me or not. That damn boy's poker face.

I take my turn. The ball rolls into the gutter twice.

Straightening my back, I watch the pins reset. Well, I'm not usually this bad at bowling. Though it's been a while since I've done it.

Behind me, Hanna is saying something, but I can't hear it because my blood is pumping in my ears.

"He's so into you," Hanna sings under her breath after her turn. Linc is up next.

"Will you stop?"

"Don't worry; I'm going to fix this."

"Fix what?" My eyes go wide. "Hanna, do not do anything! Nothing needs to be fixed." Only everything needs to be fixed.

Hanna rolls her eyes. "Trust me, babe."

"I don't trust you!"

Linc hands Jack the bowling ball for his turn since they're both using the biggest one.

Laughing, she bumps my arm. "I won't embarrass you. I'm just giving you two a little … nudge in the right direction."

"We're going in the right direction!"

Jack waits for his ball to come back before his second go. Linc is near him so he can't hear us. Thank God.

I don't have long to convince Hanna not to do anything.

"Sure, thanks to me and my blasts from the past. This is just another one of those. We're going to the cabin."

I deadpan, "How is that a blast from the past when we never went with them?"

"We heard about it. And, anyway, we've been away with them to other places, but if you want to go back to that clubbing weekend in the crappy, cold caravans—"

"Absolutely not," I reply, cutting her off.

Our local radio station hosts a weekend at a holiday caravan park every year. It's like clubbing on the road. The building becomes a club, and ticket holders stay in caravans from Friday to Sunday.

It rained the entire time, and the caravan was not like one of those posh ones that look like a house inside. It was small, it smelled bad, and the walls were paper-thin.

Not to mention, the whole time, I was on edge because I was pretending to be eighteen with the fake ID Robbie had gotten for me. To this day, my parents think we went to a normal holiday park.

"Tilly, come on. If he leaves before you realise you're as in love with him as he is with you, it will be a tragedy. There has already been too much of that."

Her words floor me and slam into my face with the force of a ton of bricks.

Hanna thinks I'm in love with Lincoln.

He turns around, his stunning blue eyes meeting mine, and I'm falling.

Oh shit.

My lungs empty as my entire future shifts.

30

Linc

I walk over to Tilly while Jack throws his ball, and she visibly tenses, the closer I get.

What the hell happened?

"You okay?" I ask.

"Uh-huh," she mutters, avoiding eye contact and shuffling past me to take her turn.

I frown after her, a ball of ice forming in my stomach. *Has she changed her mind again?*

Hanna slaps my back. "Don't fret, Romeo. All is good."

"What?" My frown deepens. "What did you do?"

"Oh my God, why does everyone think I'm going to interfere and mess things up? Relax and be ready for the cabin, okay?"

"Hanna ..."

I have a lot of respect for her. My best friend is building a life with her, and she's so good for him. But I'm not letting her screw things up for me and Tilly. Not when my whole future is resting on a knife's edge.

"Don't *Hanna* me. I promise I haven't done anything bad." She waves her hand, dismissing the conversation. "Okay, my turn!"

Tilly sits on the booth and watches Hanna. The Ice Queen is back. But I'm not letting her freeze me out. I head straight for her and sit down.

"What did she say?"

Tilly's mouth curves in the smallest of smiles that doesn't travel as far as her eyes. "Forget it."

How can I?

"We're cool?"

"Obviously, Linc."

She bumps her arm into mine and laughs. The fake sound rubs against my skin.

We're not cool.

The weekend after the tense bowling game, my bag is on the backseat of my car. I'm outside, leaning against the door, waiting for Tilly to hurry up. Her parents are at work, but I still don't want to go inside. It doesn't feel right. After what I was involved in, I can't go there unless Emma and Dan are cool with it.

We're meeting Hanna, Jack, Ian, and Mel at Jack's where they should all be by now. We should have been there five minutes ago.

Her front door flies open, and she walks out, holding a small suitcase on wheels. Her eyes settle on mine as she swings the door shut and smiles.

"Sorry," she calls. "I couldn't find my phone."

"You didn't think to come out and ask me to ring it?"

Her mouth snaps shut, and her shoulders sag. "Huh. No, I didn't." She locks the door and heads toward me.

I take her bag and put it next to mine. "Ready?" I ask.

"Yeah. Let's go!" she replies, jumping on the spot with wide eyes.

"Someone is excited."

"Cabin on a cliff *with* a hot tub. Running on the beach, eating junk food, and drinking beer. What's not to get excited about?"

She gets into the car, and her seat belt is buckled before I can get around to the driver's side. I love seeing that smile on her face, so bright and full of life.

"Jack had better pick up my beer. I gave him the money," she says, flipping the sunshade down in the car and running her fingers through her hair.

"I don't think he'll forget," I reply.

It doesn't matter if he does anyway. I have a box of bottled Coors Light in my boot.

Settling back in the seat, she turns her head to me. "Are you looking forward to this weekend? You don't seem to be all that excited."

"Just because I'm not jumping up and down doesn't mean I'm not excited."

"What do you do when you're excited then?" she asks. The innocence in her voice makes the words more amusing.

I laugh, and she shakes her head at me.

"No need to make it rude, Linc. It was a legit question."

"I know. I'm sorry." I try to stop myself from grinning, but it's pretty damn impossible right now. "I don't know what I do really." It's been so long since I've been genuinely excited for anything. I would be for this weekend, and I kind of am, but I'm more nervous than anything.

Tilly means so much.

I make a left, and we head down the road to Jack and Hanna's place. Their house is wedged between two larger houses, sitting shorter than the rest, like a doll's house. Hanna has been gardening, obsessed with having the perfect garden.

If I didn't know her and her personality, I would think she was a Stepford wife. Everything has to be perfect.

They're sitting in their cars, not making a point at all by being totally ready to leave. We're late. I pull up beside Jack's car. He grins and points to the road. Hanna waves at Tilly, who waves back. And then I drive again, passing Ian's car to lead the convoy.

"How many times have you been to the cabin?" Tilly asks.

"This will be my fifth time."

"I'm so ready for this weekend. It's going to be a lot more chill than Legoland."

"Yeah." *And I get to see you in swimwear.*

She smiles, this time fully, and it's so stunning that she takes my breath away. Since bowling, the flirting has stopped. We've only seen each other once, and that was a quick chat before she went in her house.

I've got to give her some room to breathe. She's not going anywhere.

She's not.

"Do you have a *what happens at the cabin stays at the cabin* deal, or are you allowed to talk about it?" she asks.

"What do you think we do there?" I can't keep the amusement from my voice.

"Orgies."

"Orgies," I repeat. "I love my friends, Tilly, but I have no desire to see their dicks."

The last of her tension vanishes, and she tilts her head back, laughing. "You don't?"

"You do?"

She fake shudders. "I definitely don't want to see what's inside Jack's and Ian's boxers."

I, of course, notice that she doesn't mention me along with Jack and Ian, but I sure as hell won't say anything.

"So, you really just drink and play cards?"

"There are bars a few miles away, Tilly."

"Ah, so you spend all day playing cards and chilling in the hot tub, and then you go hunting for women."

"You make it sound like we attack them. Full consent, Tilly."

She rolls her amber eyes. "I know you don't attack women." There's a pause before she asks, "How many women?"

If we were together, this would be dangerous territory, but with my general dislike of most people and the fact that the last four years have been turbulent, to say the least, I've not slept with many women.

"Five."

"Huh."

"What does *huh* mean?"

"Nothing. I just thought that it would be higher."

Okay.

"I'm not sure what to say to that."

"Well, you have so many women throwing themselves at you, and you've only slept with five of them."

So many but the one I actually want.

"I didn't sleep with the desperate ones."

"Hmm, good."

"Good?"

Biting her lip, she nods her head, her eyes lingering longer than mine since I'm driving.

Tilly

I feel like a criminal. Walking into this sacred man-only cabin is like having a police car driving behind me. I'm not actually doing anything wrong, but boy, does it feel like it.

Jack, Ian, and Linc got a lot of shit for cancelling the boys' weekend in favour of a mixed weekend, but they promised their other friends—Tony, Luke, and Marc—that they'd do it *properly* another time.

The guys take all the luggage into the cabin. I hang back with Mel and Hanna as we admire our surroundings. The cabin is up on a cliff, overlooking the sea. Jack's parents own the three acres of land the cabin sits on, so it's peaceful here.

The sun has started to descend behind the ocean.

My phone rings as Hanna and Mel walk toward the side of the cliff.

I answer and hold the phone to my ear. "Hey, Mum."

"Hi, love. Are you there okay?"

"Yeah, we've just arrived. I would have called."

She laughs nervously. "I know."

On the few occasions where I do go away overnight, she never waits for me to call first.

I swallow the lump in my throat. Mum has been sitting at home, waiting for the allotted time it takes to get from our house to here to pass, so she could call.

This is why I can't move away. What would she be like if I was living somewhere else? She's nervous enough when I go away for the weekend.

"What is the cabin like?" she asks.

"Looks good from the outside. What are you up to?"

"I'm going to read," she replies.

That means she's too anxious to go out, and she needs to keep her mind busy. I get it; I like the escape, too.

"You and Dad should make the most of the free house this weekend," I say. *No mental images, please!*

"Your dad is going to cook something nice tomorrow."

"That's good. If he does the white wine with chicken pie thing, save me some!"

Laughing, she replies, "I can't promise anything. So, everyone there is okay?"

"Yep, Jack and Ian are unloading our bags, and Hanna and Mel are looking at the view. You'd like it. Nothing but trees on one side and the sea on the other."

And, no, I haven't told my parents that Linc is here, too.

"Sounds lovely. I'll let you go. I just wanted to check in."

"I'll text you later. Love you."

"Love you, too, darling."

I hang up and try to ignore the heavy feeling in the pit of my stomach.

How long can I keep my very fragile friendship with Linc from Mum and Dad?

The thought of them finding out I've been hanging out with him makes me queasy. I don't want them to think I'm betraying Robbie.

I don't want me to think I'm betraying Robbie.

Mel and Hanna are still looking out over the ocean, so I join them.

"Why doesn't Jack bring me here for dirty weekends?" Hanna questions, frowning into the horizon.

"Maybe because this is his family's place," I reply. "No one wants to have sex where their nana has sat."

She shrugs. "As long as his nana isn't there at the time, I wouldn't care."

Lovely.

I hate it when people have sex on sofas. I don't want to sit where someone's naked, sweaty arse has been.

"How are things with Linc?" Mel asks me.

My shoulders tighten.

How are things with Linc? God, I do not want to talk about it.

I shrug with a stiff shoulder, wiping my hands on my dress. "Fine," I reply.

"Fine?" she repeats, her voice loaded with scepticism.

"It is what it is."

Hanna raises both hands. "And it is what?"

Fucking love.

Love.

What the hell was I thinking, letting him back in?

I could have ignored him for a few months. I could have crossed the street and looked the other way when leaving my house. Instead, I got caught up in nostalgia and let the old me take over.

Now, I've fallen for him, and I have no idea how to get myself out of this mess.

Paging Jennifer!

"We're friends, Han."

She nods slowly, and I want to punch her pretty face. "Sure, babe."

"Let's go inside," I say, walking between them before I push them off the damn cliff.

It's all fun and games until someone falls in love.

When I get in, the guys are loading a ridiculous amount of alcohol onto the kitchen worktop.

Linc watches them with a smirk on his face. "I'm going to be really loud tomorrow morning."

Jack gives him the middle finger. "Or you could join us."

"No, thanks," Linc replies without hesitation.

No one will be driving until Sunday, so there is no reason Linc can't have a drink, but this isn't about making sure he's always safe when in a vehicle anymore. This isn't even about him not wanting it. This is about guilt.

"I'll be joining you," I say, taking a bottle of Coors Light.

"Yes, Tilly!" Ian says, pointing at me. "Let's get on it."

Linc laughs. "I'm looking forward to your hangovers."

My lips part as I watch him joke around with Jack and Ian. He's smiling, the tension around his eyes and jaw is gone, and he is laughing freely.

"Which room is ours, Jack?" Hanna asks.

"Last door on the left. Mel and Ian are first on the left, and Tilly is last on the right. Bathroom is first on the right," he says.

"Where are you sleeping?" I ask Linc.

"Sofa," he replies.

"What?"

"It's okay. I usually get a room, so it's definitely my turn to slum it."

My eyes pull to the two large, soft leather sofas, forming an L-shape in front of the fire. "That doesn't look comfortable," I tell him.

"It's only for two nights, Tilly."

If we weren't here, he would get a room.

"Come on. I'll show you to my room," he says playfully, grabbing my small suitcase.

I follow him along the short hallway behind the kitchen area. Linc opens the door and goes inside.

This feels too right.

My heart pounds so hard; I'm sure he can hear it. The room is small. There is just enough room for a double bed and wardrobe, but it's decorated rustic-style with lots of wood, and it's super cute.

"Bed is comfortable even if it is small. The wardrobe door gets stuck. You just need to tug it."

"Okay," I reply. "Do you want to hang your stuff in there, too?"

His stuff with mine. Sounds like a good idea.

He blinks at me like he's surprised I would offer. "Thanks."

"Are you sure you're okay on the sofa? I'm smaller than you, and I don't mind."

"No," he replies before I've even finished my sentence. "I'm not sleeping in here while you're on a sofa."

"I knew you would say that."

"Ah, that's why you offered, isn't it?"

I nod. "Totally. If I thought you would take the room, I wouldn't have said anything."

Linc laughs and wheels my suitcase next to the wardrobe. "I thought as much. So, you're planning on having a hangover in the morning?"

"Yes, and I expect a big, fat greasy breakfast to fix my stomach."

"Oh, the sober guy becomes the chef?"

"Absolutely. If you're not going to drink, you have to cook."

"Is that the rule now?" He steps closer as he speaks, and I find myself taking a step, meeting him halfway until I can feel the heat radiating off his godlike body.

I pull my bottom lip between my teeth to give it a use since it wants to be attached to his.

Linc's eyes snap to my mouth a heartbeat later. It takes him a second to recover and lift his gaze. When he does, his eyes are burning with lust.

Maybe I should offer him joint use of the bedroom.

Lift the bottle to your mouth and drink.

"Would you ever consider drinking with us again?" I ask.

His eyes drift away, scanning the room. "I can't."

"Okay," I say. "That's okay. I just don't … look, if this is your decision, that's fine, but if you're staying away from alcohol because you feel guilty, don't. You weren't driving, Linc. You weren't the one who should have been sober."

His Adam's apple bobs as he swallows. "Thank you, Tilly, but I made a promise to Robbie, and I intend on keeping it."

"I understand. I just want you to know that I don't blame you, and I wouldn't think less of you if you ever chose to have a drink."

His eyes darken, and his chest expands with a deep breath. "You don't know what that means to me, Tilly."

Actually, I think I do. I can see how much it means, and it feels amazing to be able to give him that little bit of peace. Jesus, I want to do it all. I want to heal every broken part of him until he never looks at me with those tortured eyes again.

How quickly his happiness has become entwined with mine.

"Well, I'll unpack and leave some space for your things," I say, shuffling back a step and putting my hand on the handle of the suitcase.

Linc takes the hint and clears his throat. "I'll bring my bag in soon."

He leaves the room, and the door clicks shut behind him. I exhale, closing my eyes and gripping the handle. My pulse is racing, and my body is unbearably hot after our close proximity.

I wanted him to kiss me again, and I could see from his posture and the tightness around his mouth that he wanted the same.

Yet he's now gone, and I'm standing alone in a tiny room with my hormones blazing.

I take a second for my heart to calm down and then busy myself with the task of hanging my clothes. We're only here for two nights, so I don't have much, but it takes up a small slice of time that I need to calm myself down.

As I'm hanging my last dress in the wardrobe, there is a knock on the door, loud and powerful. Linc wants to come back in.

"Yeah," I call, grabbing my suitcase and sliding it under the bed until Sunday.

Linc pushes the door open and carries his holdall in. He puts it on the bed and tugs the zip all the way around the bag. "You only brought dresses?" he asks, his voice pained as he eyes my side of the wardrobe.

"We're actually having a summer, so hell yes, I have dresses, but I also have one pair of jeans and a T-shirt," I reply.

He raises his free hand while the other takes out a pile of clothes. "I'm not complaining."

"What are the others doing?"

His bow creases at my sudden change of subject. "They're getting in the hot tub with a shocking amount of alcohol."

"Are you getting in now?" I get to see him in swim shorts.

"I guess. Why?"

"Do you fancy going for a walk first?"

"Yeah." His reply comes a little too quick, but it makes my heart jump.

I just want to spend some time alone with him before I have to share him with the group.

Linc

As much as I want Tilly wet and in swimwear, I want her to myself more.

We leave the cabin after letting the others know where we're going. I know this land like the back of my hand since I've been coming here with Jack for years.

I lead Tilly along the cliff front, so we have the sea as a backdrop. With the soft orange glow of the sun setting in the distance, Tilly looks more beautiful than ever.

"I can't believe you guys have been keeping this place to yourselves all these years."

"Well, it's not mine, so there wasn't much I could do, but I'm glad you're here now. It certainly beats six guys playing cards."

"You love those boys' weekends."

"I do."

Though it hasn't been the same the last four years. We still have a good time, but then they come home, and I go back to a town that I will never feel totally happy in.

The trees on the land start to get thicker as they begin to join forestry area that doesn't belong to Jack's family. The cabin is near the boundary, but we can keep going; the land past here isn't privately owned.

"How come you didn't want to get straight into the hot tub with a beer?"

She shrugs and pushes her long hair behind her shoulders. "I don't know. Just felt like I needed a minute before we joined them."

"Are you getting as antisocial as you call me?"

A laugh bubbles from her throat. "See the influence you have on me? They're going to be super loud and obnoxious, and while I'm all up for that, I like the peace, too."

Yeah, I like nothing but the peace. I love my friends, but loud, drunk people mostly piss me off. Or more accurately, people piss me off.

A warm breeze straight off the sea rolls in and blows the bottom of her dress. The hem lifts a few inches, just above her mid-thigh. She doesn't make a move to pin it back down, rather trusting that the wind isn't strong enough to lift it completely.

I stare at her soft skin covering those maddening legs. How many times I've imagined those in my bed, wrapped around my back. Back in her room at the cabin, I felt so close to that fantasy that my body started to react violently. I was painfully hard, chest tight, pulse racing and hands clenching. I wanted to grab her and throw her on the bed. I wanted to peel that dress off her body and worship her with my hands and mouth before I slipped inside her.

But she stepped back just in time. My muscles, once locked in place, had just about sprung free to let me take her. My heart died when she moved.

"Should I be hoping the wind picks up?" I say, breaking the silence.

Her head rolls, and she glares up at me. "When on the lads' weekend, act like a lad?"

True. I've never been a full-on pervert like my friends, not openly anyway, but there are many rules I'd break for Matilda Drake—all of them if we're being honest.

I shrug as we continue to walk into the woods, the darkness starting to swallow us. "What can I say? It's the legs."

She laughs and bumps my arm with hers, her whole body leaning into mine, sending a bolt of electricity down my spine.

"All the running is paying off, I see."

"You run just for me?" I tease.

"You wish, Linc."

Yes.

Tilly stops suddenly and bites on her damn lip again. When she did that in the bedroom, I almost lost control.

"What?" I ask.

"Are we going into the woods? Because that's kind of creepy at night." She crosses her arms. "I mean, I'll go, but you'd better be prepared to protect me with your life because, if a bear or a serial killer chases us ..."

"A bear or serial killer?" I say. "Wait, now that you mention it, Jack did say the bear in the woods is particularly fierce, and that serial killer who lives up in a tree hasn't murdered for days."

She deadpans, her head tilting to the left and eyebrow arching. "If that happens, you're going to be sorry."

"I've got you, Tilly, whether it's a bear or axe-wielding psycho."

Her face brightens, a smile stretching wide. "I like that she has an axe."

"She? Our fictional serial killer is a woman?"

"Of course."

Right. Of course.

She starts walking again, and this time, her pace is a little quicker. "It's so pretty here. The sea and a forest. What more could you ever want?"

"You still walk the forest?" I ask.

She shakes her head. "Not since we last went. Have you?"

"No, it's not the same." I look over to the sea. "The sun is almost down. We should get back soon."

"You don't want to get lost in the dark with me?"

I would do anything with you.

"As long as you don't go all shrieky on me because there's no light."

Shrugging, she replies, "I prefer the dark."

"The dark isn't you, Tilly."

"Huh?"

"You're light and warm. You're the sun."

"What are you?"

My laugh is void of humour. "I'm a fucking eclipse."

"Not to me, you're not."

Her eyes, the colour of whiskey and forever, peer into mine, and I see it. To her, I'm not this dark monster responsible for her brother's death, not anymore.

"Tilly," I murmur as warmth spreads through my body.

"Please don't think of yourself like that. You're actually all right," she teases, breaking through the intensity of the moment.

"I'm all right?"

"Mostly," she replies with a shrug.

"Wow, thanks."

She smiles up at me. "Seriously though, stop overthinking how bad you are because it's bull. There are a lot of people who are glad you're here. We wouldn't all be together like this if you weren't. Mel, Ian, Hanna, and Jack hang out regularly, but I don't. You're the one who has brought us all back together."

"Thanks," I reply, clearing my throat.

She bites her lip like she's not done, but she doesn't know how to ask something.

This should be good.

"Linc?"

I hesitate. "Yeah?"

AFTER THE END

"You know we're glad you're back, but how do your parents really feel about you being here?"

I would say something sarcastic, but she's clearly not asking how they feel about me coming to the cabin, and now is not the time. The fact that she's willing to discuss my parents at all is a miracle, so I'm not ruining it.

"They were apologetic, but once they went through the figures, they knew it had to be me. There was no other choice."

"Are they in trouble financially?" Her eyes widen a fraction.

"Without the mortgage on top of rent, they will be fine."

"Good," she replies quietly.

"I don't really know what you're asking here, Tilly. They have no ill feelings toward anyone or the town, but they understand that they're not welcome there. Not after they fought so hard to keep Stanley out of prison."

My words drive a wedge between us. Tilly tenses at the mention of my brother and how he served no time for killing her brother, and I instantly regret bringing that up.

"Yeah. Well, that was ..." She shakes her head, not knowing how honest to be in front of me.

"You can say whatever you want. I'll probably agree. Stanley is my brother, but I know there is a lot he needs to take responsibility for, and my parents did nothing but let him diminish his part in it."

"Did you ever consider staying when your family left?"

"No," I reply, my chest gripping at the memory of Tilly screaming at me to go to hell.

When my parents told me we were leaving, I wanted to stay. I could have. I thought maybe, in time, Tilly and her parents would forgive me, but in that moment, I knew I had to go.

"You wanted to be with your family," she says as we walk between trees with the sea half-hidden to our left. "That's understandable."

239

"I wanted to make things as easy as I could for everyone. It was right that I left, too. But, although it's not been straightforward, I'm glad I'm here now. It's been nice to come back, better than I imagined."

"Yeah, sorry about the straightforward thing. I didn't make it very easy for you when you first got back."

"That's not on you. You don't have to make anything easy for me."

She stops again, this time grabbing my arm, so I turn and face her. "Why not? Because you don't deserve anything to be easy for you?" she says, reading my mind. Her face is marred by a frown that screams her irritation. "Why are you so hard on yourself, Linc? I know you still feel guilty for what happened, but that doesn't mean you have to be condemned to unhappiness for the rest of your life."

"Am I that transparent?"

"You're usually the exact opposite of transparent, but right now, I see you, and what you think about yourself is wrong. You are worth caring about, Linc. No one here wants you to hurt."

"Tilly," I whisper.

Her words, as much as they hold freedom and peace only she can give, also grate on my skin like sandpaper. I don't believe her.

How can I be part of Robbie's death and be worth much?

She places her palm on the centre of my chest, and she might as well have gotten on her knees. My body's reaction to the contact is brutal. I suck in a breath as my dick swells in a second flat. I ball my hands and dig my fingers into the flesh.

"Please believe that, Linc. There has been far too much pain over the last four years. I hate to think that it'll never get any better."

"Is it any better for you?" I ask.

Maybe, if it is, I can follow suit. Her happiness is directly linked with mine, entwined so tightly that I don't think I'll ever be free of loving her. The muscles in my forearms scream for release, but if I relax, I'm going to reach for her. I'm itching to wrap my arms around her.

"It is," she assures me. "Slowly, very slowly, things get a bit better. I don't know if it hurts less or if you just get used to the feeling."

"Jesus," I mutter, closing my eyes so that I can't see the look on her face. *Why did I have to ask that?*

"I'm sorry," she whispers, stepping closer so that her palm is replaced with her chest.

There is no distance, and my dick is throbbing.

"Tilly," I rasp in warning. *You need to step back.* "Don't be sorry. I'm the one who is sorry."

She smiles sadly. "We're going to go around in circles forever, aren't we?"

"I hope not."

"Can we make a deal? Even if it only lasts this weekend?"

"What's that?"

"No guilt, no talk of the accident, and no being sorry. I want one weekend of peace, and I want to have fun. Continuing with drinks in the hot tub. I bought a new bikini for this."

I want to see that bikini right the fuck now.

"Deal," I tell her. One weekend of being the old us sounds like heaven. I'll gladly take those two days. "Now, what's this bikini like?"

She takes a step back, laughing and shaking her head. She's lighter, her eyes shining bright and mouth in an easy smile. "It's small and red."

"Sounds perfect," I reply, turning around. "Let's go and get you in it."

"Wow, you are really working hard on that perverted side."

I chuckle. "There's a bad joke in there somewhere."

Tilly walks beside me as we head back to the cabin. I thought she would want to walk some more even if it's in silence, but I'm sure not going to argue with getting her practically naked and wet.

"So, did you bring swim shorts, or are you going in the buff?"

"Why? Do you want to see me in my birthday suit?"

She rolls her eyes. "If I say yes, are you going to stop and strip?"

"You go, I go, baby!"

"I like this new you. You're smiling. Hey, does it hurt your face when you do that?"

"Oh, you've gotten funnier, I see."

"I've always been hilarious," she replies, playfully scowling at me.

We reach the cabin, and she turns to me. "Give me two minutes to change before you come in the bedroom."

I don't want to.

Dipping my chin, I reply, "Sure."

Tilly heads into her room, and I grab a Coke from the fridge. Not drinking doesn't bother me at all. I couldn't give a shit what everyone else is doing or drinking. I never have. I lean back against the worktop and wait, my eyes glued to the hallway.

I hear her moving around in the room, closing a drawer and bumping something. Or bumping into something. I should check on her. She might be hurt after all.

"Tilly," I call, walking the few steps along the hall to her room at the end. "You okay?"

She's going to be okay, but I really want to see her in that bikini—or preferably, out of it.

"You can come in," she shouts.

I open the door, and the fucking world stops. Tilly looks up, her hair fanned around her face like a blonde veil. Her body, beautifully toned with curves in all the right places, is partially covered with the tiniest scraps of red material I have seen.

My heart stalls for a fraction of a second before thumping in the confines of my chest. "Shit," I breathe.

"Huh?" she asks halfheartedly, distracted as she grabs her phone and a hairband from the bed.

She stands, and I get a full view of how stunning she is. The swell of her breasts begs to be kissed. I can't keep my eyes off the little gap between her legs. Running really has been good for her, not that she wasn't perfect before.

I swallow hard as my mouth waters.

"Eyes are further north, Linc."

"And I've seen those a million times."

Jumping forward, she slaps my chest. I know she's trying to discourage me from staring, but the leap made her breasts bounce, and my dick swells rock hard yet again.

I lift my hands in surrender. "Okay, I'm sorry. You're so beautiful, Tilly."

Her mouth parts, eyes rounding with surprise at my words. "Linc."

"My turn to get changed." I grip the hem of my T-shirt and pull it over my head.

She hasn't moved an inch, and now, it's her turn for wandering eyes. Her pupils dilate as she focuses on my chest.

My God, I love you.

I reach for the buckle of my belt, and her eyes bulge.

"Linc!"

"You're changed already, Tilly. You don't have to be in here."

Her mouth pops like she didn't even consider leaving me to get changed in private.

Snatching her towel, she dashes past me. "See you out there."

The muscles in my cheeks ache with a grin that won't settle. I change quickly, eager to get outside and in the hot tub. I wish we had more time, a whole week here, enough time for her to forget that she's supposed to hate me.

When I'm done, I head out the back, walking slowly along the decking because I need a few extra moments to prepare myself for a wet Tilly.

Jack and Hanna are cuddled up along one side of the tub, and Ian and Mel are opposite with Tilly occupying another.

There's space next to her and a lot of space opposite. I should go opposite, so we both have room, but that's not an option.

I step in and sit down as blood starts to rush down south. Tilly is at the perfect height to have the top of her breasts just on show, hot water bubbling over the swell of her breasts.

Tilly turns her head and smiles as I'm seated beside her.

33

Tilly

When Linc sits next to me, my heart goes wild.

There was a moment in my room back there. Neither of us was wearing many clothes, and the air was getting thinner, thinner, thinner until I felt like I could pass out.

I sit back against the built-in seat, and my arm presses against his.

"Strip poker tonight, guys?" Ian asks, lifting an eyebrow at Mel.

"You want me naked in front of our friends?"

"I am not playing strip poker," I say.

"Why not?" Linc asks.

I turn my head and give him a pointed look. "Because I can't play poker."

"I'll teach you."

"You'll teach me wrong, so I end up naked."

Laughing, he tilts his head back. "Damn, you saw through that."

"Nice try, Reid."

His pupils dilate, mouth parting. Because I called him Reid? I used to occasionally when we were messing around and teasing each other.

My God, everything about this weekend is exactly like the old days. And it's only Friday night. Hanna was right. This is what we need. All the blasts from the pasts are filling my empty soul.

I wish we could stay here for longer. When we're here, like this, it's so easy to believe that everything is fine, that Robbie isn't dead, and I can be friends with Linc without feeling bad about it.

"I didn't take you for a prude," he teases.

"Don't try to pull that bullshit on me. I'm not seven, so I'm not going to do what you say just because you tell me you don't think I will."

Laughing, he replies, "Busted. What do you plan on doing tonight instead?"

Don't say you.

Maybe the heat from the hot tub is getting to me?

"Beer and scary movies."

Hanna groans. "No way. Come on, Tilly. You're not a sad teenager anymore."

I glare. "I'm a sad twenty-something, and I will watch people get stabbed."

"You need help," she replies. "I hope you don't think we're all going to be watching that shit. I don't care if the blood is fake; it's scary."

"I figured you would be playing strip poker with Jack."

"We're all playing strip poker, so let's stop arguing," Ian says, holding his beer up.

Mel clinks her bottle against his and grins.

I turn to Linc, looking for help since, out of everyone, he is the most likely to want to watch a horror film with me. But he shakes his head, mouth curved perfectly with his signature smirk.

"Oh my God, fine! I'll play," I concede.

I've stayed firmly in my comfort zone since Robbie died, so maybe it is time to do something I wouldn't usually.

"Yay!" Hanna cheers. "You won't be sorry."

"I already am," I reply dryly.

When I get out of here, I'm going to put on every item of clothing I brought here with me. I'm not ashamed of my body, and I don't usually worry too much if I'm showing skin, though I don't often walk around in the buff. But having Linc here changes this from a game to something much different. Something I sure as hell am not ready to explore or even think about in any kind of detail.

Tonight, he might see me naked, and I might see him naked.

The thought alone has heat pooling south.

This is a bad idea. I can't be turned on by him.

Why bloody him?

My stupid body wants what it can't have. Maybe I'm stuck as a sad teenager, unable to control my hormones. This isn't a case of *I shouldn't want the bad boy*. This is me who shouldn't want the boy who got in the accident that killed my brother.

What is wrong with me?

My stomach twists in a big knot a sailor would be proud of.

Stop. Thinking. This weekend is about fun.

Can I not even let myself have a couple of days?

"What's going on in your head?" Linc asks. "I can see you overthinking."

I sit back. "Nope. You know what? I'm not thinking. Guys, let's go in now and get set up for strip poker."

"Hell yeah!" Jack cheers while Hanna looks at me like I've lost my mind, and she's proud of it.

I think I lost my mind a while ago though.

Linc's eyes watch me as I wrap a towel around my body and head inside to change. I don't know what he's thinking because that's near impossible with his poker face, but I don't care right now.

I want to drink beer and slowly get naked.

It's a good idea, right?

Sounds fab to me right now.

In my room, I dry off and put on a pair of jeans, a tank top and a T-shirt. Thank God I didn't just bring dresses, or my part in this game might be over super quick.

When I get out, Jack, Ian, and Linc are around the table with drinks and a pack of cards.

Mel walks out of her room. "Sure you're okay with this, Tills?"

"Yep," I reply instantly. "Let's go play."

If I gave myself longer than two seconds to think about this, I would probably chicken out, so that's why I'm ploughing ahead. I walk into the main room and sit down next to Linc. There is space beside me for Hanna. I'm glad Jack left a place for her near me because, although I've seen a naked man before, I don't really want to see my friends' boyfriends in their birthday suits. Hanna, Mel, and I have all seen each other naked already.

And let's just not think about Lincoln Reid at all right now.

I bet there are a lot of women who would be hating me. Linc was very popular with the girls back in the day; everyone wanted his attention. He hated it since he didn't like many people at all. Hazard of the face, I guess.

"So," I say, leaning my elbows on the table, "how the hell do we play this?"

"I'll talk you through it as we play," Linc replies. "I can't believe you don't know how to play poker. I would have bet money on you knowing."

I shrug. "My dad offered to teach me years ago, but he was impatient, and I got bored. All I know is, you keep a straight face, which shouldn't be hard for you, and pretend like you're doing better than what you are."

So, if all you need to win is to pretend, I should win easily.

Linc laughs humourlessly. "For that, I'm going to make sure you're down to your underwear in the first hand."

"Like that hasn't been the plan all along."

I don't want that to be the plan.

I kind of do.

Linc

Getting Tilly down to her underwear has been my plan for four long years.

So, let's see how this goes.

Would I rather see her semi-naked in private? Yes. But will I take what I can get? Yes.

Jack deals the first hand of cards, and I scoop mine toward me. Tilly picks hers up as if you're supposed to show the world.

"Don't let anyone see your cards," I tell her.

She presses the cards into her chest and frowns. "Did you see my cards?"

"No," I tell her even though I know she has a two and an ace.

"I don't believe you, but I'm still going to beat you," she replies, straightening her back.

I love her confidence, especially given that she has never played before and is at risk of being naked soon.

Jack explains the rules as we go, and Tilly has a frown the whole time. I know that she understands how to play. She just has an awful poker face. Her hand isn't good.

That works for me.

She growls and tosses her cards into the middle of the table.

"What's it to be, Tilly?" I ask. *Top, please.*

Her amber eyes narrow, and she tugs a t-shirt over her head. She has a grey tank top underneath.

"You layered up?" I ask.

"Of course I did. I've never played this before!"

"What happened to you kicking my arse?" I tease.

She folds her arms. "I still will, but I needed to level the playing field somehow."

"You mean, cheat?"

"I don't recall Jack mentioning anything about layering being against the rules."

Damn, she's got me there.

I turn back to the game and try to concentrate. I want to go back outside and take a walk with her. Or get back in the hot tub, just the two of us. She's happy though. She's smiling the way she was at Legoland. Hanna is a genius.

But how long can we spend in the past?

Jack deals the next game and the next and the next.

"How do people play this for hours?" Tilly asks, fanning her cards out.

She's lost two socks. The next time she loses, it has to be her jeans or tank top.

"It's rare that the same person loses over and over and over," I reply, smirking at her.

Jack has removed his T-shirt, and Mel and Ian have each lost one sock. Hanna and I are the only ones still fully clothed.

She opens her mouth to say something witty, but she can't. Sighing, she mutters, "Fine. I can admit that this isn't my game."

"But are you going to give up before you're naked?"

She tilts her head in my direction, and her eyes search mine. "Well, wouldn't you like to see me naked now?"

Seeing her naked? Absolutely. Seeing her naked in front of my friends? Not so much.

I want to be able to get naked with her in privacy, so I can do what I'm desperate to do and explore every inch of her skin.

I seal my mouth shut because there's no way I need to speak my mind right now.

"Tills, you're worse than me!" Mel says, smiling sympathetically.

"Yeah, yeah, Tilly sucks." She rolls her eyes. "How about we play something else?"

We put our cards down, and she groans.

"Oh, unlucky!" Jack teases. "What's it to be now?"

Hanna slaps the back of his head.

"Ah, what the hell? Obviously, I'm not going to look!"

Tilly grins, and then her face falls as she realises that she's going to have to reveal her underwear. Unless she has any more layers under there.

She grips the bottom of her tank top and tugs it over her head. My chest caves. She does not have any other layers. A very crisp white lacy bra begs to be removed.

My mouth dries out in a heartbeat, and all my blood pumps straight to my dick. Her skin is perfect, smooth, and lightly tanned. Her chest. God, I'm trying not to look directly at it in case my corneas burn. But the swell of her breasts is making me lose my fucking mind.

I swallow a mouthful of sand.

Fuck. Okay, concentrate on the game.

Jack deals another hand, and all I can think about is the woman beside me—soft, petite, smelling like fucking home—and her flashing more of her skin than I could have hoped.

Why is this different to the hot tub where I saw her in a bikini?

It's the underwear. So much more intimate than swimwear, and it would look so much better on my floor.

"Linc, you're up," Ian prompts. The smirk on his face is undeniable.

I keep my eyes down. And I focus on the game, something that Tilly has just made near impossible.

We play a couple of more rounds, and somehow, I manage to not bomb completely. Hanna loses a sock, and Jack loses a T-shirt.

Tilly slumps back in her seat, throwing a particularly crap hand down on the table. "I hate this stupid game."

I love this stupid game.

"Jeans, Tilly," I sing.

Her hand comes out of nowhere, slapping me on the arm.

"Whoa. Violent."

"Why haven't you lost anything yet?"

Jack scoffs. "He's undefeated."

"I find it a bit disturbing that you guys used to play strip poker," Hanna says, turning her nose up.

"Babe, we played normal poker. I have no desire to spend my weekend with half-naked men."

Tilly stands up and unbuttons her jeans. She's right beside me, taking off her fucking jeans! I grip my cards tight in my hands.

Do not touch her.

She shimmies the jeans down and steps out of them. Jesus, her underwear is matching. The air in the cabin thins.

"Another game?" Jack asks.

"I am not taking off my underwear, so I fold!" Tilly replies, raising her hands.

That's okay with me. I will have the image of her in white lace for the rest of my life.

She tugs her socks, jeans, tank top, and t-shirt on and sits back down. I only had a few short minutes of seeing her in her underwear, but the image will remain in my mind forever.

The rest of us have only lost one or two items of clothing. Tilly is awful at poker, so we play a few more games until Hanna and Mel both get bored. Jack, Ian, and I have no desire to watch each other slowly get naked, so we end the game.

Mel takes Ian back to the hot tub. She purses her lips and pushes out her boobs, so there is no way I'm going out there with them. I'm also not getting back in that tub until the water has been changed.

Jack turns his nose up, but he doesn't protest despite it being his family's.

"Jack, let's join them," Hanna says, tugging on his arm.

"No way. You know what they're going to do, right?"

"All the more reason to stop them! I want to use that tub tomorrow. Come on."

If I didn't know better, I would think that she's trying to leave Tilly and me alone. Jack's girl always has an ulterior motive.

I sit on the sofa, and Tilly joins me with her beer.

"Do you ever feel like drinking?" she asks me with the neck of the bottle to her full lips.

Every time I look at you.

"Sure."

"Robbie wouldn't have cared if you drank. You do know that, right?"

"Tilly, I appreciate what you're doing, but I've not given up alcohol because I think Robbie wouldn't have approved of me drinking."

"Okay, I get it. I just wanted to double check that you don't think he would be angry with you." She takes a breath. "You don't have anything to feel guilty for."

Fucking hell.

"Tilly," I whisper.

"No, hear me out. I've spent a lot of time wondering why you didn't see that Stanley was over the limit. I've been angry for four years, and it's cost me those four years. I don't blame you for any part of my brother's death."

Here she is, telling me the one thing I've wanted to hear for so long, and all I can do is stare at her like she's grown another head.

I shake my head, trying to get my brain to engage.

Tilly laughs. "I know you're not a talker, but you're not often rendered speechless."

"You don't blame me?"

"No, I don't. You should work on not blaming yourself, too."

"I'll try," I tell her.

Her eyes narrow. "You're only saying that to humour me."

"Ah, I'm not such a closed book right now, huh?"

"Nope. I'm learning to read you, Linc."

"Yeah? How are you finding the book?"

Her cheeks flush pink, and she dips her eyes.

"It's X-rated?"

"Oh my God!" Her head snaps up. "It is not X-rated."

"I don't believe you. Admit it; you want me to take my top off. Your eyes look the same as they did when I got in the hot tub earlier."

"Do they?" she mutters, shaking her head with the faintest smile. "You have a nice chest, but I cannot comment on whether your book would be X-rated."

"Ah, I see. You need a frame of reference. No one reviews without trying first."

She puts her beer down on the coffee table. "Are you offering me sex right now?"

"Doesn't have to be *right* now."

Her head tilts back as she laughs. Manoeuvring, she tucks her legs underneath her and angles her body toward mine, facing me straight on.

I twist, throwing my arm over the back of the sofa.

"Wow, I'm allowed to choose when we have sex. Thank you!"

Laughing at her retort, I shrug. "I'm nothing if not a gentleman, Tilly."

"I have to admit that I'm becoming much fonder of this side of you."

"Are you?"

She nods, her cheeks flushing again. "You've never been flirty. Granted, I've never seen you on nights out, chatting up women."

That's what I'm trying to do now. Though much more carefully since I'm not just looking for a shag here.

"You want to see that?"

Her eyes cloud. "Not particularly. You should chat up women if you want though."

What?

Sighing, she gets up, and I watch her retreat to her bedroom with my mouth hanging open.

What the fuck just happened? Where did that come from?

Tilly spends the rest of the weekend flirting and then stopping herself. And I don't push anything because she has to go through this battle with herself. One minute, she's happy with me, and then the next, she's frosty. I don't mind. It's all part of her coming to terms with how she feels and accepting it.

Our time will come.

35

Tilly

It's official. I'm certifiable. That's the only explanation for my yo-yo behaviour. I can't settle on one emotion for longer than five seconds before another one takes over. What makes sense one moment seems mindless in the next.

I would make an appointment with my therapist, Jennifer, but I don't want to discuss Linc with anyone. Not in depth anyway. I don't know what I'll find there, what I'll admit I'm willing to give up to be with him.

Not my parents. Never them. But, when he's with me, my mind short-circuits, and I don't care what anyone thinks or how hard it would undoubtedly get for both of our families if we gave this a go.

What would that even look like? We spend Christmas mornings with our respective families and then meet up in the afternoon? That wouldn't work long-term.

No part of me and him would work long-term, and we have to accept that.

God, I was such a twat during what should have been an amazing weekend, turning cold the way I did after the poker game. I don't want him to chat up other women, but I should. But yeah, I *really* don't. See, Hanna's little plan is working, but too much has changed.

I've tried staying away from him, and that doesn't work out. All we do is go around in circles because neither one of us is really ready to walk away from the other. We had the best and easiest friendship, but what we're doing now isn't trying to get back to that. We're trying to make our circle shape fit into a heart shape hole of a relationship.

It's eleven in the morning, the day after getting home from the cabin, and I'm still in bed. I don't have to work today, and I'm going to make the most of that by moping around for as long as I can get away with. Mum and Dad won't be home until this evening, so I have ages.

Linc is only meters away in his parents' old house. After the weekend, he probably got up at the crack of dawn to continue work and get the hell out of here.

At the beach, he said he would fight for us, but does he still think it's worth it?

I wouldn't blame him if he ran, and honestly, that's what should happen. One of us needs to be gone, so we can both move on. If there isn't an option to spend time together, then maybe we can get past whatever has been happening between us, and I can go back to not feeling like I'm drowning in guilt every time I look at my parents.

The craziest part, on my behalf, is that I know he would walk away right now if I told him that was what I truly wanted.

I could end this now and maybe save us a whole world of hurt.

But can I do that?

Can I fuck?

Maybe I like the pain? It's been a long time since I've felt anything else as strongly as pain.

Paging my therapist!

Sighing, I throw my arm over my eyes and groan at the knowledge of my ever-sliding sanity. Linc is so perfect, so perfect for me, that I can't get over the suck factor here. I'm not being fair to him.

The shrill ring of my phone on my bedside table has my teeth grinding. *Who is interrupting my moping day?* I just need some time where I don't see or speak to anyone. I need to try to get my head on straight.

What I really need is to have a very big conversation with my parents and then Linc. But that is just about the last thing I want. It's up there with having a lobotomy and listening to my dad's horrific rendition of Bon Jovi's "Always."

I grab the phone and slide to answer.

"So, the weekend turned into a bit of a car crash. What happened?" Hanna asks. No greeting.

"I don't really want to talk about it."

"Well, too bad. I do, and you need to. Everything was going so well. We were all getting on all weekend, *so much* flirting, and then you turned into the Ice Queen. As far as I can remember, Linc didn't insult you."

"No, he didn't insult me."

He just made me fall for him and want a future with him, which is much worse.

"Then, what, Tilly? You've always been the chill one. You say what you mean, and everyone knows where they stand with you. I envy that. I don't understand what's changed. You said you didn't blame Linc for Robbie's death, but was that a lie?"

"I didn't lie about that. I don't blame him anymore, and I have forgiven him. But things between us are getting a little more ... involved." *I know Linc isn't to blame for Robbie's death.*

"So?" she says the simple two-letter word like it's nothing.

"So, we can't get involved."

"It wouldn't be straightforward, I'll give you that, but all anyone wants is for you to be happy. I've not seen you as carefree as you've been recently since before Robbie died. Lincoln is bringing you back, Tilly. Don't throw that away."

"I didn't go anywhere, Hanna." My tone is defensive and snippy, heart racing with an edge of anger.

She might think she's helping, but telling me all the shit I already know isn't.

"Not physically. Look, I know you don't want to hear this because you're still not done pretending like everything is okay, but I love you, Tills, and I hate seeing you being less than you are. Where is my fierce best friend who was always ready to take on the world?"

"What do I need to take on?"

"Your life, babe."

My hand tightens around the phone, fingertips digging into the glass screen. "My life is fine."

"But don't you want a great life? Don't you want to do all of the things you planned, go on adventures, and fall stupidly in love?"

"You sound like you're in some dramatic teen TV show, Han."

And I have fallen stupidly in love. Heavy on the *stupid*.

"Everything I just mentioned is attainable, Tilly. It's not just for TV shows."

"Whatever, Han. I need to go and do something."

"Do what?" she pushes.

Sighing, I shove myself up, so I'm sitting in bed. "Eat."

"I have to work this afternoon, but I can come over after that."

"Hanna, I love you, but I just want to be alone right now."

"Is that a good idea? You tend to think too much when you're alone, and you're already overthinking this whole Linc thing."

I open my mouth to protest, but I can't deny it. Hanna is right; I do overthink Linc. I want to jump headfirst into whatever we have going on, and I usually would. Had there been no crash or had Robbie survived, I'm sure I would be in Linc's bed now, not my own.

But those things did go down.

Ugh, I'm doing it again!

Anyone have any cures to stop your mind from constantly spiralling?

"I'm fine, Han. I'll see you later."

"Come by the restaurant for dinner."

"All right, see you later," I concede and hang up the phone.

Well, she's not going to stop now that she knows Linc and I are kind of, sort of, maybe a thing.

Hanna is like a dog with a bone. She won't give up until she gets her way. She has always been like that, getting puppies, holidays, men by sheer will alone.

Hey, if she can fix my mind, she can go to town on me.

I kick the cover off, letting out only a fraction of my frustration, and get up. My conversation with Hanna has woken me up too much to stay in bed, and my bladder is about to burst.

After using the bathroom and getting dressed, I head downstairs to drink my body weight in coffee. Hanna asked me to come to dinner while she works, which means she's going to tell Linc the same thing and she will feign surprise when we both turn up.

Bloody interfering woman.

Linc and I don't need to be set up. We've got that part down ourselves. The issue we have is being able to stay together.

If I were smart, I would do what my uncle Jeffrey did and emigrate to Australia. But I can't even move thirty miles from my parents, let alone thousands.

I bypass the kettle and go for the coffee pod machine for a much stronger hit of caffeine. Coffee used to be the answer to a lot, but recently, it's been letting me down.

I grab a mug from the cupboard and almost drop it. Either my hand is weak or the mug suddenly weighs a ton. I take in a ragged breath and grip the edge of the worktop, but I can't get enough oxygen.

My eyes bulge.

Why the hell is this happening?

Slow it down.

I drop to the floor, my knees hitting the hard tiles, and plant my palms on the cupboard door in front of me.

"You're okay. You're in the kitchen. Breathe in for five. Breathe out for five."

In my mind, it's Jennifer speaking. I listen to my therapist's soft Northern accent coaching me through the panic attack, telling me exactly what I need to do to calm down.

After a few more seconds, my lungs fill, and my tense shoulders relax.

I rise to my feet, my legs still uneasy.

You're fine. Make your coffee.

The pod slips into the machine, and I make the coffee with shaky hands.

Nothing is wrong.

My heart is racing as I take my coffee to the table and sit down. It's only when my butt hits the seat that the tsunami of emotions pulls me under, and I break down. Bending over and collapsing with my head on the table, my chest, tight and heavy, rocks with deep sobs that make me want to sink into the ground.

I need to see Robbie.

36

Linc

It took me all morning to realise that Tilly isn't going to come knocking on my door, so I went to her house, knowing her parents were working. I couldn't wait until tonight when she would undoubtedly be at the restaurant, too. *I'm on to you, Hanna.*

The first day at the cabin was perfect, until after the poker game. Then the rest of the weekend she was distant.

Why can we never have a good end?

When Tilly didn't answer, I knew exactly where she would be.

The cemetery is blossoming with a dozen different colours. Flowers line the boundary to brighten the place up and make it inviting. It's hot today, the sun strong in the sky, but Tilly doesn't seem to be aware.

It's now early afternoon. I have no idea how long she's been here, but I've been standing by my car for the last twenty-five minutes, and she's not moved an inch.

I need to check on her even if I only get a load of mouth for doing so. Hey, at least she would be speaking to me, right?

I push off my car and head down the long gravel path toward her. She left her car at home, so she must have walked here.

She hears me approach and looks up from where she's sitting by Robbie's headstone. Her eyes are red-rimmed from crying, and her cheeks are tearstained. I hate seeing her like this. But I don't know the cause.

I mean, we're at Robbie's grave, so I can take an educated guess, but she's not talking.

Before she can tell me to get lost, which is on the tip of her tongue—I can tell by the frown on her forehead—I say, "Tilly, I'm not going anywhere. Please talk to me." I sit opposite her.

She flinches as I reach down to touch her.

Fuck.

I breathe through the pain of her latest rejection. "Tilly," I whisper.

"Why did you come back? Why you?" Her face crumples, and tears spill from her eyes.

My God, that hurts like a bitch.

"What?" I clear my throat.

"You should have stayed away. Everything was okay before you came back."

I suck in a breath. "I don't know where this is coming from. Everything started off great at the cabin, Tilly. What's changed?"

My eyes flick to Robbie's headstone holding Tilly up as she lies back.

She covers her face and shakes her head. "I don't want to want this."

"Want what?" My heart thuds. I think I know where she's going, but I need confirmation. "Tilly, want what?"

"You!" She throws her arms down and scowls at me.

At the same time, rain starts to drizzle from the sky.

My lips part. One word is all it took to send my pulse into a frenzy. I've wanted to hear her say she wants me again so badly. It'll never get old.

"Can we go to mine and talk about this?" I ask.

Her eyes don't leave mine, and she doesn't make any attempt to move. So, I guess we're staying here and getting wet.

"I can't go home with you."

"Why not?"

You just said you wanted me.

"Something will happen."

"Something? You're worried about us having sex?" I'm fucking not.

"That and everything else." She clenches her hands into fists by her sides. "Tell me we're never going to happen. Tell me you've changed your mind and that you don't want me."

"I can't do that."

The rain starts to come down harder, wetting my clothes through. Still, she doesn't move, like she's not even realised it's raining yet.

"Yes, you can! Tell me you don't have feelings for me."

"No, I can't, Tilly, because I want to be with you!" The words are out before I have the chance to stop them. We've established that we're both attracted to each other but the whole idea of us being a couple has been off-limits.

Her body stills, but her eyes widen. "No," she whispers. "You can't want to be with me. Take it back."

The rain mixes with her tears, but she makes no effort to wipe either from her face. I bite back the urge to reach out.

Shaking my head, I say, "I can't take it back. I want you."

Silence stretches out before us. I can hear her ragged breath mixing with the sound of pouring rain hitting stone and grass.

The temperature has dropped drastically, but I barely feel it as I wait for a response.

She closes her eyes and leans her head back against Robbie's grave. With a breath that sinks her chest, she replies, "Linc ... I think I'm ready for more, too."

On a gasp, I reach out and grab her hand. It's instinctive. I need to touch her. She doesn't push me away, but she does cry harder. It's so fucking painful to see how much this is hurting her.

"Tilly," I say, tugging her to me.

This time, she slumps forward, straddling me, as the rain hammers down on us harder. Her chest rocks as she cries into the crook of my neck. There's nothing to be said right now, so I hold her closer and enjoy what I've been craving for years.

She's here, in my arms, and it feels like the biggest lottery win. I bow my head and breathe her in.

Tilly lets me hold her for almost ten minutes. But then her wet body begins to shake, and I know that, as much as I don't want to move, I have to.

I stand up, taking her with me. Her legs wrap fully around my waist, clamping me like a vise, as if she's worried I'll make her get down. As long as she's not letting go, I sure as hell won't.

I don't know if she's even noticed that we're moving because she doesn't say anything. I walk her back to my car through the rain. I come to a stop by the passenger door, and she finally slides down my body and stands on her feet.

"Are you okay?" I ask, cupping her chin and making her look up at me, my heart wild at the contact.

Her beautiful amber eyes are mixed with pain and love. Blonde hair is stuck to her neck and down her back, and her skin is paler than usual. Shit, I should have moved her sooner. She looks like she's freezing.

"I don't know," she admits.

"Let's get you home, dry, and warm, and we'll go from there, okay?"

Tilly nods, so I get her in the car. When I get in, I crank the heating up and drive back to hers.

"Where do you want to go?" I ask when we approach our houses.

"Yours."

Good.

Neither of us speaks as I drive. Her eyes stare out the windscreen, but they're glazed over, like she's not really seeing anything. She's lost in her thoughts.

I park in my drive, and Tilly immediately gets out. She dashes to my front door like she's scared her parents will see. I don't even think they're in since it's two in the afternoon.

"Do you want to have a shower?" I ask.

She spins around, eyes wide with alarm.

"I meant, on your own, Tilly." But I sure as hell wouldn't say no.

"Oh, er ... yeah, please."

Neither of us has yet to address the wanting to be together bomb we both dropped. I desperately want to. I want to hear her say she's mine.

I grab her some sweats that should fit her and a clean towel, and she goes for a shower. When the door closes, I force myself to walk down the stairs. Knowing that she's in there, naked and wet, is sweet torture.

In the kitchen, I make a coffee and sit at the table. Tilly drinks, but I don't have any alcohol in the house since Jack and Ian drank the last of their beer, so I'm pretty limited in what I can offer her to drink. She probably won't care though.

We have more pressing things to worry about than refreshments.

I'm not really sure how I can get her past this guilt she feels over wanting me or even if I can at all.

I'm draining the last of my coffee when she walks into the room. Her hair is damp, and she hugs her arms around the oversize sweatshirt.

You look beautiful.

The words are on the tip of my tongue. But she looks scared again. Her eyes stare at me like she's trying to figure out what the hell to do, and I don't know which way she's going to lean. Maybe she'll think it's worth the pain, or maybe she'll just want to walk away.

"Do you want anything to drink?"

She shakes her head and slowly walks to the table.

I watch her, completely lost. She's so hard to read right now, and that's probably because she doesn't know how she feels.

"Okay," she says, resting her hands on the table as she sits opposite me. "Will you tell me about that day now? We didn't get a chance before. I couldn't make it."

"Yeah," I rasp as memories of Robbie's lifeless body rush my mind.

This is the conversation she wants to have first?

I want to discuss us, but the two things go hand in hand. Maybe she needs to understand what happened before we got into the car with Stanley she can focus on what we do next. Her own imagination is her curse.

What she wants to do could depend on what I tell her now, so I'm tempted to give her the watered-down version. But I would never do that. She deserves the whole ugly, devastating truth.

"You were at the pub all day."

"There was a group of us—about ten or eleven, I think. As you know, we were celebrating my cousin's birthday with a pub crawl. Robbie and I were on the beer. Stanley had three pints before we all ate at around one in the afternoon. After that, we thought he'd switched to Coke."

Tilly's eyes fill with tears. Her fingers thread together like she's looking for comfort. I don't leave my seat even though I want to. She needs to hear this.

"At eleven, when we were leaving, I didn't want Stanley to drive at all, but he assured me he was fine." I take a breath. "Robbie assured me it was okay. He and Stanley had both driven a car after a beer as long as it had been a while. It had been ten hours since we thought Stanley had stopped drinking, and he had eaten twice since. And," I say on a sigh, "that wasn't the first time he'd had a beer and gotten behind the wheel."

"So, you both got in the car," she whispers, her eyes darkening.

"We both got in the car," I confirm. "After ten hours and him only having a few beers, I didn't think there would be a problem."

Her eyes snap shut, and she inhales.

I go on, "Stanley has always been larger than life—you know that—so it's never easy to know when he's drunk. I mean, it takes a lot, and he'd obviously not had enough to slur his words or stumble. Robbie and I believed he was okay ..." I grip the side of the table as Robbie's bloodied face slams in front of me. The picture never fades or gets distorted. I can see it in my head as if it's a photograph.

"What happened next?" she asks when the silence stretches to minutes.

I swallow. "Everything was fine at first. We were ripping Stanley for losing out with a girl to Robbie. Then, we came to a bend. Stanley started braking, but he was going too fast. He slammed the brakes on, and that's when he lost control of the car. We flipped ... I don't know how many times ... and a tree stopped us."

She bites her lip. This is stuff she knows. She would have been told by the cops about the bend and the car flipping and hitting a tree. This next part she doesn't know. No one does because I don't talk about it. The police wanted facts, Tilly wants everything between.

"I woke up, and there was silence."

"You were unconscious?" she whispers.

I nod. "Stanley was, too. I was the first to wake. I lunged forward to check on them in the front, but my seat belt was locked. For a few seconds, I fought against it, not really knowing what was going on. I was disorientated. When I took off the seat belt, I leant between the two front seats so slowly. It was eerily quiet, and I was so scared they were both dead.

But I managed to convince myself that they were unconscious, like I had been, and needed my help.

"Everything moved fast then. I checked Stanley's pulse. His head was tilted toward me, so it was easier to get to him. He had a pulse, and I could see his chest moving."

I gulp, knowing I'm coming to the part I fear the most. The part where Robbie died.

Before I checked him, I could pretend that he was still alive like Stanley and me, and he just needed to wake up. There was hope. I believed I would be able to do something to get him out.

"I moved to Robbie. My hand froze just inches from his neck when I saw how still he was. His face was ... bloody, and his eyes ..."

Fuck.

I grip the table harder, my heart tearing apart.

"His eyes what?" Tilly asks, her voice clogged with unshed tears she's trying to hold in.

"Were ... open. They looked so much like yours, same colour. He was looking at me." Well, he wasn't, but that's how it appeared. "He was already gone," I whisper.

Tears roll down her cheeks. "What did you do then?"

"I tried anyway. I got out of the car, which was difficult since the doors were bent in, and I pried Robbie's door open and tried to get him to wake up. *He wouldn't fucking wake up.*"

I dip my head. "The seat belt wouldn't come off. The next thing I heard was a woman shouting, telling me she'd called emergency services. She ran toward me and tried to help with getting Robbie out of the car. I was so scared, Tilly. I knew he was gone already, but what kind of friend would I have been if I didn't attempt to bring him back?"

She sobs, pressing her palm against her mouth.

"The seat belt was stuck. I tugged on the damn thing for ages before I managed to get it off him and lift him out of the car. By this point, Stanley was coming around. He saw what was going on and started shouting at Robbie to wake up. I laid him on the floor and was just about to start CPR when I heard sirens."

"They pronounced him dead at the scene. That's what we were told," she cries, her face crumpling in agony.

"Yeah. They worked on him for a while, but they couldn't wake him up either." I take a breath, my fingertips digging painfully into the wooden table.

Tilly rises to her feet. I watch her walk to me, not having a single clue where this is going. Hearing the details of Robbie's death must be so much harder than the facts.

I push my chair back and stand. She falls forward and into my arms. I hold her tight and press my face into the crook of her neck as we both cry.

37

Tilly

It takes a lot of willpower—because, right now, I feel like staying in Linc's arms and hiding away forever—but I stand up straight, and he moves back.

His eyes are tortured when they meet mine.

He's bled the story out to me, and he looks exhausted.

"What you went through, Linc …"

"Was nothing compared to what you and your parents have been going through."

"No, you're wrong. I know Robbie wasn't your family, but you were friends, and I know it would kill me if anything happened to Mel or Hanna, especially if I was there. Have you spoken to anyone?"

He snorts. "My parents put me in therapy."

"Did that help?"

He shrugs and looks away. "A little, I guess. But she wanted me to let go of the guilt, and that's not something you can control."

"Linc," I whisper, reaching out and curling my hand around his bicep, "I don't want you to hurt anymore."

His hand comes from nowhere, knotting into my hair and making sure I don't go anywhere. His expression is intense. "I don't want *you* to hurt anymore, but we both know it's not that easy." His eyelids flit shut. "I thought getting past Robbie's death would be the hardest thing I'd ever have to do, but wanting something I can't have is worse. You are everything good in my life and everything bad, wrapped up in one painfully beautiful, poisonous package. What you do to me, Tilly, is excruciating, but I can't stop wanting you. I can't walk away because *I love you* so much that I can't think straight."

Oh my God.

He lowers his head when I feel tears sliding down my cheeks. My heart is racing in the best and worst way. I want to make it better for him, but I'm not sure how. Hurting him is the last thing in the world I want.

"Everything is so fucked up. I killed Robbie. Not directly, but I had the chance to stop it and didn't."

"Shh," I whisper, my throat closing. "You didn't kill him."

His opens his pained eyes and looks away.

No. He has to know how I feel, how much I want him, too.

"You could kill *me*, Linc, and I don't think that would even stop me from loving you. Sometimes it feels as though you are killing me."

He takes a sharp breath, his eyes rising to mine like I hold the answers to everything. "Jesus, Tilly. We need to stop doing this. We want the same thing. Tell me we can try."

"Try being together?" My heart leaps at the same time my stomach bottoms out.

I'm always teetering on the edge of good and bad with Linc. Any contact we have can easily go either way, and my feelings for him at any given time can do the same. I'm walking a tightrope without a harness, just waiting to see if it will be him catching me when I eventually fall.

His brows rise, and he looks up at me without moving his head. "Yeah. It's all I want, and I think it's worth a shot. Don't you?"

"But what if—"

"What if we're happy?" he interjects, getting there before I can go on the negative. "What if everything else will fall into place because we're willing to make that happen?"

He makes it sound so fantastically easy. Love conquers all. Love is the reason people commit crimes of passion, but let's not explore that right now.

His fingers press deeper into my scalp, his actions as pleading as his words. "Is it not worth a chance?"

Before I can overthink—seriously, can I get my medal now?—I respond, "Yeah, it's worth a chance."

This time, his whole head snaps up, meeting me dead on, and his back straightens. He didn't expect that. His posture before was defeated. He was prepared for another rejection. I'm tired of rejecting what I want.

And I'm so damn tired of living my life for other people.

"I'm scared of all of this," I admit. "I don't want to make things harder for my parents, and I don't want the whole town talking about us and judging us."

"We can talk to your parents. The rest of the town doesn't matter. We might be news for a few days. Then, some bored housewife will have an affair with the hired help, and we'll be old news. Who cares what they say?"

The old me wouldn't have cared.

"I don't care what they say about me per se, but I do care if people think I'm betraying Robbie."

"Are you betraying Robbie by being with me?"

For the first time, although I've always kind of known, I'm sure that I'm not. There is no doubt left in my mind that Robbie wouldn't have minded the thought of me being with Linc.

"No, I'm not betraying Robbie."

"Good. People might talk, but that doesn't mean what they say is always true. The ones who knew Robbie would know he would have been behind us."

"Did you ever talk to him about me?"

"He asked me if I liked you more than a friend once, but it was before I knew I did."

"What do you think he would have said now if he were still here?"

The corner of Linc's lip curls. "I think he would have threatened physical harm if I ever hurt you, told me it was gross that I liked his little sister, but ultimately, he would have been happy if you were happy."

"He was the best brother anyone could ask for."

"He's still out there somewhere, Tilly, watching over you."

"I need to have a conversation with my mum and dad."

"Are you ready for that?" he asks, reading the uncertainty behind my words.

"I have to be."

I take a step back. I desperately want to kiss him, but it would feel wrong to officially start something before I've spoken to Mum and Dad. And if he kisses me now, that's it. After admitting how we really feel, we can't kiss without it being the start of *us*.

"Do you want me to come with you?" he asks.

"No. I should do this alone. I'll come over after, but it might be late if they want to talk." *Or shout.*

He nods. "I'll be up."

"Don't. Go to bed, and I'll wake you up."

His eyebrow lifts in the most adorable way. "Go now. I'm off to bed."

I laugh and shake my head. Linc places a soft kiss to my forehead, his lips lingering for a second and turning my insides to jelly.

"I'll be back soon," I tell him as he moves back.

I leave Linc's and go next door to my house. My legs feel heavier with each step I take, kind of like when I was walking into the hall at school to take exams. Only this is worse because Mum and Dad might end up being angry with my choice to be with Linc.

Biting my lip, I let myself in the house and go in search of my parents.

Mum is in the kitchen.

"Hey," I say, tapping my fingers against my leg. "Where's Dad?"

She raises her eyes and smiles. "He's out with Colin tonight. Do you want anything to eat?"

Damn it, he's out.

"No, I'm good, thanks. Do you think he'll be late?"

"Most likely," she replies with a laugh.

I can't wait until tomorrow because I told Linc I would do it today. I've been putting off so much when it comes to Linc. I can't wait another day. I owe him more, and I don't want to let him down again.

"Tilly?"

"Huh?"

"I've been talking to you. Where was your mind then?"

"Sorry. What were you saying?"

"I was asking what you've been up to. I've not seen you much."

Hmm, let's see ... went to Robbie's grave, had a mental breakdown, shouted at Linc, cried all over him, went back to his to discuss Robbie's death in detail, told him I love him, and then became semi-official with the youngest Reid.

Yeah, not happening.

"I went for a run."

Her eyes look through me like she doubts my words. She should; it's all a lie.

"What have you been doing?" I ask, trying to steer her away. When I tell her about Linc in a minute, I would like it to happen more naturally than with her questions.

"I've not long got home from work, so I've been reading. I'm getting quite into it again."

Mum is a massive bookworm, and she always had her head buried between the pages of a paperback. That slowed down considerably when Robbie died, so the fact that she's doing something she loves more often again, that she feels it's worth the time to spend on herself, makes me dance internally.

My smile widens. "That's great, Mum."

"Yes, it is."

I sit down at the table, pressing my palms down on the top.

Okay, start by bringing Linc up. He came on my fictional run, too.

"Tilly, is everything all right?" she presses.

"Sure. Yeah, it is actually." I bite my lip hard, my heart flying in my chest, anxiety coursing through my veins.

Please be okay with this. Please, please, please.

I don't want to hurt my parents; they've been through too much.

"So, Mum ..." My throat closes. I shove my hands under the table and wipe them on Linc's joggers.

"Yeah?"

"Well ... so ..." Sighing, I close my eyes. "You know ..."

"What's going on, Matilda?" Mum asks. She sits down at the table, slamming her hands on the wood.

My jaw drops. She's not used my full name since before Robbie died ... because she hasn't needed to. I've not done anything she's not agreed with in four years, and I'm unsure of what I've done now.

"What?"

"You're trying to tell me something. You're not sleeping well, you barely eat, and your mind is busy. Tell me what's going on because, right now, I'm worried sick."

I shake my head, but I know I have to open up. It's killing me—all the secrets, lies, and guilt. This is why I'm here right now.

Tell her.

"Linc," I whisper.

"What about him?"

"I ..." I lick my dry lips as my heart tries to break out of my chest.

"You like him," she says, tilting her head to the side. "Am I right?"

Shit.

She's more intuitive than I give her credit for.

"Yeah." My admission makes me breathe in relief.

I hate keeping things from my parents; we've always been open.

She sighs. "Oh, darling. You could have told me."

"I couldn't. You hate him. I'm supposed to hate him."

"I don't hate Lincoln." Her voice sounds affronted. "No, I don't hate him, love. I suspected you were getting close to him. He isn't in control of his brother's actions. He and Robbie didn't know how much Stanley had drunk that day. I won't lie and say it's easy, seeing him back here, but it isn't as hard as I thought it would be. Dad has said the same. We're getting used to him being home, and we're okay with it. Are you two together?"

"No."

"Why not? I think he feels the same way. I thought that back when you used to hang out together."

I squirm on the seat, now having to admit that I'm not with him because of her and Dad.

"Matilda," she says again for the second time in four years. "It's us, isn't it? You think we'll be upset."

"You were so upset when he came back."

"Because it was the first time. He's been here three months now, and although I've only seen him a handful of times around town, it hasn't hurt. I don't wake up, scared to look out the window or leave the house in case I bump into him. In fact, I suspect he's avoiding me and your dad."

"He goes out early in the morning or late at night, so you don't have to see him. He visits Robbie at stupid times, so no one will run into him."

Mum closes her eyes, pressing her fist into her heart. "That's not what I want. He isn't the bad guy here, and I don't want him feeling like he's in the wrong."

"I've tried telling him that, but he blames himself. God, he carries around so much guilt. I hate that he thinks everyone hates him, and I know Robbie wouldn't have wanted the town to shun him."

"Of course not," Mum says. "Your brother was such a loving person. He wouldn't have been angry with Stanley for long and certainly not Lincoln."

"You're not angry with me?"

"Why would I be?"

"Because Linc's brother took so much from us. In a stupid way, I feel like I'm betraying Robbie by liking Linc."

By loving Linc.

"Never have you let Robbie down, you hear me? Never. If you have a chance at happiness, I want you to grab it with two hands. As your mum, that is all I could ever ask of you. I don't care who you fall in love with, Tilly, just be happy."

Wow.

"Thanks, Mum."

She smiles at me over the table, her eyes shining with unshed tears. "Are you going next door, or do I need to repeat my happiness speech?"

I laugh. My heart warms. I didn't think I could love my mum any more than I already did, but she's proven me wrong.

"I guess we know where Robbie got his forgiving nature from."

"No, darling. There is nothing to forgive where Lincoln is concerned."

Standing up, I give her a smile. "Okay, I guess I'm going next door."

"Will you invite Lincoln over for dinner one night?" she asks.

Stopping beside her, I place my hand on her shoulder. "Only after we talk to Dad."

"Sounds reasonable."

I bend down and kiss her forehead. "Love you, Mum."

"Love you always, darling."

I leave the house, practically running, and head to Linc's.

God, I just need to see him. I'm so ready to jump into his arms and his bed. Thank God his house is right beside mine. My heart is light, my stomach filled with butterflies for our first time.

I walk up his path, and my feet stall as I look through the window.

The smile is wiped from my face with a massive slap.

Stanley is home.

Linc

I need to do something while I wait. Who knows how long Tilly's talk with her parents could take? They might have a lot to say and a lot of questions to ask. Electric energy buzzes through my body at the thought of her walking back into my house *for* me.

Okay, I need to go and take a shower. A cold one.

Heading upstairs, I check the door over my shoulder first. She's clearly not going to be here already.

I go into the bathroom and strip.

Running the shower, I step in and turn the water temperature up high. Tilly is only next door; the pull I feel toward her is all-consuming. I want her here. I want her wet, naked body in the shower with me.

Groaning, I lean my forearm on the wall. The second my eyes snap shut, she's here. Gripping my rapidly growing erection in my hand, I squeeze and pump the shaft hard and fast.

Tilly steps in behind me, pressing her breasts against my back as her hand reaches around, scratching down my abs as she heads south.

My breathing quickens.

Tilly's fingers brush over the head of my cock, and I arch into her hand, desperate for her. She runs her hand lower and curls her fingers around me. I tilt my head back and let out a long groan as she pumps her hand up and down.

"Tilly," I breathe when her teeth bite into my back.

Her free hand slides around my side, and nails cut into my flesh. I'm so close. My balls tighten, and my hips move frantically.

"Fuck," I snap and lose myself in the moment with a fantasy.

My orgasm explodes down to my toes. I grit my teeth and groan.

Twisting, I lean back against the tiles and wait for my breathing to slow. My legs are weak. If I come that hard and fast from just thinking about her, what the hell is going to happen if I have her in the flesh? I'm going to need a tactical, aren't I? I'll have to have a wank before, so I don't lose it too soon.

I wash and get out of the shower.

When I'm done in the bathroom and dressed, I head downstairs for coffee. My phone is in my hand, no notifications.

Chill the hell out. She's busy!

As I reach the bottom step, I hear a noise in the kitchen that catches my attention. I slide my phone back in my pocket, and with my heart rate accelerating, I step toward the door to find the cause of the scraping noise.

Rounding the corner, I burst into the room, ready to kick the arse of whoever has broken in. I've only been in a handful of fights before. I don't really see the point unless someone is threatening me or my family. Stanley had no problem getting into a fight. If someone looked at him funny, he would kick off. I tend to avoid looking at strangers, so I really couldn't give a fuck how they were *looking* at me.

The air leaves my lungs like they've just collapsed at my shock of seeing the culprit.

"Stanley," I say.

What the hell is he doing here?

Every time home was mentioned in the last four years, he would say with venom that he would rather die than step foot in this town again.

Yet here he is.

"What's up, bro?" he asks, smirking from behind a mug of tea. "Kettle is still hot."

"Why are you here?" I ask, folding my arms over my chest. *Shit, he can't be here.*

I wouldn't put it past him to be here because he's bored, and he wants to cause a stir in town. He doesn't care what people say about him as long as they're talking about him. He hasn't refused to come back here because he's worried about what people will say. He's stayed away, so he can deny responsibility.

He raises his dark eyebrows. "That's no way to welcome your big brother home, Linc."

"Just tell me what you're doing," I reply, exasperated.

"I thought you could use some help."

Bullshit.

He's never cared about what I've had to do before.

"What's the real reason, Stanley?"

Lifting one shoulder in a half-shrug, he replies, "Curiosity."

"What are you curious about?"

"My hometown."

"Really? So, you're going to go out, speak to people, see what's new, visit Robbie's grave?"

Stanley's jaw hardens when I mention Robbie. His cocky facade slips. "I'm here for you and our old house."

"You should go. I don't need help, and there's no reason for you to be here. It's only going to cause problems."

"Problems for you? Are we talking about Tilly?"

I walk closer, holding his gaze. "No, we're not talking about her ever. Get in your car and leave, Stanley. You're here because you can be. You love the attention, but this isn't a game. Robbie is dead."

"You think I don't know that?"

Blood pumps through my body, making my heart pound in anger. "Then, why did you come back? Don't be a dick. For once, think about someone other than yourself!"

"For fuck's sake, Lincoln! I'm entitled to come home. We're selling the house, and I wanted to see it one last time. I thought I might be able to help you. I didn't come here to hurt anyone."

"Then, think about what you're doing! Think about what you say and how you come across. You look like you don't care."

"I don't give a shit how I look to anyone else."

"Fine. Whatever. When are you leaving?"

"I planned on staying a week, but given your less than fluffy reception, I think I'll just stay a few days."

Fuck's sake.

He can't be here, not when I'm finally getting somewhere with Tilly. We need more time before we bring my brother back into the mix. She's only just okay with seeing me, not him.

And her parents sure as hell won't want to see Stanley.

I scrub my hand over my face. "Look, I'm going to level with you here, Stanley. Tilly is finally opening up and—"

"So, that's why you want me gone? This is about pussy."

"You are such a tosser," I snap. "Can you stop being so fucking selfish?"

"I knew you liked her."

"Well observed!"

He puts his mug down and folds his arms. "Family is supposed to come first, yet you want me to leave, so you can get in a girl's pants."

"She's not just any girl, and you need to practice what you preach. When have you put me, Mum, or Dad before yourself? You don't care about what we've given up as long as you're all right. Stop being such a selfish prick and do the right thing. Leave before Tilly, Emma, or Dan sees you. Or anyone else for that matter. You're going to do nothing but cause pain here."

"That's a bit melodramatic, even for you, little brother."

I slam my fist down on the countertop. "Are you going to try to talk to Emma and Dan? You never even said sorry to them after the accident."

"It was an accident," he growls.

"I know, but that's not the point." *Why can't he see it?* "How can you be so deep inside your own arse that you can't see what's right and wrong here?"

"Right and wrong. You sound like an old man, Linc."

"I'm not old anything. I'm a man, and you're acting like a petulant teenager who can't admit his own faults or take responsibility for his mistakes. I know Mum and Dad have made it very easy for you to avoid blame, but surely, you understand what you did."

"We're done here," he grits through clenched teeth.

"Go, Stanley."

He rounds the counter, staring me dead in the eye. "I don't think I will. I'm going for a nap. It was a late night. I'll see you for dinner."

"Damn it, Stanley!" I shout, turning and following him out of the kitchen.

No.

My eyes immediately seek her, like I subconsciously knew she was there. Tilly is outside, looking through the long pane of glass beside the door. I might be looking at her, but she's staring at my brother.

"Tilly," I call, striding to the front door.

My movement draws her attention, and she spins on her heel and runs.

No.

"Wait!" I wrench the door open and sprint after her. I catch her halfway back to her house. "Tilly, please, let me explain," I say, wrapping my hand around her wrist to stop her from getting away.

She stops walking, her hands clenching into fists. Very slowly, as if she's giving herself time to calm down, she turns around. The pained expression on her face, in her tired eyes, rips me apart. Pain slices through my chest.

"Why is he here? You said it was just going to be you!"

"He just turned up. I didn't know, I swear." I step closer, pleading with her to believe me. "Tilly, *I didn't know.*"

"Why is he here?" she repeats. Her voice is cold and detached, like she's asking a stranger.

I'm losing her.

"Hey," I say, tugging her a step closer. "I need you to believe me. Don't run, Tilly. Talk to me."

"I can't see him." She shakes her head, spilling big tears down her cheeks. "I'm not ready. I didn't know. He was just there, like a nightmare or something. I wasn't prepared. You said it was just you, and ..." She sobs, ending her rant, and her chest caves inward as she bends down.

"It's okay." I lean down, so I'm face-to-face with her, and I cup her chin. "It's going to be okay. He's leaving soon. If I'd known, I would have made him stay away."

Do my parents know about this?

"This is inevitable."

She looks off to the side, but I don't think she's really looking at anything. I feel her getting further away. She's in her head now, talking herself out of us.

"Don't do that. We've only just started, Tilly. Give me an hour, and he's gone. Go home, and I'll call you in a bit."

Why the hell did he pick now?

She shakes her head and backs up a step, tugging her arm from my grip.

"No," I say.

It's in her eyes—flight.

"This isn't what I want. I can't deal with him, and he's your brother. We were stupid to think it could work."

"Tilly—"

"Don't, Linc. Just stay away from me for good. I don't want this. Leave me alone."

"Tilly, no, please."

"Leave me alone!" she shouts and sprints to her house.

I hold my breath as this fucking girl tears me to pieces yet again.

39

Tilly

I walk through an aching pain in my chest and heavy legs. My vision is blurred on account of all the tears.

Mum is home, but I can't hear noise in the house, so she must have taken her book into the garden, and I have never been so grateful. I slam the front door closed, and my legs give way. I slide down the wooden door, and when my butt hits the hard floor, I wrap my arms around my legs.

Stanley is here.

He took my brother, and he has the front to show up. Swallowing the lump in my throat, I sob into my knees as the hole in my heart widens.

It hurts so much, seeing him again. Robbie didn't deserve to die. He should be here right now, living his life. I miss him more than I ever imagined was possible, and Stanley turns up like he didn't ruin my life.

A scream rips from my throat, and I give in to the pain. Whacking my head back against the door, I let the pain bleed from my body.

This is why Linc and I could never be together. I was stupid to think we could. Stanley will always be in his life, and I can't have him in mine.

I cry for my brother and for a situation so impossibly unfair until my eyes are raw, and each breath feels like cuts to my throat.

My fist grips at my top, digging into my splintering heart.

I need it to all stop. It's too much. I gasp for air, my free hand digging into the tiled floor.

Close your eyes and breathe.

I have to calm down, but the walls are closing in, darkness beginning to overpower the light. I'm sinking back into the mud. After fighting my way out and almost making it, I'm going back.

I don't want to.

Hold yourself together. Think.

I gasp again, and my windpipe opens. With my lungs inflating, I manage to push myself to my feet. All I want to do is get into bed, but handling stairs feels like climbing a mountain. I stumble forward like a drunk and grip the banister.

I can't let Mum see me like this.

Lifting my first foot, I take a step up and wipe tears as they fall. My vision is blurry, but I know where I'm going, so I make my way up by memory.

I get into my room and flop down on the bed. Curling into a ball, I try to hold myself together as everything falls to shit again.

Stanley looks normal. Nothing has changed. When Linc came back, I could see the regret in his eyes—I still can—but Stanley looks like he's never had a bad day in his life.

What if he stays until the house is done?

I can't do that. I can't bump into him all over town.

How will Mum and Dad cope with seeing the reason their son is buried in the ground?

Mum is cool with Linc, and I think Dad will be, too. I love them so much for that, but I can't expect them to deal with Stanley, too.

"Tilly?" Mum calls softly.

Shit, no.

I freeze, clenching my teeth to try to stop myself from crying. She is going to find out that Stanley is back, but I was hoping it wouldn't be like this.

Get yourself together for her right now!

I wipe my eyes and sit up. "Hi, Mum."

"Don't *hi, Mum* me. What is going on? Why are you crying? Did it not go well with Lincoln?"

"It …" Oh God, I'm going to have to tell her. Of course I am. She can't bump into him. "I didn't even get inside the house."

"Why not? Honey, we really are okay with this."

"That's not it. Stanley was there," I whisper.

Mum's face falls. Her once-rosy complexion whitens in a stellar Casper impression. "Oh."

"Yeah. Linc tried to run after me and explain, but I had to get away. I told him I couldn't do it and left him standing outside."

"Tilly," she breathes. She gulps and shuffles a bit closer to me. "Lincoln cannot control where his brother goes."

"I understand that. But it was a sharp reminder of what's between us. Stanley isn't something we can get past. He's Linc's *brother*."

"Don't make rash decisions right now."

"It's not rash. How would we make it work?"

Mum shakes her head. "The only people who can answer that is you and Lincoln."

"I don't have the answers, and I can't have Stanley in my life. Being with Linc … well, that would inevitably happen."

"Lincoln makes you happy."

"For how long? One day, he will want me to be around his family. He can't cut them off, and I would never ask him to."

"I'm so sorry, love."

My throat closes as the weight of my decision presses down on my chest.

"Me, too," I whisper and curl my fingers, nails pressing into my palms. "Are you okay?"

She's so focused on me right now that I don't think she's really heard me. The man responsible for her son's death is sitting next door.

God, I hope Linc makes him leave.

Maybe he will go with him...

No, don't think about that.

"When Lincoln returned, I did wonder if *he* would, too."

Mum hasn't been able to say Stanley's name since the accident, but we always know what she means by *he* or *him*.

I tuck my legs up into my chest and wrap my arms around them. The aching hole in my heart is spreading and making my stomach churn.

"You prepared yourself for him coming back?"

"Your dad and I have had a conversation. There is nothing we can do to prevent him from coming back, so we have to deal with it until he's gone."

Who knows when that will be?

There was a suitcase by the front door, so he was planning on at least one overnight stay.

"How do you deal with it precisely?" I ask.

My mum might be the strongest woman in the world just for getting out of bed each morning, but that doesn't mean she deals particularly well with anything surrounding Robbie's death.

"We do nothing differently. I won't hide in my house, for fear of seeing him. We've had some time to get used to Lincoln being back. His return is no longer raw, so I think we're in a better place to deal with his brother, too."

I wish I could believe that. I never wanted to see Stanley again, but I didn't think I would completely melt down like that, and Robbie wasn't my child.

How can I throw away the one thing that was finally making me genuinely happy, but my parents can go about their daily routine like normal?

Have they overtaken me? Somehow, have they healed, and I've missed it?

"Mum," I whisper, hugging my legs tighter, "everything is a mess again. I miss Linc already."

She opens her arms, and I fall into them the way I did when I was a child. Her arms, thinner than they used to be, hold me with as much attentiveness as I remember. Sometimes, you just need to hug your mum, and when you've messed up your life, yet a-fucking-gain, you need it more than ever.

Linc

Day three of Stanley being home rolls in, and I'm so fucking done with everything and everyone. Tilly is avoiding me at all costs. She won't answer her phone or reply to my text messages.

I haven't seen her despite no longer going out early in the morning or late at night. She's probably going out late and early to avoid me, knowing I've given that up.

Last night, when I was greeted with her voice mail yet again, I told myself I would give up. But I woke an hour ago, at five a.m., and realised that wasn't what she wanted. I promised her I would fight, and she told me to fight hard. So, that's what I'm going to do. No matter how goddamn painful it is, I won't give up until she can tell me she's one hundred percent sure we can never be together.

Thing is, I think she might be close to there now. She just had to talk to her parents about us first. If Stanley had only called first. If only I'd had a chance to talk to her about him, work through all that shit before he showed up, maybe we could have figured something out.

He will always be my brother; that will never change. She must understand that.

What did she think would happen? We'd never see him? There wouldn't be family occasions where we'd all have to be together?

In ten or twenty years' time, would I still be going to weddings solo because she couldn't be around him?

Did she even think of any of that at all?

If she didn't, we're in real trouble. I love the girl with every fibre of my being, but I can't have half a relationship with her. It's all or nothing, and I have the distinct feeling that it's going to be nothing.

But, hey, there's still hope, right? That old bastard that's kept me from moving on thousands of times over the last four years.

I'm in the kitchen, chain-drinking coffee, when Stanley walks in at ten a.m.

"Morning, brother," he says, scratching his head.

I grit my teeth.

"Oh, come on, Linc. You're still pissy with me?"

"I don't want to have the same conversation with you over and over," I tell him. We've already spoken about my feelings toward him being here. "What are you doing today?"

"Finishing the bathroom, aren't we? Or are you really asking when I'm going home ... again?"

"Yeah, I'm asking when you're going home."

"Not today."

"Right."

"Do you want me to talk to Tilly?"

"No." I stand up, my body moving in reaction to his words. "No fucking way. Don't go near her. She doesn't need that."

He shrugs one shoulder. "It might help."

"It won't. You can't just turn up in town and expect everyone to forgive you. Are you even sorry?"

His chest puffs with a deep breath. If I were scared of him, I'd be on guard now. "I'm trying to help you with your girl trouble."

"You are the reason I have girl trouble. If you want to help, leave."

"For how long, Linc? Have you thought ahead? What will you do when the house is finished, huh? Are you going to buy it off Mum and Dad to be with her? You're supposed to go home and start a business with Dad. Or have you forgotten that now that she's showing interest?"

Fucking prick.

"You don't know what you're talking about."

"No? What part of that did I get wrong?"

"You don't need to worry about what I'm going to do. I'll live wherever I want. But it won't be in this house."

"So, you are planning on staying here. Does Dad know?"

"Not that it's anything to do with you, but I'll sort out what I'm doing with Dad."

Stanley shakes his head. "Man, you've got no idea what you're doing."

Maybe not. But then neither does Tilly.

"I'll figure it out."

I don't like the unknown. Not like this anyway. I'm happy to go with the flow through most of my life, but when it comes to her, I need security.

I turn to leave because he's making me angry, and I need some air. Since he got here and Tilly left, I've been burning inside. The same deep anger I've felt for the last four years is bubbling back to the surface.

I'm angry with myself, my brother, and my girl.

There are mistakes that I can never run from, and I was stupid to think I could move past them so easily.

Slamming the front door behind me, I grind my teeth at Stanley shouting something after me. I can't make it out, and that's probably for the best.

I stop on my way to my car. Emma is just pulling into their drive. She cuts the engine, gets out, and freezes when she sees that I haven't left.

"Morning," I say. There is so much more I want to say than that.

I want to know about Tilly, but how can I ask that when my brother is meters away? I don't know how to talk to Tilly about anything. When I see her, I just want to apologise over and over, but I don't think she wants to hear it.

"Morning, Lincoln."

Screw it.

"Is she okay?"

Her smile softens. "She's doing all right."

All right. At least one of us is.

"Have a good day," I say and practically dive for my car. I need to drive and put some distance between me and my brother.

41

Tilly

I get into work just in time and rush into the staff room to dump my bag. It's a miracle I made it at all after only getting a few hours' sleep. I miss Linc more than I thought was possible.

Mum saw him yesterday morning. When she told me about it, I pretended it was no big deal. I mean, we live next to each other for now, so it's going to happen at some point. But it is a big deal because, although I pretend I'm doing okay and that things were too new with Linc to bother me that much, I feel like I'm dying.

No one but Linc knows that I love him. That hasn't stopped just because we're not together.

We can't be together, and it hurts so bad that I feel sick.

Stanley is staying in a house meters from mine.

How could he think it's okay to come back here? Is he trying to prove a point?

Maybe he thinks that, because Linc hasn't been chased out of town with pitchforks, he would be welcome back, too.

The town isn't all that thrilled to have Linc here, let alone the guilty brother.

No one has mentioned anything to me yet, so I can only assume he's been staying in the house. It's been four days now though.

How much longer can he hide out for?

Linc might be making him stay inside.

I chuck my bag on the sofa and check my reflection. *Great.* Puffy under eyes, barely covered with concealer, hair messily tied up—but not that cool *I meant it to look messy* messy—and blotchy skin.

No one is going to care as long as I'm bringing them food and drink, and I sure as hell don't care much about my appearance right now.

Everything is so raw still. Every time I close my eyes, I can see the look of pain rip through Linc's face when I told him we were done. It's all such a mess. Much like my hair.

I head into the restaurant, giving my colleagues a smile as I head to my section. Hanna isn't working today—thank goodness. She would have a lot to say about Linc and Stanley. She already has, but I've managed to avoid her for long periods of time so far. I love that she has my back, but listening to her bitching about Stanley isn't what I need at the minute.

Linc didn't know Stanley was coming back.

God, he's not his brother's keeper, and he certainly can't control him.

I take orders from a waiting table and go to the bar to make their tea and coffee.

"Everything okay, Tilly?"

I turn around at the sound of Greg's voice.

"Hi," I say, blinking hard to check if he's really here or not. I seem to recall him telling me we weren't friends anymore as long as I wanted Linc in my life. "Greg," I say, "you're here."

He laughs. "Looks like it."

I pick up the tea and coffee I just made. "Will you give me a minute? I'll just take these and then come back."

He nods and takes a seat at the bar. I feel his eyes on my back as I take the drinks, and I see them on my face as I walk back.

"What's up?" I ask, standing next to him.

He pats the stool next to him. "Will you sit down?"

"I would, but I'm not allowed to while I'm working. Is everything okay though? Are you all right?"

"I saw him," he admits. It doesn't take a genius to figure out that *him* is Stanley.

"Where?" I ask.

"His house. I was driving past late last night after a date and saw him getting in his car. Why is he back?"

I shrug. "I don't know why. Because he can?"

"Well, how are you? And your parents?" he asks, his voice soft. The tone he always uses for conversations surrounding the Reid family.

"I'm not all that great, and my parents haven't seen him yet."

"Do they know?"

"Yeah. They're doing okay, but I can tell it hurts, the possibility of seeing him again."

"Jesus, Tilly. You should have called me."

I tilt my head to the side and deadpan.

"Come on. No matter what happens, you know I'll be there if you really need me. What has Lincoln said about Stanley coming back?"

"He said he didn't know he was coming, but I didn't really give him much chance to talk."

Greg's eyebrows rise, and he turns his body toward me. "You two aren't together anymore?"

I sigh. "We were never together, Greg. He's a friend. He's always been a friend."

Lies.

"There's nothing more there?"

305

"No ... well, yes, but there can't be. I shouldn't be talking to you about this."

I take a second to look around the room. There are only two tables in my section at the minute. One is waiting on food, and the other was served by someone else before I got in, and they are eating.

"You have feelings for him," Greg says. He's not asked me a question because he believes he's right.

He knows I do.

"I have feelings for him. Maybe it's just the nostalgia of how things were before."

"Is that what you really think?"

No. I love him more than anything.

"Whatever. It's not a problem anymore."

I think he's pretty mad at me after the way I spoke to him. We need some distance, and I certainly can't pretend like everything is fine and hang out with him when Stanley is there.

"Do you want to meet and talk about it?" he offers, tapping his hands on the bar.

"You don't need to worry about me, Greg. I'm fine. Don't feel like you have to check up on me. I can sense your reluctance."

He frowns. "I just said that, if you need me, I'll be there."

"Yeah, but I said I'm fine, and you believe me."

He averts his eyes, gritting his teeth.

"You always were easy for me to read," I tell him.

"Right. Well, I'll be off then. Take care of yourself, Tilly."

"You, too, Greg."

I watch him walk out and then head to the kitchen to see if my table's food is ready yet. It would have been so easy to accept Greg's offer. He's always been good at cheering me up, but that wouldn't have been fair. He only asked me to be polite, so I'm not going to force him to do something he doesn't feel comfortable to do.

With a heavy heart, I take two full English breakfasts to my table.

Get through this shift, and you can go home to watch an unhealthy amount of Netflix.

Nothing scary though. Horror reminds me of Linc.
Okay, let's not think about him.

I freeze as I walk to my car after a busy shift at work. No. Not him.

What's he doing here, in the middle of the car park, by my car?

Stanley looks up, but his expression doesn't change when he sees me. His light eyes are as emotionless as ever. I'm not sure if there's something wrong with him or if he's just too involved in himself. But I don't really care.

I want to leave, but I won't let him drive me away. With my throat feeling like I've swallowed sand, I shuffle toward him.

"What are you doing here?" I ask, folding my arms.

"I want to talk to you."

"What could you possibly have to say to me after what you did?"

"Tilly," he grunts, "I am sorry about the accident."

About the accident. No, *I'm sorry your brother is dead?*

"Do you always diminish your responsibility?"

He inhales noisily through his nose. "That's not what I'm doing. I just said I'm sorry."

"But are you, Stanley? Because you certainly don't sound like it." Fire burns in my veins. "He died, and you never showed you gave a shit!"

"He was my friend."

"Yeah, that was his mistake. You're selfish, and you're acting like this is a game. You think you can give a halfhearted apology, and all is forgotten? Jesus, you're responsible for my brother's death!"

"He didn't have to get in my car."

"Are you fucking kidding me?" I spit. "Why are you here? You might not think that you did anything wrong, but *everyone* else knows otherwise, so stop lying to yourself and take a shot at being a decent person for once in your pathetic life."

Stanley's eyes twitch as he glares at me like I'm the Antichrist. "You don't know the first fucking thing about me."

"I know what I see, Stanley, and I see a spineless dickhead who will blame everyone and everything else before he admits his faults. You tell yourself what you need to, but deep down, you know what you are."

"This was a mistake."

"Yeah, it was. You should leave now. Leave your old house and leave town. Stop bringing Linc down."

His top lip curls. "Until that house is sold, my family owns it, and I'll stay as long as I like."

"Linc is okay with that?"

"He's my brother."

"That's not a yes."

"You know what, Tilly? You can fuck off." Stanley storms past me.

I ball my fists and breathe in through my nose and out through my mouth. Tears sting my eyelids at the cruelty in his words.

How can anyone be responsible for a person's death and not be sorry?

Stanley doesn't care that his irresponsible drunk driving killed Robbie, his friend.

They'd spent so much time together; they were always together, and he doesn't care.

Does he not miss him? Is he too deep into concealing his wrongdoing that he doesn't see what he did?

He blamed Robbie for getting into the car.

I do, too. My brother shouldn't have been so stupid, but who gets behind the wheel of a car, knowing they've consumed alcohol?

I'm so over today.

I get into my car and slam the door. Then, I burst into tears, gripping my steering wheel.

Linc

I run my hands through my hair and lay my head back on the sofa. Ever since Stanley came back, I've barely slept. He's being unfair to Tilly, Emma, and Dan. There is no remorse.

My brother has no remorse for killing his friend.

I don't know what to do with that. He should have gone to prison. My parents made the wrong decision when they fought to keep him out. Stanley needed it. He still does, but the door for that one is firmly closed.

Maybe, if there had been a suitable punishment for his actions, he wouldn't behave like he's a victim, too.

The British justice system didn't hold him properly accountable, so why should he?

What does that mean for him now? Will he ever be able to take responsibility for anything he does?

God, this isn't my fight. I can't force him to face facts and be sorry.

He's not apologised to Robbie's parents. Not even back then.

How can you not be sorry?

I can't wrap my mind around it. This isn't even just about Robbie's family; it's about him. Stanley and Robbie were friends. As far as I'm aware, Stanley hasn't been to Robbie's grave to apologise. He's never broken down and wished there was something he could do to bring him back.

Mum and Dad aren't happy that he's home, but like usual, they back him. Stanley has a right to be here, to say good-bye to the home he grew up in. That's their take on the matter.

They're as deluded as him.

The front door slams, making the wall rattle. I jump and turn around, looking over the back of the sofa.

Stanley storms in the room, his face red and jugular vein pulsing.

"What the hell was that?" I growl.

"Your girlfriend is a bitch, by the way."

He went to see Tilly.

My hands tremble as a cold sweat breaks out across my forehead. I stand up and face him. "What?"

"I saw her in town, and she ranted like a psycho."

"What the fuck were you doing, talking to her?" I snap. God, that is the last thing she needs. "What is wrong with you?"

He folds his arms and puffs out his chest, trying to make himself look bigger and more imposing. "There is nothing wrong with me. I went to talk to her, and that was obviously a mistake because she's crazy."

"She's not crazy, you prick. She misses her brother! Can you not see your part in this at all?"

"So, she still hates you, too?"

"I wasn't driving, dickhead, and I'm sorry for what happened." I shake my head. "You want people to forgive you, Stanley? You have to *earn* it. Hold your hands up and admit what you did wrong, apologise, do whatever it takes to prove that you're sorry."

"Why the fuck should I beg people to like me again?"

Jesus.

I pinch the bridge of my nose, feeling a headache coming on. "If you're not willing to do that, you're not willing to be forgiven. Why can't you see that?"

For the first time, I wonder if there is something really wrong with him. *Is he capable of feeling remorse?*

I don't believe he would ever potentially hurt anyone, but he doesn't seem to care that he has.

"I don't need it the way you do. I don't love Tilly."

I grind my teeth and drop my hand. "That's not the point here. This is about Robbie. Your *friend.*"

"Look, whatever. I came back here, hoping that being in our childhood home might improve things between us, but obviously, that's not going to happen, so I'm leaving."

"What? Things would be a whole lot better between us if you would man the fuck up. I can forgive mistakes, Stanley, but you have to admit *your* mistake."

"I wasn't alone in that car."

Oh my God!

"I'm not saying I'm blameless, but you're saying you are. Mum and Dad have made this so easy on you. You're not a child who needs protecting."

His eyes twitch. "So, you think I should have gone to prison?"

"Yeah, that's exactly what I think. Maybe then you wouldn't be so incapable of seeing any fault or blame in yourself."

"Are you fucking kidding me? You're my *brother*!"

"That doesn't mean I think you shouldn't be held responsible for your actions! I will have at least a fraction of respect for you if you admit to me right now that you are to blame for Robbie's death."

Stanley opens his mouth, and I can tell by the tightness around his eyes that he's about to protest.

"Not that you're the only one to blame, but you are to blame," I add, stopping him from using that bullshit.

311

"You know what, Linc? We're done. I don't need a brother like you. I'm going home." His lip curls at the corner as he walks away from me and heads upstairs.

That is fine with me. He can leave. He can want nothing more to do with me if this is how he is going to be. There is no point in hanging on to someone purely because you share DNA.

There is nothing redeeming about my brother, but I can still work on me. I can still try to make it up to Robbie's family in every way I can. That used to be by staying away, and it still might be, but I'm hoping things have changed too much for Tilly, so she won't slam the door in my face permanently.

I walk around the sofa as Stanley bangs a door above me. He must be packing.

Bloody good.

Stanley might be done, but I am, too. We're too different.

After five more minutes of stomping and slamming, Stanley thunders down the stairs, bag in his hand.

The vein in his neck is still twitching. He passes me, keeping his eyes ahead and his lips glued together.

He swings the front door open and marches out. I roll my eyes and follow him out of the open door. He rips his car door open and throws his bag onto the passenger seat.

My eyes slide sideways at the sound of a door opening on Tilly's house.

She freezes mid-step as she spots me and Stanley. Her mouth parts like she's seen a ghost. Gripping her throat, she spins around and darts back in the house.

I press my hand into the endless ache in my chest and rip my eyes from her front door just in time to watch my brother drive off without another word.

Tilly

Stanley left two days ago, but I still haven't seen Linc since. He was outside his house, and then … nothing. It's like he's disappeared off the face of the earth.

I wish I'd stayed until Stanley drove off. I should have gone over and talked to Linc.

He must think I hate him.

It's now ten at night, and I'm worried. *What's he doing?*

He's never been this absent since he first arrived. I've always seen some sign of life, like his car parked in a different position.

It's been radio silence since I told him to leave me alone the day Stanley arrived.

I didn't mean it. Seeing his brother had been a massive shock, and it catapulted me back four years to the last time I had seen him, when everything was so new and raw. I acted out of fear, but Linc might believe I meant it.

What if he thinks I don't want to see him again?

I was on my way to tell him my parents were behind us and that I wanted to be with him despite probably never being okay with Stanley.

God, I have screwed up so badly. Again.

My mum and dad have gone to visit my aunt and uncle for the night. I take the stairs far too fast and have to grip the banister, so I don't face-plant. My feet can't get to Linc quick enough.

I slam the front door and run across the grass to his front door. My footsteps squelching on the wet ground.

"Linc?" I call as I knock.

Biting my lip as nerves explode in my stomach, I lean in and try to listen for any sign of him in there. It's deathly quiet. His car is in the drive, and I've not noticed Ian or Jack come and pick him up.

I twist the handle, and the door opens.

Where is he?

Walking in, I close the door behind me and flick the light on because the house is cloaked in darkness.

Maybe he's asleep?

Whatever is going on though, we need to sort this.

I move deeper into the house, and that's when I hear a light thud, like something hitting the floor. It wasn't heavy enough to be Linc falling, but I follow the noise anyway.

When I step into the kitchen, my heart takes a nosedive.

Linc is sitting on the floor in the kitchen, leaning against a cabinet. Drinking.

The sight of him squeezing his eyes closed as he takes a long swig of whiskey straight from the bottle takes my breath away.

I did this.

He's drunk. No, he's wasted. His hair is messy, like he's been running his fingers through it the way he does when he's angry or frustrated. His small movements are sluggish.

Lincoln is drinking! He doesn't drink.

I step closer, tears stinging. "Linc," I whisper.

He stills. His eyes flick open, and the bottle freezes at his lips.

Dark blue eyes, full of pain, stare into me.

"What are you doing?" I ask, kneeling down in front of him.

He watches me as I reach out and take the bottle from him. Besides letting it go, he doesn't react.

"You don't drink."

That earns a hollow laugh from him. Shaking his head, he looks up. "Four years, not a drop has passed my lips, and three months after coming back here, I'm drunk." His voice is slurred and slow. He rolls his head to the side, and his eyes meet mine again. "I haven't even wanted a drink until you."

Ouch.

I look away, guilt settling in the pit of my stomach and making my shoulders double over. The bottle is still in my hand, and I feel like joining him, but alcohol has never helped anything for me yet, so I put it down.

"I'm sorry about the other day, Linc. Seeing him again was a shock, but I didn't mean what I said to you. I just wish I had known he was coming back, so I could have prepared myself for seeing him again."

"I didn't know he was coming back," he slurs. "I wouldn't have let him if I'd known."

"I know," I reply.

He groans and runs his hand through his hair. "How the fuck do you do this?"

"Do what?"

"Wreck me." Blinking heavily, he sucks in a breath. "It fucking hurts. Loving you only fucking hurts."

It only hurts.

The pit in my stomach widens.

"Linc," I whisper again, tears sliding down my face.

I know the pain he's talking about. I feel it, too, and I would give anything to have it be like the movies. Shouldn't we be walking on air and having sex every five minutes? Why couldn't I fall for someone easy to love?

"Don't," he says, but I only just make out the word.

His eyelids are getting heavier. There are only a few sips of the bottle left, so he's made a good dent. It's going to hurt tomorrow, especially since he doesn't usually drink.

"You need to sleep this off," I say, wiping the tears from my cheeks.

"Don't cry," he mutters. "I can't stand you being upset. Fuck, Tilly, I love you. Everything gets in the way. It's never going to happen, is it?" He doesn't wait for me to answer before continuing, and I'm kind of glad because I don't have the answer, "It's not enough. All those wankers who said love was all you needed can fucking burn."

"Linc, let's get you to bed."

We need this conversation. We can't keep going on like this. First, it was me breaking at the beach and cemetery, and now, it's him.

He groans and closes his eyes. "You should just go."

"No." I stand and bend down to get his hands.

When we touch, my heart races, and Linc's mouth parts, his eyes burning into mine, desire flaming behind the blue.

Well, that's why he wanted me to go and not to help him.

I pull because, despite not wanting to make things even worse here, I want to take care of him. He's going to hate himself in the morning when he sobers up. He made a conscious decision not to drink, and he's broken that. I've made him break that. There is no way I'm leaving him to wake up to that kind of guilt and self-loathing.

"Come on. Let me help you."

He pushes himself to his feet, still holding one of my hands, and stumbles into me. Groaning again, he lowers his head, burying his face against my neck, and squeezes my hand. I should pull away, but I can't. In fact, I find myself sinking against his chest.

I place my palm on the solid muscle over his stomach.

Linc mumbles something. I think he's telling me he loves me, but his voice is too muffled from the booze and my skin.

"You need to sleep this off."

He lifts his head a fraction. His dark blue eyes are wounded. "I drank, Tilly."

"Don't worry about that right now," I say and tug him forward.

Most of his weight is on me, and he's unable to walk in a straight line. We zigzag upstairs, Linc placing his feet so carefully on the stairs, like it's taking extra concentration to move.

I can't believe I've done this to him.

I manage to get him all the way upstairs and into his room. He flops down on his bed and swears. It looks the same as before in here—grey walls, very minimalistic, with a few classic horror movie posters from cinemas hanging up.

Rolling onto his back, he chucks his arm over his eyes. His chest caves as he takes deep breaths.

My heart shatters, as I know how much he's hurting right now.

"Linc, I'm so sorry," I say, climbing onto the bed with him.

Moving onto his side, away from me, he mutters, "I don't want you to see this." His voice is raw, slurred, and thick with emotion. His back jumps with silent sobs.

I lie down, facing his back, because even if this is all he will let me see right now, I'll take it. The remainder of my fragile heart breaks, and there is nothing I can do to stop myself from sobbing. I cry because I love him. I cry because nothing about this is easy. I cry because I want nothing more than to have him wrap his arms around me.

"Linc," I cry, sobbing harder, knowing that he's as broken as I am right now.

The pain of our situation takes my breath away.

He finally hears me over his own despair and rolls over. He looks up at the headboard, not letting me see his face, but he does do one thing I desperately need and wraps me in a tight embrace that is full of promises to fix us both.

Linc and I hold each other until we drift off to sleep. I crash hard, my body melting into his.

Somewhere during the early hours, when the sky is still black, I wake up because I'm too hot. Linc is behind me, his chest plastered to my back, arm around my waist. His breath quickens, blowing against my ear.

My top has pulled up to my belly button, and Linc's hand is resting on my stomach, right at the waistband of my leggings.

Oh my God, move that hand.

I grit my teeth in desperation as his touch ignites a fire between my legs. I'm facing away from him, so I can't see if he's awake.

All I know is that I'm supposed to be asleep, but I'm currently trying to control my hormones because my clit is pulsing. His skin grazing mine is maddening.

I press my legs together as his fingers sweep upward. Wrong direction, but it's now only inches from my breasts. My nipples are hard already. My mouth parts. Linc's touch is electric. His chest moves quicker, fingers digging gently into my skin.

He's awake and as turned on as you.

I'm throbbing, heat pooling between my legs.

I want to say something, but I don't know if he knows I'm awake. Like I'd be asleep right now.

"Tilly," he whispers so quietly.

My pounding heartbeat almost drowns his voice out.

My breath catches in my throat.

Linc's body tenses. Well, he knows I'm awake now.

I clutch the bedsheet in my fist, and he moans. I can't have any more distance between us. I'm over being away from him; it's too hard—which, coincidentally, is the current state of his dick.

I turn around, so we're face-to-face.

The bedroom is bathed in darkness, but I can just about make out his silhouette. It's dead silent with neither of us daring to breathe.

Then, his mouth grazes mine, and my heart loses it entirely.

I squirm against the burning between my legs as Linc moves his lips hard over mine. Groaning, he rolls me onto my back and kisses me with a force that makes my toes curl.

Arching my back, I desperately grind against him, needing the friction to satisfy the throbbing.

Linc obliges and arches his hips into mine, his tongue probing my mouth, flicking strong and fast, promising things to come.

His hands glide down my body, and he grabs a fistful of my T-shirt by the hem and tugs it up. His mouth leaves mine for the briefest of seconds while he whips my top over my head. He, thankfully, is already shirtless.

I run my hands down his chest, feeling every bump of his solid muscle as I go. His lips meet mine again in a rough kiss that sends me spinning. I shove at his joggers—no boxers underneath it would seem—and use my feet to kick them the rest of the way off his legs.

And that's about where my control over the situation ends.

Linc moves quickly, like *reactions of a cat* quickly, to remove my leggings and thong.

His hand brushes against my stomach, and I don't know if I want it to go north or south. I actually don't care, just as long as he's still touching me somehow.

He chooses north, and his strong hand cups my breast, squeezing. I almost buck off the mattress as his thumb and finger circle my nipple, and he moans into my mouth.

I'm going to fucking explode in a second.

I arch my hips, trying to tell him what I want. His moan is muffled by my tongue. Linc wastes no time in granting my request. He grips his cock and lines it up at my entrance. His mouth leaves mine. We're both breathing heavily, my chest caving.

Linc pushes inside, his eyes squinting shut in the dark room. I watch his face, my mouth falling open at the feel of him stretching me to fit him. He's big, hard, and perfect, and I never want this moment to end.

He fills me completely until I can feel his pelvis against mine.

"Oh," I breathe, my eyes flitting closed as I clench around him.

Nothing has ever felt this good. His skin raw against mine sends a shudder through my body. My clit pulses at the feel of him so deep.

Linc moves his hips, and my eyes fly open. I raise my butt, meeting his every stroke as he pulls almost all the way out and slams back into me. I grind myself against him every time his hips meet mine.

Oh shit!

Pressure is building in my body, the need to come overtaking everything else. I dig my nails into his shoulders and cry out his name as he plays my body like a damn musician.

"Linc," I murmur.

He groans and roughly grabs my hip. Something in his eyes changes, and he pounds into me over and over, every stroke of his hips harder than the last, sending me insane.

He's lost control, and I love it. His cock slams into me over and over in the most stunningly powerful way. I'm getting so close, I feel the fire spreading through my body. His mouth comes down hard on mine and he groans my name.

"Oh God," I murmur against his frantic mouth.

This is too good. I can feel every inch of him inside me, very quickly driving me insane.

He pulls away to kiss my neck, his tongue dragging over my skin, making my toes curl. I close my eyes when his hand sweeps up my body and finds my breast.

I want to tell him to go slower and go faster at the same time. I'm so close, it's torture waiting, but I want to make this last forever. This is us. We're together, he's inside me, and I have never felt so good in my life.

"Please don't stop," I cry, arching my body into him.

He tugs my nipple, and I gasp.

"Linc..."

"You feel incredible," he says against my neck as his teeth gazes my skin. "You're so tight, so perfect. I can't get enough."

Shit.

My hands reach up and tangle into his hair as my body coils tight. *I'm going to come.* I writhe underneath him and throw my head back, tugging fistfuls of his messy hair.

"Yes," he breathes. "Come for me, Tilly. Come around my cock."

His words are the trigger. I let go, falling into oblivion as my body shakes with an orgasm that makes me dizzy.

"Fuck." He presses his forehead to mine, his eyebrows pinched together, almost like he's in pain. "Fuck, you're squeezing the life out of me. I'm going to come inside you, Tilly."

"Yes," I pant. Oh God, I want that. "I want to feel you come." I grab the muscle on the small of his back. "Linc, come inside me."

Dropping his head to my shoulder, he moans long and loud as he pumps into me.

Linc's movements slow, and my body goes slack, the intensity of my orgasm turning my limbs to mush.

His lips lightly press down on my neck, and he pulls out of me. I curl onto my side, still in his arms, and it takes me only seconds to fall back to sleep with a faint smile touching my lips.

Tilly

I'm not sure which one of us fell asleep first the second time around, but when I wake up in the morning, we're in the same position, clinging to each other. Naked.

Linc is still sleeping. He looks a lot more peaceful now, but I know that's not going to last because, even if we manage to sort something out between us, he's still going to have to deal with the fact that he consumed alcohol—and a lot of it.

And we had sex.

Not that I think he's going to be all cut up over that one, but it is something we need to talk about. I know the sex was in the middle of some massive emotional breakdown on both our parts, but it was supposed to happen.

My body feels like I had hot sex last night. I'm sore in the best way, and my thigh muscles ache from holding on around Linc's back.

Somewhere along the road, Linc and I are supposed to be together. It's just a shame we've hurt each other so much to get to this point.

Will he be angry with me for his drinking?

He did say that he'd easily stayed away from alcohol for four years, but three months after being back in my life, and he got wasted.

I close my eyes as guilt floods my heart. He was so sure that he never wanted to drink again.

He should be pissed at me, but there's no point in me stressing over something that might not happen.

I slip out of his arms and head downstairs to make coffee and get him some water and tablets. He's going to have a banging headache; that's for sure.

I'm just finishing the drinks when I hear him come downstairs.

He looks around the corner with wild eyes, like he's lost something—me. He thought I'd taken off. When he settles on me, he releases a breath, and his shoulders relax.

"Are you okay?" I ask.

I feel like I've been run over, so he must be ten times worse.

"I thought you'd gone."

"I figured you'd need these," I say, picking up the tablets and water from the counter and handing them to him.

He takes the pills and downs them with a long swig of water. When he puts the glass down, he notices the whiskey bottle on the floor. I should have moved it, but I wasn't exactly thinking straight.

"I'm sorry," I tell him, bending down to get the bottle.

He walks past and takes it from my hand. He pours the small remainder out into the sink. "You didn't force me to drink, Tilly."

"I didn't hold it to your mouth, but we both know I'm not blameless."

"You know, I wish there could be one moment between us where there is no blame or no guilt."

"Last night," I whisper.

His burning eyes pin me to the spot.

"Or this morning, although I don't really know what time it was. I don't feel guilty for that. I don't regret being with you."

He watches me like he's sure I'm lying.

"What are you saying, Tilly?"

I step closer, splaying my hand over his naked chest, feeling the erratic beating of his heart. "I'm saying I love you, and I don't regret you."

I expected more talking because we're very good at talking in circles when it comes to us. But he doesn't say anything at all. Well, he does, but it's nonverbal because his mouth closes over mine.

My hands fly to his shoulders, and I glue my body to his. Linc's lips are strong and demanding, and he kisses me like it's the last thing he's ever going to do.

Linc pulls me close, his hand sliding up my back and into my hair. "Tilly," he moans against my mouth.

Back upstairs!

Linc nips my bottom lip as the temperature in his kitchen soars. I feel the kiss down to my toes. His tongue slips into my mouth, and I suck.

"Fuck, Tilly," Linc says, pulling back and holding my upper arms. "If you want to talk, we need to stop because I'm seconds from carrying you upstairs."

Sounds good to me.

"Okay," I breathe.

As much as I want to go back to bed and explore his body in daylight, we do have a lot to discuss. We always end up taking steps back, so I want to try to do this right now. I don't know how I could go back to the way we were after being so close to him. Last night changed everything forever.

"What happens now? So that I'm clear because nothing with us has been clear," he asks, pressing his forehead against mine.

"Now, I guess you recover from your hangover and take me on a date."

"A date? But that's so *other people* normal? Are you sure you wouldn't rather go and have an argument in the middle of a storm?" he teases.

"There isn't a storm forecast today, so we'll have to just try this instead."

His lips quirk, and his eyes dance. God, it is such a stark difference from last night. I don't ever want to see him that down ever again. Whatever happens with family, I'm going to put me and Linc first. I think we deserve it.

"Where do you want to go? Because I'm not sure I can go anyplace that'll have noise above a whisper today."

"Damn it, there's a marching band playing at the summer carnival all week."

He rolls his eyes. "They're still doing that?"

I nod. "They've not gotten any better either. How about we take a rain check on the date and stay in today?"

"Nope, not happening, Tilly."

"You just said—"

"I'm not giving you any time to talk yourself out of us going public. We're going out, and I don't care what anyone thinks. Let them talk. I'm just finally happy that we're in this place."

I curl my arms around his back and lay my head on his chest. He knows me better than I thought. The longer we leave it, the harder it will get for me to go out and face the people who will no doubt talk about the siblings of Stanley and Robbie getting together.

While I don't think people are angry with Linc anymore— at least, not all of them—they are still mad at Stanley. There will be talk, and I'm just going to have to ignore that because I can't have anything else come between us.

Like when you undoubtedly have to see his parents and Stanley.

"In that case, you can take me to dinner."

"We've been together for two seconds, and you're already making demands. Is this how it's going to be?"

"We're together?" I ask, grinning against his chest.

He sighs. "You're not funny." Linc pulls back, so I look up at him. "We're together, exclusively, and we're serious. Okay?"

I try not to laugh at how authoritative he's being, and I actually kind of love that we're on the same page. There is no way we could ever do casual and not get hurt. Hell, we can't even be just friends without it hurting. Things have moved so far past casual that it's not even funny.

"Yeah, I'm good with that. I should go. My parents are due home this morning, and they'll worry if I'm not there."

"Your parents are home now," he says, looking out the kitchen window.

I look around his shoulder. My parents' car is pulling into our drive, and I groan.

Linc drops his arms around me and takes a step back. His jaw is tight, but he doesn't look angry. Not with me anyway.

"No, I'm not worried about this. I like it here, on our own, and I was hoping to get to have you to myself a little longer, but I want you to come with me."

His eyes find mine in half a second flat.

I step closer to him. "I'm not ashamed, and I'm not hiding. We've just arranged to go out tonight."

"You want me to go to yours now?"

I shrug. "Sure."

His eyes widen. He's scared. He's not afraid of much, but being around my parents is on the list. But I know he's only scared of hurting them even more.

"They support us, Linc."

He stills. "They what?"

"The day I was coming to yours and saw Stanley, I'd had a conversation with my mum. Remember, that's why I went home? Mum figured it out right before I told her actually because she noticed that I hadn't been eating or sleeping properly. You did that to me, how I felt about you did that. She told me that, if you made me happy, I should go for it. They don't blame you, and they don't hate you. She even told me to bring you to dinner."

He opens and closes his mouth, and then he shakes his head.

"As much as I love you shirtless, you should probably put a top on before we go."

Linc stares at me like I've been speaking a different language.

"They're really okay with seeing me? When I first moved back ..."

"It was new and brought up a whole heap of semi-buried emotions, but now that they've worked through that, the way I did, they're ready to move on, and they're okay with you."

"Tilly," he whispers, frowning like this is too much to get his head around.

I take a step closer, so there's no distance between us. "Linc, I spent a lot of time blaming you when it wasn't your fault. I don't want to carry that around anymore, so I don't, and neither do my parents."

His chest rises and falls hard as he tries to make sense of what I'm saying. He never expected to be forgiven, but really, he hadn't done anything wrong. Stanley should have been sober by the time he drove. Linc and Robbie had no idea that he wasn't.

Nothing will bring my brother back, and hating everyone involved that night only hurts me in the end.

"You okay there? You've gone pretty quiet."

"I never thought this ... Tilly, I've wanted you for so long or for you to at least not hate me. This doesn't seem real. I think I need a minute to ..." He sighs, frowning adorably into the distance.

"Linc, you been pining?"

He narrows his eyes. "Okay, I'm over it." Chuckling, he pulls me into his arms, and I have never seen him look so settled. "Let me go get dressed and try to do something with my hair, so I don't look so hungover."

"You don't look hungover. You look like you had some chick tugging your hair."

"Fuck, I loved it when you did that."

"Didn't suck for me either." I shove his chest, not that he moves much, and point to the stairs. "Go and get ready."

Linc

I feel like shit. Physically, that is. Everything else is how it should be.

Tilly is downstairs, waiting for me so that we can go to her house. I'm nervous as hell to be around her parents. I don't want to cause them any pain. Even if they don't blame me anymore, my brother is the one ultimately responsible, and no matter how angry I still am with him, he's family.

I splash water on my face and run my hands through my hair. Images of Tilly writhing underneath me flash through my mind. Nothing has ever felt as good as being inside her. My right hand and thoughts of her don't even come close.

"Linc, how is it taking you so long?" she shouts up the stairs.

My watch shows that I've been up here for two minutes. Two.

"Coming."

I don't look half as bad as I feel. My head is pounding, but besides a little redness around my eyes, there's no evidence of my drinking last night. My moment of weakness is not even something I have the capacity to think about right now.

Tilly is standing at the bottom of the stairs with a beautiful smile that makes my heart race. God, I'm so grateful that my parents decided to sell this house.

"I thought you were making yourself look less rough?" she teases when I hit the bottom.

I reach around and slap her very peachy arse. "I can't believe I thought I missed you."

She laughs as I wrap my arms around her back. "It's weird, you being back now. Not bad weird, but it kind of feels like you never left, you know?"

"Hmm," I say. I can't agree. I felt every second of our four-year separation.

Stepping forward into my chest, she looks up at me. "Come on, I need to get this done."

"You're nervous."

"I just want it to go well," she replies. "They're being amazing with us, but in the back of my mind, I'm kind of scared that the reality will be harder. You know, will they really be okay when they see us?"

"Tilly, everything is going to be fine. Maybe they'll need a little longer, maybe there will be a few tough conversations, but I'm not going anywhere, and I will fight for you until my last breath. So, will you calm down, please?"

"It doesn't suck when you're being sweet, you know."

I nod. "Noted. Now, let's get out of here."

We leave my half-renovated house and head to hers. Tilly lets us in and calls for her parents. She has hold of my hand, and I squeeze.

"Where have you been, Matilda?" her mum asks. Her mouth snaps shut as she notices me beside Tilly.

"Did you just full-name me again?" Tilly says, lifting her blonde eyebrow.

Emma ignores her daughter. "Lincoln, hello."

"Hey," I reply, placing my palm on Tilly's back. I want to ask how she is, but that doesn't feel right.

"Well, come in, you two. No need to be standing in the hallway," Emma says. "Dan, put the kettle on. Tilly and Lincoln are here."

Tilly tugs me into the kitchen. Their house hasn't changed much at all, though it doesn't look at all dated.

"Lincoln, how are you?" Dan asks, turning as we come into the kitchen.

Neither of them looks like they want to kick me out, so it's going well so far.

"I'm doing okay, thanks. You guys?"

Emma smiles. "We're okay. We're glad you and Tilly have worked things out."

"Me, too," I reply.

Tilly turns to me, grinning the way she did when we were younger. Her eyes aren't carrying around any pain.

She pulls me to the kitchen table, and we sit down with Emma while Dan makes coffee.

"How is the house renovation going?" Emma asks.

Easy subject.

"Er, slow. I didn't realise how much damage the leak last year had done. Ian and Jack have helped, but it's taking time. We're getting closer though."

"Aren't you due back at work?"

"No. I left my old job to go into business with my dad. Once I get back, we're starting the new venture." Seconds after I finish talking, I realise exactly what I said. Tilly is watching me like I've just kicked her, and I will do anything to never put that look on her face again. "But I guess I need to have a conversation with my dad."

This isn't a conversation to be having in front of her parents, but that doesn't stop her.

"You were going to start up a business with your dad?"

I clear my throat. "Yeah. He's worked in advertising since he was eighteen, and I've recently found out that I'm good at it. He wants to go on his own, and I want to work for myself. Wanted."

She shakes her head. "That's not a goal you can just give up, Linc."

"Yeah, actually, it is. My own business, house, and everything else are just details. If I can't do the business from here, I'll find a job somewhere."

Her parents watch silently, and for once, Tilly seems speechless.

"You can't just decide that right now."

"It was decided the second you walked into my house yesterday."

She narrows her eyes. "You're so stubborn."

No, I'm just so over missing her. I'm not letting go now that I have her, and I will do whatever I need to do to be with her. I have money saved. I can rent here and get a job until I figure something more permanent out.

"I'm stubborn?"

She laughs and shakes her head. "I'm not that bad."

Dan snorts, and Tilly flashes him an evil look.

"Come on, love," he says.

Tilly rolls her eyes but doesn't push it. She is so stubborn. She fought against us for long enough.

"So, things are finally good?" Emma asks, her eyes flitting between Tilly and me.

"Really good," she replies to her mum and gives me a smile.

Yeah, there is no way I could leave this girl to start up a business with my dad. It'll be here or nothing.

"I'm glad to hear it." Emma taps her mug and purses her lips.

I get the impression from her silence that her question was much more loaded than that. She wanted a better response ... probably about Stanley.

"What?" Tilly asks, picking up on Emma's reaction to her brief reply.

"Well …" Emma trails off, unsure of how to put it into words.

"He left because he knew it was a mistake, coming back, so he went home. I hadn't known that he was coming; it had been a surprise to me, too," I tell her.

My heart dips as I think about the possibility of her not actually thinking about my brother. What if I've just volunteered information that reminds them who I am and who my brother is?

Emma smiles, her hands stretching around her mug. "Thank you, Lincoln. Do you think he will return again? I take it, you're sold on staying here?"

"I'm definitely not going anywhere, and I don't think he will come back."

Dan takes a sharp intake of breath. "Right. So, do you think you will be able to run a business from here?"

"Yeah," I reply.

He nods, and I think he's impressed that I'm willing to do anything to be with Tilly. That gets me points with the parents, surely.

I'll make it work, and if I can't, I'll do something else. Maybe I'll just go solo or have a sister company and work with my dad indirectly. A career is important, but when I'm old and grey, I'm going to remember my life with Tilly, not my life at a desk. I would follow her to the ends of the earth and give up anything to be with her.

"Sounds like something you need to discuss with your dad, Linc," Tilly says.

"I will, but don't worry about it, okay?"

She will always be number one.

"Sure," she replies. Her eyes burn into mine with flashbacks of last night.

I clear my throat and avert my eyes before things get real awkward and I'm sitting here with a raging erection.

46

Linc

The next morning, I'm getting dressed while Tilly is making coffee.

She is downstairs, waiting for me. Waiting. For. Me.

I still feel like I'm asleep. Like I'll wake up soon, and things will be back to normal. The girl I'm in love with will be angry and push me away at every corner, and the town will still be treating me like a leper.

But it's not a dream. She's here. She's been here, in my house and my bed. Hell, she's been in my bed *a lot*.

Her parents were okay. There was no awkwardness once we had the *I'll work from here to be with her* conversation.

They don't blame me for that night.

I rub a towel over my wet hair and take in my reflection in the mirror. I look different, even to myself. The tension around my eyes that I got used to is gone. Tilly has not only brought personal happiness, but she's also opened the door for forgiveness. I'll always regret what happened the night of the accident. While I'll never fully let myself off, I no longer wake up, crippled by it.

The towel joins my pile of clothes on the floor, and I head downstairs to find her.

The smell of coffee pulls me toward the kitchen. Tilly is sitting at the table, taking a long sip. She looks up, and her amber eyes drink me in. She puts her mug down next to the one she has already made for me.

"Hi," she says, her lips gelling together in a bid to stop a stupidly big smile.

"Hey." I sit down and lean over.

It's taken no time at all to get used to her moving closer to me rather than further away. Our lips hit, and her eyes fly shut. I snake my hand around the side of her neck and up into her hair. She makes a small sound of pleasure as my mouth claims hers.

"Your coffee will get cold," she says as we separate.

I sit back in my seat and grab the mug in both hands to stop myself from reaching for her. "I don't care."

"You'll get grumpy if you don't caffeinate … and you're already grumpy."

"Ouch. I think I've been like sunshine and rainbows the last couple days."

"Yes. Well, when you're inside me, you're pretty sunshiny."

"So, what do we learn from that? It's not coffee I need; it's you wrapped around my cock." I point to the ceiling where my bedroom sits above.

Tilly rolls her eyes with a laugh that has warmth spreading through my once-frosty chest.

"Down, boy. I'm sore."

"I'd apologise, but you were the one who woke me up in the early hours this morning."

Her smile widens. "What are we doing today? Besides sex."

"Aren't you working?"

She shakes her head. "Not until tomorrow morning, so you've got me all day."

"Okay, let's go then."

"Where?"

"Just come and get in the car, Tilly."

Her eyebrows dip together. "Okay, I'll go along with this. Am I dressed for whatever we're doing?"

I nod and drain another mouthful of coffee.

"My mum asked if you'd come over for breakfast this week. I think she misses seeing me for breakfast. Dad doesn't eat pancakes, and it's her favourite thing to make. Mostly because it's the only thing she can make that doesn't taste like it's days old."

"She's still no better then."

Every time I hung out with Robbie, we would only eat dinner there if Dan was cooking or if they were getting takeaway. Emma is a terrible cook and openly admits it.

"Nope. She still tries about every six months to make something. Those nights always end up being pizza nights."

"Some of my best memories are pizza nights at yours."

"With Robbie challenging everyone to racing games on the PlayStation and blaming the controller when he lost."

I laugh as I recall the deep shade of red his face would turn. "That damn sticking button."

"My poor Jenson Button reject of a brother. You know, I think Robbie really believed he could be a racing driver. He would always tell me how I was driving wrong and which *line* to take around a bend. Like I'm just going to follow the road, Rob."

I clamp my hand around her wrist and pull her against my body. "I miss that idiot."

Sighing, she lays her head against my chest, winding both arms around my back so tight, as if she's afraid I'll disappear. "I know. I wish he could be here. He would have been happy about us, wouldn't he?"

We've had this conversation, but given the fact that anything to do with Robbie has her second-guessing everything, it doesn't surprise me that she needs reassurance. I'll tell her a million times over until any anxiety she has over it is gone.

"Yes," I reply, placing a kiss on the top of her head.

She looks up, and her expression is full of hope and promise.

"Let's go wherever you're taking me then."

I grab my keys and phone while Tilly gets her bag and checks her makeup in the mirror. I watch her fluff her hair with amusement. She doesn't see herself how I see her.

"Ready?" I ask when she turns away from her reflection.

"I am."

We lock my front door and head to my car. I'm about three days behind on the house again, but there is no immediate rush anymore. We need to sell soon, as my folks are paying a mortgage every month, but Tilly doesn't need me to get out as soon as possible.

I'll pay the damn mortgage myself if I have to. I'm not giving up this time with her now for anything. I want to take her out and be a normal couple rather than spending almost all day, every day, renovating.

She walks ahead, a slight bounce in her step and shoulders relaxed. Across the street, one of our neighbours, Mr. Jones, watches us with a wrinkled scowl. He's old school, and he hates anyone young. He hated us as teens, and he really hates me now. Mr. Jones was one of the people who shouted abuse at Stanley when he got away with not doing any prison time.

I don't know if Tilly has stopped caring about other people or if she hasn't noticed him, too caught up in our bubble. She gets in my car and waits for me.

Mr. Jones continues to stare, his aging frame arched forward like he's losing the battle with gravity.

I raise my hand in a short wave, and that really has him spitting feathers. His mouth moves with a mumbled rambling that only he can hear, and he turns around, retreating back into his house.

Miserable old fucker.

I get into the car and start the engine. Tilly is texting.

"Everything okay?"

"Uh-huh. Just telling my parents where I am."

"Tilly, your house is right there," I say, pointing to the building meters away.

She shrugs one arm and presses Send on the message. "I don't want to stop. I'm excited."

"You don't even know where we're going."

"No, but I know you."

For someone with the ability to bring me to my knees, she sure as hell can lift me far.

"You don't know how much that means to me, Tilly."

Her smile widens. "I love you, Linc."

Those four words rolling from her lips steal my breath every time. I almost need a warning before she's about to say them.

"I love you, too," I tell her.

We arrive forty minutes later at Ted's independent cinema that has only two screens, and each of those only seats about fifty people. How they've stayed afloat with the opening of massive chain cinemas is a miracle. But it's probably because you're allowed to bring your own food and drink, and no one checks if that drink is alcohol.

The cinema has theme days, and this week is all about horror.

"What are we doing here?"

"What do you think we'll be doing at a cinema?"

She tilts her head, giving me a pointed look. "Horror week is back?"

I nod. "They're playing Halloween movies all day today. Tomorrow is all about *Friday the 13th*. I've not checked the rest of the week, but we can come around your shifts at the restaurant, if you want."

"We came here to watch *Halloween* just after my seventeenth birthday."

"I know," I reply with a smile.

No one else would come with us because our friends were all about new horror, action, or romance. They were soulless, but spending the whole day with Tilly back then is one of my best memories. I was relaxed and weightless, and I could be myself.

There aren't many people in screen two. We sit at the back, and she smiles at me.

"You're a romantic, Lincoln Reid."

"Because I've brought you to a cinema to watch a masked killer stab teenagers all day?"

She purses her lips. "No. Because you remembered it all."

There isn't one second of the time I've spent with her that I've forgotten. Tilly is one of a kind. She's someone who sticks with you, her smile and the sound of her laugh implanted in your memory.

I don't consider myself a romantic, not in the traditional sense since roses and serenading make me want to vomit, but if she thinks remembering my past with her is romantic, then just call me Mr. Darcy.

"What about you?" I ask.

Her eyes soften. "I remember it all like it was yesterday."

Tilly

I feel like I'm hungover when I turn up at work the following day. I've been drunk with all things Linc. We've spent every second together, and now, I have to do things.

Hanna and I are on the early shift, so we're not open yet, and that works because I haven't told her about me and Linc yet. If customers were here when I told her, they would hear the screaming and all of the inevitable *I told you so*s.

The chefs are in the kitchen, preparing for breakfast orders, so I head into the restaurant to lay out cutlery.

"Hey," Hanna says, looking up as she places napkins on tables. "You know what's fine?"

Her tone is flat. I'm in trouble.

I sigh. "What, Hanna?"

"That you ignore your best friend. I texted you, like, twenty times yesterday."

"It was two times."

"Oh, so your phone isn't broken?"

I roll my eyes and straighten up cutlery Hanna put out in a huff because she's annoyed with me. "No, Han, my phone isn't broken."

"So, I guess you were sick?"

My mouth twitches. "No, I wasn't sick."

Her shoulders sag. "Okay, I give in first. What's going on?"

"I was with Linc."

"Huh? You're friends with him again now?"

"No."

"What? Tilly, I'm worried. Things were getting good. You were more like yourself than you'd been in such a long time. Then, Stanley came back. And I get it; you were thrown through a hoop again, but—"

"Linc and I are together!" I cannot listen to her going on anymore. And I don't want her to be worried about me, especially when I'm *very* okay.

"Seriously? Oh my God! *Together* as in, you're having sex?"

There she is.

"Yeah, as in we're having sex."

"Tilly!" she screams, running around the table and colliding with me.

I'm knocked back, but Hanna is a lot more prepared for her assault than I am and manages to save us before we hit the floor.

"This is amazing!" she gushes. Pulling back, she holds me at arm's length. "I told you so! Didn't I tell you so? He is crazy about you; anyone can see that. I am *so* glad that you are giving him a chance; you were made for each other. Oh my God, we can go out as three couples. Mel would love that, too."

"Okay, stop before you explode!"

"This is good."

I bite my lip. "Yeah, it's good."

"You're smiling." Her fingers dig harder into my upper arms. "You're *really* smiling. I haven't seen you happy in four years, Tilly."

My eyes sting with the threat of tears. "I am happy now."

AFTER THE END

The noise that comes out of her throat is something between a squeal and a person dying.

"Tell me everything. Follow me around while I do this," she orders, holding a basket of cutlery up.

When we work early together, we each always take one half of the restaurant to get it done quicker, but I guess she doesn't care about speed today.

"Well, you know about the whole Stanley arriving fight."

"Ugh, that prick."

"Yeah. Well, I didn't see Linc for two days after Stanley left, and I was getting worried, so I went over. Anyway, things went well." I don't know if Linc would want me to discuss him getting drunk even if Hanna wouldn't judge. That seems kind of private, between us, and for him to talk about if he wants, which he doesn't because he hasn't even spoken to me about it properly.

"Specifics?"

"We talked, and we admitted how we felt and that we wanted to give things a chance. Then, we had sex."

Actually, we had sex first, but I don't want to get into that right now.

She squeals again and slams the basket down on the table. "How was it?"

"Amazing. Mind-blowing. Like we should have been doing it all along."

"Well, duh! Tilly, I'm so excited for you guys. Is he big?"

"Hanna! What the hell?" I slap her arm while shaking my head.

"Come on, Tilly. Girls talk about this stuff."

"I don't know the size of Jack's dick, and I don't want to."

She sighs. "Fine, be a prude."

I grab a handful of cutlery and turn to go to another table. "Yes, he's big."

"I knew it!" she cheers from behind me.

We're running a little behind by the time we wipe tables and get the cutlery out. They get cleaned at the end of the day, but the owners are big on dust.

345

When the doors open at seven a.m., we're just about ready. A few people trickle in, and we get orders running.

I'm cleaning a frothy milk spill from the coffee machine when Hanna nudges my arm.

"Looks like he can't keep away."

I look over my shoulder as Linc walks in.

"Do you want me to take his table?" she teases.

"Nope, I want you to finish this," I say, chucking the cloth at her to finish cleaning.

I walk over to Linc, my heart wild in my chest. He's gorgeous, wearing plain clothes and a heartbreaking smile.

"Good morning, sir. Where would you like to sit?" I say, trying to keep a stupid grin off my face.

"Wherever gets me served by you is good."

"Well then, follow me." I grab him a menu and take him to a table near the window.

Smirking, he takes the menu and sits down.

"Hanna is happy about us."

"So are Jack and Ian."

"You've spoken to them already?"

He shrugs. "Jack texted our group chat, so I figured I should tell them."

Now, I just need to tell Mel. She'll be as ecstatic as Hanna though; I have no doubt about that. My stomach buzzes with excitement of things to come—hanging out with Linc and my friends, being a couple and not pretending or holding back.

"You are so obsessed with me."

Rolling his eyes, he says, "Are you going to take my order?"

"Not yet. I thought you were going to work on the house while I was here?" I ask.

We had plans to meet up as soon as my shift finished, not that I don't want him here.

"Got hungry."

"You have food."

His smirk grows. "Got tired of missing you."

"Cheesy."

"Yes. Get used to it."

I smile. "No. Get cooler."

He laughs and chucks the menu down on the table. "I'll have a coffee and two bacon rolls, please."

"Sure." I pick up his menu, brushing his finger with mine, and I feel the touch radiate through my whole body.

"I love you, Tilly."

"Love you, too, Linc."

I float to the bar.

Tilly

Linc's parents are coming home tomorrow. This was going to come at some point. I've accepted that I'll have to have a conversation with them, clear the air as much as we can, if I want to be with Linc, but I didn't think it would be so soon.

"Talk to me, Tilly," Linc pleads, bending his head, so we're level.

I shake my head. "I don't really know what to say. I thought we had more time."

I'm not ready. Or perhaps this is exactly what I need, no time to overthink and obsess.

"Do you want more time? If you want it, you've got it."

"I do, but I shouldn't have it."

His chin lifts with understanding. "Yeah, that might be best. Do you think your mum and dad will be open to talking with them, too? That's got to happen at some point as well, hasn't it?"

"I can't rush them with this, Linc."

"I'm with you, but you should talk to them."

Groaning, I lean against him. He's home, my comfort, and my reason. Everything seems that much easier when he's right there beside me even if being with him is the catalyst for all of this mess.

"With you?"

"If you want."

I need some of whatever confidence or lack of giving a shit Linc has. He doesn't shy away from conversations that will inevitably get awkward.

"How are you so calm about this?" I ask.

If I could bottle his chill, I would make a million.

"It has to happen, so we might as well get on with it. I'm looking at the bigger picture, Tilly—a future with you—and if things have to get a bit uncomfortable for people in order for that to happen, then so be it."

"I really am glad I got my shit together and gave us a chance."

He smirks, lifting an eyebrow. "It was only a matter of time."

Behind the cocky exterior he's just put on is relief. It's still there in his eyes, a deep-rooted vulnerability over us. It's grown over the four years we were apart, and I'm determined to smash it down.

"Of course it was," I murmur against his heartbeat.

He might be surer of us now, but until days ago, I wasn't. It's taken a lot for me to see what's right in front of me, but I don't ever plan on letting him go again. I'm happy, and I know that he is, too. I won't hurt him again, no matter how hard things get or how much I want to run away.

It's time to take back my life.

Starting with meeting the parents. Again.

So, we leave his house and go to mine.

I turn to Linc as we approach my front door. "Maybe we should do this later?"

He catches me in his arms, stopping me from getting farther away from my house. "Tilly, they're coming tomorrow. There is no later."

"But ..."

"Tilly!"

Frowning, I contemplate coming on to him because I know that'll work, but he's right, and I'm just being a chicken. I let us into the house. "All right, I know. Come on. Let's get this over with."

Mum and Dad are in the kitchen, drinking wine, when we get in. They both do half-days on Fridays, so they've been home a couple of hours now. They look up in unison and smile at me and Linc.

He's been over a few times now, and my parents barely blink when he walks in. He's become part of the furniture again. He could probably let himself in, and they wouldn't care. Not that he would anymore, not without an invitation.

"Hey, guys. Can we talk a minute?" I ask, biting my lip.

My heart rate increases as I watch the lines around their eyes tighten.

"What's wrong?" Mum asks, slowly lowering her wine glass.

Linc puts his hand on the small of my back, passing strength from him to me.

"Um ... Linc's ..."

"Tilly, tell me you're not pregnant," Dad demands, his forehead creasing.

Linc coughs on air.

"No! Really, Dad? We haven't even been together long enough to know that! But I'm not! I wanted to tell you that Martha and Cliff are coming here tomorrow. Well, not here, to their house, but, yeah ..."

"I've spoken to my parents, and they want to come back and talk to me and Tilly," Linc adds, speaking much more eloquently than I managed. "We wanted to tell you, so you don't run into them without warning."

"I see," Mum says, turning to Dad to see how he feels about this.

My parents are very much a team. They don't do anything ever unless they're both in agreement. It's sweet really and something I hope Linc and I will have.

Dad gives her a small smile and turns to Linc. "Are they wanting to have a conversation with us, too?"

"They do, but they won't push."

"Ball is in your court, Dad, but it would mean a lot to me if you thought about it. I mean, at some point, we're all going to have to be in the same place, right?"

Mum slowly nods her head as if the thought has only just now occurred to her.

Is this where she changes her mind and decides Linc being back in our lives is too much?

That doesn't work for me anymore. I can't give him up now. For the first time in years, I feel truly happy.

"Mum, is that okay?" I ask.

"Yes, I do understand where this is going." She looks to Dad. "I don't know about you, but I think I need to sleep on this. How long will your parents be home for, Linc?"

"For a little while today."

"Well, I think that perhaps we'll let you two have today, there's a lot to discuss," Dad replies. "Maybe we can all get together for dinner another time?"

"They'll love that," Linc tells him.

Dad smiles. "Would you two like to join us for a drink?"

That conversation is over then. Dad has shut it down and moved on, the way he does when I try to bring up Robbie sometimes. He seems to instinctively know when Mum is emotionally strong enough to discuss something. I do worry that he's too protective, treating her like she's made of glass.

"I have to get ready for work soon, so we're going to hang out before that. Another time though."

They both nod, and we leave them to it. They're probably going to have a conversation between themselves now.

I take Linc's hand and pull him out of the kitchen and up to my room.

He's quiet until I close my door.

"Your mum isn't totally okay with any of this, is she?" he asks in a whisper, his dark blue eyes filled to the brim with worry. He looks panicked, poised and ready to grab me in case I'm also not totally okay.

I step into his arms and run my hands up his chest and around his neck. I'll never get used to the way my heart sprints every time we touch. "It's new, and she's working on it. She is one hundred percent okay with you."

"My family is a part of me, Tilly."

"I know. Give it time, Mr. Impatient. We're together, right? So, the rest of it will work out."

His arms cage me against his chest. "Ah, you're going to use my own words against me."

"Not against, but I am enjoying being the sure one for the first time. What's it like to be the irrational overthinker?"

"Tilly, when it comes to you, I've always been an overthinker. I just hide it better than you do."

"You've *always* been an overthinker when it comes to me?"

He grimaces like he's let out a secret he should have been protecting.

"Linc?"

He takes a deep breath, his chest expanding powerfully. "Okay ... Tilly, I didn't fall in love with you when I came back this summer. I fell in love with you when I left four years ago."

My mouth audibly pops open. I probably look ridiculous, like a fish coming up for food.

"You did what?" I whisper.

The corner of his mouth lifts in a smirk that makes his eyes glow. "Maybe I should have told you sooner, but there was never the right time. We've only just got together, and I didn't want to scare you off."

I want to tell him that I wouldn't have been scared off, but that would be a lie. I was petrified of everything to do with Lincoln for a very long time, but I'm not anymore.

"Linc, you know I love you, too." Not quite for four years, but I still mean it wholeheartedly.

"Good."

"So … four years, huh?" I bite my lip. My heart is going wild in my chest.

"Yeah, pretty much."

"Before or after …"

He holds me closer against his chest. "I didn't realise until there was hundreds of miles between us, but I loved you before Robbie died."

"I don't know what to say."

"You don't have to say anything."

"And, I mean, did you stop at all over the last four years? Like, you loved me, and then you got over it until we weren't hundreds of miles apart?"

"I didn't stop." He presses his lips to the top of my head. "God, how I tried to stop. It was one thing, being apart from you when I moved away, but another to know that you hated me. I wanted to contact you. There were so many times I wanted to call, but I knew you wouldn't want to talk, and I didn't want to hurt you."

"I'm sorry, Linc. I hate that you were hurting." I close my eyes in his embrace.

"I would take the pain of loving you from afar a thousand times over if it led to this moment. You're worth it."

Oh my God.

My fingers curl into his back in a bid to get as close as humanly possible. For someone who never really talks much about how he feels, Linc really has game. My stomach flutters as I swoon at his words.

But the best part is the low, breathy tone in which he speaks them.

"You should keep saying things like that," I whisper, pulling my head back so that I can see his face.

"I would tease you, but I think we both know I plan to. If it'll make you smile like this, I'll tell you how much I love you every chance I get."

AFTER THE END

"Linc, I love your words, but right now, I want your actions."

His eyebrows shoot up like he's a virgin being told he's getting a blow job. "Oh, I am all about the action."

I squeal as he picks me up and throws me onto my bed.

"Shh, your parents will hear!"

"We are not having sex with my parents in the house!"

His body covers mine. "I know, but I can kiss you. A lot."

Yes, he can. And he does.

Linc

Tilly's mum and dad are cool. There is no residual anger or resentment. They've welcomed me with open arms, and I'm so grateful for that. Tilly can't stop smiling, and in turn, Dan and Emma can't either.

I wasn't around to see them over the last four years, but I feel something healing between them all. Tilly's happiness is the catalyst for a lot of changes to come. She thought she was doing the best thing for her parents by staying here and staying still, but they need her to move forward.

Now, they all can. I know how much Robbie's death ripped them to pieces, but having a second child living her life forces them to do the same. They don't want to miss Tilly's future.

I don't want to miss Tilly's future.

So, we've all found ourselves in this new place where we've gone back to the beginning after the end.

It's kind of the perfect place to start, I guess.

I'm not here as Lincoln, the guy who was a fucking idiot one tragic night. I'm here as Lincoln, Tilly's boyfriend. I'll do everything I can to make sure that's the only person I am to them from here on out. Well, until I become Tilly's fiancé, then husband.

We went to her house for breakfast with her parents and then came back to mine to wait for my parents. They're due here any minute now, and Tilly can't sit still. She is pacing the living room, doing circuits around the furniture, occasionally venturing into the kitchen.

I just hope things can go as well with my family as it has been going with hers. I suppose that depends on their ability to leave Stanley out of the equation when they're around her.

"Will you come and sit down?" I ask in vain.

She's too wired to sit still. "Is that a car?"

I twist my head and look out the window. "Yes, but not theirs."

"Shouldn't they be here by now?"

"Anytime now, babe." I stand up because I can't watch her walk around the sofa one more time. "Hey," I say, grabbing her hips so that she can't move.

Her body is stiff as she looks up at me. "I'm nervous."

"I've noticed. What are you nervous about? You know my parents. Everyone wants the same thing here, Tilly."

"What if I react to seeing them the way I did with you? I want this to work, but what if—"

That's enough. I bend my head and seal my lips over her mouth.

With all the nervous energy she has rattling around, I expect her to push me away and make some excuse about my parents not catching us kissing in the living room, but she doesn't do that.

She grips my upper arms, tilting her head back and kissing me like it's the last time. My body responds to her close proximity in a heartbeat. I kiss her deeper, my tongue passing her lips.

Her fingertips curl into my skin, and she moans. I lose it. Rushing forward, I slam her against the wall and press my body into hers. One of my hands leaves her hip, and I reach down to grab her thigh and wrap her leg around me.

But the doorbell rings.

"Fuck's sake," I mutter against her mouth.

Laughing lightly, she pushes me away and takes a breath.

Great. My parents are here, and I'm so worked up that I think my teeth are going to snap from clenching my jaw.

"You should get that," Tilly says, straightening her clothes. Besides her lips looking a little redder, she doesn't look manhandled.

"Right," I reply, turning to adjust the massive erection she's just given me. I walk to the front door and tug it open. "You don't have a key?"

"Hello to you, too, Lincoln," Mum says, pulling me into a hug. "Your dad forgot the old house keys and didn't realise until we were over halfway."

"You didn't remember them either, Martha," Dad says behind her.

"Hey, Dad." I move aside and let them in.

Mum immediately seeks Tilly, who looks like she's ready to bolt for the back door. This was never going to be an easy meeting, but it's one we need to get through. Hopefully, things will get easier each time.

"Tilly. Hello, darling," Mum says. She doesn't move any closer because I think she also senses Tilly's reluctance.

Smiling, Tilly replies politely, "Hi, Martha."

"How are you?"

"I'm okay."

I move around my parents and curl my arm around Tilly's back. "You guys want a coffee? I can show you the new kitchen."

Well, the only new things about the kitchen are the flooring, paint, and wall tiles. I managed to salvage the cupboards by sanding them down a little and painting them grey. The oak wooden worktops have also been sanded and had oiling treatments. It looks like a new kitchen.

"Sounds good. I love what you've done in this room. The carpet and walls look great," Dad says. "The floorboards underneath weren't too bad?"

We walk into the kitchen.

"Most of them needed replacing, but it didn't take long with Jack and Ian here, too."

Tilly moves away and heads to the kettle. She's trying to keep busy.

I grab the mugs and lean close. "Relax, babe. It's okay."

Her eyes peek up at me, and she takes a breath. "I'll leave this with you then," she replies, putting the kettle on the stand and flicking it on.

I smile as she turns to my parents. She's willing to try at least.

"It's incredible, right?" she says.

I look over my shoulder to see what she's talking about. Mum and Dad look around the room in awe.

"It is," Mum replies. "So beautiful, Linc. I can't believe you did all of this."

"I had help."

Tilly nudges my back. "He's being modest. He's worked so hard."

"We're so glad you invited us," Dad says. "We've wanted to come back so many times, to reach out to you and your parents, Tilly."

Tilly nods. "I'm glad you're here, too."

Mum's eyes glow at Tilly's admission. I'm worried that she is too invested and wanting to jump straight back into how things were. I've learned the hard way; it takes work and patience to get to a place where all is forgiven.

We take drinks into the living room and sit down.

Tilly smiles at my mum, her eyes warm and free of contempt. A week ago, she wasn't sure if we could be together, and now, she's full-on forgiving. I don't know where she gets the strength.

Mum looks at Tilly like she's trying to figure out if she's sincere or not. Mum has often told me how much she misses Tilly and the relationship they had. I wonder if Tilly is feeling that now, too.

"How have you been?" Mum asks her.

"I'm doing okay now. It's been rough though."

"Tilly, I am so sorry," Mum says through emotion that sounds like it's clogging her throat. "We thought we were doing the right thing by Stanley."

"I might not agree with what you did, but I do understand it. I don't hold you accountable for Stanley's actions."

Dad clears his throat. "Thank you, but we are to blame."

Shit.

They are, of course, but I didn't think they would admit it.

"What happens now then?" I ask them because it's a little late to make him face up to what he's done.

Dad takes Mum's hand. "We have tried talking to him. He's agreed to start counselling. There is no telling if it will do any good, but it's a start."

"He agreed?" I ask, needing that confirmed.

"Yes," Mum says softly. "We should have made him talk to someone long ago, and that was our mistake as his parents. We're trying to do the right thing now for your family, Tilly. For Robbie especially."

"Thanks," Tilly whispers, taking a deep breath. It could well be too little, too late, but at least they're acting. "I don't know if I'll ever be okay with being around Stanley."

"No one will ask that of you—not now, not ever," Mum tells her, beating me to it. "We were hoping that you would allow us to be a part of your life with Lincoln though?"

Tilly looks up at me, but I keep a straight face. Her decision has to be based on what she can do, not what I want.

She smiles and squeezes my hand. "I would like that, Martha."

The relief on Mum's face would be clear from space. Her dark eyes light up. "That's wonderful. We have missed you.

Perhaps, when you're ready, you can visit? You'll like our new house. We have a hot tub," Mum says.

When Tilly was young, Mum and Emma used to take her swimming, and they'd use the hot tub. Mum would come home, gushing about how cute Tilly was. I have a feeling Mum always hoped for a girl, but I clearly am not.

"That sounds amazing," Tilly replies, squeezing my hand tight.

It's a little too soon for her. She's okay to talk to my parents, and she'll go through any long-drawn-out conversation we'll undoubtedly have, but she's not ready to play happy families again. The Reids and the Drakes were once intertwined, spending so much time together that we might as well have been related, but a lot has happened, and four years have passed.

Mum wants to jump right in, right back to when everything was good, but that's not possible. If we can even get to that point again, it's going to take a lot of work.

She's not a stranger to hard work. She fought for Stanley so hard that she lost a piece of herself, but I know it's going to hurt when she finds out that Tilly will want to take this slow. Not that she has a right to be upset. The fact that Tilly is here at all is a miracle.

Sensing Tilly's unease, Dad changes the subject, and we chat about the house renovations a little more, Tilly's job, my dad's job, and just about everything else we can think of that doesn't delve too deep. Dad and I have yet to discuss the business, but he will know that we're going to have to alter our plans, so I can work from here.

Hour two rolls around, and I'm beginning to tire of talking so much.

"We should get going soon," Dad says.

Mum's smile falters. "Oh, yes." She looks back at Tilly like she never wants to let her go again.

I know how much Mum loves her, but she is going to have to take a step back in order to go forward. I had to take about a thousand back.

"Um, maybe, in a few weeks, we can go for dinner with my parents or something?" Tilly asks.

"Only if that's cool," I tell her.

I don't want her rushing anything for my benefit. We'll get there. In the future, there will come a point where we can all be in the same room, both sets of parents—perhaps not Stanley—but there isn't a rush.

"It's cool. I'm ready to move on."

Epilogue

Tilly

Linc is asleep beside me. We're in Rome, Italy, on our honeymoon after a shotgun wedding, a year after he came home. No, I'm not pregnant.

It's mid-morning. We slept in after not sleeping much last night. I slip out of bed, wrapping one of the many sheets around my body, and open the door in our bedroom to the balcony.

I step outside, and the hot air slams me in the face. Rome is stunning but bloody hot. As much as I love the view of the Colosseum, I have instant regret of leaving the air-conditioned room.

"Tilly," Linc calls. I turn as he props himself up on his elbow, his naked body in perfect view. "Why are you on the balcony in just a sheet?"

"No one can see," I reply. Well, probably not. I can't see anyone else on their balconies, so I assume that means I'm not being seen.

He holds his hand up. "Come here." His voice is deep and demanding and makes my insides burn.

"I can't."

"Why not?"

"Because, if I do, we'll be there for hours, and I want to explore some more on our last day."

Linc narrows his eyes and sits up. "We've been everywhere we wanted already, so by exploring, do you mean, shopping?"

Laughing, I step back into the room. "Guilty."

I can't believe that, ten days ago, I married this man. *How bloody lucky am I?*

We had a small ceremony with only family and close friends. It was perfect, and the fact that my family and his got along warmed my heart. We did have dinner with Linc's parents and mine. At first it was awkward and even got a little heated, but the air was cleared.

Linc hasn't said anything, but I think his parents will move back soon. Slowly but surely, they've been rekindling their friendship with Mum and Dad.

Stanley isn't coming back. He moved in with two friends and took a job at a local bar. Linc didn't seem surprised, and neither did their parents. The whole subject is still a bit sore, so we don't visit it that often. I know the bare minimum about Stanley's life, like how well he's doing at counselling, and although I don't wish him any ill will, that's how I want to keep it.

"If you'll come shopping today *without* moaning, I'll let you join me in the shower now, *and* I'll blow you on the balcony tonight."

Linc flies out of bed, his erection standing tall against his belly.

I laugh and reach for him. "Eager much?"

"On the balcony? Really?" His eyes are saucers, wide with hope and longing.

"You're so cute, but yes, on the balcony. *No* moaning."

"I will be the most supportive husband on a shopping trip there has ever lived."

I grin—not because he's like a kid at Disneyland, but because he called himself my husband. I know that's what he is, but, Jesus, it feels good to have this man completely. We're a married couple now. It's us against the world—officially, legally. I know we're forever, but the ring on my finger is the security we both need.

Nothing will come between us ever again.

Acknowledgments

A*fter the End* is a book that has been in the back of my head for a long time. I didn't tell anyone about it until I was chilling with my friend (and blogger/beta reader/event planning extraordinaire). Zoë, your enthusiasm, which I think was heard throughout the hotel, spurred me on every time I was sure I couldn't finish this. Thank you for always championing my writing.

Joe, Ashton, and Remy, thank you for being my reason for everything. When I'm having a bad day writing or something just isn't clicking, I know I can always turn to you guys.

The Indie Girls, I don't even know where to begin thanking you. There has been a lot of stress with two close deadlines and back-to-back edits, and you have all been so amazing with each one of my meltdowns. You're all so inspirational, and I'm lucky to have you to lean on.

Sofie, all I ever give you is the title of the book, an incredibly brief description, and if I like a certain colour. Somehow, you send back the most perfect cover. I promise to never get too involved in my covers. LOL!

Jovana, I could not do this without you. Thank you so, so much for being the best editor on the planet.

And thank you, readers! I hope you enjoyed Linc and Tilly's story.

About the Author

U K native Natasha Preston grew up in small villages and towns. She enjoys writing contemporary romance, gritty young adult thrillers, and of course, the occasional serial killer.

Follow Natasha on social media:

Goodreads: https://goo.gl/nWsYRC

www.facebook.com/authornatashapreston

https://twitter.com/natashavpreston

www.instagram.com/natashapreston5

Made in United States
North Haven, CT
11 July 2023

38822656R00226